Consuming Passions

Consuming Passions

Freda Bright

Consuming Passions

Pan Books
London, Sydney and Auckland

First published 1990 by Pan Books Ltd,
Cavaye Place, London SW10 9PG

9 8 7 6 5 4 3 2 1

© Freda Bright

ISBN 0 330 31592 7

Phototypeset by Input Typesetting Ltd, London

Printed and bound in Great Britain by Billing & Sons Ltd, Worcester

To Justine Valenti,
who first urged me to write novels.
With thanks, I think.

Prologue

Seeing her walk up Park Avenue that morning, a trim figure in a linen suit, you would not have taken her for a woman bent on revenge.

The stride was brisk. The pitch of the shoulders, confident. The tailoring, immaculate. In one hand she held a tan attaché case of shiny new leather. The effect was that of a smart young professional on the rise.

Only the mouth betrayed tension. The lower lip was bitten raw.

When she came to the church, she turned right into the side street. It was a short tree-shaded block, lined with turn-of-the-century mansions. Each building had its manicured plantings, its ornamental plaster, its polished brass doorknob. Each had its Banham Burglar Alarm in clear view.

Look, the houses teased, *but don't touch. You are in the presence of power.*

Halfway down the block, the woman paused at the entrance of a massive brownstone. There was no sign of life within. The curtains were drawn, the windows closed despite the heat. The geraniums in the window box looked forlorn.

Five shallow steps led to the front door, where a brass lion's head caught the sunlight. She checked her watch. Three minutes early. The appointment was for twelve sharp.

Damn! she cursed under her breath. She did not want to appear over-eager, like some hungry little terrier hot for blood. Control was everything. Control was how one gained the upper hand.

She would wait till the precise stroke of noon before ringing the bell. After that, nothing less than divine intervention could stop her. In any case, what difference would these few minutes make? Let her victim enjoy a fool's paradise for another few sweeps of the second-hand. The young woman could afford to be magnanimous. Already the taste of victory was sweet on her tongue.

For the hundredth time, she pictured the scene ahead in graphic detail. Each step was as familiar to her as a home movie.

She would ring the bell. Enter the hall. Sweep up the stairs past the Sargent portrait. Hand over the contents of her briefcase without dramatics or embellishments. Wait courteously. Then pose a single question: "Is there anything you care to add for the record?" After which, she would take her leave.

The whole scenario could be managed in a quarter of an hour. And when it was over, power would have passed from one generation to another.

Old lives for new: it was the way of the world, and only a fool or a professional bleeding heart would wish it otherwise.

Reflexively, the young woman tightened her grip on the briefcase, jiggling it gently to assure herself that the contents were still intact. Her efforts were repaid with a soft gratifying rattle. She had forgotten nothing.

The dozen sheets of typescript were within, encased in a manila folder. One safe deposit key. Three photostats. The entire package weighed less than a hand-gun, but in its way it was as lethal.

Already she could envision the headline.

DEATH OF A LEGEND.

She could envision the byline, too. Heady stuff.

She checked her watch.

One minute to go. One more sweep of the second-hand before she, "Little Miss Nobody from Nowhere", toppled a national monument.

For the object of this exercise was none other than Geraldine O'Neal, that mythic combination of beauty and brains, of wit and style, the woman who had charmed the pants off America for over three decades, rôle model to the millions. And when it was over, the "monument" would be back in the gutter she sprang from. Undone, not by violence, but by cunning and guile. The selfsame tools the victim herself prized most highly.

It was more than revenge, the young woman believed. It was poetic justice.

Times without number, she had sat at the idol's feet in rapt adoration, imbibing her wisdom, learning how to cheat, to lie, to climb, to manipulate, how to cover her ass, how to smother all qualms and grab the brass ring.

Those hours had not been wasted. The student was about to outstrip the mentor.

Now, at last, she was ready to move onward. To grasp the career opportunity of a lifetime. And nobody – least of all Geraldine O'Neal – could condemn her for that.

On the avenue, a church clock struck noon. The young woman's heart thudded in response. For one wild moment, she had an urge to cut and run. Some tender-hearted instinct imperfectly suppressed suddenly clutched at her conscience. In that moment, she was swept by a dozen conflicting emotions: love, hate, jealousy, fear, the rage of hero-worship gone awry. There was no denying the enormity of what she was about to do. No mitigating the consequences. Beneath her breath, she uttered her credo. It consisted of three short words. "Go for it!"

Then, with a visible effort, she pressed her thumb to the doorbell, gave her name on the intercom and waited.

A minute later, the buzzer admitted her into a dimly lit foyer. Inside, the air was stale and motionless. There was a smell of rotting flowers. For a moment, the young woman stood disoriented, adjusting her eyes to the semi-darkness.

"Where are you?" she called out.

There was no response.

From the foyer, she could just make out the life-size Sargent at the head of the staircase. It was a portrait of a green-eyed Edwardian beauty, sumptuous in black satin *décolletage*. "My alter ego," Geraldine often called it, and indeed it bore a sharp resemblance to its owner. They shared the same jade eyes. Now those painted eyes stared at the intruder with contemptuous silence.

Another minute passed. Then an overhead light

switched on and a tall, striking figure emerged from the upstairs study to stand alongside the portrait.

In the gloom, she appeared gaunt, almost spectral. The face was pale and hollow-cheeked, the dark hair wild beyond apology. She wore a crumpled silk peignoir of indeterminate colour. Both the garment and the woman had seen better days.

Nonetheless, the presence was imposing. Regal, in a way. Still beautiful. Now, the magnificent spectre leaned over the newel post to peer down at her visitor.

"What is it you want?" Her voice was harsh, as though speaking to a tradesman. State your business, the tone implied, and begone.

The young woman's eyes went smoky with rage.

"What I want is a reckoning," she replied. "A quid pro quo."

She waited breathlessly for some acknowledgement and when none came, brandished her briefcase like a deadly weapon. "Do you know what's in here, Gerry? I expect you do. I have your past . . . your future . . . your fate."

Wordlessly, the spectre turned on her heel and walked into her study without a backward glance. Geraldine O'Neal had selected her turf. The battle was about to be joined.

The young woman crossed the foyer to the foot of the staircase and placed her free hand on the banister. Beneath the light layer of dust, the mahogany was silky to the touch. It was a handsome staircase, gracious in the manner of an earlier epoch. No one built like this nowadays.

She winced, knowing that in all likelihood she would never set foot in this house again. She had loved this place. This beautiful home full of the accoutrements of wealth and taste and power. Full of the memory of happier days.

And even as she ascended the staircase, an unbidden image sprang to mind. An image of the first time she came here.

The house had been en fête on that occasion, ablaze with light. There had been laughter and music and the omnipresent tinkle of champagne glasses. And masses of flowers in buckets, vases, great silver bowls.

And she herself, a stranger to the city, had crossed the threshold with a heart full of hope and dreams and promise – and stepped into a miraculous new world.

It had been the happiest night of her life.

It was hardly more than a year ago.

part one

one

Lee Whitfield spread the contents of her wardrobe on her bed and groaned. It was a very small wardrobe and a very narrow bed.

What to wear?

In face of womankind's oldest dilemma, she was tempted to throw her hands up in despair. For all her twenty-four years, she felt as wide-eyed as Dorothy in Oz.

"Something tells me we're not in Kansas anymore," Dorothy had said. Or in Lee's native Nebraska for that matter. And come to think of it, New York gave a pretty good approximation of Oz.

Back in Cedar City, an invitation to someone's house of an evening meant pot luck and penny-ante card games. You wore a pretty skirt and blouse. As for a night out on the town, that signified beer and burgers and best jeans.

Nothing in her social experience had readied her for the nuances of a Manhattan "reception" at the home of a glamorous celebrity.

Yet there it was, on a thick creamy stock, handsomely engraved.

Geraldine O'Neal requests the pleasure of your company for a reception (such an oblique word!) *in honour of Taki Yoshimura.* (Whoever he was!)

The RSVP had been crossed out. Instead, there was a scrawled notation. "Tried to reach you. Couldn't. Do come! G."

It had been hand-delivered a half-hour earlier and the festivities were slated to begin tonight at eight.

Did that mean sharp? Lee wondered. Or was it better to arrive fashionably late? Did "reception" connote dinner or just drinks and nibblies? Maybe she should have a bite before she left, to be on the safe side.

But all those questions were dwarfed by the ultimate poser: what to wear? The wording of the invitation gave

15

no clue. There was, fortunately, nothing so daunting as "Black Tie" in which case Lee had nothing to wear. On the other hand, "reception in honour of" seemed to imply an evening dripping with diplomats, in which case Lee had nothing to wear. On the third hand . . .

She groaned, perplexed. Three weeks in New York had left her reeling from culture shock. People here dressed differently, talked differently, moved to different rhythms. She couldn't figure them out.

Every night, after a hard day's job hunting, she would return to the grubby furnished flat on East 12th Street, plunk herself down on the battered sofa, turn on the TV, plug into the six o'clock news and try to take the pulse of the city she had pledged to conquer.

But what followed was less a pulse than a tidal wave. Rapes. Robberies. Drug busts (many of them right around the corner on 11th Street). Beggars. Hustlers. Wife beating. Teacher beating. Turnstile beating. Vigilantes on the subways. Cops on the take. Every night, Lee absorbed this half-hour catalogue of crimes and outrages with a sense of bewilderment. Even the weather report struck her as excessive.

Each day had to be the hottest or the coldest or the wettest or the nicest in the history of the bureau. Nothing less than superlatives would do.

At first, this fixation on the weather puzzled Lee. If the folks around here wanted to know what hot was, what cold was, they should visit the Great Plains. Besides, it wasn't as though New Yorkers had crops to worry about. They spent most of their lives indoors. But before long (for Lee was essentially a quick study), this local peculiarity began to make a kind of crazed sense.

It was New York macho, in its simplest form: the belief that everything that occurred here – from muggings to pollen count to the price paid for a one bedroom apartment – must necessarily break some kind of record. Not only did such an attitude automatically make New York the standard-setter for rest of the world, it also identified New Yorkers as supreme survivors. Crime here was better (or worse, depending on your point of view) than anywhere

16

else on earth. People were louder, meaner, kinder, tougher. The pace was faster, the subway smellier, the cockroaches smarter. The lowliest cabbie knew more about Life with a capital L than the sagest resident of Denver or Chicago (let alone Cedar City) could ever aspire to. For it went without saying that any place west of the Hudson River was, collectively, irreversibly "the boonies".

That much was clear to Lee; other conundrums remained. The language of graffiti. The bursts of steam that emanated from midtown manhole covers. The bathtub in the middle of her kitchen. And now, that most immediate and nagging of questions: *what to wear.*

With a baleful eye, she re-examined the display on the bed.

Her good grey suit? Blah! Businessy. That suit had been on so many interviews since her arrival, it could practically write its own résumé. It deserved a night off. And after that, a day at the cleaners.

The ice-blue chiffon? Now that little number had wowed the guys in the stag line at her senior prom. Instinct told Lee that tonight's audience would be a tad more sophisticated.

Her floral silk print? It had "hick" printed all over it.

The green-and-white check? It bounced.

As for the skirts, the shirts, the Fair Isle sweaters, the cowboy boots – every item seemed as provincial as varsity letters.

Which left the black wool A-line. Period.

No matter that it was far too warm for this weather and a trifle severe. It was "classic" as her mother used to say.

"With basic black and a simple string of pearls," the maternal wisdom ran, "you could call on the Queen of England."

Lee couldn't testify as to the dress code at Buckingham Palace, but that was hardly tonight's problem. The Manhattan social whirl was. And on that score, her mother's advice had thus far proved hopeless, despite the fact that Nancy Whitfield was New York born and bred.

Thirty-seven years is a long time. The city had changed

17

beyond recognition since the day when Lee's parents had left it as newlyweds. Their memories were frozen in time.

The cosy midtown cafés her mother recommended with such gusto were long gone, razed to make way for office blocks. Gone too were the Fourth Avenue bookshops, Lewisohn Stadium, the Bond Clothing sign at Times Square, the 52nd Street jazz joints her father always spoke of, to say nothing of S. Klein's, the Automat, Ebbet's Field, Moondog and (to Lee's dismay) cheap bed-sitters on the Upper West Side. Slums had become luxury areas, grand hotels had degenerated into slums. The city of her parents' youth and romance was extinct.

Indeed, the only New York tie that had survived the decades (and a tenuous one at best) was Nancy's link with Geraldine O'Neal. The two women had gone to college together. For a couple of intense years, in the Gospel according to Nancy Whitfield, they had lived in each other's pockets, been the most intimate of buddies, the joint stars of their class. Had been two of a kind.

Gerry had been maid-of-honour at the Whitfield wedding, after which their ways diverged. Nancy's path had led to contented years (at least Lee presumed they were contented) of marriage and motherhood in Cedar City.

Whereas Geraldine O'Neal!

Her accomplishments could fill a book and doubtless would one day. Scholar. Show girl. Columnist. Lecturer. Executive. Feminist. Diplomat. Hostess. Currently head of her own PR firm. About the only thing she hadn't done was marry. The contrast between the two lives could not be more profound.

Yet time and distance notwithstanding, she figured prominently in Nancy's chatter. It was "Gerry O'Neal this" and "Gerry that", dropped with studied casualness at bridge clubs and PTA meetings and church suppers. "You know [beat] Geraldine O'Neal, the celebrity."

Concerning Gerry's fame, Nancy was as good as a clipping service, with an eagle eye for relevant printed matter. A picture in *People* ("Look, there she is with Paul Newman . . . Norman Mailer . . . Mario Cuomo . . . King Hussein.") The mention of her parties in a Liz Smith column. ("It's where the wheeler-dealers gather," Nancy explained, as though privy to their lofty secrets.) When Geraldine O'Neal made the cover of *Time*, Nancy bought out the news-stand.

David Whitfield took this obsession with good humour. Other men's wives had hobbies – soap opera or evangelical religion or painting on velvet. Nancy was entitled to hers.

Thus Lee grew up with the image of Gerry O'Neal always before her. Her own feelings were mixed. There was a might-have-been quality in her mother's adulation that was troubling. A note of yearning, of loss. Lee sometimes wondered if this vicarious brush with glamour hadn't provided the sole note of drama in Nancy's unromantic life. Perhaps it had.

The reverse, however, was highly unlikely. Geraldine O'Neal, Lee was certain, did not drop Nancy Schroeder Whitfield's name on all occasions. Lee doubted she thought of Nancy any oftener than once a year. Indeed, Lee might have questioned the very existence of this fabled friendship were it not for the birds.

Each Christmas, without fail, she sent Nancy a little ornamental bird, exquisitely wrapped, from wherever in the world she happened to be. Its arrival was a great occasion in the Whitfield home. The birds might be made of china or glass or carved wood or (when O'Neal had been Ambassador to Togo) of inlaid ivory. One year, in a stunning departure from tradition, she sent an authentic Audubon print. David said it must have cost a fortune.

The miniatures were set out on the living room mantel, the Audubon print above, where they served as conversation pieces and points of pride. Lee thought of it as The Gerry Corner. Like the Poets' Corner in Westminster Abbey. A sort of shrine.

"Why birds?" she once asked. "Is there a special significance?" Her mother had responded with a dreamy smile.

"Trophies," she said. "Trophies of a friendship."

That friendship, Lee noted, did not extend to phone calls, birthday cards, letters, visits or the other, more common forms of mutual esteem. Lee assumed the birds were simply part of a gift-giving pattern, a routine courtesy

19

handled by a secretary. To her mother, they implied a deathless tie.

"Call her the minute you get in," Nancy Whitfield had insisted on the eve of Lee's departure. "She'll be delighted to help."

Lee was sceptical. Why should a celebrity like Geraldine O'Neal knock herself out for the daughter of a schoolmate not seen in decades? The woman must be besieged with special requests, such being the curse of fame. Lee's claim upon her was the slenderest.

Lee Whitfield was not shy. Two years as a reporter on a Midwestern daily had taught her how to make cold calls, elicit facts, ask blunt questions. But this once, she felt intimidated. Geraldine O'Neal had achieved myth status among the Whitfields, cast a shadow across two thousand miles. Now that the physical distance had been bridged, Lee was wary of viewing the legend close-up.

Suppose O'Neal were to brush her off as just a pushy pain-in-the-ass? Suppose Lee couldn't even get through? Being snubbed in the exercise of her profession was something she could handle. Being snubbed on a personal level, something else. How would she explain it to her mother? Day after day, Lee put off making the call. The potential for humiliation was just too great.

"Well?" her mother would phone from Cedar City every Sunday. "How's the job hunt going?"

"Slowly," Lee would reply – the understatement of the year.

"Have you called Gerry?"

"Not yet."

"Why not? Honestly," she would cluck, "for someone who claims she wants to set the world on fire, to pass up a connection like Gerry O'Neal! Besides, I'm dying to know how you find her."

Ideally, Lee would have landed some super job on her merits, after which she would have felt easier about introducing herself. Then she could call not as the daughter of an old friend nor as a supplicant, but as a journalist attached to one or another prestigious publication. She

20

and Gerry would meet, if not as equals, at least as fellow professionals. It was a question of dignity.

But the weeks of interviews had not only exhausted Lee's resources; they had also weakened her resolve. If she was going to survive in this city, an increasingly doubtful proposition, she needed all the help she could get. So, on a Monday morning, swallowing both qualms and pride, she called the midtown office of O'Neal Associates.

And called and called and called. Not once did she get beyond the secretary. At any given moment, Ms O'Neal was, according to this tartar, in Washington, in conference, in flight, in a meeting, on another line, "unable to speak with you at this time".

Six attempts had sufficed. By Friday, Lee had given up hope of getting through. Instead she wrestled with the problem of explaining to her mother that in the glittering world of Geraldine O'Neal, the Whitfields were *persona non grata*.

And then – this afternoon without warning, this extraordinary invitation arrived.

Lee was utterly bewildered. Had it been extended out of genuine warmth? Or was it a means of getting Lee off her back with the minimum of one-on-one time? A snack, a drink and a fare-thee-well was, conceivably, the total worth of the Nancy-Gerry tie.

Yet even if the invitation led to nothing more than a one-night stand, Lee couldn't help but be thrilled. Tonight, she would enter the social stratosphere – and through the front door at that. It was the stuff of fairy tales.

Here she was, a raw newcomer, suddenly being afforded an insider's glimpse of New York. The other New York. The one that didn't appear on the Six O'Clock News. The New York of the bright and the beautiful and the powers that be. The city she had come to conquer. Such a chance might never arise again.

Impossible not to spin fantasies. Not to see this as a turning point in her fortune. A Rupert Murdoch might be there. A William Paley or Abe Rosenthal, only too happy to give an aspiring young journalist a break. Especially since that young journalist appeared to be an intimate of Geraldine O'Neal's.

Lee clasped her hands behind her head and gave herself over to a shameless daydream.

"Whitfield . . . Whitfield . . ." – the tycoon would furrow his brow – "are you by any chance the Whitfield who did that terrific series on the silo scandal?"

Lee would smile modestly and acknowledge this was so. "I'm surprised you're acquainted with it," she might add. "It was a story of strictly regional interest."

"I make it my business to be aware of superior journalism wherever it occurs," the great man would pronounce, after which he would offer her a slot on *The Times* or CBS or *Newsweek* or *The Village Voice* or whatever. And a byline, of course.

Careers had been launched on flimsier encounters, she supposed, and New York being Oz, who could say where tonight's adventure might lead? With a happy laugh, Lee returned to the matter in hand.

What To Wear?

It would have to be the black wool, after all. Safe, sophisticated, always-in-fashion black, capable of infinite interpretation. Enhanced for this evening with a double strand of pearls (not real, but who would know? who would care?) and matching ear-rings. Black bag and (for lack of ruby slippers) a pair of well-polished leather pumps.

The all-purpose outfit. How could she go wrong? Better understated than overdressed. She ran her fingers through the wealth of thick blonde hair. No hayseed fell out.

She must remember to pick up a nice bottle of wine for her hostess so as not to arrive at the party empty-handed. Lee hadn't been raised in a swamp after all. She knew a few things.

two

"Don't tell me!" The green eyes widened in delight, the mouth shaped itself into an ecstatic O. "Nancy's daughter!"

Well before Lee had a chance to introduce herself, Geraldine O'Neal's arms were wrapped around her in an exuberant hug. She smelled of Opium. "How splendid that you could come! Now, Nancy's daughter!" She stepped back to get a better view. "Let me look at you."

As she did, Lee too made a swift appraisal.

A bird of paradise, was the image that sprang to mind. A magnificent creature of fabulous origin, refulgent in silks of hot Venetian colours – russet and crimson and malachite green – that swept the floor in a luxurious rustle.

She was even taller than Nancy had intimated, the regal height extended further by spiky heels and a mass of upswept dark hair. Bigger than life, Lee thought, and twice as vivid, from the glowing skin to the husky voice to the innumerable silver bracelets that set up a musical jangle when she clapped her hands. As she was doing now.

Incredible to think this brilliant, dazzling, utterly gorgeous creature, this colour plate from some children's fairy book, was the same age as her mother. That both women came from the same modest background. Belonged to the same species, even!

Now she was embracing Lee with her generous smile.

"You're the image of your mother . . . the very image!"

"Thank you, Miss O'Neal. I take that as a compliment."

"As you were meant to. Your mother was one of the cutest gals in Hunter." Lee must have blinked, for her hostess gave a quick sharp laugh. "'Gals'! Sounds antique, doesn't it? Especially when I'm talking about your own mother. But that's how we thought of ourselves in the old days. Now please . . . call me Gerry. Everyone does except the tax man."

"Gerry then," Lee grinned, feeling momentarily at ease.

23

She was early, though thankfully not the first arrival. A dozen guests were mingling in the drawing room, while waiters glided among them bearing champagne in tulip glasses.

Only then did Lee realize she was still clutching a bottle of wine. The silver-foil gift box that had looked so festive in the liquor store looked so foolish now, as provincial as her "little black dress". This was not, she realized, a bring-your-own bottle do. Least of all, when the bottle was a sweet Italian wine.

In panic, she looked about for a place to stash it unobserved. Behind a vase . . . in the umbrella stand, perhaps. Too late! For Gerry had already caught sight of the package and swept it from her in a seamless gesture.

"Wine," she exclaimed. "Oh Lee . . . how sweet. Well, if it isn't – " she read the label – "yes it is! Asti Spumante!"

Lee alternately reddened and paled, but Gerry fixed her with those magnificent green eyes and smiled with genuine warmth.

"Why, I haven't had Asti Spumante since your mother and I were in college. And only then, on very special occasions."

Behind Lee, the front door opened to admit a fresh cloudburst of guests. They were moving toward Gerry – handsome worldly people, superbly dressed, about to claim the attention of their hostess. But Gerry's gaze never left Lee's face. "It was very thoughtful of you to remember and if you don't mind," she placed the bottle on the hall table, "I'm going to keep it for myself and enjoy it at leisure. In memory of those wonderful days. Thank you, Lee."

A patent lie, but so graciously done that Lee found herself believing it. Touched beyond words, she tried to frame a reply, but Gerry had already turned to greet the newcomers.

"Terry darling!...Alice! How splendid that you could come . . . You're looking marvellous, lambchop!" followed by a warm embrace. Lee headed through the double doors into the heart of the fray.

Soon, the spacious living room was dense with bodies – smooth-shaven men and elegant women, grouping and regrouping into an endless variety of clusters, spilling out into the back garden, into the dining room where an elaborate buffet had been set out, into the library, the front hall.

With each new arrival, the decibel level rose. Lee gathered snatches of dialogue here and there. Code words meaningless to her, but familiar currency among the other guests. And names names names – of people, places and things.

The Hamptons . . . Punch . . . Wedtech . . . Felix . . . Ivana . . . BAM . . . Vartan . . . Mortimers . . . Skadden-Arps . . . the Bess Mess . . . Robo-Toke.

This last, which Lee inferred to be some kind of gadget, was usually voiced with a nod in the direction of the guest of honour, a stocky Japanese with a fixed smile and hard eyes. What the link was she couldn't fathom. Another mystery to add to the pile.

She felt like a kid outside a pastry shop, nose pressed to the window. Everybody knew everybody, the happy babble confirmed. No one knew her.

Such hopes as she had of being rescued by Gerry quickly vanished. There were a hundred other guests to attend to. Lee felt abandoned.

Lord knows she tried to fit in. She smiled at total strangers, looked as friendly as she could, but nothing came of it. A half-dozen times, she managed to inject herself into an on-going conversation, but all she got for her efforts were vague nods and blind eyes. She might have been speaking Greek.

It was easier to storm the gates of heaven than to gain admission to these tight little clusters. Her clothes, her ignorance, even (or perhaps especially) her youth marked her as an outsider, a newcomer to the ranks. Except for the waiters, she was the youngest, most negligible person present.

Miss Nobody from Nowhere. The self-defined image stung.

As for those fancied encounters with Rupert Murdoch et al, Lee could only wince at her *naïveté*. The New York Establishment was not looking for recruits, thank you very much; its members were perfectly content with the status quo.

She would give herself till ten, and if nobody spoke to her by then, would slip out silently and send a "thank you" note in the morning. The social debt on both sides, hers and Gerry's, would then be discharged.

The minutes dragged by. No one breached her silence, though one elderly gent did sneak her a wink, more out of amusement than lust. She nibbled the passing canapé, nursed a second glass of champagne, then began inching toward the door. Her woollen dress felt hot and scratchy. It was cooler in the hall.

People were still arriving, others already leaving. Busy folk, she assumed, for whom a party like this was not a social milestone, merely another entry in a crowded Filofax.

Ten o'clock came and went and yet she lingered, still reluctant to write the night off. She wasn't likely to be in such a place again (at least not until after she was rich and famous), and it seemed a pity to let the opportunity go for naught.

She was, after all, a writer, an observer of the human cavalcade. If she couldn't wangle a job at this party, she could at least wring a story out of it. A satirical piece, ideally, designed for consumption back home. A piece slightly wicked yet meticulously observed. Because if there was anything that Midwesterners loved, it was seeing New York and New Yorkers skewered.

Briefly, she considered titles. TWINKLE TWINKLE was one possibility. Or PUTTING ON THE GLITZ. Yes. That was better. With a subhead, *How the Other Half of One Per Cent Lives*.

The journalist in her was now in charge, taking mental notes, imbibing atmosphere, studying the scene as lucidly and coolly as if the guests were specimens under glass.

It was a gift Lee had. The knack of creating an emotional distance between herself and the objects of her scrutiny, while sopping up telling details. A fly on the wall was how she defined her role, watching the action close up with sharp eyes and palpating antenna. In the picture but not of it.

26

She had developed these skills on the *Bismarck Tribune*, when she'd had to interview victims of sudden grief. Instant widows, bereft mothers, plane-crash survivors, foreclosed farmers, city officials caught with their hands in the till: the basic grist of the reporter's mill. You couldn't let it touch you, any more than a surgeon could afford to be squeamish at the sight of blood.

The trick was, to think of everything as a story.

Outside of that, Mrs Lincoln, how did you enjoy the show?

Tonight's story for instance, would be *Home Town Girl Views Life Among the Lofty*. She couldn't actually interview her fellow guests, that would be a breach of hospitality. But she could speculate. Enhance. Create vignettes that were part fact, part fancy, all style, in the manner of the New Journalism.

She inventoried the physical setting – the high-ceilinged rooms, the flowers, the furniture, the magnificent portrait at the top of the stairs – then moved on to what interested her most: a closer study of the people.

There was no dearth of material here. Despite the common factor of middle age and pricey clothes, they were a heterogeneous lot, with a healthy sprinkling of foreigners. Diplomats probably, given Gerry's background. Lee made out a dozen familiar faces, although she couldn't put a name to each one. Then she began zeroing in on types.

That portly fellow in the grey worsted suit, for instance, looked the classic Irish ward boss. Peddling influence or canvassing campaign funds was her bet.

Or the aging blonde soubrette in the green chiffon. Any moment, those spaghetti straps threatened to slip off her skinny shoulder and reveal a naked breast. When worst came to worst, would she run for cover or brazen it out?

Or the cute little priest standing by the buffet popping shrimp by the handful. He had everyone around him in a thrall. Was he taking confessions or telling racy jokes?

Listen hard (she penned the words mentally) *and you could get an inside tip on the market or the racetrack or the next hot*

Tex-Mex joint or hit Broadway show or the name of "my own personal trainer".

Shamelessly, Lee gave herself over to the role of voyeur.

The most intriguing object was Gerry herself. Wherever Lee looked, there she was – a darting splash of colour, in what Lee would describe to her readers as "golden palazzo pants sashed in a stab of red silk". She was working the room like a politician, with Mr Yoshimura in tow. Very tactile, Lee observed. Constantly touching, hugging, kissing, pressing flesh, creating physical contact in every encounter. Now and again, her laughter would float across the room, full-throated and musical. Clearly, the fun was wherever she was.

Lee watched, engrossed. Someone tapped her on the shoulder.

"No fair sitting on the sidelines. This is not a spectator sport."

He was tall, black and handsome in a beautifully tailored pinstripe suit. And under a hundred years old. Under forty even.

"Oh but it is!" she said, thankful for company. "I'm keeping score. Lions ten, Christians nothing. I'm Lee Whitfield, by the way."

"Jake Matthews." He offered his hand. "I'm Gerry's lawyer. I haven't seen you here before."

Lee explained her presence, then, absurdly grateful for his attentions, dropped all pretence of journalistic cool. "You know, you're the first person to address one word to me all evening. I was beginning to feel like the Invisible Man."

"No one could ever mistake you for a man," he said gallantly, "invisible or otherwise. But if Gerry hasn't introduced you around, don't take it to heart. She's on the job tonight, promoting a client. That's what they pay her for." He looked at Lee more closely. "You mean, you really don't know anybody here at all?"

"Not even by name," the words tumbled out. "A lot of people look familiar, and I suppose I ought to recognize them. Like the illustrations in history books. You know, group portraits where everybody's a somebody. Like *The Congress of Vienna, The Night Watch*, what have you. Only in the textbooks, they have a little sketch on the opposite page, with all the people shown in outline. Each one is keyed, so you can figure out who's who."

Jake laughed. "Perhaps I could provide the same service, although this particular group looks more like a Harry Hirshfield drawing than a Rembrandt." He scanned the crowd with a knowledgeable eye. "Apropos of art, that's the Director of the Guggenheim. Kissinger of course you recognize . . . George Steinbrenner . . . That bald fellow's Eli Austrian . . ."

"Any relation to Austrian's Fifth Avenue, the department store?"

"He is Austrian's Fifth Avenue."

"Now the shorty with the ferocious mustache and elevator shoes?"

"That's Señor Oliveira. He lives here." And when Lee raised her eyebrows, Jake explained that the diminutive Bolivian occupied the garden apartment of the brownstone. "Gerry invites him to her parties now and then. Now if you look over at the piano, you'll see . . ."

Lee listened rapt as he culled faces from the crowd, often supplementing his recital with telling anecdotes. There were investment bankers, fashion designers, senators, sportsmen, leading lights from the UN: everybody operating at full steam, wheeling, dealing.

The beefy Irishman (she was delighted to have her guess-work confirmed) was indeed a politico, a City Commissioner, no less. Her shrimp-popping priest on the other hand was revealed to be . . .

"Cardinal Novak?" she marvelled. "Himself? Are you sure? I thought cardinals always wore red."

"It's after hours." Jake laughed. "Although His Eminence is probably still on the job. He's been after Gerry's soul for ages. Now that fellow by the mantel . . ."

Behind them, the front door swung open for yet another latecomer, a youngish man, pale-haired above lashless blue eyes.

29

He strode into the hall, peeled off his topcoat and gloves, then with hardly a lateral glance, handed them to Jake.

"Lawrence Winterbourne," he said, expecting to be announced.

Lee froze. What had happened was all too clear. The new arrival, seeing nothing beyond a black skin, presumed Jake was hired help, existing only to fetch and serve. Jake, stunned, said nothing but his eyes were an open wound.

A split second later, Gerry emerged from the crush, and in that instant, Lee knew she had witnessed it all.

Now she strode toward them like a toreador entering the arena.

"Larry darling!" Gerry crooned as she embraced the awful man with a killer grip. "How splendid of you to come. You're looking terrific. And I see you've already had the privilege of meeting our very very distinguished guest" – she continued without skipping a beat – "Prince Jacob Matawele of the Burundi legation. Such an honour to have a member of the royal house in my humble abode! Do be a lamb, Larry, and take His Excellency's things. You can put them in the upstairs den next to the landing. Then fetch him a drink. That's a pet!"

Lee was mute with admiration.

As for Winterbourne, his face had turned a blotchy red. He didn't know whether he was being euchred or not, but had no choice except to do as told. Lips clenched, cheeks afire, he retrieved his coat and gloves and marched upstairs.

Her face beaming with malicious glee, Gerry watched him go. "Prick!" she muttered to his back. "By the way, he absolutely loathes being called 'Larry'. You might want to keep that in mind."

Then, in an abrupt shift of mood, she stretched her arms wide, putting one around Jake, the other around Lee and drew them to her.

"Now let's put the unpleasantness behind us," she said. "What are you two kids doing out here anyway? This is supposed to be a party, goddamit. Jake, love, do me a favour. Get people over to the buffet table or I'll be eating this stuff for a month. Lee . . . you're too pretty to be

30

loitering in hallways. Go flirt. Have fun! That's an order."
She blew a kiss and headed back into the living room.

"What a woman!" the erstwhile "Prince" shook his head
in wonder.

"Fantastic!" Lee murmured.

The incident had a galvanizing effect on her. That Gerry
should treat her as an intimate, a fellow conspirator,
seemed to Lee the ultimate compliment. Whether it was
the sudden rush of "belonging" or the third glass of champagne or a general warming of the atmosphere, Lee didn't
know, but from that point on, she felt as though she were
born to be here in this room. With the other "insiders".

She permitted Jake to move off (having already hogged
an unconscionable amount of his time) and began socializ-
ing in earnest, determined to speak to everyone at least
once during the evening.

"I'm Lee Whitfield and I don't believe we've met," she
introduced herself around, this time without fear of rejection. Within minutes she was mingling, laughing, making
small talk. Unconsciously, picking up the style of her hostess, she opened each gambit with a bit of flattery, deserved
or not. ("I loved your book . . . what a stunning dress . . .
I'm absolutely thrilled to meet you.")

The natives were friendly when stroked, and even world-
renowned celebrities, she realized to her astonishment,
managed to absorb yet another bit of fulsome praise.

Jake's remark came back to her, about this being a professional occasion. Not just for Gerry, he had indicated,
but for most of those present. She had a swift keen sense
of deals being made right and left. A merger might be born
here. The financing for a new Broadway show. A bank
loan for a million-dollar project. In these precincts, anything was possible.

In a corner of the room, Gerry was huddled with Mr
Yoshimura and the City Hall panjandrum. The three of
them looked utterly rapt. It pleased Lee to think that Gerry
was pulling off some fabulous coup demanding both verve
and acumen. Then the little group broke up and Gerry
moved on, always with a hug, a laugh, dispensing love,
reaping admiration, mixing, fixing – who knew what!

It gave Lee a shivery feeling, this proximity to power. For the first time in her life, she had a sense of what life was like at the heart of the action, the hub of the universe. And it was intoxicating.

The crowd gradually moved into the dining room. Lee followed.

The food was sumptuous, of an order that she had never known. Great silver platters heaped high with salmon, lobster, smoked trout, half a dozen different kinds of pâté.

"Gerry always does put out a terrific spread," the man behind her said.

"Yes, doesn't she?" the new insider murmured. In her joy, even the dread black woollen dress was forgotten.

She took a plate, sat down at one of the little tables between a Broadway producer and a Wall street CEO.

The discussion turned to crime in the streets and something called the Guardian Angels.

"The religious organization?" Lee asked.

The producer laughed as though she'd said something witty. The Wall Streeter furrowed his brows.

"I take it that the crime rate doesn't worry you."

"Personally, I think it's vastly over-rated," Lee said. The fourth glass of champagne had made her euphoric. "A creation of the Six O'Clock News. Why, I've been here nearly a month and I haven't been mugged or raped even once."

"Where are you from?" the financier asked.

"Cedar City."

"And where's that?"

Lee looked at the crayfish *quenelles* on her plate. At the glass of Piper-Heidsieck in her hand. At the banker in his thousand-dollar suit. At Beverly Sills sitting at the next table fishing something out of a gold mesh handbag. At the room . . . the china . . . the flowers in their silver bowls. . . . the crystal chandelier . . .

"Cedar City," she pronounced slowly, "is about as far from Manhattan as you can get, without actually leaving the planet."

There was general laughter. A few feet away, Gerry O'Neal caught Lee's eye and winked.

Then, far too soon, the party was over. As if at a signal, people were gathering wraps, exchanging kisses, saying their farewells. Lee joined the departing stream, not wishing to leave, not daring to be the last one out.

"It's been a wonderful. . . ." she began.

Gerry snared her by the wrist.

"You stay!" she whispered. "We haven't talked. I'll meet you upstairs in the den."

three

WHOOSH!

The silver-kid sandal came flying through the air. It caromed off the wall and hit the floor with a thud.

Gerry O'Neal had entered the study, a Diet Pepsi in hand.

Then WHOOSH! Another high-kick worthy of a Radio City Music Hall Rockette – and the second silver shoe followed suit.

"God!" she exclaimed. "I was born to live barefoot. Sit sit sit!" – for Lee had sprung to her feet – "and let me catch my breath."

With a rustle of silk and a jangle of bracelets, she collapsed into an over-sized sofa, stripped off her belt, unbuttoned her waistband, peeled back the tab on the can and swallowed off half the contents in a gulp.

"Total bliss," she sighed. "The finest moment of the day, I swear! Like being let out of prison. I've been on the go non-stop since eight this morning. You can take yours off if you like. Shoes, that is. Or anything else that you care to. Aren't you hot in that dress? Just give me a second or two of quiet, then we'll chat."

That said, Gerry laid her head back, shut her eyes and proceeded to doze off. Lee used the moment to observe her at close range.

Her first impression had been wrong, Lee acknowledged.

In repose, Gerry no longer appeared to be so dramatically her mother's junior. It was her animation that fostered the illusion of youth. Awake, Gerry exuded sparkle, glamour, a raw vitality that mocked the passage of time, making her seem almost girlish. Sleeping, she couldn't mask the fifty-odd years.

That said, she remained an astonishingly handsome woman. There was a touch of poetry about the face, the romance of some half-forgotten Irish ballad in the dark cloud of hair. The lips might be a trace too sensual, too wide, the eyes too deeply set, but only a perfectionist would quibble. The sculptor had done his work well.

Yet though the years had dealt kindly with Geraldine O'Neal, they had dealt with her nonetheless. Close to, Lee observed a network of fine lines etched across the forehead, around the eyes; the waist not quite so slender, nor the jaw so firm as appeared at first glance. Beneath the glittering array of silver bracelets, the large capable hands bore a weathered look.

Her nails were short, Lee observed. Business-like. Perhaps she bit them. An odd failing to a woman so *soignée*. It indicated that the idol was vulnerable after all.

Studying the sleeping woman in such intimate detail, Lee began to grow uncomfortable. Should she stay? Leave? Lock the door behind her? As if on cue, Gerry's green eyes snapped open.

"Did I doze off?"

"Five minutes," Lee replied.

"Five minutes out of both our lives," Gerry laughed, suddenly alert. "God, I hate sleeping. It's a total waste of time."

Her voice, low and sexy, was younger than her face. It snuggled into Lee's ears. Beneath the words ran a current of fun, exuberance. Like a teenager, the night before the prom. Now she rubbed her hands with anticipatory gusto. The nap had given her second wind.

"Be a love, Lee. Pour us a pair of nice hefty brandies, then fill me in on what's been going on back home. I want to hear all the family lowdown. What they've been doing, thinking all these years. The works! To begin with, how's your mother?"

Face up-tilted like a theatre goer at a long-awaited show, Gerry was all eyes and ears and expectations. If only, Lee wished, she could dazzle her with racy anecdotes, riveting dramas of domestic life. But Lee had only meagre stock with which to work.

Tolstoy was right. Happy families *were* all alike, and of the Whitfields there was little to say without getting mired in boring detail. No triumphs, no tragedies, no soaring heights or lower depths.

Her mother was fine, thank you very much. Active in the Literary Society. Mainstay of the Women's College Club. And now that all the kids were out of her hair (Lee was the youngest, did Gerry know?), she'd got herself elected to the Town Council. It entailed a lot of running around for very little money, but she seemed to enjoy it. Said it made an interesting change from the PTA. In answer to Gerry's question – yes, Nancy still plugged away at her poetry when time allowed. Who knows? Maybe some day she'd get published. They kept their fingers crossed.

Her brother Drew was a chemist with a biotech firm in Omaha that specialized in developing new strains of hybrid corn. Her oldest sister had married a Volkswagen dealer and was raising three kids in Cedar City. Her other sister was divorced and selling real estate in Fond du Lac, her husband having run off one fine summer evening with a former Miss Wisconsin Cheese.

"The one note of high drama in our lives," Lee said wryly.

"Miss Wisconsin Cheese," Gerry laughed. "The mind boggles. The stomach churns. And your father? He's well?"

"Dad's terrific."

For over two decades, David Whitfield had been the Director of Music in the Public Schools and "it may not seem like all that much to you," Lee said, fishing for some example of family distinction, however modest, "but Dad's built the Cedar City Wolverines into one of the finest High School marching bands in the entire Midwest. They won the Sousa Medal at the State Fair three years running . . . the only small-town band that ever did."

Gerry hummed in acknowledgement. "Playing *Seventy-Six Trombones*, I have no doubt. It all sounds so . . . well, like a page out of Garrison Keillor. I can't quite picture it. You see, I remember your father as a dashing Juilliard student. Very bohemian for that time, with the most wonderful head of long wavy hair. In fact, he was about the only fellow I knew who didn't have a crew cut."

"Dad's still kind of dashing," Lee said, "although you

can forget about the long wavy hair. He's, to put it kindly
– thin on top."

"Not bald!" Gerry looked distressed.

"Let's just say that compared to dad, Kojak is a hairy
ape. The Resident Bowling Ball, Mom calls him. Anyhow,
he plans to retire the end of this year."

"So young?"

"He'll be sixty-two in August, which is when the School
Board likes to pension 'em off. They want to make way for
a younger man. Dad claims that he's looking forward to
having time for himself, but I'm not so sure. . . ." Gerry's
lips pursed and Lee guessed that the topic, with its inti-
mations of mortality, upset her. "I'm sorry," she said.

"I always think of your parents as young, I suppose. But
of course they were when I saw them last."

"Dad's very active," Lee softened the blow. "He fishes
and does carpentry. He'll manage to keep busy."

"Of course. And your mother . . . she's happy with her
life?"

It was question so outrageously personal as to leave
Lee speechless. However, Gerry apparently didn't expect a
prompt answer, for she continued in a pensive voice.

"She could have been a contender," Gerry mused. "Yes
indeed. Nancy was just bursting with talent, practically
exuding it through her pores. A regular fireball. And full
of plans! My God! She was going to write an epic verse
play or the Great American Novel or whatever, remake the
world with a stroke of the pen. We were very big on social
justice at the time, up to our eyeballs in ideals, your mother
even more than I. Of course, I'm talking about when we
were nineteen, twenty – before she met your father." Gerry
caught Lee's eye and smiled, as though apologizing for
this bout of nostalgia. "In those days, you see, we women
faced a much clearer set of choices. It tended to be either/or.
As it happened, your mother chose the *either* and I chose
the *or*. Today, of course, it's another story."

She shrugged. "You probably think I've no right to ask
such an intimate question, apropos of your mother being
happy, but Nancy was very close to my heart. Naturally,
I'm curious as to how things worked out."

Lee, to whom this recitation of her mother's early glories seemed wellnigh incredible, now felt a catch in her throat.

"All for love or the world well lost? Is that what you're asking? Did my mother make the right decision back then?"

"I only asked you if she's happy."

My parents have a terrific relationship, Lee was tempted to respond, presuming that would suffice. In Cedar City, women of Nancy's generation tended to consider themselves happy or otherwise largely in terms of their marriages. In which case Nancy was happy.

But was there another case to answer? Lee didn't know. Try though she might, she couldn't match Gerry's image of her mother as a rising star in the literary firmament with the comfy chatelaine of 38 Elmhurst Place. It was ludicrous. Her mother was . . . well, "Mom": maker of beds and casseroles, mender of scraped knees and small appliances, comparison shopper, Saturday night bowler, marathon phone gabber, popular with the neighbours, active in the town, complaining only about the weather and a touch of arthritis.

That this was not a role in life Lee fancied for herself seemed beside the point. Gerry's question remained – was Nancy happy?

"Yes . . ." came the equivocal answer. "She certainly seems to be."

Gerry looked thoughtful. "Good. I'm glad for her. Now let's talk about you. You haven't told me, what brings you to New York?"

It was the chance Lee had been waiting for all evening. She took a deep breath and plunged.

"Ambition."

The word boomed. Reverberated. Seemed to hang for a moment in the air.

"Ambition!" Gerry echoed. "That's such a pregnant term. It says so much and so little. What precisely is it that you're ambitious for?"

"I want . . ." Lee cleared her throat, uncertain where to begin. Gerry was watching her with an odd expression.

"I want . . . to be somebody! To make my mark in the big world." She saw the flash of quick sympathy in Gerry's eyes, the spark of recognition, and knew she had struck a chord. "I want to be famous, to have my name stand for something. I want a hush to fall when I enter a room. I want heads to turn . . . people to murmur 'that's Lee Whitfield'. I want to live centre stage, know the finest minds of the century, mingle freely with the brilliant and powerful. I want to be one of their number, to have my opinions count. Exchange ideas, make a contribution. I mean no disrespect for my family, Gerry. I love them. They're good kind people, but I don't want that sort of life for myself. You can't imagine what it's like, Gerry, growing up in some stagnant little backwater, feeling that the world is passing you by. It's like being invisible. My mother, as you know, is a great poetry quoter and there's a line she's fond of – from Gray's *Elegy*, perhaps you know it – 'Full many a flower is born to blush unseen. . . .'"

" ' . . . and waste its sweetness on the desert air.' " Gerry nodded, leaning closer. "Therefore you came to New York. I understand. And I fully sympathize."

She sees! She knows! Lee was suddenly borne aloft by the heady sensation of having found a champion, a sharer of the dream. At that moment she would have gone to the stake for Gerry O'Neal.

"I'd rather die than live out my life as that desert flower," she said. "I came here quite simply because this is the toughest, grandest, most challenging, most exciting city in the world, and if you don't make it in New York, you just don't make it. All those superlatives New Yorkers claim for themselves are true. Everywhere else is bush league. I learned that tonight."

"Why? What happened tonight?"

"Tonight," Lee said, "I had a glimpse of how fantastic and varied the great world can be. Talking to Henry Kissinger . . . meeting a cardinal. Why, just watching you, listening to you was a revelation! You're so sophisticated, so plugged in. That's how I myself hope to live some day. You're my model, don't you see? You prove it's all possible."

She sat there, cheeks flushed, having blurted out more

than she intended. "I guess I sound like a half-baked freshman," she began, but Gerry was riveted.

"That's very flattering," she said at last. "Irresistibly
flattering. However, it isn't enough to dream the dream.
You have to pursue it. What is it you do, Lee, that's going
to propel you to the heights? Do you dance? Act?
Paint? . . ."

"I'm a writer."

"Like your mother . . ."

"No, not like my mother. She's more of a romantic. I
deal with facts, not poetics. I'm a good observer, a sharp
reporter. My dream is to be a feature writer for either
newspapers or major magazines. Maybe eventually edit
one of my own. I've got a good sense of style, a sharp turn
of phrase. I think I could be another Tom Wolfe, given the
chance. The trouble is, I can't get a toe-hold in this town.
I'd be willing to take any kind of job in any kind of publication – run copy, proof-read, write obits. . . ."

"Getting down to specifics," Gerry broke in. "How's
your résumé?"

"I happen to have one right here in my bag."

"A girl who comes to a party bearing a résumé." Gerry
laughed. "I like that. OK . . . let's take a look."

She scanned the single page of typescript with a knowing
eye.

"Twenty-four years old . . . Cedar City High where you
were Yearbook editor. Then college . . . Phi Bete, that's
good . . . at Midwestern U." She made a face. "That's bad.
They go for Ivy League types here in New York, as you
may have observed. However, not a helluva lot you can
do about the old college tie. Editor, campus newspaper . . .
good, good. Researcher, *Cedar City Times* . . . sounds
dinky."

"That was a summer job," Lee interjected.

"Change it to 'reporter'. More impressive. A small-town
paper, no one's going to check up on you. Now . . . Run-
ner-Up, Haversham Prize . . . whatever that is. Change
that to 'Winner'. Again, who's to know?"

"But . . ." Lee spluttered.

"Listen, sweetie. Everybody lies on résumés. It's standard procedure. You can be damn sure whoever reads yours is going to knock off fifty per cent as pure hype. So give yourself that fifty per cent edge for openers. Now, we get to the heavy-weight stuff. Two years with the *Bismarck Tribune* . . . City Desk. . . . Feature Writer . . . Award-winning series on – " the brow furrowed "- 'silo leasing'?"

"It was a major coup!" Lee explained. The preceding year, she had uncovered a price-fixing conspiracy among the agribusiness giants and revealed it in a six-part exposé. To Dakota farmers, the story was an eye-opener, with repercussions in the State House.

"You have it in your portfolio?"

"I do. It's my most important sample."

"Well. We don't have an awful lot of grain silos in Manhattan, I'm afraid. Still, I suppose a story's a story." Gerry smiled and handed Lee back her résumé. "Now what I want you to do is fix this up along the lines I suggested, then bring it around to my office on Monday. One of the girls will run it off on a laser printer. It looks more professional that way. Next – what do you wear when you're on interviews?"

"A classic-tailored grey flannel suit."

"With . . . what kind of accessories?"

"A white silk shirt, black pumps, pearl ear-rings. Very conservative and business-like." Lee was proud of the effect.

"And forgettable, too." Gerry shook her head. "You want to give them a jolt of colour. If you insist on wearing grey flannel, at least spice it up with something outrageous. Here!" She slipped off her ear-rings, huge glittery medallions of silver and emerald green, and handed them to Lee. "Try them on. Go ahead . . . don't be shy. Oh, yes. Just smashing! Take a look in the mirror. You like? Keep them . . . they're yours."

"Oh, but I couldn't . . . absolutely not!"

"They're only costume," Gerry said. "No big deal. Besides, they look better on you than on me. And they have absolutely nothing to do with grey flannel suiting, which is a plus. Take it from a pro, Lee. One of the quickest ways to get people to remember you is to wear something startling. It doesn't have to be expensive, just big and frivolous! Tough but feminine – that's the image you want to project. And maybe even a little reckless. Or something sexy with scarves. You know what God's greatest gift to the poor working girl is? The ability to accessorize! That and good legs. Now you have the full secret of my success. So no more arguments, take the ear-rings."

Lee laughed. "Thank you. I'll wear them with pleasure."

"Now," Gerry said, "the real nitty-gritty. Where have you been interviewed?"

Lee went down the list, beginning with *The New York Times* and the glossy magazines, moving downscale to the trade papers, the scandal sheets, the supermarket digests. "I even applied for a job at something called *Astrology Today*."

"My favourite reading," Gerry grinned. "What did they tell you?"

"That I didn't figure in their future."

"Probably just as well. Who'd you speak to at *Time-Life*?"

"A woman in personnel."

"At Condé Nast? Enterprise Publications?"

"Ditto. They take my résumé and say they'll keep it on file."

Gerry rolled her eyes. "A total waste of time. Personnel departments are notorious for never hiring anyone above the level of washroom attendants. Anyhow, they know fuck all about writing. You should be power-lunching every day with editors, cultivating friendships with senior staff. Connections are crucial – especially in the media business. The people who make the news tend to hang out with the people who write it. It's all one huge network, a kind of mutual backscratch society. I'm not saying that talent counts for naught, it's vital! But as you must be aware, journalism is considered a glamorous profession, which means that there are probably twenty qualified applicants for every entry-level job. Kids from the best schools, the best families. And half of them are willing to work for peanuts. It's tough to get anywhere without connections."

Lee, whose "power lunch" that day had been with a paperback book on a stool at Yogurteria, could only groan.

42

"But I don't have connections."

"Of course you do," Gerry said crisply. "You have me! What do you think old friendships are for? Now, grab your pen and let's make a list . . ."

She began reeling off names of key people at *Fortune, Newsweek, Vogue, Manhattan Inc.* while Lee scribbled furiously.

"Tell you who'll be invaluable in your situation. Bobby Obermayer. I'll drop him a note tomorrow. You know who he is, of course . . . The head of Enterprise Publications. That's half a dozen magazines right there, plus a new one they're starting up. What the hell . . . Bobby owes me one. Not that my note will actually get you in to see the great man – he communes only with God these days – but he'll pass it along for action, which guarantees you a respectful hearing farther down the scale. So call there Tuesday. Insist on speaking to his personal secretary, a Miss Mintchik. Tell her you're the gal I wrote about, she'll set up the appropriate interviews. Well, that's the list," she concluded. "I can only get you in the door. After that, you're on your own. And don't forget to wear your new ear-rings."

"I don't know how to thank you." Lee threatened to burst into tears, but Gerry deflected her.

"I'll think of a way some other time. And, if you don't mind taking another bit of advice from me – I seem to be in my 'Dear Abby' mode – when you're being interviewed by old-timers, try to get them to talk about themselves. Everybody in the office has already heard their war stories a million times, poor bastards. They're delighted to get a fresh audience. Just sit there and look googly-eyed and you'll be doing them a service. Yourself, too. I expect a full report from you before the end of next week. But enough shop talk. How's New York treating you otherwise? How's your apartment?"

"The pits."

"The rent?"

"Exorbitant."

"The neighbourhood?"

"Junkie's paradise."

"Your social life?"

"Thus far, limited to Saturday night at the laundromat."

"No one special guy, I gather?"

There had been, Lee explained, back in Bismarck, a computer whiz with whom she'd been living for over a year. A lovely man. "Robbie wanted to get married, but it wasn't in the cards."

"Oh?" Gerry had risen from the sofa and began fussing about the room, emptying ashtrays. To Lee's astonishment, she picked up her brandy glass and poured the contents back into the decanter. "This stuff costs fifty bucks a jug. No point wasting it. You were saying about your guy back in Bismarck. What happened?"

"Just that our careers took us in different directions. He was starting a job in Silicon Valley and of course I was coming here. I couldn't let my feeling for Robbie get in the way of my future. Maybe that sounds callous but I'm willing to do whatever's necessary to establish myself, short of committing a capital crime."

Gerry smiled, and Lee, pleased with her reaction, continued.

"I want you to know, Gerry, I'm not a sentimentalist. I've got what it takes to make it to the top!"

"And what is that?"

"Ambition! Burning ambition."

Gerry turned and looked thoughtful.

"Everybody's ambitious, Lee. In this town you could throw a glass of water out the window and be guaranteed to splatter twenty ambitious people, each of whom would blithely climb over their grandmother's body for the next step up on the corporate ladder. Ambition – even burning ambition – isn't enough to carve out a place for yourself. You need something more."

"I know," Lee concurred. "You need smarts."

Gerry shook her head. "Everybody's got that too. Christ! you young people are so smart and capable, it's scary. What I'm talking about is passion."

Lee stared at her, not comprehending.

"Passion," Gerry repeated slowly. "It's not a word that's particularly popular with your generation. Like idealism. Also an unfashionable term. Perhaps they're one and the

44

same. I don't know. But whichever word you choose, it's the difference between competence and greatness. True, heartfelt, consuming passion. The will to commit yourself totally to whatever you believe in, whether it's business or love or politics or writing for a magazine – even if it means throwing caution to the winds. Passion is how you know that you're alive. And it's the one factor they don't teach you in college, not even in psychology courses!"

"Passion," Lee echoed politely.

"Passion. The ability – no, more than that, the need to put every inch of yourself on the line. Even when it's dumb. Especially when it's dumb. The world is full of pussy-footers and pragmatists and technocrats and zombies, kiddo. Don't you forget it. People who take the joy out of living, the zest out of success. You have to fight them with everything you've got. And fight those impulses in yourself. Sometimes the smartest thing you can do is be stupid. I should know. I've done it time and again."

She paused and saw that Lee was mystified.

"You don't know what I'm talking about, do you?"

Lee groped for a cue.

"You're saying I should fling myself wholeheartedly into my work and not take any shit."

"Not exactly." Gerry hooked her arm through Lee's and guided her toward the staircase. She sounded amused. "Forget I opened my mouth. An old-timer's rambling. Now, in your mother's absence, suppose you let me do the maternal number for a bit. I want you to take some of this wonderful food home with you. Don't give me an argument. I bet you're subsisting on canned tuna and Kraft Macaroni and Cheese . . . am I right? Of course I am. Yours truly is absolutely psychic on such matters. Better than those creeps at *Astrology Today*. So," she led Lee into the kitchen where the woman from the catering service was cleaning up the remains of the buffet, "give my young friend here some of that lovely roast beef. No no!" She elbowed the caterer aside, with a brusque gesture. "You call that a slice?" Then, bangle bracelets clinking, silks swishing, she proceeded to hack off a two-pound cut. "Now, let's see . . . what else? How about some shrimp, gravlax, a little pâté? Those *quenelles* went like wild fire. I must order them again. Fresh figs. Do you like chèvres?"

Lee reddened. "I'm not quite sure what it is."

"French goat cheese," Gerry said. "You either love it or hate it. But you won't know till you try. I'll cut you some."

Lee watched, fascinated, as Gerry tossed beef, seafood, fruits, cheeses, French bread, *petits fours* – enough groceries for a week – into two Gristede shopping bags until they were filled to bursting. "There!" she handed the parcels over. "Better than the Automat or wherever it is you kids eat nowadays. Now, I don't want you to even think about the subway at this time of night. Full of loonies and grifters. Take a taxi home. On some things it's worthwhile splurging. Cabs are one. Now! I expect you to call me by . . . let's see, Thursday afternoon and tell me how it's going. Better yet, come around to the office and have a drink. Five o'clock. Super!" She ushered Lee out of the door. "Good luck on your interviews – and don't you dare not wear those ear-rings! That's an order!"

four

Gerry's injunction to the contrary, Lee Whitfield did not take a taxi home. Nor the subway. She walked the sixty-odd blocks. More accurately, she floated – anchored only by two bulging Gristede bags and a pair of jumbo earrings.

While ambulances raced and sirens screeched, Lee inhabited a private cloud, unseeing and unhearing, wafting past bleary-eyed doormen, past mansions that housed sleeping millionaires and trust fund babies, past Bloomingdales and Banana Republic, past seedy gay bars where male hustlers were peddling flesh and fantasy, past late-night head shops and all-night delis, past the spanking new offices of *Trend Magazine*, past a team of Con Ed workmen drilling for a Better New York, past a trio of armed robbers holding up a Cuban social club, past Bellevue Hospital, past garbage-lined streets and dank alleys, past bag ladies and muggers and winos and junkies and leatherboys with purple hair, past dog walkers and dope dealers and lovers and loonies and a man wanted in four states for multiple murder, past them all until, towards two in the morning, she arrived unscathed at her doorstop.

It was a journey that – when she was some weeks worldlier – she would have better sense than to repeat. But on this chilly spring night, Lee was wrapped in a mantle of grace. As with saints and simpletons and new-born babes, Fate smiled upon her ignorance. Nothing mean or low could touch her. She felt – transcendent.

It is given to few mortals to read the future, but for the first time in her life Lee Whitfield felt possessed of that power. She had seen the woman she wanted to become. Would become! Must become! It was a splendid and heartening vision. It was awesome.

Gerry O'Neal sat up in bed, unable to sleep, listening to The Best of the Big Bands on tape. Alone – worse luck! –

as was most often the case in recent years. The days of wine and roses had long since given way to nights of being curled up with nothing more lubricious than a Ruth Rendell mystery and a box of crackers. She was suffering from what it pleased her to call Post-Party Depression.

"You're gettin' old, kid," she announced to no one in particular.

Getting careless, too.

Twice this evening she had inadvertently referred to Yoshimura as Yamamoto. A war criminal, for Chrissakes! She had linked her prospective client with the man who'd master-minded the attack on Pearl Harbor. Mercifully, Gerry had caught herself before anyone else did. Besides, how many people remembered who Yamamoto was? Hell, who remembered Pearl Harbor any more? The actual day, that is, and what you were doing when you heard the news. Not Mr Yoshimura, to be sure. He wasn't even born then. But Gerry remembered. She had been reading a Batman comic book.

Her ambivalence concerning Mr Yoshimura had nothing to do with nationality. She was beyond that type of prejudice. On the positive side, the man appeared to be a lavish spender, an admirable quality in a client. But he expected value for money, and how much value remained to be seen.

Taki Yoshimura was the marketing director of a Japanese computer company. He had approached Gerry a month earlier and asked for her help. Being unfamiliar with the New York power structure, he needed a PR firm to get him launched. His target was the city's Transit Authority. His product: an electronic turnstile.

RoboToke (as the device was called) was state-of-the-art: vandal-proof, robbery-proof, labour-saving, superior in every conceivable way to the antediluvian model currently in use in the subways. The only glitch: it would cost in excess of $50,000,000 to put in place.

Gerry heard him out with growing scepticism. The subway system was a catalogue of problems: crime, dirt, graffiti, aging trains. It was as much as the Transit Authority could do to keep the cars on the rails, she told him, let alone spring for an outlay of this size. Mr Yoshimura faced a very hard sell.

Moreover, she was puzzled as to why he'd come to her, since his problem was one of economics rather than image. At that, Mr Yoshimura grew effusive. Even in Tokyo, he insisted, she was renowned for her tact, her charm, her powers of persuasion. The O'Neal touch would be invaluable to his enterprise. And of course the O'Neal connections. All he asked was that she put him in touch with the right people and say a few words on his behalf.

"We Japanese prefer to deal with friends than with strangers," he explained, "and the way to do that is to turn strangers into friends."

Gerry mulled his proposal over for several days, although his intent was perfectly scrutable. Yoshimura was in the market for high-level contacts. He was looking for a power broker.

Her instinct was to turn him down. She was neither an influence peddler nor a lobbyist, and he was clearly a man who expected personal service. The whole thing smacked of giant headaches. But, as so often before in her life, practical considerations prevailed. A client was a client, a fee was a fee and business having been slow of late, Gerry agreed to give it a go. Besides, where was the harm in putting interested parties in touch? In one manner or another, she'd been doing it for years.

Tonight's reception had been the opening barrage. The guests were drawn largely from her "A-List" and provided a nice *mélange* of glitter and clout. Not that the Kissingers or Cardinal Novak were likely to extend themselves in the promotion of electronic turnstiles, given their broader interests, but their presence lent the gathering cachet. And there had been a number of equally powerful if less glamorous figures (city officials, investment bankers) who were precisely the type of "friend" Yoshimura had in mind. By the evening's end, he had declared himself satisfied. Come Monday, he would sign the contract, and Gerry could congratulate herself. The party had been a roaring success.

Yet her after-the-ball sense of anticlimax remained. Ensuring other people's fun was strenuous work. She hardly ate on these occasions (who could spare the time?) and rarely drank (who could risk the indiscretions?) By the time she'd kissed the last guest goodbye, she was in a most peculiar state. She felt mentally revved up and physically drained. Her eyes still smarted from cigar smoke, her mouth muscles ached from perpetual smiles, yet some part of her was geared up to push on into morning. A night club, a cosy after-hours spot, a ride through Central Park in a hansom, topped off by breakfast at the Empire Diner. Ham and eggs with fried potatoes and a paper napkin on your lap. The works!

Now *that* would have been a fitting conclusion to the evening. Trouble was, nobody kept those hours these days. At least not people her age. And on those occasions when they did stay up all night, it was for business, not pleasure.

On the stereo *The Woodchoppers' Ball* gave way to Helen Forrest singing *Skylark*. Gerry folded her arms and let the music wash over her. So beautiful! So romantic!

Someone should erect a stone to Hoagy Carmichael, she thought. They don't write tunes like that anymore.

It was true. Indisputably true. How could you compare *Skylark* to that unintelligible garbage on MTV, or Helen Forrest to Motley Crue?

As a rule, Gerry grew testy when people of her generation waxed sentimental about how great everything used to be in the good old days and how the world has been going downhill ever since. "Mush alert!" she once hollered at a dinner party when her escort started wandering down Memory Lane. "I'm sick and tired of hearing about the goddamn Brooklyn Dodgers. They've been gone for over twenty years. Isn't it time you switched your allegiance to the Mets?"

Instant nostalgia set her teeth on edge: it stamped her whole generation as out-of-date, mastodons saddled with the past. If Gerry prided herself on anything, it was keeping up with the times, being contemporary in the fullest sense.

She was the first person in her circle to buy a word processor, a microwave oven. She thought the automated cash machines (another of the old-timers' favourite bleats) were simply terrific, far better than standing in line at the bank.

But now and then, in the solitude of her bedroom, she admitted the old farts were sometimes right – at least about certain things.

The songs *were* lovelier when she was young, the movie stars more glamorous. Food was tastier. (Why, kids today didn't even know what authentic vanilla ice cream was like, let alone real tomatoes!) And, at least in her own mind, the women were more passionate, the men more ardent. She didn't miss the snows of yesteryear. She missed the fires.

Skylark ended. The tempo picked up, romped, stomped as Count Basie swung into the *One O'Clock Jump*. You couldn't hear it without wanting to tap your feet.

"Groovy," as Andy Novak used to say – she smiled at the antique word – when he would put the record on his wind-up Victrola – carefully, those 78s were so fragile – and the two of them would try out the latest jitterbug steps.

She'd been – what? twelve, thirteen? a tall, gawky kid, flat as a pancake beneath her sloppy joe sweater – when she and Andy finally graduated from stickball to loftier pursuits. They used to meet after school in his parents' front parlour and devote themselves to mastering the lindy-hop.

"I'm gonna be a famous dancer some day," she'd warn Andy, then proceed to career madly into tables and chairs.

"Yeah . . . sure," he'd pick her up off the floor, "and I'm gonna be the Pope."

"Well, a famous somebody, anyhow!"

Inevitably there came a point when Andy's mother could endure the threatened destruction of her furniture no longer. Then Marta Novak would storm in from the kitchen and scream at the top of her lungs, "You're going to do permanent damage to your ears listening to that!"

Her own mother agreed, while adding the novel theory that jitterbugging was the cause of acne, something to do with excess motion stimulating the sebaceous glands of the skin. It also led, for good measure, to immorality and madness.

Gerry winced at the memory. What innocent times those were!

And how hot she had been to be the best of everything. The best jitterbugger, the best bowler, kisser, speller, Latin student – though where precisely these minor excellences would lead her, Gerry hadn't a clue at the time. All she knew was that she had to be on top of the heap, and when her English teacher asked where this fierce sense of competition was leading, she could only reply: "I wanna be somebody."

"*Want to*, Geraldine," Miss Bishop enunciated slowly. "With two t's in it. You *want to* be somebody."

The very words Nancy's daughter had spoken tonight.

Recalling Lee's outburst, Gerry smiled. She had found the girl both awkward and touching, almost an echo of herself when young. There were the same enthusiasms, the same passion to succeed, the same aching desire to stand out above the crowd. What Hank Winterbourne defined as "fire in the belly".

Notably absent in Lee's wish list had been all mention of money, an omission Gerry heartily applauded. The one prejudice she confessed to was a dislike of New York's so-called Yuppies. She found them greedy, more interested in acquisitions than ideas. *Whoever dies with the most toys wins,* ran the motto on the T-shirt.

It appalled her that the brightest of her friends' sons and daughters set their sights on becoming Wall Street lawyers or arbies or investment bankers, not out of any love for the nature of the work, but because that was where the big bucks were. They were people without ideals and they never drank at lunch. Like that MBA by last week, who answered her ad for a business manager. He gave her firm the once over and pronounced that it was "not part of my game plan".

"What is your game plan?" Gerry asked.

"I want to make ten million dollars by the time I'm thirty."

"Why?"

"Why?" Her question baffled him.

"Yes, why? To save the whales? To save the world? To retire on a tropical island? To enter politics? To go to the south of France and paint pictures? Give me something I can understand."

The young man had looked at her as though she had taken leave of her senses, then explained: "Because money is the way you keep score."

She had heard that line before. It was the current cliché, but she was damned if she knew what game it was that had all these scorekeepers scrambling. Whoever dies with the most toys – dies anyhow. And probably sooner than the rest of his fellows.

Perhaps that was what she found so refreshing in Lee Whitfield. The girl had a calling, a mission that needed no rationale.

Naïve, perhaps, but there was no forgetting that look in her eyes, a look that bordered on reverence. Gerry was her idol, her model. The words had cut deep. For a moment, it was almost like having a daughter of her own. Immensely gratifying.

Gerry was not, on the whole, a woman who wasted time on regrets. Given the circumstances of her life, she would choose the same again. Lord knows she had had chances galore to marry. And, on two occasions, to mother. She had opted for abortion each time. They were pragmatic decisions and she felt neither guilt nor remorse. Child-rearing had never held any particular charm for her. Then as now, Gerry cherished her freedom. Beyond that, it was pointless to second-guess.

Yet she could see the merit of children once they'd grown up. Once the first messy years were sweated out. You could do things together: travel, exchange ideas, foster their careers and their love affairs. And be guaranteed at least minimal companionship in old age.

In fact, she wouldn't at all mind having a grown daughter such as Lee. In this regard, she could almost envy Nancy. Tonight, in the study, Gerry had felt a tender, adoptive surge of affection.

It would be a pleasure to take the young woman under

her wing. She could play the role of sponsor, guide, fairy godmother. Steer her around the shoals. The notion was intoxicating. It appealed to her sense of justice, of service. She herself certainly could have used a powerful mentor – a Geraldine O'Neal, if you will – when starting out.

But Gerry had not been so fortunate. She had begun with nobody, with nothing. Had begun at the very bottom with nothing but a dream. And made herself up as she went along.

five

She grew up barely a dozen blocks away in a part of New York then as now called Yorkville. Except for its nomenclature and the occasional German deli, the neighbourhood has changed out of recognition.

Today Yorkville is a gleaming upthrust of luxury apartment houses, inhabited by the new ebullient rich: buildings that style themselves the Monarch, the Sovereign, Claridge House, Kenilworth. In keeping with their lofty names, these edifices boast roof-top swimming pools, health clubs, multistorey garages and prestigious lobbies guarded by doormen whose uniforms would do credit to a royal retinue.

But listen closely to those doormen, particularly the old ones, and you may still hear the accents of Central Europe. For in its previous existence, the area constituted one of the city's noisiest, most bumptious, ethnic enclaves. It was Mittel-Europa transported to uptown Manhattan, complete with breweries and strudelshops and turnvereins. Germans, Croats, Hungarians, Czechs: the mix was as pungent as the cooking smells that emerged from a thousand tenement kitchens. The only thing its denizens had in common was membership of the working-class.

Gerry was born in one of those polyglot tenements, a small squat yellow-brick affair with wrought-iron fire escapes and ill-fitting windows that rattled every time the Third Avenue El roared by. Across the street was a brewery, whose billboard thoroughly dominated the view from the living room. In lieu of trees and sunshine, Gerry looked out upon the twenty-foot high likeness of a bosomy squaw. MOHAWK MAID, the slogan ran, QUEEN OF PILSENER BEERS. She wore a feather in the middle of her forehead and a brief leather-fringed skirt. In the background, painted mountains and waterfalls touted the freshness of the brewer's wares. Every night at dusk, the billboard burst into illumination with enough wattage to light up the entire front of Gerry's building. You could read, knit, do home-work by the light of Mohawk Maid. The one thing you couldn't do was turn it off.

For the first sixteen years of her life, Gerry's evenings were passed in the unrelenting glare of the billboard, until such hour as she would draw the blinds and hunker down for the night on the sofa bed. Yet even asleep, or so she swore, she felt the light beating down on her eyeballs. Mornings, she awoke to the clop-clop of the Mohawk Maid dray horses as they pulled out of the courtyard with the day's delivery. She developed a life-long aversion to beer.

The O'Neal household, something of an anomaly, was composed in its entirety of three generations of females.

At the top was Gerry's grandmother Eva Kandrassy, a red-wigged harridan of Hungarian birth with a temper as fierce as her chicken paprikash. Without ever getting the hang of English, except for a few choice expletives, Eva nonetheless managed to terrorize the neighborhood, vent-ing her displeasure at life upon everyone in sight from the pork butcher to the iceman to the kids playing stickball in the street. Amidst the stream of Magyar invectives that issued from her mouth was her claim: "I was a countess in the old country." She was not. She was, in fact, of pure peasant issue and very close to certifiably mad. A firm believer in the witches and vampires of her native Carpa-thia, she slept with a clove of garlic between her lips.

Next was the pale-haired Mimi, as docile as her mother Eva was tempestuous, as genteel as Eva was foul-mouthed, a decent hard-working dentist's assistant of modest accomplishments whose most ardent wish was for dom-estic peace in her time.

And finally, making her appearance early in the Depression, was Mimi's only child. From the moment she made her debut, in the delivery room of Metropolitan Hos-pital, kicking and squalling ("My gracious," the nurse had said, "that's an active baby."), Gerry was utterly unlike her mother in both appearance and temperament. So much so that as a little girl, she was inclined to believe the stork had brought her and delivered her to the wrong address.

There was no stork. There had been nothing more mir-

aculous than green-eyed Seamus O'Neal, a casual labourer
fresh from County Cork who loaded barrels at the Mohawk
Maid brewery. Seamus had lingered in Yorkville just long
enough to marry Mimi Kandrassy, impregnate her and
endow their only offspring with his Irish name and eyes
and good looks, before leaving for parts unknown. Mimi
never blamed him. She never discussed him either. And
being Catholic, she never filed for divorce. Years passed
with Seamus hardly being given a second thought.

In fact, this semi-wedded state suited Mimi perfectly.
She enjoyed the status of matron, while free of the myriad
nuisances that derive from living with a man. Thus, no
effort was made to find a replacement for Seamus O'Neal.
The issue of sex barely arose.

"Men want just one thing," she would mutter darkly on
occasion.

"Oh yeah? What?" Gerry loved to pretend total innocence, knowing that this was guaranteed to make Mimi
blush and turn away.

But perhaps the poor creature eschewed male companionship simply because she had no stomach for further
emotional ructions. As it was, the household was in a
constant state of war. Time and again, Mimi found herself
caught in a free-fire zone while Eva and Gerry engaged in
contests of will. Theoretically, Eva was in charge of bringing up her grandchild while Mimi went forth to earn a
living. In reality, the flat was too small to contain such a
pair of volatile temperaments. Perhaps New York was too
small. Given the combination of a high-strung old lady and
a headstrong adolescent, explosions were inevitable. Eva
gave orders. Gerry took pleasure in flouting them, with
the result that the two spent much of their time exchanging
epithets at maximum volume.

"Pick up your socks."

"Make me!"

"Slob!"

"Greenhorn!"

"Bitch!"

"Crackpot!"

A final curse, and the old woman would spit and cross herself.

"Momma," Gerry would shriek when her mother came home, "she called me a vampire!"

Domestic relations hit a new low when it was reported to Eva that her granddaughter had been seen kissing Andy Novak in the hall. With their mouths open, yet. And he, a boy headed for the seminary!

"You'll wind up in a brothel," the old woman screamed.

"And you'll wind up in a looney bin!"

Poor Mimi! Too terrified to take sides in these convulsions, she sought refuge in the comparative quiet of Dr Kittelhorn's office. Far from complaining about her job as the family bread-winner, she looked forward to it, often volunteering extra hours. The sound of the good dentist's drill pulverizing tooth enamel was, relatively speaking, music to her ears.

Gerry too had found an escape hatch. Her haven of choice was a rococo movie palace on East 86th Street where, for ten cents on a Saturday afternoon, she could immerse herself in a double feature, a March of Time, a Pete Smith short, a Fox Movietone News – a full four hours of paradise. On the ceiling of the theatre, fluffy white clouds wafted across a dark firmament a-twinkle with stars. On the screen, another type of star cast its spell.

There was Myrna Loy, slinky, whippet-thin in bias-cut satin, her dialogue as hard and sparkling as the diamond bracelets that marched up her arm. Roz Russell, smart and sassy in a man-tailored suit, decimating all the guys in the newsroom with her wisecracks. Bette Davis, imperious in tailored skirt and riding breeches, dismissing unworthy suitors with a snap of her whip. Katharine Hepburn giving Spencer Tracy what for!

What women they were! Reporters, detectives, lawyers, tycoons, foreign agents. Smart, beautiful, chic, powerful, clever. Fiercely independent. And not a dental technician among them! Every week Gerry fell in love anew.

Oh, to be such a personage when she grew up. They were her models, her heroines, her teachers without portfolio. They showed her how to enter a room, how to toss her head, how to eat peas, how to greet a British duke. How to kiss, too, for that matter. And if Gerry couldn't be as beautiful as her idols, she could at least be as smart. Her Saturday matinees at the Orpheum translated themselves into honour grades at school.

Then one day in her fifteenth year, Gerry looked into the mirror and discovered – to her astonishment – that she was beautiful.

It hadn't happened overnight, this physical glow, but it had indisputably happened. It was her awareness of her beauty that was new. The dread acne had been vanquished, the gawky height had evolved into a statuesque bearing. Skinny had become willowy. Even the bane of her life, the pancake-flat chest, had swelled into a provocative bosom.

Transfixed, Gerry stared at this stranger in the mirror, made note of the shiny dark hair, the dancing eyes, the face full of wit and intelligence.

Yes, beautiful! It hit her with force of an epiphany. And as, bemused, she knew this gorgeous creature to be herself, she was granted yet another revelation.

She had what it took to conquer the world.

Geraldine had always been possessed of drive, cleverness and a certain jaunty self-confidence; there could be no holding her back. At least in her own mind. For as surely as movies had happy endings, as surely as life must follow art, Gerry believed her own history would emulate the triumphs of those celluloid goddesses. Fate decreed that she too would someday dwell in a Park Avenue penthouse, with a closet full of Adrian gowns, a gaggle of adoring men at her feet, that a maid would bring her breakfast in bed while she read about herself in the papers. A universal object of envy. Just like Myrna Loy.

That afternoon she blew a whole week's allowance on Chen Yu lipsticks, one bright red and one fuchsia, in shiny metallic tubes. Enough of that dime-store Natural Tangee. Beauty must have its due.

But "looking swell" was not enough. That same night she tackled the other outstanding obstacle between her and what she considered her destiny. She announced her decision to go to college.

Mimi was flabbergasted. Secretarial school, possibly. Or a course at the beautician's academy. But college? No Kandrassy had ever pursued higher education, and for a girl, such an event was unheard of. Besides, Mimi pleaded, who could afford such luxury? She had been counting on Gerry's getting a job once she finished high school. As things stood, it was all Mimi could do to support the three of them.

Gerry didn't back off. Instead she bulldozed. To college she would go, and nothing her mother could say would stop her. Her sights were set on Hunter, where tuition was low and academic standards high.

Gerry expected to work part time. Nights, weekends. Sling hash, sweep streets. Do whatever was necessary to help defray the cost. But one way or another, she would earn her degree. Moreover, she wasn't asking, she was telling.

"If you're sure . . ." Mimi bowed beneath the onslaught.

"Of course I'm sure," Gerry barked, inwardly relieved that her primary goal had been achieved with so little struggle. Willpower was everything in these situations, she realized. Subjected to a show of strength, her mother could be counted upon to cave in. So, probably, could most people. But another major battle still loomed.

"And something else just as important. I want a room of my own."

If Gerry was going to compete with the smartest kids in the city, she explained, she'd need a decent place to study, to think. Otherwise, her whole education might go to waste. She was fed up with sleeping on the sofa year in year out, like an overnight guest.

"I need a door I can close. I need privacy!"

"But where?" Poor Mimi was perplexed. The flat was so tiny. "You want me to give you my room?"

Gerry shook her head. "Too small. Besides, you work. You need your sleep. Let *her*—" she jabbed an angry finger in Eva's direction "—sleep on the living room sofa. Let *her* enjoy the company of the Mohawk Maid. Let *her* wake up to the goddam traffic at 4 a.m."

"You want Grandma's bedroom?"

Mimi quaked. Her worst nightmare was being realized, a showdown between the two females she dreaded most. Already Eva was turning a blotchy purple. The smell of blood hung in the air.

"Why not?" Gerry shot back, shouting over the rising stream of Magyar curses. But now, heady with the scent of success, she was in no mood to flinch. Great dreams called for great measures.

"Why not Grandma's room? What has she done to deserve it? She doesn't work. She doesn't contribute. All she does is sit around and stuff her mouth with your food and nag and scream obscenities. This is your house, Momma. You pay the rent. You can put her where you damn please . . ."

"Such language!" Mimi gasped.

"And if I don't get my way," Gerry wheeled around to glare the old lady down, "if I don't get Grandma's room, I will leave this house and sell my body to all the men in the 86th Street cafés. And when I do, when I am the shame and scandal of the neighbourhood, I will tell everybody – the landlord, the mailman, the Novaks, Mr Kraus at the hardware store, Dr Kittelhorn, Father Andros, EVERY-BODY! – that the so-called Countess Eva Kandrassy has sent her granddaughter out into the streets to whore."

"Blackmail!" Eva clutched her breast. "This is black-mail."

The following week, Gerry had a room of her own.

six

In the decade following World War II, Hunter College was the gateway for thousands of Geraldine O'Neals. A place where bright girls of modest means and soaring ambitions could break free of their backgrounds. The consummate bootstrap for working-class women.

NEW YORK CITY SPOKEN HERE, a wag once posted a sign outside the English Department, in homage to the Bronx nasals and Brooklyn vowels that echoed down its halls.

You could look in vain for ivied walls or grassy quads. A hardy utilitarianism pervaded its 68th Street "campus" (there was another such in the Bronx). There were no sorority houses, no dorms. Those amenities were superfluous. Most of the students lived at home. The Subway Scholars, they styled themselves, as ineffably New York as the IRT.

Each morning, they would battle the rush hours, toting their heavy canvas bookbags, noses buried deep in Dostoevski or Sartre (why waste a minute of precious time?), then dutifully return home each night to sleep. Straphangers all.

In the days before the classless ubiquity of blue jeans, Hunter girls were more likely to be outfitted by S. Klein's on the Square (DO NOT DISGRACE YOUR FAMILY, said a sign in the communal dressing room, THE PUNISHMENT FOR STEALING IS JAIL) than by Peck and Peck or other fashionable purveyors of the cashmeres and tartans then *de rigueur* on out-of-town campuses.

But if Hunter lacked the panache of Radcliffe, the ambiance of Vassar, the cachet of Smith and Bryn Mawr, it offered an education second to none. In a school where merit was the sole ticket of admission, where family and money didn't count but achievement did, there were few backsliders or social butterflies.

And more than compensating for its deficiencies of bricks

and mortar, vaster than anything the Seven Sisters could offer, was the fact of Hunter's true campus: New York City.

No ivory tower sheltered these students. Escape simply wasn't allowed. Wherever they looked, the "real world" swirled about them – vibrant, messy, competitive, demanding, alive with the latest in art and theatre, ablaze with new ideas, aroil with intellectual ferment. That sense of the city pervaded the classes, giving a sharper edge to the academic content, a fresh urgency to every debate.

It was here, in this citadel of idealism and dissent, that Gerry enjoyed her first taste of what was to become a lifelong trait: a love of disputation.

Her college years coincided with a particularly turbulent era in American life. The Korean War was raging. The Russians had unleashed the A-bomb, the result of espionage many patriots said. On the domestic front, a brash young senator named Joe McCarthy was finding treason and conspiracy from one end of the land to the other. Hysteria was rife, emotions rampant. "Are you now or have you ever been . . ." became the hottest question of the day.

And even as the air filled with loyalty oaths, the airwaves were filled with something else. With Uncle Milty and Gorgeous George and dancing cigarette boxes and roller derbies. America, which had held firm against the communist threat, succumbed totally to the invasion of television.

In short, there was no dearth of issues for Gerry to fling herself into, no shortage of targets on which to vent her undergraduate spleen. She joined everything in sight: the debating team, the chess club, the dramatic society, the literary magazine, Americans for Democratic Action, fans of Le Jazz Hot, and a little group of fellow-aesthetes who duly trooped all over the city in search of *recherché* foreign films.

This whirlwind round of activity, crammed as it was between her studies and a part time job, left Gerry with something less than six hours' sleep a night. Notwithstanding, she thrived, physically and academically. Every semester she headed the Dean's List.

63

All that was lacking to make life ideal was a circle of intimate friends. Gerry was not popular with her fellow students. Nor could she understand why. Yet time and again, she felt a pulling away, a parched wariness among her colleagues and peers. They never invited her to parties or out on double dates. She hadn't a single close girlfriend. When she ran for student council at the start of her sophomore year, she was badly whipped by a girl with only half her gifts.

"What is it?" she cornered Irma Zaplinski after her defeat, knowing Irma was not the kind to pull punches. "Do I have bad breath? Smelly armpits? Do I talk too much?"

Irma folded her arms and viewed Gerry with a quizzical expression. "You mean you really don't know?"

"I swear, Irma . . ."

"It's not that you *talk* too much." Irma looked away, uneasy. "It's that you . . . well, you *are* too much."

Gerry still didn't get it. "You mean I try too hard. That's it, isn't it? The other girls think I'm too competitive."

Irma shook her head. "We're all smart and sharp and competitive or we wouldn't be here."

"Then what . . ."

"But do you have to be beautiful on top of everything else?" Irma burst out. "It's simply not fair!"

Gerry was dumbstruck.

What did they think – these classmates of hers? That she was going to rob them of their boyfriends, their fiancés, their brothers? And what on earth was she supposed to do? Bury her head in a paper bag? Hide her body beneath sackcloth and ashes? You would think beauty was a curse, not a blessing, she marvelled. That it constituted a personal offence.

What particularly stung was that she had chosen Hunter over the co-ed city colleges precisely because she wanted a serious atmosphere for study, without the distraction of boys. She had looked forward to building the friendships of a lifetime, and instead found herself a kind of pariah.

It was extraordinary! There were organizations that fought for the rights of Negroes and refugees and unfairly

64

dismissed professors, but it had never before occurred to her that she too belonged to a discriminated-against minority, albeit a highly enviable one. The beautiful girl, the dazzler, far from being welcomed by her sisters, was a perpetual object of fear and mistrust. It was a hard lesson to learn so young. Not that Gerry would have swapped one bit of her endowment for Sandra Becker's thick ankles or Irma's downy upper lip. Still, it was impossible not to feel resentment.

This sorry state of affairs continued until the arrival, in her junior year, of Nancy Schroeder from the Bronx. The two young women met in a Lit class and discovered they shared a passion for Henry James. And hot pastrami. And Gregory Peck. And Picasso's Guernica. The two hit it off instantly.

"It's spooky," Nancy said, "how much we think alike. Like the siblings in Cocteau's *Enfants terribles*." Her references were almost always literary, usually French.

"Or the Bobbsey Twins," Gerry laughed.

Nancy was a slight, curvy blonde, not pretty but cute in a pixieish kind of way. Her face was salvaged from forgettability by a pair of startling blue eyes that glowed with intelligence. She had, moreover, a kind of pliant disposition that was unthreatened by Gerry's fierce beauty. Far from being envious, she was flattered. To be befriended by such a spectacular personage seemed the ultimate compliment. Perhaps Nancy hoped that some of Gerry's glamour would rub off on her or provide inspiration. She spoke of immortalizing Gerry in a play.

For at nineteen, Nancy already had a keen sense of vocation. She knew exactly what she wanted to do with her life. Nothing less than revitalize the American theatre.

"Look at what's happening in France," she harangued Gerry over macaroni and cheese at Horn and Hardhart. "Genet. Claudel. Giraudoux. The marriage of verse and drama, of form and content. Plays that deal with matters of social substance, primal themes, yet full of poetic imagery. Of course, among the French, it's an honoured tradition, dating back to Corneille and Racine."

"We had Shakespeare," Gerry interjected. "As I recall he did a pretty fair job of it."

"Had!" Nancy waggled her finger. "That's the operative word. Had! Besides he was English. Look at what's happening on Broadway today. *Life with Mother . . . Bagels and Lox!* Pul-leeze, Geraldine! How can you compare! Our poets don't write for the public any more, that's the tragedy! They only write for each other. But what can you expect, given that we live in a land where mediocrity rules." She trotted out her favourite epithet. "America has become a nation of philistines," she declared. "Bourgeois philistines. Anti-art. Anti-culture. Interested only in pursuing the Great God Mammon. Oh, Gerry, wouldn't you just give your soul to live in Paris?"

It was Nancy's dream to travel there upon graduation and sit at the feet of the masters. Then one day, their wisdom absorbed, she would return, a glamorous exile rich in life's experience, bearing the plays that would rouse the American theatre from its torpor. Already, she had amassed a considerable body of work, including a two-hour drama based on Sacco and Vanzetti and a dozen notebooks crammed with verse. Early in their friendship she showed her output to Gerry who thought it was terrific, particularly the short poems.

"Unpublished of course," Nancy sighed, having sent a selection of her work to half a dozen literary magazines. She talked of papering her bedroom with rejection slips. "Some days I despair of ever seeing my name in print."

"Unpublished as yet," Gerry amended.

The remark, said as a courtesy, nonetheless started her thinking. For if Nancy was flattered by Gerry's friendship, the reverse was also true. It was wonderful having an acolyte, a true fan, a follower, and she looked for a way to show her own appreciation of Nancy's worth. Without a word to anyone, she worked out a plan.

In those days, *The New York Times* ran an inquiry column in its Sunday Book Review. Readers would send in a half-forgotten snatch of verse and ask if any fellow-readers could identify its source. As a rule, some eagle-eyed correspondent came through with poem and author. If the piece was short enough, *The Times* would often reprint it in its entirety.

Accordingly, a Miss G. O'N. of Manhattan submitted a couplet from one of Nancy's sonnets along with a query. Unsurprisingly, the week after the request appeared, a Miss M. E., also of Manhattan, identified the work in question as "Sea Mist" by Nancy K. Schroeder. In the subsequent issue, the sonnet ran in full.

"There it is! Your name in print, kiddo," Gerry handed the Book Review to a delirious Nancy. "I should only write so well!"

"But what does M. E. stand for?" Nancy asked.

"It stands for *me*, you dodo!"

"I'll never forget this. Ever. I don't know how to thank you."

"A postcard from Paris will do."

"Tell you what," replied the worshipful Nancy, "I'll dedicate my first book to you. Or my first baby, as the case may be."

For the other great topic of discussion between the two friends was marriage. It engrossed them over a thousand cups of coffee.

Gerry had already racked up two proposals, the first when she was fifteen from her erstwhile jitterbug partner, Andy Novak.

"How can I marry you if you're going to be a priest?" She thought he was kidding.

"I could reconsider if we were engaged."

But whether he was serious or not hardly mattered. Gerry couldn't possibly entrust her fate to someone who was two inches shorter than her. It was against the law of nature. And being engaged would mean she couldn't date other boys. Andy's parents, however, felt sufficiently threatened to ship their son off to the seminary post-haste. Years later, his "proposal" would serve as a running joke.

There was no doubt, however, about the intentions of her other suitor. Geoff Barbour was a handsome medical student whom Gerry had met in her sophomore year. Clever, ambitious, from a prosperous family, what the conventional wisdom called "a catch", Geoff was as smitten by Gerry as she seemed to be by him. They dated exclusively for several months, happy as lovebirds. He introduced her to his parents. All signs were positive, including his gift of a two-carat diamond ring. But when Geoff suggested announcing their engagement in the papers, something within Gerry snapped.

"I'm too young to get married."

"By the time I finish med school you'll be twenty-one."

"Suppose I don't love you then . . ."

"That's why people get engaged, Gerry," came the reasonable answer. "It will give us a chance to test our feelings."

"Suppose we find each other boring."

"Boring!" Geoff was stunned. "Are you telling me I bore you?"

"No," she admitted, "but sooner or later we might . . . well, run out of things to say to each other. You know me, Geoff. I can't decide how I feel about Karl Marx from one day to another. Or black olives or miniature golf. You're looking at somebody who couldn't get more than halfway through *Beowulf*."

"In other words, you have a short attention span."

They argued for at least an hour as to whether she was temperamentally suited for the long haul, shuttling the theme back and forth, hashing and re-hashing. Geoff was hurt and uncomprehending. Gerry, significantly, was growing bored. Was this a preview of wedded bliss, she wondered as she handed back the diamond ring.

"We're friends?" She gave what she hoped was a gracious smile.

"No!" He shoved the ring in his pocket with an angry gesture. "Certainly not!"

And that was that.

Which didn't mean that she had ruled out the prospect of marriage, but that that particular heaven could wait. More urgent was the dilemma posed by "going all the way".

"Would you?" Nancy asked. "If you were really in love?"

That, Gerry conceded, was the $64 question. She liked to think of herself as having a passionate, romantic disposition. No slave to out-moded convention she, but a free-thinking generous creature far far above the petty morality that equated virginity with "virtue". Such small-mindedness made her sneer.

Yet she lacked the courage of her convictions. The thought of getting pregnant scared her half to death. It would be the end of her freedom, of all her dreams. On every side, the risks were appalling.

It wasn't only her Catholic upbringing that kept Gerry on the straight and narrow: it was the whole temper of the times. Abortion was illegal. Immoral, expensive, shameful. It would scar a woman for life, the common wisdom declared, not just physically (a very likely outcome of dangerous back-room procedures) but emotionally as well.

One simply didn't dare take the chance.

Nancy agreed. And while both girls liked to suppose that one day they might conceivably shuck off the conventions and enjoy glamorous affairs with rich and brilliant lovers, in the meantime they both assumed that sex would have to wait upon marriage. Ideally, marriage with Mr Right.

The year was 1951. Before the pill. Before Roe v. Wade. And they belonged to the last generation of American women ever to be so trusting, so romantic, so innocent. So young!

Now and then, Gerry would find herself caught up in Nancy's fantasy of going to Paris. To travel anywhere abroad was no doubt a wonderful thing. And it postponed that awful decision of what Gerry would do after graduation.

She envied not only Nancy's talent but her clarity of purpose. To know exactly where your gifts lay, to have such a precise set of goals was light-years beyond Gerry's own vague notion of "being somebody".

For all her achievements, Gerry hadn't a clue as to a career. Her talents didn't translate into any known *métier*! They were generalized, diffuse. She could neither paint nor sing nor play a musical instrument, was bored by anything to do with either numbers or research. She lacked Nancy's literary style and doubted if her French was good enough for the Foreign Service. As for becoming a teacher (the usual fate of liberal arts majors), the idea filled her with instant ennui. He who can, does (she recalled Shaw's maxim), he who cannot, teaches. Could there be a clearer admission of failure?

Law, politics, medicine, finance, publishing – those great avenues that a quarter-century hence would be the natural choice for spirits such as hers – such possibilities never even occurred to her. She'd as likely have considered a career in the boxing ring. There was men's work and women's work. That was the reality

She began her senior year with a bellyful of misgivings.

"I suppose you'll be rushing off to get married," her student adviser commented tartly. "The pretty ones usually do."

"Someday, I suppose." Gerry chewed her nails. "But right now I have no plans. For marriage. For a job. For anything! I don't even know what kind of work I'm suited for."

"Then think about applying for the Goldman Fellowship," the adviser counselled. "It was made for girls like you. You could gain a few more academic credentials and also see something of the world. New York is not the universe, you know."

The scholarship was named after the late Florence Ernestine Goldman: socialist, suffragette, champion of birth control, a founding mother of The League of Women Voters, and wife of a successful cloak and suit manufacturer. Upon her death, the bereaved Mr Goldman endowed Hunter College with a grant in her memory.

Only honour students were eligible, with the prize going to the entrant who wrote the most compelling essay on 'The Future of Women'. In addition to being awarded the Florence E. Goldman Medal of Merit, the lucky winner received a year's study abroad, travel and tuition paid, plus a modest stipend. Goldman scholars had studied at Oxford, Cambridge, the Sorbonne. It was a veritable plum.

For Gerry, it also represented a year's breathing time. She applied for the grant. As did Nancy. As did a score of other top students. But early on, consensus had it that the

70

race would turn into a showdown between the bosom buddies. Gerry would walk away on academic grounds, but Nancy had the edge in essay-writing.

The competition threatened to put a strain on their friendship.

"You won't take it personally if I win, will you?" Nancy asked, shortly before the Christmas break, although she knew the answer in advance. Gerry responded with the conventional "Of course not! We're friends."

Yet despite her affection for Nancy, the thought of coming in second rankled her. Gerry hated losing anything – even to a friend. Perhaps especially to a friend. It was a topic that didn't bear close scrutiny.

"You won't be seeing much of me over the holidays," she told her friend. "You or anybody else." She was determined to spend the entire vacation working on her essay.

True to her word, Gerry holed up in her bedroom for the next three weeks with a used typewriter and two reams of Hammermill bond for company. There were no parties, no dates. No jazz down in the Village. Nothing but the blank sheet of paper before her.

It was hell.

Not that she lacked for ideas. Gerry was teeming with things to say. A born talker, fast on her feet, she was rarely at a loss for words – in public. In open debate, she usually mopped up the ground with the competition. Her personality often carried the day.

But setting forth these same thoughts in a classical essay, clothing them with elegance and lofty imagery – that was another matter. She was not a "literary" type. In the solitude of her room, she had no way of evaluating her work. Each line of text was revised a hundred times. The wastebaskets overflowed. The silence deepened.

"You're driving yourself crazy," her mother, entering on tiptoe, would whisper. What Mimi really meant was, *you're driving me crazy*. By the time the vacation ground to its close, Gerry had hammered out her 10,000 words. It was good. But was it good enough? Could it hold a candle to Nancy's? She returned to college in a dour, sheepish mood.

The first morning back, she ran into her friend-and-nemesis in the corridor. By contrast, Nancy was positively glowing. Happiness oozed from her pores. Why not? Gerry brooded. She'd probably polished up her essay with a few more felicitous phrases and now the scholarship was in the bag.

"Twelve o'clock in the lunchroom!" Nancy could hardly stand still for excitement. "Be there. I've got earth-shaking news!"

But when noon rolled around, Gerry was stunned to discover that her friend's buoyancy derived from a vastly different source.

"I'm in love!" Nancy gushed. "He's the most wonderful man in the world and I'd walk over hot coals just to be with him."

His name was David Whitfield and he was, Nancy assured her, not just another boy but "a man!" A real man, twenty-five years old, a Korean war veteran, wildly gifted, finishing up music school on the GI Bill. A great future before him.

"Plus . . . six foot two and gorgeous, into the bargain!"

She had met him at a cousin's wedding in the Bronx. He was playing trumpet in the band. Although someday, mark her words, David would be a famous composer.

"The moment I saw him, it was BOOM! like Héloïse and Abelard – a true romantic affinity! Something out of the storybooks. For him, too, Gerry. He thinks – well, would you believe? – that I'm the cutest thing on two feet since Judy Holliday."

Nancy giggled. She was unused to being the recipient of fulsome male compliments; it simultaneously pleased and embarrassed her. As for Gerry, she could only wonder about the very different frames of reference this particular pair of "romantic affinities" had brought with them. From Héloïse to Judy Holliday in one breath. That Nancy should be flattered by a comparison with a comedienne who specialized in playing dumb blondes was simply astonishing. Nancy – who turned her little button nose up at anything less sublime than Mozart! Yet here she was, rhapsodizing about a guy who played catered affairs!

"When are you seeing him next?"

"Tonight . . . every night . . ." Nancy crooned. "He says he wants to see me every night of his life. And every morning. Isn't it romantic?" She drifted off to class in a semi-stupor. It wasn't till after she'd gone that Gerry realized neither one of them had touched upon the Goldman fellowship.

For the next few weeks, Nancy turned up at school late, bleary-eyed, lips swollen, neck dotted with bright red hickeys. Her concentration was nil. Then, the moment class was over, she would tear off to the Mannes School of Music where "he" was spending the afternoon in a practice room. She seemed to have no time for friends.

If this was love, it far surpassed anything that Gerry had felt for the unlamented Geoff. Her own feelings were mixed. There was a twinge of envy, a tweak of resentment, a note of uncertainty as to how all this would affect the essay contest. And, of course, curiosity about David the Divine. It occurred to her that Nancy was keeping him hidden. Was she ashamed of David? Perhaps he really wasn't "six foot two and gorgeous". Or perhaps he was – and Nancy was afraid that Gerry would take him away.

"I hardly see you any more!" Gerry let her hurt be known. "And I gather you don't ever intend to introduce me to David. That's hardly fair to me. After all you are my best friend. I won't flirt with your precious David. You have my word."

Swallowing her misgivings, Nancy finally arranged a meeting and and the three spent a pleasant evening together in the Village. David proved to be the requisite six foot two and, if not quite the Adonis Nancy had described (more of a string bean, really), a most presentable young man with an engaging smile and a head of exuberant blond hair.

He had a self-deprecating humour, in sharp contrast to Nancy's high seriousness, with his easy talk of baseball and bebop and the poker games at Mannes and his thoroughly undistinguished career as an army private. After graduation, he planned to go to Hollywood and write music for the movies: "It's about the only place where a composer can make a buck these days." His conversation was refreshingly free of cant.

Gerry found him charming, though not quite her type. Besides, he was clearly head over heels in love. In that respect, her friend hadn't exaggerated a whit. As for Nancy, she spent the evening revelling in the approval of the two people who mattered most to her. She'd been so afraid that Gerry might be critical of her choice.

Once Gerry's approval had been gained, there was no stemming the flow of her confidences. Nancy was totally absorbed in her romance, consumed by its ebb and flow. Every day, in exquisite detail, she kept Gerry informed as to the current status and her own analysis of same. It was like watching a fever chart, full of tiny squiggles up and down. And with each squiggle, Nancy was zeroing in on the most crucial issue of all: would he or would he not pop the question?

Sometimes he seemed to veer quite close to the precipice. Then as if suddenly alerted to the inherent dangers of the situation, he would quickly change the subject. Or even worse, laugh and say "only kidding". Nancy couldn't figure out where she stood.

As the essay deadline neared, she suffered agonies of indecision. "Suppose I win the darn scholarship!" she cried. "How could I go away and leave him for a year? He wouldn't wait. He's not some teenage kid, after all. He's a grown man. He'll find somebody else. Somebody who'll go 'all the way'. But then, what if I turn it down and then he *doesn't* propose . . . ! Oh God, Gerry, what am I going to do?"

"You'd really give up a year in Paris just to get married?"

Gerry was stunned. Despite the knowledge that her own best interest lay in having Nancy out of the way, marriage struck her as such a radical step. Especially at twenty. David was sweet, but he wasn't the only man in the world.

Nancy must have read her mind, for she burst into tears.

"I may never have another chance," she wept. "I'm not like you, Gerry. I don't kid myself. You're beautiful, you'll be able to pick and choose for years to come. You've already had two proposals. Whereas me . . . I doubt if I'll ever find anyone as terrific as David, at least not anyone who cares about me so much. I love him!"

"In that case," Gerry bowed to the argument that pre-empted refutation, "what if you took the initiative? Could be, he's just shy."

"You mean I should do the proposing?"

For a conventional girl, Nancy seemed less than shocked by the suggestion. "I've thought about it, believe me. And I've thought about what happens if he turns me down . . . ! Omigod, Gerry, I'd have thrown away my best chance. He'd never ask me, after that! Never!"

Yet drastic measures were called for. And this once, Nancy – who usually avoided anything that smacked of flamboyance – decided to take matters into her own hands. The scholarship deadline was one week away. The time for shilly-shallying had passed. She had to know.

Nancy lived in the Bronx in a two-family house with her parents and a crusty old grandfather. David, being a gentleman, always took her home after an evening out. It was a long tiring haul on the D train, but his reward was an hour or so of furious petting in the darkened living room, where Nancy's parents gave the couple a clear berth. They trusted their daughter, with good cause.

So it was that on a Saturday night in early February, the two love-birds were entwined on the sofa in their usual state of disarray when Nancy "accidentally" knocked the coffee table over. That was the signal. Suddenly, the living room lights switched on and, through what seemed to David a half-dozen different doors, Nancy's entire family burst in upon them, the downstairs neighbours but a step behind.

"Congratulations!" In a twinkling, the young couple found themselves surrounded with well-wishers.

"Yes sir, you're a lucky fella!" Grandpa Schroeder pumped David's hand while the lucky fella was trying to tuck his shirttails back in. Nancy's father had already brought out the best Scotch. As Nancy herself might put it, the *fait* was *accompli*.

David could have objected. He could have run like hell. In fact, he was relieved to find the dread burden taken from him. For a man who had performed creditably in the face of enemy fire in Korea, he simply couldn't muster up the courage to propose. Now that it was over, he accepted the situation with good grace.

(Years later, without going into specifics, Nancy would laugh and tell her children, "Your father never actually proposed to me, lovies. We just sort of happened." And David would look at her and wink.)

For the rest of the term, it was all Nancy could do to get to class on time. Her days were full of plans plans plans. The wedding was set for the first Sunday in June. The next morning, the newlyweds would set off on what promised to be an epic honeymoon. "Four weeks at least," Nancy burbled. "Driving clear across America. We want to see as much of it as possible before we settle down in LA and David starts his career."

After which, fame and fortune would duly come.

"You'll continue your own writing, I hope," Gerry said.

"Of course!" Nancy nodded. "Just because I'm getting married doesn't mean my brain turns to Jello. Maybe I'll write screen plays once we're out in Hollywood. The movies could use a touch of class."

Later, however, she admitted that the prospect of marriage had taken the zing out of her ambition. Since no family was big enough to harbour two rising stars, it was sufficient that David alone should succeed. She would be happy living in his shadow, enjoying his eminence. And maybe write a little poetry from time to time.

But . . . "My role in life is to be his helpmeet," she explained. "The woman behind the man of the house. That's what marriage is all about. Say what you like, Gerry, that Future-of-Women stuff notwithstanding – and don't forget that Florence Goldman was the wife of a successful guy. She could afford to indulge in rhetoric. I can't. Why kid ourselves? Look at the real world – the world of politics, the arts, business. A man's career will take precedence, whereas a career girl is usually assumed to be a dilettante. Besides, when David becomes a somebody, then I'll be a somebody too. And proud of it!"

To Gerry this turnabout was a slap in the face, a betrayal

76

of everything they'd talked about. At the first opportunity, before she'd even tested her wings, Nancy had junked all her dreams and skittered off into the security of being engaged. Was this what she'd worked so hard for in college? To live in a man's reflected glory!

"Mrs David Whitfield," Gerry said sourly.

"*The* Mrs David Whitfield," Nancy replied, then dropped the subject rather than venture on dangerous ground.

A couple of days before the wedding, however, it surfaced again when Gerry took her out for what she called "The Last Supper".

They went to the little Italian restaurant that had been their favourite hangout "B. D." as Nancy said. Before David.

Gerry ordered a bottle of Asti Spumante, which struck them both as very cosmopolitan, and then proposed a toast. "Here's to the future. May it exceed our expectations."

They clinked their glasses. Nancy's hand shook.

"You getting pre-opening night jitters?" Gerry asked.

"No." Nancy blinked back a tear. "I was just thinking, here we are going off in such different directions. You with the scholarship, me with David. I can't help wondering if we'll ever see each other again."

"Of course we shall," Gerry insisted. "When we're both rich and famous. Only next time, we'll be drinking real French champagne."

"Maybe by then, you'll be married, too."

Gerry shook her head. The sparkling wine had loosened her tongue.

"Maybe . . . but I doubt it. Something inside of me rebels at the idea of settling down with one man, doing all the wifely things. Frankly, I can't picture myself picking up somebody else's socks. Hell, I don't even pick up my own. In fact, I'm such an awful slob I doubt if any guy would put up with me. No!" she clarified. "That's trivializing the question. What it comes down to is, I can't be Mrs Anybody Else, play second fiddle. Too self-centred, I suppose. But I want more out of life. I want to be free, unencumbered, explore all kinds of different experiences," her voice rose,

"and have grand love affairs with lots of distinguished
men. I want to see the world from the heights instead
of . . . instead of . . ."

"Instead of settling for the view from the kitchen
window," Nancy completed her thought and sighed. "I
used to think we were birds of a feather. I guess it took
David to show me that we're not. I'm a nester at heart, a
basically domestic creature. A wren if you like, whereas
you . . ."

"Yes?" Gerry waited.

"Oh you . . . you're an eagle!"

"Hoo ha!" Gerry flushed. "An eagle indeed."

But drunk though she was, the image pleased. As so
many times before, Nancy had chosen *le mot juste*.

The following Sunday Nancy and David were married in
a chapel on the Grand Concourse. It was a joyous occasion.
David's family came up from Texas. Nancy's parents had
pitched in to buy the couple a used but serviceable Nash
coupé. Gerry was the maid of honour.

"We'll keep in touch!" Nancy hugged her before leaving.

"Always!" Gerry swallowed the lump in her throat.

The following week, it was Gerry's turn to say goodbyes
aboard the SS *Queen Mary*. The departure point for the
eagle's first flight proved to be a cramped airless cabin on
D-deck, well below the water-line. Not the heights, she
observed wryly, but the depths. Although from here there
was no place to go but up.

"My daughter graduated first in her class," Mimi informed Gerry's cabin-mates, a trio of elderly schoolmarms
from Vermont. "And now she's going to study French
Literature at the Sorbonne."

"Oh Momma!" She tapped her feet with impatience. The
accommodations were as spartan as Girl Scout Camp. The
Goldman fellowship did not extend to frills.

Mother and daughter went up on deck. The New York
skyline looked glorious in the morning sun. Gerry was
wearing white cotton gloves, beige pumps and a green-
plaid shirtdress above a voluminous petticoat. She felt herself quite the sophisticate.

78

"Now be a good girl in Paris!" Mimi shouted over the blast of the funnel. "Don't drink too much of that French wine. Write. Be sure to hang up your clothes every night and change your underwear every day. And don't leave a ring around the bathtub. After all, I won't be there to clean up after you."

An hour later, both Gerry and the *Queen* were underway.

God, what an awful dress that was!

Even after all these years, the memory made her laugh. For a moment, she succeeded in picturing herself as a young and blooming twenty-year-old, standing on deck with the wind blowing her hair, watching New York harbour recede. Instinctively she touched her face as if to recapture the moment, reclaim the years. It seemed like a century ago. Another person. Hell, it was!

Nancy's daughter must have brought on this fit of nostalgia, Gerry concluded. Lee had that same hopeful look: the fledgeling voyager, bright and innocent, ready to take on life at full tilt.

Those were the days!

With a sigh, she picked up the Bill Blass outfit off the floor, and inspected it. Thank God she hadn't dribbled on it. That would have been three thousand bucks' worth of gravy. She draped it over a chair. ("Hang up your clothes every night," she could hear her mother's ghost nagging. *Give up on me, Mimi. I never learn.*)

Regrettably, the ensemble would have to go back tomorrow to the design salon at Austrian's. Such a pity. It had looked marvellous on. Still, it was nice of Eli Austrian to let her borrow so liberally from his store. He really was a love.

Then, remembering her promise, Gerry went to the little escritoire and wrote a note to Bobby Obermayer. It was the least she could do for old times' sake. Nancy would be grateful. The girl as well.

Like most of her ex-lovers, like Eli and dozens of others, Bobby could be counted on to come through with small favours. That was about all you could count on them to manage any more.

Yes, indeed, those were the days, when she had more men about her than she had lines in her diary. And such men! Virile, energetic, full of style. *Surprise me*, she would command. And they did. Life was so thrilling then, full of drama and passion. So grindingly dull now.

That was the real curse of aging: the sameness of everything. Or perhaps it was the temper of the times. As things stood, she'd already given up almost all the fleshly pleasures: inch-thick steaks, fried potatoes, deep suntans, double martinis, casual love affairs (although the truth was, they had given *her* up, worse luck!). Even her beloved Gauloise cigarettes had been forfeit – in some ways the greatest sacrifice of all.

Which left only work. But after thirty years of hustling, the day-in-day-out exigencies of building a career had lost both charm and challenge. Work had become a pain in the ass.

Besides, she'd done it all. In her more grandiose moments, she could weep along with Alexander the Great that there were no more worlds to conquer. No more men either. Life had gone as flat as last week's Veuve Clicquot.

Tonight, for instance, the only real spark of fun had been when she pulled the rug out from Lawrence Winterbourne. Poor sod! He was probably blasting her with antique curses this very moment. That had been truly naughty of her, she smiled. But what the hell – she would have done it again. One needs a few laughs now and then.

On the other hand, it was about time she started acting her age. The sensible thing would be to plan for retirement, develop a hobby or two. Gardening, say, or weaving. Or writing her memoirs. Something appropriate to the fullness of her years.

"Ugh!" she said out loud. Anyhow, there was no one to hear her.

For the house was very quiet, now that the help had gone home. Home to husband, she reckoned, and children. Maybe she should have had a child after all. Or at least a permanent man. Why, at this very moment, Nancy Whitfield was probably spoon-snuggled up to good old David. Still happy after all those years, to hear Lee tell it. There was that to be said for the long run of marriage. You weren't condemned to go the last lap alone. It was enough to make one jealous.

Here she was, closer to sixty than to fifty, practically a candidate for Social Security, and what did she have to show for it? An empty bed and a borrowed Bill Blass. The woman with a thousand friends and no one to share her loneliness in the hush of the night.

She tried to sleep, but tonight the bed seemed larger, lonelier than usual. Colder too. Perhaps she might have fallen asleep had there been a warm body beside her. Or just someone to chat to. Was tonight a preview of all nights to come?

Conceding defeat, Gerry switched on the light. It was nearly three o'clock, almost nine the next morning in Bonn. Wishing desperately for a last Gauloise to give her fortitude, she picked up the phone and dialled West Germany direct.

"British Embassy," came the clipped acknowledgement.

"I'd like to speak to His Excellency," the formal designation made her smile, "Ambassador Sir Campbell Simms."

A minute later he came on the phone, sounding faintly harried.

"Who is this please?"

"Did I catch you in the middle of a diplomatic crisis?"

"Gerry!" She could hear the pleasure in his voice, along with a faint Scottish burr. "What a delightful surprise."

"I have what I hope is an even better one," she returned. "Tell me, Campy, do you still plan to retire at the end of the year?"

"I do." He sounded puzzled.

"And when you do, will your offer still be good?"

"My offer!" He gave a happy laugh. "You mean of marriage? Yes yes, of course it will be good. Is this a theoretical question, darling, or may I hope that you've finally changed your mind?"

"Well, my love – " her voice grew intimate "– let's put it this way. If you're still game, when your tour of duty's over . . . I want you to make a Lady of me."

seven

A dozen blocks to the south, in a vast, overheated Park Avenue apartment, Lawrence Winterbourne stretched naked on the Ispahan rug. He was spread-eagled, motionless, except for one flaccid organ which was, at that moment, being earnestly worked over by Risha Lindstrom.

Occasionally Lawrence would open his eyes to glimpse Risha's platinum head bobbling up and down between his legs. She promised to produce the first real pleasure of what had been a dreadful evening. Dear Risha! So loyal. So understanding.

The "Oriental Salon" was an apt setting for such activity. It had been his father's favourite retreat, a large square chamber lavishly furnished in an unorthodox mix of Eastern styles. The effect was simultaneously eclectic, expensive and vaguely erotic. A rich man's fantasy of a sultan's harem.

The walls were lined with Moorish divans inviting one to drowse or carouse. The windows were latticed in wrought iron, sensuous and serpentine. Low-slung coffee tables of teak and inlaid ivory held trays of Persian miniatures, each designed to whet the jaded appetite. Even the fireplace, imported intact from an Anatolian palace, managed, in the intricate calligraphy of its blue-and-white ceramic tiles, to suggest novel forms of copulation. In the manner of Middle-Eastern interiors, the art and furnishings were scaled for the horizontal rather than the vertical occupant.

The appropriately recumbent Lawrence Winterbourne raised his eyes. Above the fireplace, in a heavy gilt frame, hung an enormous Delacroix, *La nuit algerienne*. The painting, some ten feet across, depicted a fair-skinned odalisque clad in gauzy harem pants, lounging on a nest of silken cushions. This lady – every inch of her ripe for erotic endeavours – was being fanned by sinewy Nubian slaves with strapping thighs. They looked ready to jump her bones. She looked ready to receive them.

The picture had always disturbed Lawrence, with its suggestion of what he deemed to be "peculiar practices", specifically sexual congress between black and white. Worse yet, tonight it conjured up once more the humiliation that he had endured but a few hours earlier at the hands of Geraldine O'Neal. Prince Matawhatsis indeed! The man had turned out to be nothing more than some shabby lawyer in Gerry's entourage. One of her studs, he presumed. They were probably performing lascivious acts this very moment. And this was the man for whom he – Lawrence Winterbourne of Park Avenue, Bar Harbor and Lyford Cay – had stepped and fetched. The memory made him groan.

"Am I biting too hard, Lawrence?" Risha's head shot up at the sound.

"No no . . ." Lawrence pleaded. "You're doing fine. Just keep up the good work."

"It's only good if you relax, you know. Now, Lawrence." The voice was as soothing as a lick of honey, which was a relief. Risha could be terribly strict sometimes. "I want you to imagine you're a Viking hero . . . a blond god being borne across boundless seas after the magnificence and torment of battle. This very day you have conquered a primitive tribe of Abyssinians," (the woman was absolutely psychic on occasion) "and I, the humblest of servants, have been sent to heal your wounds on the long voyage home. Where does it hurt, Master?" Risha's inquisitive tongue began licking the base of his scrotum with a light rotary motion. "There?"

The "Viking deity" shut his eyes and gave himself over to the contemplation of his favourite fantasy.

For Lawrence Winterbourne was consumed by a passion that gave shape to his life: the so-called Mott-Ilkington Stone.

This remarkable monolith, unearthed in 1882 by a Michigan beet farmer named James Ilkington, has long been an enigma. The stone is a granite slab measuring approximately three feet by two. One side is incised with geometric

83

markings which Ilkington and his wife Edna took to be the decorative work of the Chippewas. Indian art being held in low esteem at that time, the stone was left to moulder on the Ilkington front porch and might be there still were it not for an itinerant Bible salesman who spotted it in 1893. Granite was not native to that part of the country, Ephraim Mott observed, thus leading him to conclude that the stone was of miraculous origin. The incisions he surmised to be an archaic form of writing (Aramaic or Ancient Hebrew) most probably containing divine revelations, on the order of Joseph Smith's golden tablets. At considerable expense, Mott transported his "find" to Philadelphia where a team of antiquarians determined that his supposition was only partially correct. The incisions were, indeed, ancient writing, though hardly divine. They were eleventh century Viking runes. The granite appeared to have been quarried in New Hampshire.

Thus began one of liveliest disputes of the ensuing decades. If indeed, the Mott-Ilkington Stone was genuine, here was indisputable proof that some five hundred years before Columbus, a team of hardy Norsemen had not merely set foot in America, but explored deep into its heartland. Ergo: the history books were wrong and Columbus a Johnny-come-lately, so to speak. A Michigan-based movement petitioned Congress to declare a national "Leif Ericson Day", to the chagrin of all Italian-Americans.

The conflict raged unabated until 1920 when a Harvard philologist put paid to such speculation by declaring Mott-Ilkington nothing more than a clever fake. The Italian community once again breathed easily, Columbus was reinstated in his proper niche and the stone vanished from the public consciousness.

In 1952 it was purchased for the sum of $750 by Henry Winterbourne, a man inclined to amass odd bits of Americana, and stored without further ado in a Jersey City warehouse, alongside such other novelties as Adirondack furniture, a matchstick model of Mount Rushmore and an assortment of early baseball gloves. Amidst this indiscriminate clutter, Mott-Ilkington was all but forgotten.

Then, two years ago, the Winterbourne Estate hired a

graduate researcher from Oberlin to catalogue the collection and put it in order. Thus it was that Risha Lindstrom entered Lawrence's life.

She was six foot three, handsome in an Amazonian kind of way, superbly muscled (she lifted weights in her spare time), twenty-four years old to Lawrence's thirty and terribly terribly clever. She often spoke in parables, claiming to possess psychic powers. Lawrence was certain she did. He adored her. She put him in mind of a pythoness he had once seen swallowing a small furry animal. He longed to be that small furry creature, to be devoured whole by this magnificent column of flesh.

Every afternoon he would disappear inside the Jersey City warehouse where the two of them would alternately catalogue his father's curios and couple furiously amid the dust on the Adirondack chairs. He explained his absences by announcing an interest in nineteenth century Americana. Gerry O'Neal noted this new-found enthusiasm with approval.

"I'm glad," she told him at their quarterly meeting, "you've found something better to do than waste your time on that Hare Krishna crap of yours . . ."

"It wasn't Hare Krishna, it was Rahjneesh."

"Well, whatever the hell. All those joyboys are alike. In it for the money. This is much more appropriate." She went so far as to suggest he take a course in librarianship, concluding: "A man your age should develop some useful skills."

As always when Gerry offered advice, Larry seethed internally while managing to mumble something suitably innocuous.

"I hate her," he later confided to Risha.

"You hate her because she has power over you."

"You have power over me, Risha."

"Ah . . . but mine is a power for the good."

"I still hate her."

"Hate is the gate that closes the street but opens the way."

"Did John Lennon say that?"

Risha merely smiled, that cryptic smile of hers that

implied there was a meaning behind the meaning of the words.

He was with Risha the day she came across the Mott-Ilkington stone. She recognized its significance instantly. "Feel!" she took his fingers from her breasts and placed them atop the stone. "Ancient vibrations of your Nordic ancestors. Listen and feel, Lawrence. The Gods of Nifflheim are reaching out to us."

Risha explained the legends that the stone had engendered, about Viking giants who conceivably bestrode the land centuries before the Genoese adventurer. Lawrence listened, enthralled.

He had never cared much for Italians. Not since Lucia Mangianaro slapped his face in the servants' pantry for what was little more than a friendly gesture. And some of the Latins were so dark. . . . well, you could scarcely be certain which side of the Mediterranean they sprang from.

"But you say the theory was disproved by a Harvard scholar."

"Not disproved, Lawrence." Risha watched him with a thoughtful expression. "Disparaged . . . derailed. But not disproved. By a professor with the interesting name of Bruno Goldstein. Need I say more?"

They talked long into the night about the true meaning of Mott-Ilkington, talked of runic mysteries and of a heroic northern race. With each passing moment Lawrence became more firmly convinced of the stone's authenticity and all it implied. By dawn, the theory that the first white men in America were northerners had become, for him, a historical necessity. It explained his country's greatness.

"I would like to endow a Chair at Columbia to that end," he declared.

Risha shook her head. "The Eastern educational establishment is little more than a conspiracy to maintain the status quo. The university would take your money, apply it to their own projects, then call you a crank behind your back. Your ideas are not fashionable, you know. No, my friend, with your millions, you have the ability to take matters into your own hands. Found your own school. The Institute of Nordic Studies," she crooned. "Better yet, the

Lawrence T. Winterbourne Institute of Nordic Studies. With you as the director and me by your side! Think of it, Lawrence – a powerful intellectual community guided by your vision, your faith! Perpetuating your name!"

He thought about it. Non-stop, in fact, from that day to this very moment, lying naked on the Ispahan rug with Risha on her knees before him. He had already selected a site for the Institute, a hundred-acre estate in Katonah. Two days earlier, he had put down a binder on the property. Risha had been so pleased. "I'm proud of you," she'd said. He lived in constant fear that she might find him weak and ineffectual, perhaps leave him one day. Purchasing the estate would be proof of his resolve. But before the dream could come to pass, he had to prise control of at least a part of his fortune from Geraldine O'Neal's mean, grasping hands. She would make him beg. She always did. Was ever a man so badly served by a trustee? He made it his business never to see her socially. He had gone there tonight only at Risha's urging. He wished to sell the Delacroix.

"What for?" Gerry had asked. "It's a lovely painting."

"I want to buy myself a house in Westchester." He saw no point in mentioning The Institute. The one time he had confided his vision to her, she'd dismissed it out of hand. "It's fifty rooms, an excellent investment property, prime acreage . . ."

"How much?" she'd cut him short.

"Three million, five."

"Really Lar," Gerry had clucked. "The last thing you need is another white elephant. How much space does a bachelor require, anyhow? As for selling the Delacroix, it's out of the question. If you dislike it that much, I'll approve a donation to the Met. As for your next request, no. I can't advance you money from the fund for such foolishness. Who put you up to this – that albino girlfriend of yours? What's her name . . . Rambo?"

"Risha is not an albino! She's . . ."

"Yes, I know . . . a Viking princess," Gerry had mocked. "Larry, my dear, I'm doing you a favour by saying no. Those estates are a drug on the market. Believe me, one of these days, when you come into your inheritance, you'll thank me for having been so prudent on your behalf."

As always after a bout with Gerry, he had returned home feeling impotent, unmanned. Only Risha could heal his wounds.

"I hate her . . . I hate her . . ." he intoned, his buttocks now moving in rhythm with Risha's ministration. "I hate her. . . ." Why even now – it simultaneously pained and aroused Lawrence to think of it – Gerry was probably writhing lasciviously under the black man's thrusting cock. At the thought, his own member began to thicken and rise.

Yes – Lawrence could hardly control his response – he pictured the two of them grinding, sweating, roiling, faster and faster . . . deeper and deeper . . . up and down . . . in and out . . . *Oh god! Oh god!*

"Oh god!" he cried. A burst of jism shot into the air.

"There!" Risha said triumphantly. "Isn't that better?"

Lawrence fell back flat, utterly exhausted, his penis limp against his thigh, while Risha towelled him off.

"That woman . . ." he breathed.

"There'll be another time, Lawrence. Another approach."

But Lawrence had not finished his thought.

"That woman . . . killed my father."

eight

J. Fletcher Birnbaum, or Fletch as he was known to those who loved and feared him (usually the same people), possessed numerous gifts. He had the ability to maintain a day's growth of beard throughout the workweek and (hardly less prized) the knack of creating physical havoc in even the most ordered environment.

In the month since being named Editor of *Trend Magazine*, Fletch had transformed the polished hi-tech decor of the corner office into what his wife called "Early Pigsty". Every available surface was littered with newspapers, books, magazines, manuscripts, tear-sheets, press releases. The floor was a jungle of layouts, defying even the most nimbled-footed visitor. There was, however, method to his messiness. One half of Fletch's job consisted of keeping abreast of the times. The other half depended on forging ahead of them, thus ensuring that *Trend Magazine* lived up to its name.

He peered, now, across a paper mountain, to examine the young woman who stood before him with respectful attention. She was attractive in a hick sort of way, with a small, piquant face and bright eyes wedged in between a pair of outlandish green ear-rings. Fletch was prepared to loathe her.

"Sit, sit," he growled. She looked about her for a safe surface, and finding none, gingerly removed a pile of papers from a chair.

"Tidy little minds create tidy little magazines," he said by way of explanation, then reached for her portfolio. "OK, Miss Whitebread. Knock my socks off!"

By nature he was not a sweet-tempered man, but today he felt particularly entitled to be rude. A man in his position should not have to succumb from pressure, least of all when the strings were being pulled on behalf of some inexperienced chit of a girl.

All Obermayer's note had said was *Do you think you can*

find a place for this young lady? Yet despite the innocuous wording, within the forty floors of Enterprise Towers, the tycoon's request had the force of command. Which meant Fletch would probably have to hire this kid above more qualified candidates, then dream up something to keep her busy. He only hoped she could read and write. But considering Obermayer's reputation, he suspected her talents lay elsewhere. *Lay*, being the operative word.

He riffled through her articles with a cursory eye, barely hiding his contempt.

Silo Scandals in North Dakota, for God's sakes. You gotta be kidding, his pursed lips seemed to say. Farm foreclosures. The Decline of the 4-H Clubs. Just the kind of inside poop Manhattanites were dying to read! For Chrissakes, where did Obermayer find this bimbo – in a corn field?

He flipped more pages, then something caught his eye. He stopped to read a short piece.

"They really got a Prison Rodeo there in Bismarck?"

"Believe me, Mr Birnbaum, I wouldn't make up anything so outrageous."

"Why not?"

He flipped some more pages, pausing to read an interview with a 110-year-old woman who claimed to be the product of General Custer's union with an Indian squaw. The piece was entitled "Custer's Last Stand?"

Still doing his best to avoid eye contact, Fletch handed back her work. OK, so the girl could read – he begrudged the admission – maybe even write a little.

"You seem to have a certain modest talent for treating oddball topics in a mildly entertaining manner," was the most he would grant. "I might be able to use you for the front-of-the-book."

Each issue of *Trend*, he explained, would carry a one-page layout called O.P.B. – an acronym for Other People's Business. The feature would consist of half a dozen brief items, covering unusual occupations and enterprises that could be found in New York City. They might be trivial, awesome, looney – the range was infinite. He only asked that they be entertaining.

90

"Like, umm. . . . bagel-makers?" she asked.

"Boring."

"Million-dollar currency traders?"

Fletch faked a yawn.

"Would the Other People's Business have to be legit?" she asked.

For the first time, Fletch looked at her with real interest.

"What did you have in mind?"

"I'm not yet sure. First, I'd have to know what your concept is for the magazine."

Her question took him by surprise. Not everyone realized that *Trend* was his concept, the beloved child of his middle age. Despite himself, Fletch began to unwind.

Trend, he explained, was an upscale weekly, aimed at households of $100,000 a year and up. However, it was edited not just for pace-setting Manhattanites but for pace-followers as well, that wealthy army of readers who watch the goings-on of the rich and infamous with their tongues simultaneously hanging out and clucking. And although the magazine was being written in New York, its potential reach was enormous.

"Even people in," he glanced at her résumé, "Cedar City have a vicarious interest in their betters, I dare say. Especially if they've got the money to follow suit."

Each issue would cover finance, politics, fashion, restaurants, the lively arts, contemporary manners, always with an emphasis on keeping ahead of other publications. Exclusivity was all.

"What *Trend* eats and wears and thinks this week, New York will be eating and wearing and thinking next week and you'll see it in *People* Magazine the week after that. Maybe a month later, in the *Enquirer*. Only by then, we'll have moved on to greener pastures."

"The *Enquirer*?" She was riveted. "Isn't that a scandal sheet?"

"What's the matter, kid? You think the fat ladies in the check-out line at Safeway are the only ones who enjoy a bit of spice? Well, let me tell you . . ."

The rich, F. Scott Fitzgerald to the contrary, were not really that different from the rest of us, at least not when it came to main-lining sensation. They were just as hooked on scandal, just as intrigued by the broad range of human misbehaviour.

"We're all prurient sonsabitches, if we only admit it, never happier than when we're sniffing round the garbage can. The trick is, if you're a quality magazine, to make the garbage look kosher."

It was simply a matter of presentation, he maintained. Take Picasso. Why, his sex life was every bit as sleazy as Presley's! Except when it's Picasso, a Wall Street broker can sop up all the lurid details without losing caste. Indulging in smut? No way! Dear Reader was simply furthering his education in art.

Nor must stories be limited to the lofty. There was, Fletch pointed out, no behaviour so gross, so deviant that it couldn't be transformed into reputable reading by getting a few quotes from some social scientist. In fact, given the fortress mentality of city dwellers, he personally wouldn't rule any topic out of bounds, provided it was timely and handled with panache.

In a single trenchant article, Fletch had turned a subway vandal into a respected "Graffiti artist". On another occasion, he had profiled a Mafia enforcer as a modern-day Renaissance Man.

"I had him photographed with a machine gun in the Strozzi Palace. It was a gorgeous story. As I said, style is everything." He then proceeded to get off one of his favourite lines. "You know the difference between an art film and a porno flick? Subtitles."

She gave an appreciative laugh. One thing Fletch could say for this girl: she was a helluva good listener.

Of course, he continued, the juiciest reading for *Trend* subscribers concerned the scandals that touched their own inner circle. "Claus von Bulow, Ivan Boesky, Bess Myerson . . ." he licked their names with his tongue. "Those are the ideal. An editor's dream. Believe me, there's nothing that affords people greater pleasure than watching the competition fall from grace. The guy you had dinner with last Saturday – better yet, the guy who never even invited you to dinner, that snob! – suddenly hauled off in handcuffs by a Federal marshal. What's not to like? It's circulation dynamite. I remember once when I was at *Esquire* . . ."

He chattered on happily for another twenty minutes concerning his editorial philosophy, his aspirations, his coups, while she listened, clearly spellbound. Then the intercom buzzed.

"Gotta go!" He stood up and put on his jacket. "Any questions?"

"Just one," she said. "Am I hired?"

He looked at her with a puzzled expression. "What the fuck have we been talking about for the last half hour? Report tomorrow morning, first thing. Oh, and about salary . . ." He stopped at the door.

"Yes sir?"

"You start at the bottom."

"Yes sir!"

"Yes sir, Fletch!" he corrected with a laugh. "Please get the nomenclature right."

nine

Five o'clock as agreed, she turned up at Gerry's office bursting with news. It was Lee's first visit and her curiosity was at its peak.

O'Neal Associates proved to be an elegant suite of rooms in Rockefeller Plaza with a commanding view of the skating rink some thirty floors below. The view excepted, the place afforded a stunning contrast to the decor at *Trend*. Gerry's hand, warm and intimate, was everywhere: in the fresh flowers, the English furniture, the Dufy prints on the walls with their gay depictions of Paris and Deauville.

A secretary – a plain, capable-looking woman – ushered her into the sanctum with a cordial smile. "The boss is expecting you."

Gerry was on the phone. Or to describe it more accurately, the phone was on her, scrunched between shoulder and chin while she roamed about the room talking, making calls from a list, simultaneously thumbing through papers on an antique partner's desk.

She was wearing a hot pink silk shirt and deep crimson skirt, the jacket draped over her chair. Chanel. Lee recognized the look. It spoke of confidence and power. As Gerry paced, one arm jangled with silver bracelets. She was a perpetual motion machine.

Sit sit, she mouthed. Lee perched on the sofa, feeling like a kid in a classroom, privileged to eavesdrop and watch an artist at work.

All the while she talked on the phone, a stream of underlings and apprentices marched through her office with questions to be resolved, papers to be signed, copy to be approved or annotated.

The office staff consisted of young well-groomed men and relatively mousy women. Lee couldn't help wondering if there wasn't an element of casting involved. A sense of dramatics. Gerry must relish the role of Queen Bee.

"Herman Herman Herman!" she would shout from time

to time, and a tall pale fellow of uncertain sexuality would come bolting through the door ready to execute her commissions. From what Lee gathered, he was second in command. But a distant second, to be sure. Geraldine O'Neal ran her own show.

Lee listened and learned.

On the phone, Gerry's voice was alternately seductive and businesslike. She worked from a list, ticking off each call when completed.

". . . two lovely boys, just the type of child who belongs at Dalton. Do find a place for them, Gardner. It'll mean so much to their father, knowing they'll be attending the most exclusive prep school in New York, I wouldn't be surprised if he came through with an endowment. The name is Yoshimura. Should I spell that . . . ?"

". . . exactly the kind of kids you want at Trinity, from a lovely Japanese family. You'll find a place for them, won't you, Robin? Their father will be thrilled at the prospect of having them attend the absolute best prep school in New York. I'm sure he'll find ways of expressing his appreciation. That's spelled Y . . . o. . . . s . . ."

"Hello, Judge Barkis, how good to hear your voice. You missed a splendid party last Friday and we missed you. Oh dear! Sorry to hear that. Her sinuses again? Poor Rosie. Give her my love. I have an oddball question, Jack. Maybe you can help. I'm curious about whether you think there might be a causative relation between fare-beaters and increased violence in the subways . . . ?"

"Sharon!" Gerry buzzed the intercom. "Send a couple of dozen tulips to Rosalind Barkis. The old gal fell off the wagon again. Did you get my call through to Commissioner Metesky? Don't even bother trying him at the office. And for God's sakes, don't call him at home. He's at his boyfriend's between five and seven. The number's in there under Ralphie Q. Q. as in Queen. Meanwhile, get me Judith Klinger . . ."

"Judy, honey! How are things in the wonderful world of market research? Yeah, good with me, too. Listen, I'm going to throw some work your way. I need a survey done of subway riders. What they hate most about the stations – grime, crime, crumb-bums, et cetera with a particular emphasis on outmoded turnstiles. That's right, turnstiles. The tokens get jammed. They're slow . . . unsafe. People are sick and tired of seeing kids beat the fare . . . time for a complete overhaul. Right? I'm not asking you to skew the results, Judy. That would be unethical. Just skew the questions. You know what I mean . . ."

"Marvin, how are things in the wonderful world of broadcasting? Really! You're leaving NBC? How come? Uh . . . huh." She began scribbling furiously. "My . . . my! Ouch! Yup, I agree. Integrity is everything. Well, GE's loss is America's gain. No, sweetie, I won't say a word to anyone till it's announced. Wild horses and all that jazz. . . . Best of luck with your memoirs."

"Jack, lovey. How is everything in the underpaid world of public service TV? Tut tut – such language! Listen, bud," she motioned to Lee to fetch her jacket, "you didn't hear it from me but NBC is going to be looking for a very senior news producer in a few weeks' time. Big big bucks. No, I can't say who's leaving, but pick a name, any name. Un . . . unh. Pick another. Now you're talkin'! In the meanwhile, you can do me a favour." She held out her arms for Lee to help her on with the jacket. "How about Channel 13 doing a panel show on 'The Shame of our Subway Stations'? They really are revolting. I'm getting some research in to prove it. If you like, I can line up a few talking heads for you." Phone still clamped to her chin, Gerry had pawed open her bag and was checking her lipstick. "Think about it. We'll have lunch next week, OK? And good luck at you-know-where."

"There!" She ticked off the last name on the list, hung up the phone and rubbed her chin. It was as red as a violinist's. "Done."

"Wouldn't it be easier if you got a speakerphone?" Lee asked. "You could talk and keep your hands free."

"It wouldn't be so intimate," Gerry said. "I like the feeling of personal contact. Well, Lee, I understand congratulations are in order."

"You mean about my job?" Lee was flabbergasted. "How did you know?"

"I've got the world's best grapevine, speaking of which I would say this calls for champagne. What's your new boss like, by the way? You can tell momma! I understand they used to call him Fletch the Wretch at *Esquire*!"

"He's fat," Lee began. "Fortyish. Funky. Flakey. Five o'clock shadow . . ."

"A fan of alliteration, I hope," Gerry smiled. "But what makes you say flakey?"

"For some reason, he seemed to look at everything in my book ass-backwards. All the good stories, the pieces with content, he sneered at. I felt like a dolt. The only stuff he seemed to like was trash and trivia. It was such a put-down, I couldn't help but think it was calculated. Frankly, I'm amazed that he hired me."

"Oh?" Gerry said. "I'm not. In fact, I was certain he would."

Lee found Gerry's confidence puzzling. "How can you say that? You've never seen any of my work. For all you know, I could be a total klutz. Although I'm not, I hasten to add."

For a moment, Gerry seemed taken aback, then she smiled. "Of course you're a good writer. I could feel it in my bones. Now, don't ask me how I know these things, darling! I just do. And I'm sure you did a dynamite interview."

"I think that's what did it," Lee confided. "The interview. I took your advice and let him talk his head off. Then every couple of minutes I'd grunt an amen. It really worked. God, the man went on forever about his 'concept' for the magazine."

"Which is?"

Lee thought a moment. "Designer sleaze, essentially.

97

The low down on the high and mighty. A mix of crass with class . . . gold-plated gutter. I'm paraphrasing, of course."

"I get the picture," Gerry laughed. "Sounds to me as if *Trend Magazine* is destined to succeed. And you too." She checked the clock. It was 5:30. "Tell you what . . . let's get our butts out of here. I've been sitting in the office all day. Makes me antsy. Do you have any plans for tonight? No? Splendid, because I've got a couple of tickets to something or other at the Imperial . . ." She buzzed the intercom. "Sharon, what the hell do I have on for this evening? Is that a musical or what? Right. And make me an early dinner reservation. Côte Basque, I think. Yes, for two . . . !"

She turned to Lee. "All set, then. First, we go over to the Oak Room for that champagne toast I promised you, then have a pre-theatre bite. It's a musical so it doesn't matter if we run late. . . ."

"I insist you have the Grand Marnier soufflé." Gerry waved away the dessert menu. "It's a speciality here and just scrumptious. A million calories, but you're a skinny young thing. You can handle it. As for me, I'll settle for a cograc and coffee. You don't mind terribly if we miss the first act, do you, Lee? The trouble with the theatre is that you can't talk while the show's going on. Well, you can, actually, but people seem to take it amiss. Although with some of the shit I've seen lately, I think you'd probably be doing both author and audience a favour. I have an idea for your column, by the way. There's a woman in Soho, a Madame something-or-other, I have no doubt, who communicates with the spirits of dead pets at fifty bucks a pop. And they communicate right back, arf arf. All bark and no bite, so to speak. Strikes me as the ideal pet. I've heard of medium poodles, but poodle mediums? Anyhow, sounds like a marvellous hustle. Why don't you call Betsy Gaynor in the morning and get the details? You know who she is, the Senator's widow. She's in the phonebook, Gaynor, with a 'y', East Sixties – make a note of that, Lee. Shame shame, you must always keep a notebook on you. Well, ask the waiter. He'll provide. Anyhow, it seems Betsy's been communing with her late Lhasa Apso ever since he was kidnapped last fall. She paid the ransom twice over, but all she ever got back was his name tag and a lock of his fur. Of course, that's a story in itself, Betsy and that dog. They had matching sable coats, would you believe? I mean, we are talking rich canine here. His birthday parties were famous, catered by Petrossians, no less! Poor Betsy! She was absolutely devoted to the beast. They say–" Gerry leaned over to whisper something scabrous in Lee's ear, then reared back and laughed. "Well, tongues will wag, in every sense of the word. I personally am inclined to doubt it, a Lhasa being such a wee small creature. But then, of course, so was the Senator . . ."

They never did get to the theatre that night, and when Lee rolled home at close to midnight, she felt slightly tipsy, wholly happy. Life couldn't be better. Then, emptying her handbag of a collection of hastily scribbled notes (there must have been a dozen in all), she flung herself on the bed and indulged in a recap of the evening's highlights. So much wonderful food. So many great story ideas. Gerry just dripped talent from her fingertips. Lee felt honoured to have such a friend.

On Saturday, Gerry promised to take her shopping for clothes at some discount place in Jersey. Gerry said she should spring for one good outfit. Lee could hardly wait. Gerry herself wore nothing but Chanel suits to the office. It solved problems, Gerry said. "Who the hell can think straight at eight in the morning? This way, I simply reach in the closet and I'm ready to go!"

Imagine having fourteen Chanel suits! Of course, you kept them for years and years so they were basically an economy, Gerry said.

Gerry said. . . . Gerry said . . . Gerry said. . . .

"I bet your mother's over the moon about your job," Gerry said.

Lee, who had begun drifting off to sleep, sat up with a bolt. Ye Gods! It had been a week since she'd phoned home.

She shot out of bed and grabbed the phone, then hesitated, feeling guilty as hell. She'd hardly given them a thought these last few days. They didn't even know she'd met Gerry. It was only a little after ten, now, back in Cedar City. Her parents would still be up, watching the news in the downstairs den. And wondering what the hell had happened to their darling daughter! Lee gritted her teeth and dialled.

A minute later, Nancy was on the line.

"Hi Mom! Remember me? Your long lost daughter. What is it with you guys, anyhow?" she lied. It seemed easier that way. "I've called a dozen times, but I never seem to catch you gadabouts at home any more. Or maybe it's the time difference. Anyhow, I've got sensational news. You sitting down?"

"Sounds like our baby's doing OK!" David Whitfield nursed the single shot of bourbon that he allowed himself each night before retiring, while Nancy just sat there, looking thoughtful.

The conversation with Lee had disturbed her.

"Do you think we're gadabouts, honey?" she finally asked, but as usual, David managed to read her mind.

"If Lee says she called, she called. And even if she's exaggerating a bit, she only did it to spare your feelings."

But Nancy wasn't satisfied. "She forgot, pure and simple. You notice something else? Lee never once asked how we were. It was all Gerry this . . . Gerry that . . ."

"That's not quite fair. First of all, nothing ever happens here to tell . . . you know that. Second, you were the one who kept insisting that she look Gerry up. And by the sound of things, the two of 'em have really hit it off. Champagne at the Plaza! Not bad for a kid from Cedar City. And if Lee's excited and, OK, a bit forgetful about phoning, so what? It's not a Federal case."

Nancy folded her arms and looked her husband dead in the eye.

"You think I'm jealous, David, don't you?"

"I'm jealous too, babe. What sensible person wouldn't give their eyeteeth to be in Lee's shoes . . . young and cute and making it in Manhattan? Thanks, bud, I'll take half a dozen."

100

"I didn't mean of Lee," Nancy said, then got up and plucked an unlit cigarette from her husband's lips. "Stop that nonsense, David. You know what the doctor said."

"He said no smoking . . . he didn't say no gumming." Convinced that his wife was suffering from empty-nest syndrome, he was happy to change the subject. And he liked being fussed over now and then. "Let's put it this way. Suppose instead of giving up cigarettes, I give up matches and lighters. I'll even give up ashtrays, as a sign of good faith. We got a deal? OK, boss, you win. Here's the pack."

"And no sneaking 'em out behind the house, either." She leaned over and planted an affectionate kiss on his gleaming pate. "I want to keep you around for a while, David. You're all the family I have left these days. Now off to bed with you. I'm going to read for a bit."

"Don't stay up too late," David cautioned, as she settled back into the sofa. "We've got a big day tomorrow."

"We do?"

"Prize Day. My last. Talk about forgetful . . . !"

He peered to see what she was reading. *"Eleanor of Aquitaine and the Four Kings.* Some kind of romantic novel, is it, or are the four kings from a poker hand?"

"It's biography," Nancy said. "She was an extraordinary woman. An anachronism, really, considering she lived in the Middle Ages. A crusader, politician, a patron of the arts, married to Henry II, mother of Coeur de Lion . . ."

"Uh . . . huh. Sounds like a million laughs. My wife, the mainstay of the public library," he said fondly. "Don't know how they'd survive without you. Anyhow, enjoy the adventures of your middle-aged lady and I'll see you in the a.m."

After David had gone upstairs, Nancy lowered the light and tried to lose herself in Amy Kelly's lustrous prose. The book *was* a romance, of course, in the finest, highest sense of the word. What could be more romantic than a real life pushed to the limit, played out on the grandest scale? But tonight the richness of the imagery palled, making her restless and inexplicably sad. She closed the book with a sigh.

How, after all, could you compare Eleanor's triumphal progress into medieval London with the thrill of Prize Day at Cedar City High!

That was unfair, Nancy kicked herself mentally. And petty to boot. Prize Day was David's baby. He had begun it twenty years earlier as a stimulus to musical activity, and it had grown into an important local event. Practically everyone from the mayor on down turned up to hear the best kids in the band as they competed for a silver cup and a $500 Savings Bond. The award usually went to whichever of the trumpet players did the fanciest version of *Ciribiribin* (David's *hommage* to his idol Harry James), although last year a tuba took the honours. That made a change, she thought. Real front page news.

Taking care not to disturb the nocturnal quiet, Nancy opened the door and stepped out onto the wooden porch. It was a crisp spring night. The air was heavy with the scent of budding lilacs, the sky dazzling against the blackness of the prairie. Cedar City was asleep. There was no sound of life anywhere, except for the plaintive hoot of an owl, no light but the cold glitter of the stars. A thousand miles of wheat and corn lay between here and Chicago. A thousand miles of desert and mountain between here and the fabled "Coast". The Gold Coast of California where she and David were going to find their own El Dorado.

Mr and Mrs David Whitfield of Hollywood and Beverly Hills. With a swimming pool out back.

Only, through nobody's fault, it hadn't happened that way. Or if there was a culprit, then it had to be that '47 Nash. No wonder the make was long since gone bust.

From the moment she and David had set out on their honeymoon, the jalopy had been nothing but trouble. If it wasn't the distributor, it was the brake linings. If it wasn't the brakes, it was the carburettor. By the time they reached Buffalo, Nancy was as knowledgeable as the average garage mechanic. If they hadn't been so much in love, the journey would have been a nightmare. It was an adventure, instead.

All through that rapturous summer, they camped out,

befriended hobos and farmers' wives and waitresses in roadside coffee shops, made love in the rumble seat under the stars, in haylofts, in cheap motel rooms, enthralled by the newness of it all. So what if the trip ran a month or two longer? Fame and fortune awaited at the end of the line.

In Muncie, David ducked into Woolworth's for a can of yellow paint and a brush, then festooned the hood of the car with a giant lemon, while Nancy applauded. In Decatur, the clutch began to go. In Davenport (and how could David not make a pilgrimage to the birthplace of Bix Beiderbecke?), he and Nancy had their first minor argument.

"I'm not sure that the idiot child" – David's term for the Nash – "is going to make it through another month, sweetie. Or the money, either. I suggest we get onto Route 66 and head non-stop to LA."

"Without seeing Mount Rushmore?"

"It's way out of our way."

But Nancy, feeling some obscure point of honour was at stake, had been determined to prevail. "When you wanted to visit Davenport for your own private reasons, I went along without a squawk. Well, what about my interests, David? Don't I get equal say in this family?"

"OK." David bowed to her logic. "But let's just pray the weather holds out."

The weather didn't. Nor did the money. Nor did the Nash. In the midst of a freak snowstorm in that featureless stretch of prairie where Nebraska touches South Dakota, the "idiot child" gave a bone-rattling shudder, then collapsed beyond all hope of resuscitation. David stumbled out of the car and with bare frozen fingers knocked the snow off a roadside sign.

WELCOME TO CEDAR CITY, Pop 18,860
Kiwanis Meet Wednesday at Grange Hall
"A Nice Place to Live"

"I sure as hell hope so," was David's comment, "because it looks like we're going to have to stick around for a bit, at least until we get our grubstake back. I'll look for some kind of work tomorrow." He kicked the sign in disgust.

"Cedar City, your population has just soared to a boffo eighteen thousand, eight hundred and sixty-two."

Nancy got out of the car and promptly threw up. It was her first intimation that she was pregnant.

"Make that sixty-two and a half," she said.

"Oh Jesus!" First he turned pale, then he reddened, then he reached for her hand. "Don't worry, honey, everything's going to be OK. Worst comes to worst, we'll stay here a bit longer."

They walked the rest of the way into town.

"It was as though," Nancy recounted that historic moment in a letter to her parents, "the old Nash came here to die, holding out just long enough to deliver us to safety. Thank God David's rustled up a job teaching music. California will have to wait till next year."

To this very moment standing on her porch amid the scent of lilacs, Nancy believed that some capricious kismet had been at work.

Whether out of malice or charity (she never could decide), the Nash had robbed them not merely of a destination but of a destiny. Yet perhaps it was for the best. Over the years, Cedar City had been good to them, and vice versa. They had friends, a place in the community. Their children had grown up straight and strong. When it came to what the demographers call "quality of life" – safe streets, clean air, good housing – the family had fared better than all but the wealthiest residents of New York and LA.

The Whitfields finally did get to California some sixteen years into their marriage, when they took the kids on a trip to Disneyland. But by then, New York was a memory, Hollywood a dream and Cedar City the sole reality.

"How come you never went back East," Lee used to ask her, "at least for a visit?"

On cue, Nancy would dredge up a dozen valid reasons. The kids were too small. The trip too expensive. Her parents had retired to Florida. Maybe next year. . . .

But tonight, standing on an creaky wooden porch at the edge of a prairie, Nancy knew those were alibis, excuses. The truth lay much deeper than that.

She had left home with such high hopes. How could she return with her tail between her legs? It was asking too much. In Cedar City, at least she was a somebody, a good-sized fish in a modest pool. Her neighbours looked up to her, respecting her learning, her (relative) sophistication. In fact, she was the embodiment of what passed in Cedar City for high culture and the locals were grateful to have her.

But once back in New York, there would be no denying the chasm between what she had wished for and what she was, the gap between her youthful picture of David as a conquering hero and the small-town bandmaster now snoring peacefully away upstairs. Here, David was a husband to be proud of. But in Manhattan – she shuddered to think!

Thirty-odd years in Cedar City had transformed him into a complete provincial. He loved the simplicity of small-town life, the lack of fuss and phoniness. To him, Cedar City encapsulated all the abiding values in an increasingly turbulent world.

"Look at that!" He would point to some report of Los Angeles gang wars or drug abuse among the Hollywood greats. "Such craziness. And to think we once actually wanted to live there!" He spoke as if Cedar City had spared them great dangers. Perhaps it had. But it had spared them great opportunities as well.

Had David ever been as brilliant as she once thought him, or had Nancy simply been bedazzled by love? The latter, she suspected, and though she loved him still, loved him dearly, it was for qualities other than the "genius" with which she had endowed him years ago. He was good. He was sweet. He was loyal. He was patient. But he was certainly no intellectual. Bless his heart, the man never read a book, except the occasional Tom Clancy. "My Nancy," he would say with an air of total contentment, "reads enough for both of us. She's so smart."

Go back to New York? For what? for whom? Any dream of returning in triumph had long since died. And while logic told her that most of her Hunter classmates were leading lives just as routine and perhaps a good deal less pleasant – suburban housewives or overworked school-teachers – there was always the haunting picture of Gerry.

Gerry – with her fame, her glamour, her clothes, her wit, her worldliness. Gerry – the supreme example of what might have been, what life might have held, had she not sacrificed everything for love.

ten

Lee settled in quickly at *Trend Magazine*. Quickly being the operative word, for to her surprise, the pace of a weekly magazine was hardly less hectic than that of a daily newspaper. And unlike her job at the *Tribune*, there was no second edition in which to rectify goofs. For better or worse, each golden word of prose that found its way into print remained current for one full week.

Her "office" consisted of a desk, a chair and a word processor, located some ten feet from the water cooler, twenty feet from the door of the Men's Room. Not a glamorous setting, but, she soon realized, well-placed strategically, for in the course of a business day, every male who worked at *Trend*, from the mighty Fletch down to the lowliest office boy, had occasion to pass her desk. Often as not, they'd stop to chat or trade a bit of gossip, the end result being that Lee was usually the first to learn what was going on.

"Smart ploy," Gerry had commented. "Internal politics are crucial." Lee agreed, although she would cheerfully have ceded her vantage point for a private office or even a modest cubby hole. Those amenities, however, were reserved for the handful of "names" who pulled down top salaries.

Everyone else – journeymen writers, fact-checkers, copy editors, proof-readers – was huddled into an open area as dense and noisy as a factory floor. *Trend*'s reporters might spend their days chronicling the life-styles of the wealthy, but they did so from an extremely modest base.

Fletch was a skinflint who believed in minimum staffing and maximum hours. For the most part, the magazine was turned out by half a dozen reporters, a handful of columnists and a small core of contributing editors who lent their expertise on special topics. Without exception, the writing staff was young, fresh, knowledgeable and ebullient. There was Bea Jones, in her punk hair and outlandish minis, covering the world of high fashion. Teddy Goodman, son of a famous financier, dishing up the dirt from Wall Street. Rich-kid Bill Frazier, nipping into the washroom each afternoon at five to swap his T-shirt for restaurant-critic clothes. Some bright young turk from the New York Film School who delighted in giving the Hollywood establishment what-for. Throughout, the tone was brash and irreverent, marked by a "look-ma-no-hands" sort of sassiness.

Now and then, when a subject was hot, Fletch would buy a feature article from a free-lance writer, but these cash outlays invariably left him in a foul mood. "Why do I have to pay through the nose for some piece of shit about the Brawley case when I've got all these writers just sitting around on their ass collecting salaries!"

His goal was that the magazine be entirely written in-house, to which end he would assemble the editorial staff every Monday and discuss features for forthcoming issues. No theme was too outrageous to be considered. Very few were outrageous enough.

Fletch himself was a wellspring of ideas. "How 'bout we do a piece on three-year-olds being tutored for admission to the fancy nursery schools. I hear getting into Harvard's a snap by comparison. Fred, look into it for me. Sally, has any one ever done a guide to the best Ladies' Rooms in midtown? Where are they . . . Saks? Four Seasons? How the hell do I know? We could rate them like movies . . . one, two, three stars. And be sure too to check the stalls for graffiti. X-rated Ladies' Rooms – I love it! OK, who've we got can get an interview with Woody Allen? Want to know his views on fatherhood, has it changed his life, all that crap. Francesca, you have connections."

But his own fertility did not suffice. He demanded ideas from every writer on his payroll. "Knock my socks off!" he'd preface each meeting, then cross his feet atop the conference table.

This was the cue for each staff member to begin lobbying for this or that pet idea. The scene reminded Lee of a college seminar, all those hands shooting up with a "me, me, teach" eagerness. Only at stake here was more than passing grades. It was linage, column inches, exposure for your name. Conceivably, fingers crossed, a cover story. Write enough sharp features and who knows? That window office could be yours, baby. Or an offer from a bigger magazine.

Thus, each meeting was for a free-for-all. Yet fast as proposals popped up, Fletch shot them down. "Wakey wakey!" – he would heap scorn left and right. "I read about it in *St Nicholas Magazine* back in Nineteen Ought Two." Or worse – ". . . in last month's *Vanity Fair*."

Even those stories deemed worth developing had to run a second obstacle course. "My wife . . ." Fletch would say, and the groans could be heard a block away. Fletch's wife was a top model, all ninety-eight pounds of her, the incarnation of chic, capable of shredding any item that was less than trendy with a swipe of those perfect cheekbones.

"My wife found this tacky," Fletch would say. It was the kiss of death. For good measure, he'd add, "And so do I."

Still too new to New York to have developed a gut feeling for local issues, Lee bided her time at first, watching and learning, profiting by her colleagues' mistakes. The problem was, she had no primary sources other than Gerry, and one lone woman, no matter how famous, hardly constituted a celebrity network. There was some slight satisfaction to be derived from noting that her competitors, despite Ivy League backgrounds and connections, were faring no better.

At every meeting, she scribbled dozens of notes, analysing which subjects intrigued Fletch, which bored him silly. One of these days, she would come up with the big story idea, the exclusive that would put her on the map. Until then she spent her days scouring for prospects for Other People's Business.

Her opening column had included Gerry's suggestion, the medium who communed with dead dogs. The piece had gone down well, earning a grunt of approbation from Fletch, but it was proving a tough act to follow, given his can-you-top-this mentality. Each week, Lee ploughed through over a thousand press releases, to say nothing of trade journals, patent applications, court dockets, the classified ads, even the New York Yellow Pages, in perpetual search of the odd and the offbeat. She chased down plant psychiatrists, the inventor of the Gorillagram, a sweet little housewife who baked erotic cakes for Blue Birthdays Inc., a health nut who marketed pure Vermont air in flip-top cans, the 72-year-old blacksmith who shod horses for the NYPD mounties – to say nothing of cranks, crackpots and publicity hounds.

It took fifty phone calls to develop ten decent leads, ten leads for the one crunchy paragraph. Thus, filling the column to Fletch's satisfaction represented a full week's sweated labour. It made for lightweight reading, pleasant enough but hardly the groundwork for a dazzling career. She felt, on the one hand, proud to be associated with a hot new magazine; on the other, faintly ashamed of the trivia she was writing.

"Read it and weep." She showed a handout to the passing Bill Frazier. "Some guy wants to import Hailsham Castle from England and turn it into a New Jersey shopping mall. Can you beat that for gross?"

"Don't know as I'd want to," he laughed, followed by, "What are you doing for dinner tonight? There's a new Thai place I want to try out . . ."

As *Trend's* restaurant critic, Bill was in the enviable position of having a *carte blanche* expense account for four dinners each night, that number offering sufficient scope for him to test the cuisine. The foursomes were usually composed of whichever colleagues were available in addition to what Bill called his "Muffy of the Week". He usually had one on tap, some clean-haired girl from last year's Greenwich cotillion – bland, sweet and empty, with Ralph Lauren clothes and perfect teeth. They all had beautiful table manners, Lee observed. The restaurants Bill chose were newish and pricey, with the better ones being visited another two or three times for what he called a "comprehensive overview".

On paper, the job sounded more like play than work, outdone only by the post of theatre critic. However, dinner with Bill imposed its obligations. It was no fair saying that all you wanted was shrimp cocktail and a steak. Duty demanded that each of his tablemates plough through at least three courses, with the emphasis on the odd and elaborate, in addition to a full complement of wines. Bill sampled every dish that came to the table, though never in view of the staff, for he guarded his anonymity with zeal. "I don't want the chef knocking himself out for *Trend Magazine*," he confided. "I want to be treated like everyone else."

He certainly didn't look like a professional gourmet. Lean and athletic, appearing even younger than his twenty-seven years, he seemed to be nothing more formidable than a college kid in town on a spree. Waiters often ignored him, maître d's sat him at the back, but all the while, he was scribbling arcane notes into a tiny lined pad that might later appear in a scathing review.

"How'd you get to know so much about food?" Lee once asked him.

"My mother," Bill replied.

"She cooks?"

"She has cooks."

She also had husbands, Lee gathered, some half-dozen of them, each one wealthier than his predecessor. Bill's father, who figured early in the sequence, had been chief of protocol at the State Department. The then-Mrs Frazier helped build her husband's career by entertaining often and lavishly. "By the time I was six," Bill said, "I could tell a cêpe from a porcini at twenty paces."

"What's a cêpe?" Lee asked, assuming she could also find out what a porcini was by indirection.

"Come to La Venezia with me on Friday and I'll show you."

When she had nothing else to do, she would join him. The food was usually good, the ambiance pleasant, and if Bill's date didn't add much to the conversation, there was always another colleague who did.

"So how about tonight at the Thai place?" Bill said. "Fred and Renata are coming, and you and I make four."

"No Muffy this week?"

Bill laughed. "The last one I had was brain dead. Also

a calorie counter, even worse. I thought maybe you'd like to sub."

"Thanks a lot," Lee said, mildly wondering if he was interested in her as something other than a willing palate. It was hard to tell with Bill, given his easy-going style. "But I'm afraid I already have something on."

"Anyone special?" he asked.

"Dinner with Geraldine O'Neal," she pronounced with a flourish, as though to say: See, I know important people, too.

Bill, however, was only mildly impressed. "I believe she and my father had a thing going a few centuries back," he said amiably. "I remember my mother being very pissed off. Is she still such a looker?"

"Fabulous!" Lee replied. "What's your dad's name, by the way? I'll give Gerry regards from his son."

An hour later, she was sitting in Gerry's study, her second visit that week. Already Lee felt herself a familiar, like a house cat or a favourite niece. She could find her way around the kitchen, knew which chairs were comfortable, which bathroom to use. Had learned to mix the Campari and soda that Gerry enjoyed at day's end.

If her hostess wasn't ready, Lee would bring the drink upstairs and sit on the edge of her bed while Gerry put the finishing touches on her ensemble, chatting as she fussed. Lee watched and learned.

On occasion, Gerry would turn off the phone ("that's what answering machines are for") and give Lee her undiluted attention. The hell with the outside world, she seemed to say. Nothing matters to me more than your company. These moments, as intense as they were intimate, made Lee feel like a member of New York's most exclusive club. The inner circle of Gerry O'Neal. They occurred with increasing frequency.

When Gerry found herself with time on her hands and no one to share it, she'd send for Lee to "come save my life". Sometimes the invitation was issued as marching orders ("I absolutely forbid you to miss Baryshnikov!") sometimes they were sweet seductions ("I've just received

112

two huge Maine lobsters and one has your name on it.") Either way, she wouldn't take no for an answer. Lee jumped at the chance.

Such evenings were packed with glamour. As a rule, Gerry had some gala entertainment on tap: a Broadway première, the opening of a smart new gallery. And though Lee suspected she had been asked only after other (presumably male) escorts had proved unavailable, it hardly mattered. To be caught up in Gerry's whirlwind was a privilege.

More was on offer than the obvious thrill of catching the best show in town from the best seat in the house. It was a chance to meet the rich and famous, to see and be seen, to be perceived as the intimate of a great celebrity.

Lee was always introduced with a flourish. "The rising young light of *Trend Magazine*," Gerry would say, or something equally flattering. Lee learned not to blush. It was almost true. No longer quite the cipher, she was becoming a somebody. It was intoxicating.

But if nights on the town were a treat, even better were the cosy evenings at home. Gerry had given Lee a set of housekeys so she could let herself in and mix them both drinks, before settling down in the den for a "just-the-two-of-us" chat. On those occasions, Gerry would open her heart, talk simply and earnestly, imparting the wisdom of a lifetime's experience. The sessions might have been subtitled: *How to Succeed – A Lesson from the Master*.

"You kids don't know what struggle is," would precede the flood of anecdotes that, taken all together, provided a comprehensive road map to the top. There were cautionary tales, Machiavellian in their complexity, of how she had battled discrimination, nabbed clients, curried favour, broken rules, charmed and cajoled, pandered and pummelled, played dumb and played smart depending on circumstances, but always always played to win. There were war stories, most but not all ending in victory, but even defeat could bring enlightenment. Yet the underlying theme was always the same. *Go for it*. The only failure, she claimed, was the failure of nerve.

Lee listened, absorbed, filing away bits of advice. "Don't

stand when you do business with a bald man. They think you're staring at the top of their head." "Never trust anyone who speaks of himself in the third person." "Always check the silver after having Congressmen to lunch." When Lee got home at night, she'd jot them down.

"You ought to write a book," she once said.

"And give this stuff away for twenty bucks a copy?" Gerry laughed, which remark made Lee feel all the more flattered to be the sole recipient of such an education.

Yes, there were lessons to be gleaned here, and not only on the tactics of business. For every lesson that touched upon the complexities of office politics, there were others, equally useful, on the intricacies of eating artichokes and tying silk scarves and handling cab drivers. Gerry's tutelage knew no bounds.

"I don't pretend to be a professional make-up artist," she said, plunking Lee down before her dressing table, with its vast array of pots and brushes, "but I've learned a few tricks in my day. Let's try some different faces just for fun. . . ."

An hour later, Lee viewed her reflection open-mouthed. Gerry had worked a transformation. And yet there was nothing you could put your finger on and holler "*Fake!*" It was indubitably Lee who stared back at her, Lee and no one else, but a glamorous Lee, with heightened cheek-bones, sensual mouth and lustrous eyes. Even her button nose had, with a few carefully placed strokes of blusher, taken on an aristocratic tilt. A Lee who could carry off those gigantic ear-rings that were becoming her trademark back at *Trend*.

Gerry rubbed her hands and looked pleased. "You're an absolute knockout!" she said. "Now you see how it's done . . . twenty minutes is all you need. And don't ever let me catch you wearing that peculiar shade of lipstick again!"

About ten o'clock, if they were staying in, she would call to have food delivered. Nothing fancy, Chinese or barbecued chicken or on one occasion even pizza "with everything on it". Lee was amused that despite the lavishness of her entertainments, Gerry was modest in her personal tastes.

She lived alone, which Lee found astonishing for someone so wealthy. No cook, no lady's maid, just a doughty middle-aged housekeeper named Ida who worked from nine to six, a once-a-week seamstress and such casual help as was needed from time to time.

Except for the leftovers from Ida's lunch, the refrigerator was usually empty of everything but olives and champagne.

"I don't like a lot of staff breathing down my neck," Gerry explained. "I live enough of my life in public."

Lee was delighted. On nights like this she had Gerry all to herself. This evening, Gerry had sent out for lamb chops and a salad. "We could make those just as easily," Lee commented.

"Well, maybe you could," Gerry said, "but leave me out of this. I think, I talk, I travel, I write, I read, I hire and fire, I dress, entertain and run a business. Don't ask me to cook into the bargain. Now be a love and mix us some aperitifs."

Lee brought in the drinks and a jar of macadamia nuts to hold them till the food arrived.

"By the way," Lee said when they'd settled down over Camparis, "I work with a guy whose father is Austin Frazier of the State Department. I gather from what Bill says, you and he were – well, what the columnists would call a 'romantic item'."

A week ago, Lee would have hesitated to bring up such intimate matters, but now she knew Gerry better. Far from exercising discretion about former lovers, Gerry was disarmingly forthright.

Now, however, she furrowed her brow. "What'd you say the father's name was?"

Lee repeated it. "Of the Philadelphia Fraziers. He was a big wheel in Washington in the early sixties. Chief of protocol, in fact."

"Vaguely rings a bell," Gerry said after a pause, although Lee could see that it didn't, "but I can't place him off hand. I'll take your friend's word for it that we were a hot ticket.

In the early sixties, you say. That would be the Kennedy administration. No, I don't remember Frazier, but did I ever tell you about the night I spent with JFK? It was at the Carlyle, here in New York. Well, it's a good thing for the country that he performed better in the Oval Office than in the sack. It was Bim, bam, thank you ma'am. . . . although I find that often the case with powerful men . . ."

And she was off and running.

Lee never knew what to make of these reminiscences, beyond the obvious conclusion that Gerry loved recounting her triumphs. By turn, Lee's eyes flew up in awe (What memoirs these would make!), widened in shock (Gerry had no qualms about naming names) and blinked in occasional disbelief.

For if even half of these affairs had taken place, then Gerry O'Neal's career was an even greater phenomenon. Where in God's name did she find the time? The energy? Was she pulling Lee's leg?

And yet . . . and yet, the relics of that gallery of men were omnipresent. There was the huge cardboard box in her dressing room, crammed with snapshots and love letters galore. The bits of memorabilia – paperweights, carriage clocks, books with passionately inscribed dedications, framed photos, a crystal ashtray bearing the White House seal – that were strewn about the rooms with a cosy abandon. There was the Sargent portrait in the hall bequeathed by Henry Winterbourne. The little garnet ring she never took off and of which, with uncharacteristic reticence, she would say only that it was a memento "from someone I loved very dearly".

Yet with the dazzling exception of the Sargent and possibly the ring, the value of those gifts was clearly more sentimental than real.

"I never took expensive presents from lovers," she told Lee. "If I had, they might have assumed proprietary rights."

No, the lovers hadn't owned Gerry either body or soul. But she, in memory, owned them.

In retrospect, she seemed to have adored them all – even the ones characterized as shits. Shits they may have been,

116

but they were *her* shits, and that (Lee inferred) gave them merit.

For a woman who claimed to lack acquisitive instincts, who insisted there was something comic in Andy Warhol's cookie jars and Ivana Trump's dresses and the army of aesthetes who haunted the auction houses in search of yet another piece of Ming, Gerry took a true collector's pride in her lovers.

They were her wealth, her trophies, her prized possessions. When the mood was on her, she would trot out the choicest pieces with the gusto of a Hearst showing off the treasures of San Simeon. In lieu of artworks and jewels, Gerry's collection consisted of hearts and scalps, to say nothing of other more intimate attributes, each one of which she appraised with a connoisseur's eye.

"Fabulous in bed . . ." might be the judgement, or "sexy, but no sense of humour . . . a superb specimen . . . a three-alarm snorer . . . the last of the big spenders . . . brilliant, but a psychopath . . . a lousy lay . . . a sweetheart."

Thus were the great and glorious put to rest.

Throughout these narrative, two lines recurred with frequency. "He was crazy about me." Alternately, "I was crazy about him." Occasionally, though not often, both lines were quoted in conjunction.

"If you were so crazy about him," Lee was once emboldened to ask, "then how come you never married?" At which remark Gerry had shot her a long hard look. "There's crazy and crazy," she said. Yet for a moment Lee suspected her of leaving something unsaid. A secret agenda, perhaps? A lover reserved for her declining years? The moment passed.

Gerry declared herself a believer in "thunderbolts", that swift, erotic discovery that can zap even the wariest across a crowded room.

"Love at first sight? Oh my god, there's nothing like it!" Suddenly her eyes went misty. "You see him, this wonderful creature, maybe at a meeting, a dinner party. I once fell madly in love at the shirt counter of Bloomingdale's. It can happen anywhere, but when it does, it's an epiphany. You don't know his name, anything about him. If he's got a wife and five kids in the country or is wanted in ten states for embezzlement. And what's more, you don't care. There's something about him that speaks to you. Perhaps the timbre of his voice, the set of the shoulders, a scent, an aura – God knows what. You exchange glances, smiles – and bingo! the whole world falls away. In that moment, nothing else exists. It's a physical assault – like a rush of cocaine or a whiff of pure oxygen. Your heart beats faster, your mouth goes dry. Every perception is heightened, but somehow distanced too. You can feel your capillaries contract, I swear. And there's this strange high music everywhere, blotting out the workaday world. It's realer than real and at the same time a kind of myth, a fairy tale with you as the princess. When he looks at you, time freezes. You know that feeling, Lee," – but Lee didn't. Gerry might have been speaking Chinese.

"Such bliss!" Gerry went on. "And all you can think is that you want this man more than anything else in creation. He's your ideal, the only one who can fulfil your fantasies, make you feel truly beloved. Then you actually meet, and the roller-coaster ride begins. Will he call? Will he like you in green velvet? Will he touch your cheek, take your hand in his? Will he laugh at your jokes? Tell you his secrets? Will you become lovers tonight? Or ever? God help you – is he gay? And then, just when life is approaching the unendurable, the moment arrives . . ."

Lee was unsure if Gerry was teasing her. "Romantic rubbish" was the term that sprang to mind, Gerry being such a pragmatist, yet she hesitated to strike the wrong note.

"And do you . . . ?" she asked, non-committally.

"Become lovers?" Gerry gave a short brisk laugh and returned to the concrete present. "Probably. I amend that. Practically always. Of course, the first time is paradise, but after that, my dear, it's all downhill. You see his petty weaknesses, his patterns. The mystery vanishes. Boredom begins to set in. Restlessness too. And you're ready to fall in love with someone new. D. H. Lawrence was right – sex is all in the head."

Lee felt relieved. Gerry had been teasing her with all this foolish talk of romance on the hoof. Now Lee offered a knowing smile.

"So much for love at first sight!"

"I wouldn't knock it, though, Lee. There's nothing else in life quite as exciting. It's the tenth sight, the hundredth sight where the going gets sticky. I suspect I have a short attention span. But my God, I've known some marvellous men in my day!"

The list of her lovers was daunting: international in scope, wide-ranging by profession, cheerfully democratic in matters of race, religion and colour. In Gerry's memoirs, a Charlie Parker might rub shoulders, metaphorically speaking, with the Shah of Iran or an Albert Camus or a Welsh rugby star or the late, great Henry Winterbourne. For they all had rubbed shoulders and more with Gerry.

This was explained by Gerry's remark that well-known people usually sought each other out and tended to sleep with one another early on in their acquaintance. And while many of her couplings were affairs of the heart, most had their origins in curiosity.

"Haven't you ever wondered what some film star was like in bed?" she asked Lee. "Sure you have! Well, the fun of being a celebrity is that you can find out. Because, you see, your counterpart is probably just as curious about you. It's one of the perks of fame."

Tonight, however, although Gerry had rooted around in the sixties all through dinner and dredged up at least a dozen liaisons, the ghost of Austin Frazier remained at bay.

"No," she conceded. "I'm afraid I don't remember him, although it was certainly within the realm of possibility. But you may tell your young man to give his father my regards if he chooses. Is he attractive, by the way?"

"Which . . . the father or the son?"

"Both," Gerry laughed. "Either."

"I can't vouch for the father but Bill's quite cute in a preppy sort of way."

"Are you sleeping with him?"

The directness of the question caught Lee off guard.

"No . . . certainly not," she spluttered. "Whatever gave you that notion?"

"Well, you did say he was attractive, so naturally I assumed . . ."

"Then you assumed wrong!" Lee was miffed.

It hurt that Gerry should have so little respect for her judgement. Gerry, such a fount of wisdom about professional matters, surely realized that going to bed with Albert Camus was one thing; going to bed with Bill Frazier quite another.

"I don't want to get involved in office romances," Lee protested. "It's dumb. Word gets around so fast. And when the affair breaks up, where are you? Out of a job, likely as not. Honestly, Gerry, you know my priorities . . ."

"OK, OK." Gerry refused to be ruffled. "I didn't mean to offend your sensibilities. Anyhow, I gather casual sex is extinct. You poor kids," she added, "what with AIDS and herpes and all that other crap going around, it's a wonder you have any sex life at all. I suppose I should thank God that I'm out of the romance business. At least I had mine when the going was fun."

Lee got up and cleared away the table, threw the empty cartons into the garbage, then put their plates in the dishwasher for Ida in the morning. Gerry, bless her, never lifted a finger, as was her wont. She would have left them there all night. But Lee liked things tidy.

By way of recompense, Gerry drove Lee home.

"Aren't you going to invite me in?" she asked when they pulled up on 12th Street. "I'm curious about how you live."

Lee flushed. "It's a rat-hole," she said, "but if you insist . . ."

"I do."

Lee opened the door to the sound of creaking floorboards and switched on the light. Gerry took it all in at a glance: the naked ceiling fixtures, the bathtub with its chipped porcelain standing in the middle of the kitchen, the Keith Haring posters doing their boldest to mask the plaster peeling off the walls.

"In my day we put up bullfight posters," she mused.

Gerry opened the kitchen cupboard. A cockroach scurried out.

Lee crimsoned with shame. "I'm sorry having to subject you to this dump. As soon as I get a raise, I'm out of here. Upper East Side, preferably. Maybe even swing a mortgage on a condo . . ."

"My, my!" Gerry teased. "Condos! Mortgages! How quickly you've become the rising young New Yorker. What next, Lee? A BMW with a car phone?"

But Lee missed the irony. "God willing," she said. "I didn't come to this city to bury myself in a tenement."

"Of course not," came the good-natured reply. "Still, this place isn't so bad. At least you've got a bathtub, and, I bet, hot water too. Believe me, sweetie, your so-called rat-hole is a palace compared to how I used to live. And I see they leave the light on in the hall." Her voice had taken on a curious note – romantic, nostalgic.

Lee was puzzled. "You make it sound like the landlord's doing me a favour with that lousy little 60-watt bulb."

But Gerry scarcely heard her. "A light in the hall." Her eyes clouded with memory. "I once thought that was the height of luxury. But that was another place. Another time."

The place was Paris. The time, 1952.

eleven

The light on the staircase was timed for exactly twelve seconds.

If you were fast on your feet, possessed of good legs and lungs, you could scramble to the safety of the landing with a second or two left over – just time enough to push the button that lit up the next flight of stairs.

But if, God forbid, you were tired or distracted or a little bit drunk, then CLICK! Out went the light, and you were left stranded, blinking in sudden darkness. It was scary – not just the pitchy black, but the physical danger. The stairs were steep and narrow and it was a long way down. You'd have to negotiate the rest of the stairs by feel alone.

The best way was to get down on all fours, then grope your way up step by step, until you attained the safety of the landing. Then on your feet – slowly slowly – and start fumbling along the wall with both hands, fingers splayed, in search of the nipple-shaped button that would (Glory be!) light your way up the next flight of stairs.

For precisely another twelve seconds.

And so it went, until in triumph you arrived at the *5ème étage* ("which means fifth floor in English, mom, though it's really our American sixth") of the Hôtel de la Harpe.

It was a lesson in French thrift.

As were the newspapers.

Each morning, the previous day's newspapers were collected, cut into pieces some seven inches square, stacked, then spiked onto a nail in the W C on the third floor landing, to be used for toilet paper.

At first, Gerry wondered whether the landlord's choice of journals (*Le Figaro* and *France-Soir*) indicated an endorsement of their views or, whether, on the contrary, it was the means by which he conveyed a scatological contempt. The former, she concluded, the *patron* being too frugal a

122

person to deny himself maximum usage of anything for which he had paid good money.

Still, it gave Gerry an odd feeling to wipe herself with the likeness of General de Gaulle or Premier Mendès-France. In any event, the stuff was slick and non-absorbent. The toilet itself dated back to the early days of indoor plumbing. She had never seen anything like it: no seat, no bowl, merely two foot-holds over a shallow pan. When you flushed, you had to jump clear.

Like the lights, the plumbing fixtures provided a challenge. The fact that the hotel had once served as a brothel for the Wehrmacht (lower ranks, only) merely added to the sense of adventure.

Gerry's room was on the top floor, a small damp chamber made smaller by being wedged against the mansard roof. The overhead light, just bright enough to illuminate the stains and lumps on the mattress, was barely sufficient to read by and prone to power failures. She kept a supply of candles on the night table.

For the rest, the furniture consisted of an overstuffed chair with frayed fringes, a wardrobe, a cigarette-scarred chest of drawers that doubled as a desk and dressing table, and a sink that ran tepid water twice a day at specified hours.

Beneath the sink, on a wobbly iron stand, stood a dusty bidet of chipped porcelain.

"*C'est pour laver les cheveux, n'est-ce-pas?*" she asked the chambermaid who promptly burst out laughing then enlightened Gerry as to its proper function. Blushing, Gerry asked to have it removed. Impossible, Lisette said. It was there by law, as it was in every hotel room in France, being a necessary aid to health and cleanliness.

Which struck Gerry as odd, since her room, and indeed the entire Hôtel de la Harpe, boasted neither a bathtub nor a shower. Twice a week, armed with soap, shampoo and as much dirty laundry as she could smuggle in under her clothes, she would treat herself to an afternoon in the public bath house, wallowing up to her ears in sudsy water. As for the days in between, perfume was relatively cheap, good cologne even cheaper.

123

She regarded none of this as hardship, merely another part of the grand adventure. Yes, her room was tawdry, but it had windows – oh such windows! – with a view that took her breath away. To wake up each morning and gaze out upon serried rooftops, and beyond the rooftops, a glimpse of the Seine: surely, this was a boon worthy of any bathlessness. In that brilliant grey light peculiar to Paris, everything – the weathered slates, the patchwork of chimneys, the river – looked as clear and crisp as a stage set.

On Sunday mornings, she would fling open the window and listen to the peal of church bells – the bells of St Etienne and St Julien *le Pauvre* and (at least she chose to think) from the cathedral of Notre Dame itself. Crane her neck and she could just make out its spires, dizzying against the movement of the clouds.

She could have roomed more economically with a French family, but why should she? She could have stayed in America, for that matter. Freedom was what she had come for. Freedom and privacy, even at the cost of smelly drains and coarse sheets.

"*Au 'voir!*" She blew a kiss to the memory of the Mohawk Beer billboard some three thousand miles away, and felt herself liberated, a genuine expatriate.

"Paris is everything we ever dreamed of," she rhapsodized in a letter to Nancy shortly after her arrival, omitting the tackier aspects of her circumstances. "*C'est la vie de bohème* come true."

Then she lit a Gauloise Bleu and blew the smoke into the thin blue envelope, hoping that some wisp of it might survive the trans-Atlantic journey and afford her friend a vicarious pleasure.

And if she minimized the particular tawdriness of L'Hôtel de la Harpe, she was within her rights. Except for the view, the room was incidental. She went there only to sleep and change clothes. Then down the five flights (far easier than up) to deliver herself happily into the crowded streets, one more young student joining the ocean of students that eddied through the twisted streets and alleys into the tree-lined avenues of the Latin Quarter.

124

Only to Gerry, this wasn't a "quarter" of Paris at all. It was virtually the whole of it: a magic triangle bounded by Boul' Mich', St Germain and Montparnasse. The Left Bank was her turf. She loved it with a fierce and uncritical partisanship.

Once a month, she would cross the river to collect her hundred dollar stipend at the American Express. She would cash it on the black market, then hurry home to hide the money in a jam jar outside the window where it would be safe from the chambermaid's sticky fingers. Except for that journey and occasional trips to the museums, she considered the Right Bank to be the exclusive venue of the wealthy and of American tourists. Lord knows she wasn't the one. God forbid she be taken for the other! Her fondest hope was to be mistaken for French.

From the start, her academic life was perfunctory. Although the Sorbonne was only a few blocks away, she went there less and less, attending the minimum of lectures, perfectly content to scrape by. Her interest in Racine was waning fast.

Had she chosen to, she might have become a passable scholar, but real life was more tempting. Her French, which she feared might prove inadequate to her studies, was excellent for literary purposes. Everyday usage was another matter. And although six years of study had made her fluent in such fine points as the pluperfect tense and the vocabulary of classic drama, they had not taught her how to order a meal or use a pay phone or tell the bottom-pinchers in the Metro to bug off.

"*Avez-vous une plume?*" she had asked her landlord on being handed the register to sign. "*Une plume . . . une plume . . .* " he'd repeated with a shriek of delight. Only later did Gerry get the joke.

"Imagine!" she wrote Nancy. "The very first word I learned in French One is as *passé* as the horse and buggy. Did you know that a *plume* is a feather pen?"

She promptly set out to remedy this gap in her education, though not in the lecture halls of the Sorbonne.

The cafés were her true campus. The bustling *terrasses* of St Germain-des-Prés, the lively brasseries of Boul' Mich', the smoky *boîtes* and *caves* tucked away in the myriad side streets. There were hundreds of them, each with its own ambiance, its own group of "regulars". Even years later, when she was living in what had once been (at least for her) unimaginable luxury, she would light a Gauloise and then, the fumes potent as incense, conjure up their names the way a more godly woman might have invoked the names of saints. Dives they might have been, noisy and raffish, yet they were holy still, at least in memory.

Le Mabillion, crowded and seedy. La Rose Rouge, where heavy-lidded Moroccans dealt in hashish. Le Dôme, its broad terrace awash in memories of Hemingway and Scott Fitzgerald. The notorious Pergola, with its mix of students, hustlers and pimps. The dimly lit hole that was Café Montana, where Edith Piaf sometimes sang after hours. And, for the price of a dark and bitter *café filtre*, those twin citadels of existentialism: the Café de Flore and Les Deux Magots. If you were lucky, you might see Sartre himself commanding a table of acolytes, and maybe pick up a philosophical pearl to pass along later ("As Jean-Paul said . . ."), over onion soup at the Brasserie Lip.

Racine? Corneille? The great tragedians she had purportedly come to study? They soon sank to the level of a minor interest. For how could the glories of the past compare with the temptations, the dynamics of the world about her? A world full of iconoclasts and budding geniuses, of builders and destroyers, where everyone was under thirty – with such notable exceptions as Sartre and Cocteau and the ectoplasmic Raymond Duncan, brother of Isadora, who wafted through the streets in sandals and a Grecian toga. This was real. This was life. And even if you couldn't be young, then be either famous or outrageous. Preferably both.

Within a month of her arrival, Gerry's appearance had undergone a transformation. She developed a café slouch, a Gallic shrug and had mastered the art of raising one eyebrow in sceptical disdain.

Gone were the white gloves, the crisp cheerful shirtwaisters with matching pumps. In *hommage* to the existential spirit, she dressed only in black: cotton turtlenecks, narrow

126

skirts with a slit, lisle stockings that seemed to make her legs run on for miles. It was the colour of *café filtre*, of the tobacco in her Gauloise Bleu, the quintessential tint of bohemianism, appearing even more dramatic against the whiteness of her skin.

The effect was smashing. *"La belle Américaine"*, some of her companions called her. Or *"la belle Gerry"*. They pronounced it *Zheri*, almost like *Cheri*. It made her feel racy, like a page out of a novel by Colette.

Yet beneath this sexy sophisticated exterior, Gerry hid a woeful secret. Here she was, almost twenty-one years old and still a virgin. Shame. Shame.

No one would have believed it of her. She could hardly believe it of herself. It was a loathsome condition, an embarrassment, utterly at odds with her vision of herself as a woman of the world. What had seemed prudent back home seemed wildly out of place here, her precious virtue as outmoded as *la plume* of her eighth-grade textbook. Everybody seemed to sleep with everybody, and no harm done. Why must she be so backward!

All that was wanting to correct this deplorable state was the man of her fantasies. He should be handsome and clever (she asked little else), a first love that would give her joy to look back on.

It was only a matter of time until she found him.

Until then, she spent her evenings in a circle that was predominantly male, as free-wheeling in its composition as it was urbane. Her new friends were students, writers, artists and philosophers, to say nothing of the would-be-writers-and-artists et al. who put their creative energies into café-sitting rather than work, into talk rather than action.

"I'm studying at the Academy Julien," one fellow insisted, though he spent his days at the bar of Le Mabillion. But when Gerry voiced scepticism, he took umbrage. "What do I have to do to prove I'm a painter?" he growled. "Cut off my ear?"

Not all of them were French, by any means. There were Swedes, Danes, Dutchmen, a sprinkling of Americans over on Fullbrights or the G.I. Bill, British students living in good-natured penury, and a surprising number of young men from behind the Iron Curtain, including a lanky six footer known only as Prince Boris, who claimed to be descended from the Tsars.

What they had in common, these diverse guests of the Fourth Republic, was a desire to be more Gallic than the Gauls. Even the Americans underwent a sea change. Indeed, no one was quicker to damn the evils of Yankee imperialism, Yankee materialism, than these self-imposed exiles from the suburbs. They considered themselves honorary Frenchmen.

One knew people by first names, nick-names, by their theories and eccentricities and pretensions. This one was writing a paper on Schoenberg or a new kind of play without dialogue. That one was a Nihilist or a protegé of Jean Arp or kept a capuchin monkey on a string. The prevailing tone was profoundly anti-establishment. Daring, impudence, panache; those were the qualities that counted. Bourgeois thinking was the unforgivable crime.

Gerry drank it all in. The European men, especially, impressed her. They were utterly different from the crew-cut clean-cut Chucks and Bobs back home. Still in their twenties, with longish hair and a core of self-assurance, they seemed older, more sexual than any boys she'd known before. The best of them radiated a sense of danger.

Such girls as joined the circle didn't interest her half so much. And the feeling was apparently mutual. There were no overtures of friendship on either side. For the most part, they came to the cafés either to be with lovers or to find them, moving from one man to another with a freedom that was breath-taking. When there were no attractive prospects in sight, they drifted off, one by one.

This absence of female solidarity struck Gerry as eminently sensible. What was the point, after all, of cultivating girlfriends, of putting in all that time and effort, only to be dumped as soon as the next man turns up? That much she had learned from Nancy Schroeder.

Why waste her time with women at all? It was a man's world, clearly. And it only awaited the right one to make it ideal.

128

His name was Jean-Claude something-or-other. All she knew about him was that he came from Nevers, considered himself a devotee of Sartre's and was indecently handsome – tall and lean, with blue-black hair and the chiselled features of a film star.

He turned up one night at Le Dôme, joining the table where Gerry was seated with half a dozen of her boon companions. He was, in the casual manner of introductions, a friend of a friend of a friend. No further credentials were required.

From the moment he sat down, she could scarcely take her eyes off him. Every movement he made, every gesture, was informed with physical grace. He, too, was wearing a black turtleneck. It struck her as a romantic affinity.

The cafe was crowded that night, and at their table, the talk, which rapidly grew heated, was of Samuel Beckett. Should Beckett be properly considered a glory of English literature, of Irish literature or of French? Should he be considered a glory at all?

Rikki for one preferred the comedies of Laurel and Hardy. Denise disagreed. This new play *Godot* was unutterably profound. What did Jean-Claude think?

Gerry leaned over to hear his answer, when suddenly a drunken voice boomed out "Beckett . . . Beckett!" followed by a string of obscene epithets.

Gerry looked up in astonishment, to see a middle-aged whore with hideous orange hair, her face a smear of greasy make-up, staggering towards them like a runaway locomotive.

"And yet so wonderful in bed," the awful creature began to weep, mascara running down her cheeks. For a moment, it looked as though this visitation would collapse onto their table. Gerry snatched her Pernod out of harm's way.

Then, even more astonishing, Jean-Claude sprang to his feet and kissed her hand with a gallant gesture, steadying her as he did.

"*Chère Madame.*" He indicated his empty chair with a formal flourish. "Would you do me the honour of joining us for a cognac?"

The monster swayed for a moment, then responded by

grabbing at his genitals. He ducked. They wound up in an ungainly embrace.

"Some other night, my beautiful boy . . . I'm often here. But first, give me a kiss . . ."

Then she lurched off to another table, leaving Jean-Claude with a smear of cheap lipstick on his chin.

He turned to his companions with a laugh.

"Does any one have a handkerchief?"

"Here," Gerry said. "Let me wipe that muck off."

Jean-Claude grinned and pulled up a chair beside her. At close quarters, she observed with rapt fascination, he was even handsomer. Aristocratic, almost. His teeth were white and even.

This man, something within her sang, perhaps this man.

"Who was that . . . that *putain*?" she asked with a shudder of distaste. "Not a friend of yours, I hope."

"Why, that was Kiki," he replied. "Kiki of Montparnasse."

In her youth, he explained, she had been everybody's friend, one of the surpassing beauties of the 1920s. She had sat for Man Ray, Utrillo, Modigliani, Soutine, Foujita, providing each with inspiration and more. Kiki was, in fact, trebly famous: for her looks, for her lovers, and for her lack of pubic hair.

"Really!" Gerry found this last item extraordinary. "Do you say that out of first-hand knowledge?"

"Please," he laughed. "I have never slept with Kiki. Not even once. Although," he reconsidered, "on the other hand – *pourquoi pas?*"

"*Pourquoi pas?*" Gerry echoed. *Why not?* It was a phrase he would use time and again.

"Why not indeed? More improbable things have happened. It might be an interesting experience. To be in touch so intimately, so baldly, one might say, with the artistic heritage of France."

Gerry stared at him.

"You're teasing me," she said. "You made it all up . . . about Kiki's hair, I mean. She probably dyes that orange, too."

130

Jean-Claude shook his head. "I'm a student of myths," he said. "They usually hold the key to the truth."

There were myths about everybody in Montparnasse, he told her. Even the people at this table.

Rikki, for example, wasn't Danish as claimed, but German. Myth said that he had once been a member of the *Hitler Jugend*. André, who passed himself off as the ultimate rake, had a wife and child in Clichy to whom he dutifully returned every night. Dominique smoked hashish. Henri was being kept by a Cambodian prince.

"And me?" Gerry had to ask. "Is there a myth about me?"

"Ah you." He held her gaze. *"La belle Américaine."*

"That's not a myth, it's an epithet. Tell me, what do they say?"

He whispered the words, his lips brushing her ear, his breath warm against her cheek. Then he leaned back. "Is it true?"

She felt a sudden surge of sensuality, enhanced by the Pernod and talk of Kiki. It was followed by a surge of fear. She might never see him again. Their world was so unstable, evanescent. And he was so beautiful. Kiki was right.

Deep inside her, a tiny motor began to whirr.

"Would you like to find out?" she asked, meeting his eyes with an unflinching gaze.

"When?"

"Tonight."

"Pourquoi pas?"

They made love by candlelight.

Its amber glow informed the familiar shape and objects of her room with an extraordinary beauty. The unmade bed, the pattern of the wall paper, her naked flesh: all were the colour of liquid gold.

And the most magnificent object of all was surely Jean-Claude.

"Let us begin," he said "by touching."

He had long beautiful fingers, sensual and caressing, and beneath them, she began to discover her body, her points of joy and trembling, as surely as he did. Then he put his mouth on her breast. On her belly. On the tangled mat of her pubic hair.

At first she lay awed and silent, observing him in help-less fascination. She was afraid to move for fear of fumbling, of breaking the rhythm, loath to reveal the depths of her inexperience. She must watch, learn, for if she shut her eyes it would be all over – too soon, too sudden. She wanted to remember every detail of this night, the most important of her life so far, the one that would mark the transition from girl to woman.

But soon, she fell into the rhythm of his lips, his fingers in a kind of slow-motion dance, an attenuated sequence of desire and when he finally entered her, smoothly, relent-lessly, her eyes were already shut in rapture. In the distance, she heard someone cry out in a kind of madness. Only later did she realize that the voice was her own.

"*La petite morte*," Jean-Claude said afterwards as they lay entwined in the light of the guttering candle. The little death. It was the French term for the moment of orgasm.

"Will you stay the night?" she asked.

He stayed the night, the morning. Towards noon he got dressed to leave. "So," he looked at the bloodstains on the sheet. "The myth was true, after all."

Gerry flushed. At least, no one would ever again call her The Virgin Queen.

For the next several months, she spent nearly every night in Jean-Claude's arms. Yet at the end of that time, she knew hardly more about him than she had learned that first evening. Where he lived or with whom remained a mystery, and she was reluctant to press. This was a man who preferred to keep his own counsel.

Perhaps, she speculated, he had been wounded by other women. That would explain his cynical pose. At least she hoped it was a pose. In her mind, no man could be so agreeable, so playful in bed if he truly were indifferent to feminine charm.

Yet though he was physically tender, claiming sex was

132

better when unhurried, intellectually, he displayed a brutal streak.

God was dead, he jeered. Property was theft. Marriage was slavery. Tragedy was farce. And given the absence of all values except pleasure, anything was permitted, *pourquoi pas*, except the crime of being bourgeois. Everyone should experience everything.

He forbade Gerry to sustain any illusions about their relationship and certainly what little she could discern about his past was hardly conducive to long-range fantasies.

Sent to Paris at twenty to study engineering at the École des Mines, he had found the work tiresome, his colleagues more so. Within a month, to the anguish of his parents, Jean-Claude had squandered a year's allowance, quit school and declared his independence. Education was for fools, he insisted, and work was for flunkies. All told he would rather be a thief, in the manner of his idol Jean Genet, than a gentleman.

That was four years ago. Gerry pegged him as having wound up somewhere between the two extremes.

He passed his days drifting amiably in the bohemian demi-world, haunting the bookstalls and the galleries, talking philosophy in cheap cafés. He was wonderfully well read, shrewd, and on occasion, amusing.

When it pleased him, he could behave with the most beautiful manners, betraying his origins in the despised upper class. But when he did so, it was with an air of mockery. For the rest, he had no trade, no ambition, no discernible income. He lived only for the day at hand.

Gerry could never anticipate his moods, whether affectionate or merely affected. Indeed she was never certain when she would see him next. Jean-Claude was bound by neither clock nor calendars.

Every afternoon, between five and six, she would come by Le P'tit Maroc, a cramped little café where he often took an aperitif. It was inexpensive and Beni, the bartender, was friendly. If Jean-Claude was there, as he was oftener than not, they would join forces for the evening. A cheap meal at a student restaurant was followed by an hour or

133

so of café-cruising and chatter, then back to her room to make love. And on that particular, she could find no fault with him.

He brought to this one endeavour an enthusiasm that was otherwise absent in his life. They made love constantly, eagerly, wherever the occasion and the desire arose. On the bare floor of the landing, one night when the hall light had caught them short. Beneath the sky, against the slope of the mansard roof, naked in the midday sun.

"Who will see us?" he laughed over Gerry's protests. "God?"

One evening early in April, when the weather turned warm, he met her as usual at the P'tit Maroc. To her astonishment, he was wearing a proper suit and a tie.

"Tonight, my pet, we're going to enjoy one of life's supreme pleasures. A three-star dinner. I bet you haven't had one since you've been in Paris. Laperouse, I think, would be appropriate. Yes, that will do."

He insisted in walking her back to her hotel so she could change. Yes, her best dress and high heels, even a silly garter belt and stockings. Tonight was an occasion.

"How very elegant," he said.

An hour later, Gerry was studying the menu and the prices of the famous restaurant in a state of terminal shock. Had he robbed a bank? Inherited a fortune? She had never been in a place like this. Even the walls were covered with art. How could he afford this?

"Here!" Jean-Claude was amused at her discomposure. "I'll order for both of us."

They dined on langoustines, and salmon and an extraordinary duck, amidst a cavalcade of vintage wines. Gerry, whose taste buds had already undergone a major transition (even the cheapest bistros were an improvement on her grandmother's goulash) felt that she had been granted a preview of heaven. To be eating soufflé Grand Marnier with Jean-Claude by her side: life could offer nothing more divine.

By the time they returned to the hotel, she was giddy with pleasure and wine and desire.

134

"Ah me!" She collapsed on the bed face down, too drunk to undress. "Help me, *cheri*."

She could feel his hands, tender and smooth, removing each garment in leisurely turn. It was good to lie there, passive and sensual, while the world swam gently round her. Good to be undressed, to be made love to, woozy as she was.

"Don't move," he said when she began to roll over to offer herself to him, open-legged. "Stay on your stomach just as you are and I'll make you happy."

He placed a pillow beneath her hips and arranged her body to his pleasure. Then she felt his cock tracking an unfamiliar path between her buttocks.

"Please!" she said with a sharp intake of breath. "We've never done this before. I'm afraid."

"It won't hurt," he promised, sliding his hands under her, holding her breasts to brace her. "You'll like it."

Against the flat of his palms, her nipples hardened in swift response. "See?" He began to enter her. "You like it already. A little trip to Sodom. *Pourquoi pas?*"

It did hurt. She did like it. Or at least as much as she remembered, for when she woke the next morning, bruised and hung over, head throbbing, bottom aching, he wasn't there to tell.

"Oh God, what a night!" she groaned and went back to sleep.

Toward noon, feeling very fragile, she got dressed. It was the third time this week she'd missed class.

The sensible thing would be to go out and have a bite of lunch and strong coffee. Then maybe a good long soak in the public baths.

Opening the window, she reached out onto the roof for the jam jar and enough cash to get her through the day. The jar was empty. She froze in disbelief.

All her money! Nearly a hundred dollars' worth of francs. She had cashed her check but the day before yesterday. A whole month's worth of living was in there.

"Lisette!" she cursed the chambermaid. That goddam Lisette had found her hiding place and stolen her blind.

She would call the cops, launch a complaint with the *patron*. What kind of fleabag was this anyhow!

Then, in a swift, sickening moment, she knew the thief wasn't Lisette at all.

"Have you seen Jean-Claude?" she asked the bartender at Le P'tit Maroc, knowing in advance what the answer would be.

Beni shrugged, as if to say, *ces jeunes hommes*.

"Do you know his last name . . . where he lives?"

Beni shrugged again.

She spent a panicky several hours making the rounds of every café, every restaurant he frequented. No, no one had seen him. No one really knew him. Perhaps he'd left town. Rikki had heard a rumour that he had gone to Stockholm with a Swedish girl friend, but Dominique said no, it was the south of France. Trouble with the law, was Prince Boris's conclusion, though whether for anarchy or drug-running, he couldn't say.

A little past midnight, Gerry dragged her weary body back to the P'tit Maroc in a last desperate hope.

"Still no sign?" asked the sympathetic Beni, then poured her a stiff jigger of Hine.

Gerry reached into her purse and came up with a handful of near-worthless aluminium coins. Seventeen francs. Not even enough for the brandy. The enormity of her situation hit her with hurricane force.

She had nothing. No reserves. No money. No lover. No hope. No illusions. She was flunking out of the Sorbonne for good measure. Young women jumped into the Seine for less cause.

She pushed the drink away from her. It spilled across the marble counter. More foolish waste. She burst into tears.

"I'm broke," she cried. "He took everything I had. I can't even pay for the drink. What a nightmare!" *Quel cauchemar!*

Beni's answer was to pour her another.

"So, now, I suppose, you will be going back to America."

Gerry gulped it down, then shook her head in despair. Anything but that. She would starve before she sent home for money, die the death rather than return whipped by the exigencies of life.

Oh Jean-Claude, you swine! You beautiful sexy vicious swine. Rot in hell!

The knowledge that she had been well and truly fucked in every sense of the word momentarily overwhelmed her.

But she hadn't the time to indulge herself in the full-scaled hatred of Jean-Claude whoever-he-was. Rage was a luxury. If she succumbed to it, she would be lost.

Right now, she had to deal in necessities, not luxuries. And the greatest necessity of all was survival. It pushed every other matter out of her mind.

At whatever cost, whatever effort, she had to eat and pay the rent and hang on to that precious freedom that had come to mean the breath of life itself. That was the reality. From that, there could be no retreat.

But how? What choices did she have? Briefly Gerry toyed with a vision of herself walking the streets with a smile and a swinging handbag or hustling suckers at the bar of La Pergola.

Impossible. Geraldine O'Neal did not sleep with a man for money. She had too strong a sense of self. It was against her nature, her inherent arrogance. Worse yet, it was the very antithesis of freedom. Even here, three thousand miles from home and desperate, she was convinced there were alternatives.

"I'll manage," she snuffled. "I'll get a job."

"Doing what?"

It was Gerry's turn to give a Gallic shrug. "What can I do?"

Beni leaned over the counter thoughtfully.

"You're so tall. Pretty, too. Perhaps. . . ."

His sister-in-law was a dresser at the Folies Bergère. According to Renée, there was a rapid turnover among the show girls. They came, found rich lovers and left. They were Amazons, these girls: tall, well-built, long-legged. Who knows? Perhaps if she fit the costume . . . ?

"I don't dance, I don't sing," Gerry said.

"You walk around and parade your flesh," Beni said. "How much talent does that take?"

Gerry looked at him and sighed.

"Pourquoi pas?"

The make-up took a half-hour to put on, the costume marginally less. But then, the costume was skimpier than the make-up.

Twice daily Gerry went through the ritual in the noisy communal dressing room that dated back to the days of gas-light.

Her outfit consisted of an ounce or less of gold sequins strategically placed (she had to shave her pubic hair) and topped off by an enormous feather headpiece. A pair of high-heeled mules completed the costume and when all the paraphernalia was in place, Gerry cast a silhouette over seven feet high.

It was the feathers that inspired her choice of stage name.

"Miss Mohawk?" the business manager went to put her in the books. "How do you spell that?"

Gerry obliged. "It's an old Indian name," she explained.

He wrote it down, unblinking, and she had the odd notion that a number of the girls took similar liberties. Like the men of the French Foreign Legion, she thought, they were eager to obscure either the present or the past by assuming a false identity.

Her name was the only secret she had left. Everything else about her was in full and unblushing display in Egyptian Fantasy.

On stage she was one of forty show girls, essentially nude, whose job it was to mount a mirrored staircase, moving at a stately pace so the men could get a good look, while the orchestra played a medley of vaguely Eastern airs. Then once in place on the pyramid, she would strike the appointed pose and hold it unmoving for perhaps twenty minutes while the star acts did their turn. She was a *tableau vivant*, a living picture, a minor ornamental piece in a lavish production.

This was followed by a trip back to the dressing room to change into a different co-ordinate of sequins and feathers for an almost identical routine. Only now, the theme was Man in the Moon.

138

It was the most boring work she had ever done. It was also hell on the feet.

The long wait backstage was hardly better, but at least there she could study for exams.

The other girls passed the time in an intense scrutiny of their faces and body – plucking, tweezing, creaming, polishing nails, squeezing blackheads – while keeping up an easy chatter about the things that mattered most: men, clothes and good-natured gossip.

Looks were everything to her new colleagues. They were the common currency, the stock in trade, the only ticket to a secure and happy future. Thus, no greater tragedy could be envisioned than the loss of youthful beauty.

"Marie wanted to come back after the appendectomy," Gerry heard someone say, "but how could she? She has a scar four inches long!"

"Poor girl!" There was a sigh of general sympathy. "Her whole life in ruins."

Gerry burrowed further into her book.

The money wasn't bad, although she earned considerably less than the dancers or the girls who came wafting down from the balcony on garlanded swings or Carmen, the little blonde who rode a live black panther in the Egyptian routine.

Those girls had skills, or in Carmen's case, courage. Gerry did not. The salary was, however, sufficient to keep her afloat, and the hours such that she could still attend classes at the Sorbonne. Looked at from a scheduling point of view, the job was ideal. Setting about her studies with a new sense of purpose, she asked only to pass the exams. That would be quite enough to salvage from the fiasco.

"All in all, not too bad," she thanked Beni with a kilo of ham her first pay day. At his advice, she had shown up at the "audition" wearing her most form-fitting dress and high heels. In the glittering night spots of Place Pigalle, Beni warned her, the existential look was out. Glamour was in.

The next morning, Gerry wrapped up the uniform she had worn so many months – the black turtle neck, the dark

139

lisle stockings, the now-threadbare skirt – and handed the package to Lisette.

"Take it," she told the chambermaid. "And if you can't use them, burn them!"

Her bohemian days and Left Bank nights were over, as dead as her love for Jean-Claude. She refused to think about him. The only time he invaded her consciousness was when she dined at Laperouse.

She ate there often now, as well as at Prunier's and Maxim's, expensive feeds being the sole significant perk of her new career.

After every show, there was always a supply of men hovering at the stage door, eager to take the girls out to dinner. They were rarely Parisians, more usually provincial businessmen and foreign tourists who asked nothing better than to boast to their buddies back in Clermont or Antwerp or wherever that they had gone out on the town with a Folies beauty. And perhaps to convey, with a wink, that they'd enjoyed a little "bonus" as well.

Gerry ate their dinners. *Pourquoi pas?*

After all, she reasoned, it was marvellous food, beautifully served, for the price of a few hours' companionship. And she could usually pick up an extra hundred francs "for the ladies' room".

Let her escorts think what they will, boast what they wish, enjoy their little fantasies. Gerry was firmly in control. They knew neither her name nor her address. And tomorrow, they would be gone.

After the emotional fevers of the preceding months, she required a certain time for convalescence.

For the most part, her dates were content with the bargain. They rambled on about themselves, their families, their cars, their business exploits while Gerry busied herself with the choicest dishes on the menu. It was her one meal of the day; she made the most of it. "I think a dozen oysters to start . . ."

As for those few with larger expectations of the evening, men who saw the price of the meal as an entitlement, she knew how to handle them. Just before the dessert course, she would smile flirtatiously, cadge money for the ladies' room, then excuse herself. "For just a moment, *chéri*, and do order me the *pêches Chantilly*."

Every restaurant had a back way out, especially if you made a point of befriending the mâître d'. The money was her cab fare home.

She stayed at the Folies long enough to recoup her finances, learn volumes about *haute cuisine* and squeak by her final exams at the Sorbonne. The last day of term, she turned in her feathers and quit.

"It's been," she told the manager, "a revelation."

"But Mlle Mohawk," he protested. "So soon . . ."

She responded with an Indian yell.

Yet the experience sat with her, undigested. She suspected it was unique, or at least sufficiently novel to be put to profitable use.

A week later, almost as a dare, Gerry submitted a short piece to the *International Herald Tribune* entitled AN AMERICAN SCHOOLGIRL AT THE FOLIES BERGERE.

The tone was wry and anecdotal, and though she made her brief theatrical career sound more amusing that it was, with its tales of stage-door Johnnies and wild escapes from Maxim's, she tried to convey the essential ennui of such a life. *Show Biz is no biz for me*, her closing lines ran. *This girl is going home.*

The *Trib* bought the piece for a princely hundred dollars, then ran it in their weekend edition, with an accompanying photo that emphasized her fresh clean beauty. By Monday, the US wire services had picked the item up and served it to domestic readers. In one form or another, Gerry's "revelations" ran in over a hundred newspapers, and turned her into a mini-sensation.

The response surprised her. Unwittingly, she had hit upon a theme then very popular at home: that of a wholesome American girl hanging on to her wholesome American virtue and values amidst the ancient cesspools of Europe.

That had not been her intent. All she'd wanted to do was earn a few bucks. Instead, she had her first taste of fame, her first glimpse of the power of publicity.

The media flurry lasted a couple of weeks, during which she found herself besieged with offers. Would she consider modelling for *Glamour*? Becoming a Rockette? Auditioning for Milton Berle? Endorsing Old Gold Cigarettes? Signing a contract with MGM?

Her instinct was to turn them all down. She'd had her fill of standing around looking beautiful. It was numbing to the mind, soul and body.

But the scout from Metro was persistent. "Begin as a starlet," he argued. "Give it your all and who knows? You might wind up in the big time. Think about it. Think of the kind of life that goes with being a movie star. The glamour. The fame."

She thought about it long and hard. She also thought about what happened to the starlets who didn't make the grade. The pretty girls with nothing but their looks and smiles, whose most important roles were on the casting couch. Giving their all, no doubt. Where did one go from there? If not up, then down. A starlet at twenty. A hooker at thirty. A has-been at forty.

A Kiki at fifty. God forbid!

Her answer – to the scout, to all the others – was an unequivocal No. The excitement died out as swiftly as it had begun.

She learned a great deal during that year in Paris.

She learned how to put on make-up, handle a fish fork, eat ortolans, do clever things with scarves, argue with landlords, speak a fluent and ear-perfect French.

She learned to put her money in banks rather than jam jars.

She learned that if you have something to say, and say it simply and with good humour, people will listen.

She learned that women who try to get by on beauty alone are at the mercy of fate and the inflamed appendix.

And although it was many months before she could look back on Jean-Claude and their affair with anything like equanimity, she learned from that too.

She learned that sex is one of life's supreme pleasures.

And that men, even the most enchanting of them, are

inherently dangerous creatures; therefore each woman must make her way alone.

Over the years, she was to thank him profoundly for both lessons. Even long after she'd forgotten his name.

twelve

Harlow Farnsworth was one of the country's outstanding fly-fishermen: patient, subtle, tenacious, unflappable and ever willing to explore new waters.

They were qualities that stood him well in the practice of his profession, for Farnsworth was a senior partner in the Wall Street firm of Slater Blaney. His hobby was his passion. Even his appearance came to resemble that of his quest: he was sleek and icy-eyed as the rainbow trout. In addition to the mandatory cabinets and club chairs that bespoke the successful lawyer, his office boasted a museum-worthy collection of antique flies, housed in a breakfront of polished rosewood. He had earmarked it for the Smithsonian in his will.

And wills were very much the topic of discussion today. In particular, a most unusual testament, as much an oddity as the ancient Osceola "deer tail" that was the pride of his collection.

Like any good fisherman, or, indeed any good lawyer, he knew the value of silence. When money talked, Harlow Farnsworth listened hard.

It was talking now, through the lips of Lawrence E. Winterbourne.

"If you could solve my problems," the young man was saying, "I would be happy to have your firm handle all the business of my father's estate. The administration fees alone, so I'm told, are quite substantial. And once I'm in control, I would generate a great deal more legal work, I assure you. I plan to start a foundation, you see. A vast and important undertaking that will have significant bearing on our perceptions of America, but first . . ." He paused. Risha had instructed him to downplay the heroic aspects of their shared venture and speak only of his fundamental rights. *Keep It Simple, Sweetheart*, had been her last word on the matter.

"First," he added lamely, "I have to get my hands on

144

the money. It is my money, after all. Winterbourne money. And I'm the principal and rightful heir. Yet due to this woman's connivance, to her selfish and capricious nature, I'm being cheated of my patrimony. You've studied my father's will, I suppose."

"Exhaustively."

"And the trustee arrangement?"

"From every angle. You appreciate that it's a carefully worded document, Mr Winterbourne. Quite explicit. Simply put, Miss O'Neal has control of your income until your fortieth birthday or such time as you prove to be self-supporting, whichever comes first. I grant it's unconventional; however the intent is clear. And there is no doubt but that your father was of sound mind at the time of its execution. Regrettably, I find no basis for contesting the provision."

"He was bewitched," Lawrence spluttered. "That woman had him in her clutches. She's a greedy . . . gluttonous . . . g-g-g-"

"Gold-digger?" Farnsworth completed the thought. "Is that what you want us to establish?" Then he frowned. He had met Geraldine O'Neal at a dinner party a year earlier. She had struck him as a witty, charming woman, more interested in good talk than in trinkets. "Nothing points to it, I'm afraid. Miss O'Neal herself received only a Sargent painting which, although valuable, is a minor bequest in relation to the total size of the estate. In addition she takes a modest fee for acting as trustee. A venal person would have come away with millions. And even had she benefited greatly, it wouldn't warrant legal action. Greed is considered commendable nowadays. In any case, sir, hardly grounds for contention."

"I don't care what grounds you use," Lawrence said, "as long as you can break that damned trusteeship. There must be some way to get rid of her. Replace her, perhaps, with a different trustee, someone who cares more about my happiness and well-being. I have in mind the curator of my father's memorabilia, a highly intelligent person who is sympathetic to my projects and would be delighted to work hand-in-glove with your firm. Anyone but Gerry

O'Neal! It's unbearable, a woman like that having such power over me. She's utterly unfit!"

"In what way unfit?" the lawyer asked.

"You can ask that? My God! When I think of all those husbands she's gone through!"

"Really? I thought she never married?"

"I meant other women's husbands," Lawrence said. "By the dozens. The hundreds! Surely, a case can be made that here is a woman with no scruples, no moral standards . . ."

Farnsworth sighed. "We live in enlightened times, my dear fellow, and adultery no longer outrages the public sensibilities. Except of course, when committed by TV evangelists or Presidential hopefuls, and Miss O'Neal is neither. I'm afraid her sexual peccadilloes, while no doubt interesting, hardly disqualify her for her duties. I would need proof of misconduct more germane."

"Well, there's the business with her hydrant."

"Her hydrant?" Mr Farnsworth wondered if he'd heard correctly.

"Hydrant . . . fireplug . . . whatever you call 'em."

Parking space was at a premium on the Upper East Side, he explained. Gerry O'Neal had devised her own solution.

She parked her Mercedes in front of her house. Whenever she took the car, she would plant a fake hydrant on the sidewalk alongside the just-vacated spot to prevent the space being used by anyone else. Upon her return, the hydrant duly disappeared. All the cops on the beat knew about the imposture. Lawrence said, "But she's probably charmed the pants off them too. And if that isn't illegal, I'd like to know what is."

Mr Farnsworth considered.

"Oh, it's illegal all right, but I wouldn't care to prosecute her before a jury of frustrated Manhattanites. They'd applaud, likely as not. People in this town have been known to kill for a decent space. I'd say Miss O'Neal's action reveals more about her resourcefulness than her criminality. In any event, these are not charges I would care to take before a judge. She is a former ambassador, you must remember. A respected figure, parking habits aside, with a reputation for fiscal probity. And that's what

146

we're concerned with here. After all, your own auditors are satisfied with her handling of the trusteeship. By all appearances, there's not a penny amiss."

"You mean she's never been caught with her hand in the till."

"Precisely."

"So the only kind of wrong-doing that counts would be financial wrong-doing. Embezzlement, misappropriation of funds . . . that sort of thing."

"More or less. In any event, a serious lapse – one that would cast doubt upon her judgement, her honesty, her capacity to continue as a responsible trustee. And one that could be substantiated in a court of law."

Lawrence groaned. "I wouldn't know where to begin."

"Take heart, Mr Winterbourne. There's always something, some fatal flaw, as it were, by which the unwary may be hooked. In my experience, few careers can withstand total scrutiny, least of all one as long and varied as Miss O'Neal's."

"Total scrutiny," Lawrence echoed. "In other words I ought to hire a private eye and get the goods on her. Believe me, I've thought about it, but what's the point? She ran for Congress a few years back. Lost, thank God. But if there'd been any deep dark secrets, they would have come to light at the time. Every reporter in the East was digging in the garden, so to speak, and came up with zilch. So why should private investigators succeed where the journalists have failed?"

"Perhaps because they have even fewer scruples than reporters. Naturally, as a lawyer, I would never dream of recommending that you employ illegal measures to, as you say, 'get the goods on her' . . ."

"What illegal measures?" Lawrence pounced.

Instead of answering, Farnsworth rose and strolled over to his breakfront display.

"Do you fish, Mr Winterbourne?"

Lawrence strained forward trying to grasp the import. He was sure the lawyer was trying to convey a message of worth.

"Should I?" he asked.

"Every man should," Farnsworth said with a smile, then opening the breakfront, selected a fly from its depths. "To be a successful fisherman requires a well-stocked stream, a good deal of patience, and the proper equipment."

He came around to where Lawrence was sitting and handed him a tiny object, carved with such verisimilitude as to pass for life.

"Pretty thing, isn't it? It was made by John Harrison Keene in 1888. He was the son of Queen Victoria's water keeper at Windsor and the master fly-maker of his era. As you can see, this particular gem is whittled into the shape of a . . ." For some reason, words failed Mr Farnsworth. He turned to Lawrence with a helpless shrug. "Of a . . . a. . . . You help me."

"Of an insect?" Lawrence essayed, but the lawyer continued to hover, dissatisfied with the response.

Lawrence studied the item more closely. Then –

"Of a bug!" the triumphant answer rang out.

"Quite so." Mr Farnsworth looked pleased. "Of a bug. A little bug that can be cast into a stream and perhaps catch the unwary fish. Provided the fisherman is willing to wait."

Lawrence set the fly down on the desk with a cautious respect.

"They are much improved these days," he ventured. "Bugs I mean. More technologically advanced."

"I have no doubt they are," Farnsworth replied. "Smaller, more sophisticated."

"Small enough to be concealed in a telephone?" Lawrence queried.

Farnsworth nodded like an amiable Buddha.

"Sophisticated enough to do duty in a conference room?" Lawrence pursued. "Or go unnoticed in a private office?"

Farnsworth picked up the little artefact and placed it back in the breakfront with a seemly reverence. Then he smiled.

"I wouldn't be a bit surprised."

thirteen

Sir Campbell Simms was an adept at keeping secrets. Discretion was his stock in trade.

At sixty-five, he could look back over four decades of service in the diplomatic corps, a career distinguished by the unceasing exercise of judgement and tact. Equally, he could look forward to the rosy prospects of a comfortable retirement and second marriage. His years of widowerhood would soon be at an end.

There are, however, secrets and secrets, and the hush-hush atmosphere surrounding his engagement was a matter of increasing concern. He had friends, family, colleagues of many years standing, all of whom he wished to share his joy.

After four decades of eating unspeakable foods in unbearable climates, of shaking the hands of petty dictators and tribal chiefs, of suffering fools and villains with unruffled grace, of smiling and bowing and dressing for dinner, of keeping both his temper and counsel on behalf of Her Majesty's Government, he was counting the days until he was a free man for the first time in his life. Free to speak his mind and sleep undisturbed and watch cricket at Lords and enjoy a good Arbroath smokey of a Sunday morning. Free from the demands and restraints of his profession. And what better companion for the long-sought freedom than the inimitable Geraldine O'Neal?

A marvellous woman! She made him laugh, she made him happy, she made him feel like a lad of twenty. In every respect, Gerry was a bride of whom any man could be proud. She was the rare bird captured, the treasure attained, and it was natural to want to boast of such a conquest.

Two months had passed since they had agreed to marry, yet she seemed reluctant to set the date. They chatted on the phone almost daily, managed the occasional romantic rendezvous here and there. The previous weekend they had met in Bermuda, ostensibly to plan their future. However Gerry refused to be pinned down.

"Sun . . . sea . . . sand . . ." she rhapsodized as they basked on the beach. "Let's enjoy the present instead of worrying about the future."

"All I ask is that we put a notice in *The Times*."

"Not quite yet, darling. Let's keep it our secret for just a while longer."

But Campbell, who had kept enough secrets in his life, persisted.

"How long a while?"

"Until the Queen's New Year Honours are announced."

Gerry had taken it into her head that he would be granted a peerage upon retirement and thought that the two "fusses" might be combined into a single round of festivities.

"But that's months off . . ." he'd protested.

"But darling, we're not getting married till months off," she said, then, typically, softened her rebuff with a dose of flattery. "You just want an excuse to fend off all those gorgeous widows who are after you. I won't have you breaking their hearts sooner than absolutely necessary. Now be a lamb," she rolled over on the beach blanket, precluding further conversation, "and do my back."

A more intemperate person than he might have seen such procrastination as nothing other than a selfish desire to have her cake and eat it. For months yet, as an "unattached woman", Gerry could continue to enjoy the social whirl, the dinner dates, the men dancing attendance, all the while secure in the prospects of an excellent marriage.

Sir Campbell was not an intemperate man. He was a sensitive and sympathetic one, correctly attributing her reluctance to sublimated fear. A woman who had never married (he reasoned), who had never surrendered her privacy, never bowed to a husband's tastes and decisions, might well view such a radical change of circumstances with alarm. In short, "Geraldine the Fearless" was afraid.

He smiled at the epithet. She had earned it in Africa during an international conference, in a reception line for the self-anointed Emperor of Chad. Protocol demanded that she mutter her respects and move on. Instead, Gerry seized the opportunity to chew him out in front of an astonished assembly. That the Emperor *was* a megalomaniac, a crook and an assassin struck Sir Campbell as quite beside the point. This particular assassin happened to be their host and a head of state, to boot. Neither of which considerations fazed Gerry.

How dare he, she harangued Bokassa in flawless French, besmirch the reputation of Black Africa by his callous indifference to human misery? What right had he to deck himself out in rubies and diamonds while his people starved in the streets? Was he unaware that his actions were stoking the fires of bigotry around the world? For shame!

In the ensuing silence, you could hear a pin drop. Or a head.

Her secretary looked as if he was about to have a stroke, and with good reason. Given the volatility of the Emperor's moods, Gerry might be murdered in her bed that very night. And devoured the next morning, if the worst of the rumours were true.

"Madame Ambassador," the secretary whispered. "You can't talk to the Emperor like that. It isn't done."

Gerry turned to him with a confident smirk.

"Don't tell me it isn't done, sonny. I just did it."

It was at that moment Sir Campbell fell irretrievably in love.

"You do like taking risks," he said to her that night at dinner.

"I do indeed," she laughed. "The bigger the better."

With one exception, he mused. The risk of marriage.

Today, however, he had wrung a major concession on the phone, and he believed that once a public commitment was made, she couldn't back out.

"A limited announcement," he'd insisted. "My children have a right to know. They'd never forgive my keeping it secret."

Besides, he added, certain matters had to be addressed. His flat in London, for example. It had to be redecorated and unless Gerry herself coveted the job – "No no!" she declared. "I have no patience for that sort of thing!" – he'd ask his daughter Morag to handle it. She was one of the most successful decorators in London.

Gerry softened. Sir Campbell smiled, perceiving a small but significant victory.

"I'll ring her up today. She'll be delighted."

He pushed a little further.

Agreed then. The engagement could be announced to his brother, his two married daughters and – very well! – a few intimates in the Foreign Office and here at the Embassy. It was the decent thing to do.

He hung up, ecstatic. Now that the matter was settled, he fell to envisioning homely details of their lives together. It was a gratifying occupation.

They would have a proper wedding (he had wrung that concession from her, too). A service at St Margaret's, preferably, followed by a reception for a few hundred friends. After which they would domicile in London. That was a given. To be deprived of urban pleasures would surely be torture to a woman of Gerry's temperament. She was utterly cosmopolitan, a person born to live at the hub of power. Thus, the flat in Albert Mansions should do them both nicely, at least in season. They would cultivate friends, entertain, enjoy the theatre, the shops, the galleries, the satisfying bustle of London life.

But like most of his compatriots, Sir Campbell believed that man – and woman too – can only know true contentment living in close harmony with nature. He thought himself a country squire at heart.

He owned a house in the Perthshire Highlands, a fine Georgian manor that had been in the family for two hundred years. And though he had spent most of his life abroad, he considered Scotland his home.

Come summer, they would repair to Aberuthven, he fantasized, and indulge in rustic pleasures. Garden a bit, maybe raise the odd lettuce. Ride. Go for brisk splendid walks in the rough, a faithful sheltie playing about their heels.

And of a fine June Morning, perhaps rise with the sun

to seek out one of the sparkling streams in which the area abounded. Then try their luck angling for trout.

Sir Campbell gave an audible sigh.

Fly-fishing!

How he had loved it as a boy.

Truly, one of the hardships of a life spent in the foreign service was that it afforded such meagre opportunities to fish. Not a decent trout stream in all of Africa!

He believed that Gerry would enjoy the sport too, once she gave it a try. Indeed few activities in life were more rewarding. The inner peace. The quiet satisfaction. The healthy weariness at the end of the day.

Fishing answered a spiritual need. An aesthetic one as well, he had no doubt. Was it not Izaak Walton who had called it "an art worthy of the knowledge and practice of a wise man?" What a wise man Walton was!

Even the flies, those humble accoutrements of human-kind's profoundest pastime, were often objects of exquisite beauty.

One of these days, he vowed, he would try his hand at carving his own. It struck him as an excellent hobby in the leisured years ahead.

When his aide came in with the dispatches, Sir Campbell was leaning back in his chair casting off imaginary flies and humming a tuneless Scottish air.

She had never seen him looking happier.

fourteen

"And I'll have the trout," he told the waiter. "Simply grilled with a slice of lemon, no butter. And a bottle of Perrier."

"My my!" Lee couldn't resist twitting him. "What happened to your oath of office? 'On my honour I shall eat all the richest fanciest items on the menu.' You can be defrocked for what you're doing. Or pelted to death by last week's bread sticks."

Bill Frazier responded with a graceful smile. "Tonight, with due apologies to my readers, I'm on my own time. No *sauce béarnaise* . . . no Charlotte Malakoff. Just nursery food. A man gets weary of being force-fed like a Strasbourg goose. At the moment, the only *foie* I'm concerned about is my own. My liver is enjoying a well-earned day of R & R."

"Rock and Roll?"

"Rest and Recuperation. I hope you appreciate, Lee, that what we have here is a genuine social occasion, the antiquated term for it being 'dinner date'. Surely you're familiar with the routine from old movies. Doris and Rock . . . Fred and Ginger . . ."

"Fay Wray and King Kong?"

"You're not being helpful," he advised. "I think Fay was the dinner, not the date. What I had in mind was those romantic comedies where boy meets girl. Boy asks her out to dinner. Boy even pays the tab unassisted. If he's lucky, his reward is a good night kiss. He goes home singing in the rain."

"And if he's unlucky?"

"He enters a monastery . . . something like that."

"I'm impressed. Although if I'd known that this wasn't an expense account meal, I wouldn't have ordered the porcini. Thirty-two dollars! You didn't even wince."

They exchanged smiles. A month ago she hadn't known a porcini from a pork roll.

154

"Order to your heart's content, Lee, in honour of the golden oldies. When Fred took Ginger out to dinner, did she look at the right side of the menu? Never! Neither should you."

"Well, three cheers for nostalgia, although for the record, let it be said I'm willing to go halvesies."

Bill shook his head. "Tell you what. You can reciprocate by asking me to dinner at your place one day soon. I'd like that."

The smile froze on her face.

"I don't cook," she said. "I think, I talk, I write, I research, I interview people. Don't ask me to cook into the bargain."

Bill pulled a long face.

"Does this mean you don't do windows, either?"

Lee put down her Campari and eyed him critically.

"Why do you always feel obliged to tease me?" she asked.

"Why do you always feel obliged to declare your independence?" he replied. "It wasn't being called into question. Honestly, Lee, inviting a friend over for a drink and an omelette does not connote a major loss of professional stature. I'd cheerfully do the same for you."

She shifted in her seat, uncertain of her ground. Even to her own ears, the I-don't-cook speech sounded brusque. Gerry had done it with greater flair. And at this stage, Lee was of no mind to insult Bill Frazier. He was a valuable player.

"I know you would, Bill, and I bet you make a sensational omelette, way better than anything I could manage. I didn't mean to sound ungracious, especially when you're being so sweet. I'll ask you over some time soon – promise! It's just that I have a lot on my mind at the moment. In fact," she lowered her voice in an approximation of intimacy, "I've been looking forward to this evening for quite a while. Just the two of us, tête-à-tête."

He leaned across the table and placed his hand atop hers.

"Well, here we are, tête-à-tête, as you say, and hand-in-hand."

Encouraged, Lee continued. "You're a savvy guy, Bill. One of the brightest people I know. I want to pick your brain for a bit."

He must have been hoping for a less cerebral form of contact, for he withdrew his hand and signalled the waiter.

"We're going to require a bottle, after all. I think a good Montrachet will do nicely." He then turned to Lee with a quixotic expression. "OK, Lee, now that you've duly buttered me up, what's the problem? I presume that you want to talk shop."

"I knew you'd understand," she said with relief. "The thing is, Bill, I've been knocking myself out at *Trend* for three full months and getting zilch in return. No bylines, no good assignments. Which probably means no chance of a raise. It's Fletch. He's had it in for me from the start. Whatever I come up with, he shoots down, that is when he's not ignoring me totally. Lee Whitfield, Invisible Woman."

She then proceeded to lay a string of complaints at Bill's door. She was stifled, stymied. Time was racing by and Lee was being left at the post while her competitors were romping down the fast track to fame and fortune.

"It's not a horse race, Lee."

"The hell it isn't! Look at Samantha Loring. She's my age, but to judge by her clothes, she must be pulling down twice what I earn."

"Sam has an independent income," Bill remarked. "Frankly I'm puzzled. I remember how ecstatic you were when you landed the job."

"I was, but I expected to make much quicker headway. I guess this makes me seem very greedy, or worse – envious. I'm really not." A tear glistened in her eye. "And I certainly don't want to sound embittered. It's just that New York has changed my perceptions."

Seeing how people lived, what they possessed, what they wore – all this had been a revelation. How could she move in the midst of such wealth and remain unaffected? What had been tolerable a few months ago was onerous now. Her ambition had outstripped her progress.

156

"I don't want to rot forever in an out-of-the-way desk by the men's room. Is it a crime to want something better?"

The wine arrived, was uncorked and sampled. Bill polished off a glass in a single unepicurean swig, then poured himself another.

'Lee," he said. "You're being unreasonable. Three months is no time at all. Be patient."

"I can't. I have a timetable, and if I'm going to stick to it, I have to start moving up now. Which means a major cover story between here and next April."

"What happens in April?"

"I turn twenty-five."

"Jesus, that's no great age."

"By the time Gerry O'Neal was twenty-five she had a nationally syndicated column."

"On the other hand, by the time John McEnroe was twenty-five, his career had peaked. It's an arbitrary milestone."

"Not for me. Because unlike Miss Samantha Loring, I do not have an independent income. Or a closet full of Donna Karans."

"Why pick on Samantha?" he wondered. "I have a small income myself, which is what we're dining on tonight. Unless you have moral qualms about unearned money."

She shook her head. "You prep school types! You're all alike, and I don't say this as criticism. But you really don't understand the simplest things. You ask why I've never had you over for a drink. It's because I live in a rat-hole. OK? And I'm going to live in that rat-hole until I either become a bylined writer or get a better offer from another publication. I give myself eight months to do it in."

"And then . . ."

"Then my timetable allows another two years labouring in the vineyards till I make Feature Editor." Her voice suddenly dropped, grew more intimate, as though she were sharing precious secrets with a lover. A silvery thread played in and out of the mundane words. "I'll confide something in you, Bill, but you must promise not to laugh. By the time I'm thirty," she turned to him, suddenly radiant, "I hope to be sitting in Fletch's chair!"

"Will Fletch be in it too?" Bill asked without blinking. "And how about Bobby Obermeyer's? Why not set your sights on becoming the next chairman of Enterprise Publications? The old boy can't live forever."

"There you go," she cried, "baiting me again."

"Lighten up, Lee. We all have timetables, agendas. As for your particular scenario, be assured that you share that deep dark passion with at least twenty other guys in the office."

"Of whom you're one?" Her eyes grew suspicious.

"Believe me, I'm not in competition."

But she didn't believe him. Not one word.

"You're content to be a restaurant critic for the rest of your life? Bullshit. I don't buy that for a minute. You're much too bright to stay put. Like you said, we all have agendas – you included. Now that I've poured my heart out to you in embarrassing detail, I'm surely entitled to a quid pro quo. What's in your timetable, Bill? Do you dream of being Managing Editor? Publisher? You've got your own deep dark passion I'll bet. So give!"

"You really want to know?"

She nodded.

"I have two plans going. Timetable Number One, I want to write the Great American Novel before I hit thirty."

"Have you started it?"

"Only a dozen times! The trick is in finishing it."

"What's it about?"

He paused. "Do you know, that's the first personal question you've ever asked me?"

The waiter came with the trout and the vitello porcini. Bill ordered a second bottle of wine.

The food was excellent. She lit into it with diligence, the subject matter of Bill's novel already forgotten.

"Fabulous mushrooms," she said. "How's the trout?" for Bill was picking at the fish in a desultory manner.

"Good. Fresh." He put a morsel on her plate. "I can see why the guy at *The Times* gave this place three stars."

Lee tasted the fish. It seemed a trifle bland, but then she hadn't yet developed a gourmet palate.

158

"I bet I know what the second item on your timetable is," she said confidently.

He put down his fork. "I'm certain you don't. Thus far, it's been my secret. A hidden agenda, so to speak."

But Lee felt suddenly insightful. "You're angling for Bryan Miller's job at *The Times* and you don't want Fletch to find out."

Bill looked bemused. "You couldn't be wronger. You know, Lee, not every goal in life has to do with professional advancement. People have private goals, as well."

"Aha! Now I am intrigued. You've aroused the investigative reporter in me. What is this dark secret passion of yours? Gotta know."

"Do you really?"

"I insist. Otherwise, I'll speculate that it's something truly scurrilous. Young boys, maybe, or plotting the overthrow of the republic. Come on," she teased. "Let's have it, I promise you my lips are sealed. OK, Bill Frazier's Number Two goal in life is . . ."

He paused. "You."

Lee's smile faded. "I'm serious!"

"So am I." His tone was easy, almost conversational, but his eyes never left her face. They, at least, were intense.

"I want to make love to you, Lee. Tonight, if that's not too extravagant a dream, but if not, then in the very near future. I've been brooding about you for weeks, like a goddam high school kid. I don't know that I can explain it rationally – whether it's the shape of your nose or the sound of your laughter or the way your back arches when you hang up your coat in the morning or the curve of your throat or those humungous ear-rings you always wear or the endearing fact that you never split infinitives. But rational or not, I have a bad, possibly terminal case of the hots. I want to make love to you, Lee. To you, with you, for you, at you. Does this come as a total surprise?"

"Yes . . . no . . ." She dithered, then settled on an equivocal nod. "I guess I was aware you were interested," she granted.

He pounced in triumph. "So! You have thought about it. About me."

"The thing is, Bill . . ."

But having seen his advantage, he refused to surrender the lead.

"What can I say on my own behalf? I'm clean, decent, warm-hearted, relatively honest, disease free if you don't count hay fever, and I've never been convicted of anything worse than doing 60 in a 50-mile zone. Practically a Boy Scout, by local standards. On the down side, I eat crackers in bed. But I could change, given sufficient incentive. You understand, Lee, that I haven't a clue as to where all this will get us. Maybe just a brief rollicking encounter, maybe it'll develop into a great sloppy passionate affair that will leave us both scarred for life. There's only one way to find out. Let's become lovers. What is there to lose? You can always throw me out in the morning."

"The thing is, Bill . . ."

She tried to pick her way through his jungle of words, to sort out what was alcohol and what was genuine emotion. Given his prep school accent and the underlying irony of his style, it was impossible to judge his sincerity. Perhaps he himself didn't know. Rich kids, she reflected. The children of privilege, convinced that all they have to do is ask. She felt a flash of irritation.

"Everything comes so easily to you, Bill, doesn't it? Style. Money. Wisecracks. Women too, I venture. You just stretch your hand out and they're yours. But I don't come easily."

He reared back as if stung.

"I had no intention of insulting you, Lee. I'm far too fond of you for that."

"And I'm fond of you. Flattered too, in a way. You're a very attractive guy. But please, let's not turn this into a Federal case. What I want to convey is – and I hope to God you don't take this personally – I don't believe our having an affair is a good idea at this juncture."

"May I ask why?"

"It's too much of a risk. Sorry, Bill, but I simply can't afford to get involved."

"I don't charge," he said evenly.

"I meant, emotionally involved, and you know it. Please try to understand. I think you're terrific fun, but I'm not

160

into casual sex. And at this stage of my life, anything more complicated than a one night stand . . . well, it would get in the way of my game plan. The last thing I need is grand passion, whatever that means. It would simply fuck up my life. I've got too much invested in the job right now, too much of my time, my energy, too much of myself, to have anything left over. It's not got to do with you personally. It's got to do with me."

He poured himself another glass of wine and looked at her through narrowed eyes. She could feel the temperature drop.

"I see we've graduated from timetables to game plans. Tell me, should I consider that a step forward or back?"

"Spare me your sarcasm, Bill. I'm not attacking you. As I say, it's nothing personal."

"Of course," he murmured. "There is nothing the least bit personal about rejection. I must remember that for my novel. As far as I'm concerned, Lee, the subject is closed." He pushed his plate away from him in a gesture of distaste. "You said you wanted to talk about Fletch. Very well. My advice, which is doubtless why you've honoured me with your company tonight, is that you don't sit around and wait for the great man's endorsement. You have an idea you want to develop? Then go ahead, work it out on your own time. Write the fucking piece and hand it in complete. That way he doesn't have to envision the finished product. Two things happen. Either (a) he likes it and runs it. Or (b), he doesn't like it and you try again. It's that simple."

"In other words, I should write on spec? Jesus, Bill, that never would have occurred to me. I've always worked to order. You're probably right, though. A little initiative wouldn't hurt. Trouble is, where the hell am I going to find the extra time?"

"I wouldn't worry about that, Lee. You'll have all those solitary nights ahead. Did you want dessert?"

She shook her head no, still brooding about his suggestion.

The waiter came to clear away.

"Everything satisfactory, sir?"

"Yeah!" he growled. "Just dandy."

161

"The trout was acceptable?"

"It was good, in fact. Fresh. Compliments to your fish-monger. We'd like two *café filtres*, please, and I'll have the check."

"Thanks," Lee smiled.

"For buying you dinner?"

"And for the advice. You make a lot of sense and I appreciate it. You really are a good dear friend." She paused, then asked warily, "We are friends, aren't we?"

"What else?"

They sat for a while in imperfect silence. The waiter returned with an elaborate confection of fresh raspberries and ginger ice cream and *marrons glacé.*

"I didn't order that," Bill said.

"With the compliments of Monsieur Henri," the waiter beamed. "It's been a great pleasure serving you."

Lee looked impressed.

"They recognized you," she said. "Isn't that exciting? See, already you've become a name to conjure with."

"Yeah . . . big deal," Bill sneered. "To be known and feared by head-waiters. A lifetime's aspiration."

"I wouldn't mind. I wouldn't mind at all."

He stared at her, struck by the note of longing in her voice, then paid the bill.

"Shall I get you a taxi?" he said when they emerged into the street. Her answer was to put out her hand.

"Friends," she said, then disappeared in the direction of the subway.

Bill watched her go with a mixture of sadness and relief. Then standing here, he recalled the sound of her voice. It had throbbed with love, an aching kind of intimacy, when she spoke about her dreams. Would she ever speak to him, to any man, with such passion?

He hailed a cab and headed for home. It had been a very prickly evening.

fifteen

As usual, the IRT was a cesspool.

She wedged herself in between a mumbling drunk and a three-hundred pound woman. The drunk reeked of beer. Oh, the indignities of subterranean travel. Lee retreated into fantasy. She was in the back of a limo being shuttled home from the theatre. Better yet, she was at the wheel of her Porsche . . .

"Laaaiiize and gemmem . . ."

A bearded scarecrow, greasy with the filth of a hundred bathless nights, had entered the car, shouting at the top of his voice. He had a small grubby child in one hand, a Dixie Cup in the other.

"I'm a Veet Nam vet and I need bus fare t'go home to 'Bama . . ."

Instinctively, Lee recoiled further. If she'd wanted to live among beggars she would have moved to Calcutta. She shut her eyes, hoping thus to become invisible.

Someday – someday soon – she would get an apartment in the Upper East Side and be freed forever from the curse of subway ridership. If she couldn't swing a condo, then a rented studio would do for now. With a proper decorator, even a shoe box could be made habitable. All that mattered was that the shoe-box be in a building that was smart, convenient and equipped with a lobby, a doorman and an address that she could divulge without cringing.

"The Sovereign, driver," or "I'm just off Park in the Sixties . . ."

The drunk beside her gurgled gently.

Pretending for the sake of argument that she'd been willing to share her bed with Bill Frazier, how could she conceivably have brought him home to East 12th Street? Even cabbies looked askance when she gave the address. Who could blame them!

Not that she seriously contemplated an affair with Bill.

163

For one thing, she disbelieved three-quarters of what he'd said.

The sound of your laughter . . . the curve of your throat . . .

For another, it would be all over the office in no time.

What was in it for her, anyhow? The Muffy of the Month Award?

Had Bill honestly expected she would succumb on the spot to such flattery? He must think her the world's biggest sucker or else he was as drunk as Mr Budweiser Breath on her right.

"Quarter, lady?"

The "Veet Nam Vet" had thrust the paper cup in her face. Lee looked away. Next to her, Mr Bud Breath fished into his pocket and dropped a dollar bill into the pan-handler's cup.

A drunk supporting a junkie, Lee thought. Perfect! She watched the beggar's progress down the car. He scored off three other riders. Maybe it was because of the little girl. She was cute, poor kid.

Yeah sure, he was going home to 'Bama. By way of the neighbourhood pusher was her bet. What a scam. Lee wouldn't be surprised if he cleared a couple of hundred a night.

A year ago, she would have handed him a dollar. She'd wised up since then. The truth was, you couldn't trust anyone in this town. Whether the spiel came from a subway pan-handler or a clean-cut Bill Frazier, or the vendor selling "genuine Rolex watches" on 34th Street, you could be reasonably certain it was founded on fraud and motivated purely by self-interest. People looked out for Number One, in her experience, and if you showed a stick of vulnerability, be it through *naïveté* or kindness, you were guaranteed to be ripped off.

Gerry was right. Never trust anybody one hundred per cent! And Lee didn't – except of course for Gerry herself.

Since moving here, she had had her pocket picked (twice), her raincoat filched from a peg in a coffee shop, and – worst of all – a perfectly good idea stolen from under her nose.

It had begun, innocently enough, during a conversation

164

in the Ladies' Room at *Trend*. Samantha Loring had come in from lunch smelling marvellous and Lee had asked what she was wearing.

"Fleurs du Mal. They're giving out whiffs of it at Saks."

"Did you buy some?"

Samantha shook her pretty head. "Too bloody expensive."

"You know," Lee said thoughtfully, "you could live in this city and probably never buy perfume at all. Just walk down the aisles at a good Fifth Avenue department store and help yourself to samples. They're all out there. You have your choice of brands. In fact, that might be a cute idea for a column. How a girl could manage to look and smell terrific completely on freebies – perfume samples, testers for eye shadow, make-up, hand lotions, et cetera. Most top cosmetic lines have testers on the counter, so you could look like dynamite without spending a cent. I'd write it up tongue in cheek, of course, but with practical suggestions. Maybe illustrate with a pretty model. What do you think, Sam? Would Fletch go for it?"

Samantha paused for a fraction of a second, then caught Lee's eye in the mirror.

"And offend our retail advertisers? Not only would Saks and Bloomie's howl, but Fletch would have your head on a tray."

Which made sense. Lee put it out of her mind until two weeks later, when she saw the galleys for "Fabulous Freebies". She read it in a state of near-paralysis. It was brisk, shrewd, funny, just as Lee had suggested. Only the byline read Samantha Loring.

"How could you!" Lee stormed Samantha's desk, her voice trembling with pain. "You stole my idea!"

"I don't know what you're talking about." Samantha's blue eyes widened in innocence.

"Our conversation in the Ladies' Room."

"What conversation? I haven't a clue what you mean."

In that moment, Lee realized it was hopeless. There had been no witnesses, no proof. Now there was nothing but her own aching rage. Yet to make a scene would be not only futile, but dangerous. Against Samantha's doll-faced wonder, Lee would come off sounding like an envious crank.

"What can I do?" she wept that night at Gerry's.

"Well, next time around, don't share your bright ideas."

"But what can I do to her?" Lee wanted to know. "It's so unfair. I feel as if I'm entitled to . . . well, revenge."

"Take comfort," Gerry said. "Be patient. Your turn will come. Anyhow, revenge is a dish . . ."

". . . best eaten cold?"

". . . best eaten regularly, year after year."

Then she'd told her a story.

Upon returning from her student year in France, Gerry hit the job market with a resounding thud.

"We're talking early fifties," she reminded Lee, "and as for equal opportunity, the phrase hadn't been coined. So I ask you, what kind of job could an ambitious gal hope to find?"

Lee, seasoned in the myths of prehistory, answered with assurance. "Secretarial!"

"Are you kidding?" Gerry snorted. "Being educated, naturally I didn't type or take shorthand. How could I aspire to anything so grand? You may laugh, but at the time, secretaries were making excellent money. Excellent for women, that is. No, my friend, the best I could manage was a job proof-reading at Winterbourne's."

One of America's oldest firms, H. E. Winterbourne & Sons was a mail-order giant placed a healthy third behind Sears-Roebuck and Montgomery Ward. From its catalogues, one might furnish a house, outfit a family, plant a garden, order anything from a baseball bat to a bridal trousseau to a twenty foot barracuda, stuffed and suitable for mounting in the rec room.

The wealth of printed matter so germane to the company's success emanated from a barracks-like building near Canal Street, some eighty blocks and a light-year away from the glamorous corporate headquarters on Fifth Avenue. It provided occupation for photographers, art directors, stylists, copywriters and, tucked away in a base-

166

ment area jocularly known as Siberia, a small army of female proof-readers.

They were responsible for checking facts, catching typos, spotting errors, rescuing dangling participles: in short, for ensuring that every Winterbourne publication was as grammatical, as accurate, as a doctoral dissertation. The job demanded a high degree of both literacy and concentration. Accordingly it was rewarded with the minimum legal wage.

"There were a dozen of us," Gerry amplified, "mostly with advanced degrees from good colleges. Very lady-like types. A lot of 'em had been stuck there for years."

Not Gerry, she determined, and launched a concerted effort to climb out of the trough. She began by ingratiating herself with the elderly gent in charge of Production. An enthusiastic handicapper, Mr Plimpson (nobody knew his first name) was happy to delegate the numerous petty tasks of his office to this energetic and competent girl while he pondered the mysteries of horseflesh. The more deeply he immersed himself into the Racing Form, the more responsibility Gerry usurped. She extended the job far beyond its perimeters: rewriting copy, haggling with suppliers, riding herd on typesetters and retouchers, even placing the occasional bet for Mr Plimpson. Within two years she was running the department with an efficiency that boggled some and irked others.

"I was not well beloved by my peers," she recalled. "The other gals felt that it was bad form to hustle. We were ladies, you see. We didn't consider ourselves professionals. The term hardly existed in relation to women. At most, people would call you a 'career girl'. It was a sneer, not a compliment, believe me, the implication being that you couldn't snag yourself a husband. But whatever the term, I had no intention of spending the rest of my life in Siberia. I set my sights on taking over when Plimpson retired. My goal in life was eventually to make $100 a week. To me that signified untold riches."

The fact that there were no executive women in the company didn't deter her. She believed she could change the pattern. Besides, she had made herself indispensable.

"Or so I thought. I was capable, smart. And I worked so fucking hard that even at a hundred bucks I would have been a bargain."

As soon as Mr Plimpson announced his retirement, Gerry went to Personnel and made a strenuous pitch. The Personnel Manager smiled, even did her the courtesy of filing the transfer request along with a fulsome letter from her boss. In a burst of confidence, Gerry blew an entire month's pay on a tailored suit. She was dressed for success.

Then came the announcement. The new Production Head would be one Frankie Cavallo.

"If he'd been smart," Gerry said, "or experienced, I could have understood and forgiven. If he'd been a man with a family to support, I might have sympathized. But Frankie was my age. A lout! A jumped-up mailboy from Queens with a command of English that made Francis the Talking Mule look like Shakespeare. His sole qualification was gender. He called everybody 'doll', including the ancient Ph.D.s. And hands! Jesus! – the sonuvabitch had more hands than an Indian deity. You'd think we were his goddam harem."

The loathsome Cavallo celebrated his elevation with the ultimate symbol of executive clout, a leather attaché case from Mark Cross. He carried it everywhere, even to the men's room and took it home nightly in a plastic wrap.

Gerry suffered it all – the grammatical *bêtises*, the wandering hands – for about a week, simmering all the while.

Then one morning he breezed in late, patted Gerry on the rump and said, "Hey, doll, the man wants coffee. No milk, two sugars."

Gerry duly went to the coffee wagon and complied.

"OK doll," he said when she brought it into his office. "Help yourself to a quarter from my petty cash."

He was lounging at his desk, feet up, arms folded, the Mark Cross case spread open for maximum display.

"Please," Gerry said. "Accept the coffee with my compliments."

With that, she poured the steaming brew into the depths of the attaché case.

"Ruined it completely!" Even telling Lee about it three

decades later, she chuckled at the memory. "Plus all his precious paper work. You should have seen the expression on his face, the little turd. I don't recall whether I quit first or he fired me, but it was a glorious moment."

"And that was your revenge?" Lee was puzzled. It seemed delightful, but short lived.

"Good Lord, no!" Gerry gloated. "That was only the beginning. You see, after all these years, the beloved Frankie Cavallo is still in the same cruddy job, still living in Queens, still making the same lousy kind of money. Well, every year, at income-tax time, I send him a copy of my return – so the poor bastard can read it and weep."

Lee savoured the story. As usual, Gerry had managed to put matters in a fresh perspective, and by the time Lee got off the subway at Union Square, she was feeling almost cheerful.

The "Veet Nam vet" also got out at the stop, with the little girl no longer in tow.

Had he rented the kid for the occasion? Lee wondered, as she watched him turn into an all-night bar. Probably.

Decidedly, you couldn't trust a soul in this city. Couldn't take anyone's word for anything.

With the shining exception of Geraldine O'Neal.

sixteen

Collar button open, tie askew, this was clearly a young man in a hurry. He gave the impression of having just barrelled out of one meeting and being perilously late for the next. Lee sensed that unless she nailed him down pronto, he'd vanish in thin air.

"I'm the reporter from *Trend*," she said, stopping him at the door outside his office, "and we have an appointment for three-thirty, remember? Sorry if I've caught you at an awkward moment."

"All moments are awkward these days," he said cheerfully, then after a second's hesitation motioned her inside. "But – better awkward than critical. Anyhow, it's as good or bad as any. If you'll make yourself comfortable and permit me one phone call, I promise my undivided attention after that."

He was gorgeous, she thought. The word, though opulent, best described the total effect. Tall and beautifully muscled with olive skin, black curly hair and enormous dark eyes, he might have stepped out of a Byzantine icon. Somewhere along the line his nose had been broken, spoiling the classic perfection of the profile. But broken nose and all, he was gorgeous.

She couldn't keep her eyes off him. Or her ears.

From what she could glean from his phone conversation, he was breaking a dinner engagement with someone named Max. Lee felt relieved that it wasn't with a woman. He caught her eye and winked. Embarrassed, she looked away.

The office was very flash. Pale and sleek, full of the conventional power props: stylish graphics, Saporiti Italia furniture, electronic gadgets from Sharper Image. Leased, for all she knew – right up to and including the Baccarat ashtrays. Short term, any entrepreneur with a bank loan behind him could rent whatever image he chose to project. Long term was something else.

She knew the type from a hundred interviews. Promoters. Venture capitalists. Dreamers. Hustlers. No matter what they called themselves the pattern was familiar.

To hear them tell it, they were always on the edge of a fabulous deal, on the brink of making a billion. Sure thing! Sensational! Can't lose with this baby. You turned up a month later to learn that the "sensational" venture had gone down the tubes and they were already into something new. Only this time, they absolutely couldn't miss. Fabulous! *How'd you like a piece of the Brooklyn Bridge, my friend? Or buy off on the greatest engineering breakthrough since the wheel?*

Yet she liked them as a breed. They usually sported the wrong names, the wrong complexions, the wrong clothes compared to their Wall Street brethren, but they had a derring do that made for lively copy. They were the freebooters of the business community. More flash than cash, including the rented art and the leased Mercedes.

The fast-buck buccaneers. She jotted down the phrase. A good lead-in for the story. Then jotted down the name. Michael Avesian.

The one item in this office that was indubitably the property of Mr Avesian was the scale model of Hailsham Castle. It was as intricate and convoluted as a wedding cake, a triumph of the model-maker's art. Custom-made, clearly, and damned expensive, like that creamy silk shirt he was wearing. She smothered a smile. A couple of hundred bucks of top-flight custom shirt-making and he'd rolled up the sleeves like a garage mechanic. Typical.

Except the man on the phone seemed to defy easy categorization. He struck her as classier than most promoters, or maybe it was just that he was better looking. Certainly, his scheme was bigger, even crazier than the norm. She could picture the magazine photo, very striking, with Avesian, black-eyed and vivid, posed alongside the off-white of the replica. They'd shoot in colour, obviously. This man was made for colour photography. She'd make sure they ran the right caption. Ideally one that captured the flakey yet romantic nature of the enterprise.

Meet the New Master of Hailsham Castle. Or . . . *The Earl of*

K-mart. No. It should mention New Jersey in there somewhere. It was the Jersey angle that made the story so piquant.

"I'm sorry to have kept you waiting." He had hung up the phone and was offering his hand. "My name is Michael Avesian. Michael to my friends. To my enemies, too. May we get off on an informal foot by my calling you Lee?"

She shook his hand. It was warm and strong and welcoming.

"Have you eaten?" he asked.

Lee nodded.

"Then do you mind if I do? I've been on the move since six this morning. Sally!" He punched the intercom. "Send out for a Reuben sandwich on rye, a couple of dills and coffee. What's that? Do I want Russian dressing? I don't know." He turned to Lee as though her opinion were crucial. "Do I want Russian dressing?"

"Hold the Russian," she murmured.

"My consultant here says hold the Russian." He laughed, showing sharp white teeth. "And the phone calls too. No interruptions for the next half hour, I don't care who. Except the delivery guy from the deli. He's priority. Well, Lee, have you had a chance to study the model?"

He strode over to the replica and patted it with paternal pride. "Hailsham Castle. Ancestral home of the Haslemeres. It's going to be the biggest import to these shores since the Statue of Liberty. And eventually as famous a landmark."

Lee stood beside him and examined the piece more closely.

The model was scarcely three feet high, yet even in miniature it conveyed a sense of vastness, of chivalry, the sweep of history. No salient detail had been omitted, from the turrets with their silken pennants to the crystal prisms that glittered in the ornamental pool. A topiary garden had been laid out in symmetric perfection. Was it here that the young Elizabeth had spurned the advances of the third Earl of Haslemere? Or was it in the fabled North Tower? She would check the brochure when she got back to the office.

"Marvellous," she said.

"Not as marvellous as the real thing. Hailsham Castle is one of the glories of Britain. And next year it will be one of ours. The keep dates from 1415, but it's been added to over the centuries and completed under Queen Anne. It's what's called a 'calendar house'. There are three hundred and sixty-five rooms, fifty-two staircases, twelve court-yards. And to complete the inventory, one resident ghost."

Lee whipped out her notebook.

"And you plan to bring it over here in its entirety?"

"Brick by brick and stone by stone."

"Including the ghost?"

"If I can get him a green card . . . you betcha!"

"I think what's called for is a haunting licence."

Michael laughed dutifully. "Actually, he may not want to come. He's been with the Haslemeres for generations."

Michael went on to explain the decline of the family fortunes since the heyday of royal favour. A combination of bad race horses, roulette bets and marriages had reduced the noble clan to penury. The art works, the precious silver and porcelain and furnishings had long since been sold off. By the nineteen eighties, there remained only the bricks and mortar (but what bricks and mortar!) – and the death duties.

Upon his accession to the title, the sixteenth Earl had put the estate up for auction at Sotheby's with a floor of ten million pounds, enough to pay the taxes and provide him with a blissful retirement in Monte Carlo. Michael had to outbid an Arab sheik, the Moonies and a safari-park promoter, but what was money compared to such a mag-nificent acquisition? Even as they spoke, the castle was being dismantled. It would be ready for export by year's end at which time it would be shipped and lovingly rebuilt – brick by brick and stone by stone – on a spacious site in New Jersey. New gardens were already being planned and planted. The finest decorators and designers had been engaged for the interiors. Would she like to see the layouts? The plans and sketches? That would give her a better idea.

Lee listened, absorbed. His enthusiasm was contagious. Key phrases began forming in her mind. Only the scepti-

173

cism of a trained reporter kept her from being swept away by the image.

"Why are you doing this?" she asked. "For money? Fame? A chance to get your name in the Guinness Book of Records?"

"A bit of all three, but mostly because I'm in love with the project. I'm a hopeless romantic, I suppose, but. . . ." He then discoursed at some length about his vision of bringing Old World graciousness into a corner of New Jersey, a unique opportunity, a challenge not to be denied.

"Sorry!" He stopped short in mid-litany, and gave an embarrassed grin. "I tend to go on and on and you have a column to get out. I won't waste your valuable time, but if you have specific questions, just shoot."

"I'd like this to be more than a column," Lee said thoughtfully. "There might be material here for a feature story. Not that I can guarantee it'll come off, but I'll do my damnedest. And I do appreciate your candour, Mr Av– "

"Michael!"

"Michael," she echoed. "What our readers would most like to know – hell! what I'd like to know is how you feel about turning one of Europe's landmarks, the glory of Britain as you put it into – well, let's face it – a Jersey shopping mall."

"Ouch!" Michael groaned. "That makes it sound so tacky. Hailsham Castle will not be a shopping mall in the ordinary sense of the word, There'll be no K-marts or Woolworths or Blimpies here, I assure you. The operative word will be 'luxury'."

What he had in mind was the most elegant concentration of shops in America, a centre that would rival Rodeo Drive and Worth Avenue. Discerning customers, those who appreciated the rare and the beautiful, could choose the cream from designer boutiques, top furriers, internationally renowned jewellers and craftsmen. A three-star restaurant was being planned in conjunction with London's Connaught Hotel. There would be chamber music in the topiary garden and the Great Hall would house a repertory theatre.

"In short, Hailsham Castle will be a place where people

174

of taste and means can pleasantly spend a day. And an evening."

"And a bundle of money," she interjected.

He didn't deny it. Profits were the honey that would attract prospective investors to his venture. Success was dependent on the leasing of space to premium retailers.

"As for the Jersey location, good question. Joking aside, New Jersey happens to be home to many of the wealthiest people in America. So much for clichés."

Moreover since the site was within easy reach of both New York and Philadelphia, it would attract big spenders from both metropolises.

Why doing it? Lee scribbled. *$$$.*

"You see, there's no sales tax on clothes in New Jersey which makes it a shopper's paradise for luxury goods. You're a smart lady. I don't have to tell you what the savings would be on an Armani suit or one of those crazy La Croix gowns. Ah!" he exclaimed, "from the ridiculous to the sublime!" for at that moment, his secretary bustled in with the food from the deli. Without further ado, Michael unwrapped the foil and bit into the steaming sandwich. His face lit up.

"A great invention, the Reuben. You want half? I never heard of 'em till I came here. New York's gift to the world. Not even a bite?"

Lee smiled. The man derived deep pleasure out of simple things.

"You keep on eating, Michael, and I'll just fire away. How about some background? Readers are always interested in getting to know the man behind the idea, the dreamer of the dream, so to speak. Family, education, job history. You came to New York from . . . ?"

"From Baltimore. Or Bawlamer, as the locals call it. I grew up in a very ethnic neighborhood – Irish, Poles, Lithuanians, Armenians. A sort of downmarket UN. My father ran a dry cleaning shop."

Like many an Armenian immigrant, Gregory Avesian was fiercely ambitious for his son. The boy would go to Johns Hopkins. Become a doctor, a lawyer, a credit to his family. Fulfil the American dream.

Michael too was ambitious but although clever enough to gain entrance to the distinguished university, he had no patience for the scholarly life. He ached to join the "real world". His first semester he spent more time organizing an investment club than attending classes. His second semester, he cashed his father's tuition check and plunged every penny of it into the purchase of hatch covers from a local ship chandler.

"He had a warehouse full of them, salvaged from old boats. He thought I was buying them for firewood. But they were beautiful. Big. Solid wood. I gussied them up and resold them as coffee tables. My father wouldn't talk to me for weeks. Then he saw the sales figures."

The deal had netted Michael over twenty times the investment. With cash in hand, he applied for a credit card at a local bank. He got a line for $4000.

"Once one financial institution deems you credit worthy," he explained, "a dozen others are eager to match it. Which means, essentially, your $4000 can be parlayed into $40,000 capital, short range. It's a way of getting the banks to finance you."

Thrilled by the possibilities, Michael dropped out of school to devote himself to whatever the next venture might be. He was all of eighteen.

Since then, he had done extremely well investing in a variety of odd-ball enterprises. There was the farm in the Virgin Islands where he tried cultivating mongooses for fur.

"The world's meanest critter and the fur doesn't hold up in cold weather. They weren't meant to be tamed. I wound up selling the farm to a condo developer. Turned out to be a good deal though."

He had netted two million dollars. Next, he tried his hand at what was deemed a "technological impossibility": raising a Spanish galleon from the Atlantic floor.

"According to the history books, she was loaded with treasure plundered from the Aztecs. Gold, jewels, the stuff of legend. Anyhow, we hoisted her to the surface at enormous expense."

"And?" Lee held her breath.

"Barnacles and fish bones! What a disappointment! Luckily for me, I'd presold the film rights to TV. It ran as a documentary on CBS."

More stories followed in this vein, one offbeat coup after another, and Lee, her notebook filling rapidly, observed a pattern.

Michael was quick, canny, flexible enough to switch ventures in midstream. If one approach threatened to self-destruct, he would scrap it and improvise an alternative solution. Either way, he managed to come out ahead, while preserving a sense of excitement.

Regardless of outcome, his ventures all had a quirky nobility. Domesticating the mongoose. Raising a fabled ship. Now he was speaking of how Hailsham "would build a new link between the two great English-speaking nations". Lee must have looked at him askance, for suddenly his eyes flashed fire.

"There are three kinds of businessmen," he explained. "Those who dream and dream but don't work. Those who work and work but don't dream. And those who dream, then work to make their dreams come true."

She flipped back in her notebook and crossed out $$$. In its place, she substituted *vision*.

He lowered his voice. It became intimate. Conspiratorial. For your ears only, he seemed to say.

"Hailsham is the biggest challenge of my life. And the riskiest. I've sunk every penny I own into it. The eventual cost will be over a billion. If I had any sense, I'd be scared shitless at this juncture." Then he laughed. "But in my bones, I know I can pull it off!"

Looking up at him with bedazzled eyes, Lee had to agree. He was a winner. A powerhouse. The quintessential man with the golden touch.

The allotted half hour had long since run its course. She hoped the interview might run into dinner-time. Michael was free, since Max what's-his-name had cancelled. And she had no plans of her own.

Throughout the afternoon, the multiple lights on his telephone had been lit up like a pin-ball machine, indicating a barrage of waiting calls. Periodically, a sheaf of faxes was slipped under the door. Michael didn't blink. The office itself might have been on fire, yet never once did his attention wander. He was talking to Lee – that was the immediacy – and while he did, the outside world ceased to exist.

Such single-mindedness! Such undeflected drive! Doubtless, the key to his success. However, if Michael Avesian was oblivious of these external demands on his time, his secretary was not.

"Michael!" Sally appeared at the door, clucking like a mother hen. "Give me a break! I can only hold the fort so long. You're already late for that meeting at Mercantile. Harry Bernstein's been trying to get through all afternoon, Senator Coleman called three times . . ." She appeared both adoring and exasperated.

Unfazed, he nodded and thrust up five fingers.

"Call the car, Sally, and I'll be down in five."

Then turning to Lee with a dazzling smile, he took her hand in both of his, as though they had concluded a secret pact.

"Thank you, Lee, for being so generous with your time and so patient with all my babbling. I hope the story works out well, for both your sake and mine. If I or my secretary can be of any further help, feel free to call. Any time!"

She tried to hide her disappointment. No cosy dinner for two tonight, but there would be – she was sure – other opportunities. A photo session, for one.

Then, glancing down at his enfolding hands, she saw it: the narrow gold wedding band. Idiot! Lee kicked herself mentally. *And you consider yourself a seasoned observer!* Had he mentioned that he was married? Had she asked him?

"One last quickie. . . ." Lee swallowed a stab of pain, even mustered a non-committal smile. "Just to round out the details, a little personal background. Are you married, Michael?"

"Yes," he said simply. "For over ten years. I married my high school sweetheart from Baltimore. We have two little girls, they're back at school now in Maryland."

Her heart skipped. "Then your family didn't come with you to New York. You commute?"

178

"Weekends," he said. "I get home weekends by helicopter. We have a house overlooking Chesapeake Bay."

"Sounds strenuous," she probed, "living half in Manhattan, half in Maryland."

He smiled and switched gears. "For my next major enterprise, I develop the thirty-hour day. Christ, five o'clock already. I have a car waiting, Lee, heading downtown. Can I drop you somewhere?"

"Thanks, but I'm just a few minutes' walk. Anyhow, I have a lot of material I want to digest. We'll be in touch."

She moseyed back to the office in a preoccupied state. Michael had set out to take her by storm and largely succeeded. But was he interested in her on a personal level? The messages he sent were mixed, ranging from businesslike to friendly to flirtatious. More to the point, Lee asked, was she interested in *him*? Having an affair with a married man was not among her priorities. Especially with a happily married man, if that was the case.

The reluctant mention of his wife was significant. But of what? Of reticence? Evasion? He had volunteered the minimum. Perhaps he thought Lee's enthusiasm would increase, that she would go the extra mile, if she mistook him for an eligible bachelor.

That made sense. From the start there had been an element of manipulation about the interview. She believed him when he said he was in love with the project. That kind of zeal couldn't be faked. Yet most of what he'd told her (or hadn't) was self-serving.

For all the friendliness of his tone, never once did he forget that she was a journalist. But if his truths were selective, Lee understood and forgave. There was a fundamental rule to such interviews. The subject tried to project the image of Superman while the reporter sought out the feet of clay.

More to the point, Lee could be self-serving too. There was a story in the man, lively and colourful. Precisely the kind of story that might advance her career. In short, she and Avesian could use each other. Beyond that . . . ?

Beyond that, she tried not to think.

The fact was, she was powerfully attracted to Michael.

He made her feel alive, electric. Bill Frazier's sarcasm nothwithstanding, she was human. She craved love, affection, a warm body beside her in the cool of the night, like everyone else.

What she didn't want was to be embroiled in an emotional morass.

Looked at in that light, maybe she ought to go to bed with Michael Avesian. What could be cooler than an affair with a married man? Gerry herself had enjoyed a lifetime of such dalliances and no harm done. It made a kind of sense. With Michael, there could be no question of commitments, no diversions from the thrust of career. Lee would be able to keep it simple and safe. Exercise total control.

Decided! She would call him in the morning and ask for another interview. And then another. As much time as he could spare, on the theory that familiarity bred . . . well, familiarity!

Back at the office, Lee spread her notes on the desk. Of course the facts would have to be checked, with the research being done on her private time. A good two weeks' work. After which she would write the bejeezus out of it. Essentially, however, she saw it as more of a personality profile than a business story, full of zip and surprises. Her bet was Fletch would bite. As for Michael, if it ran, he'd be profoundly in her debt. Why not? It was a million dollars' worth of free publicity.

She switched on the word processor, doodling, testing openers, hoping to capture some of the glow while it was fresh.

At 34, handsome dark-eyed Michael Avesian . . .

No! Pap. Fan-mag stuff.

Despite the yuppie clothes and chiselled good looks,
Michael Avesian is a romantic at heart . . .

Yuppie . . . a real yecccch! word. And romantic? What did that mean any more? She started again.

Michael Avesian is

Then again.

Michael Avesian is
Michael is . . . Michael is . . .

She stopped, folded her hands and stared at the screen, hypnotized by the blink of the cursor, trying to conjure up his image and make it real. Words words words. They were hopelessly inadequate. They didn't begin to convey his charisma. His appeal.

For the first time since her arrival at *Trend*, the glib phrases eluded her. She felt confused. Disoriented. More than a little bit scared. It was an unfamiliar sensation, rather what she imagined seasickness to be.

You are not in love, she rebuked herself. Ridiculous even to entertain such a notion. One didn't fall in love of a single afternoon, despite Gerry's belief. Love was a long process, as much mental as physical, requiring mutual trusts and values and interests.

No. What she felt for Michael Avesian was nothing more than a momentary case of the hots (no harm in that!) that might or might not blossom into a brief affair. Plus a perfectly commendable desire to help a personable young man publicize an interesting exciting project. That was all.

Absolutely positively not in love!

When Bill Frazier came by on his way to the men's room, she hardly saw him or heard his hello. Her eyes were shining, her face lit from within.

He peered at the screen.

Michael Avesian is driven by a dream.

Bill tapped her on the shoulder. She turned around with a start, completely unfocused.

"Hey Lee," he asked, concerned. "Have you been doing coke?"

seventeen

If Lee ever did write a piece on Gerry O'Neal (which she wouldn't dream of doing without permission), she'd have to include a line or two about the O'Neal temper. Pure Irish, Lee thought. Apt to flare up at odd moments.

For the most part, Gerry exercised commendable control, gracious even with those she disliked. But now and then, she would indulge in some bit of gutter behaviour that left Lee groping for words.

Such as the time they were sitting in a Broadway theatre and District Attorney Mariano arrived. The DA was a controversial figure, a man of burning ambitions, unfettered zeal and a thirst for publicity. As he made his way down the row to his seat, Gerry spiked him with the heel of her shoe.

"I'm sorry," she smiled sweetly.

"The hell you are!" he said, his face thin-lipped with pain.

"Fascist bastard," she retorted in a stage whisper, while Lee prayed to God that no one heard her. But Gerry was unrepentant.

"Never pass up a chance to fuck a fucker."

To watch Gerry watching the news on TV was a show in itself. In the privacy of her own home, she could let her righteous indignation rage unchecked. This senator deserved to be drawn and quartered. "No, *eighthed!*" she added for emphasis. That Supreme Court Justice should be in the dock. Almost any appearance by the President was greeted with an obscene third-finger jab. Just this President, Lee wondered, or all Presidents? All, she decided.

At heart, Gerry had an anti-authoritarian fix. "Anyone with more than five million dollars probably belongs in jail." Which was an odd remark, Lee thought, coming from someone like herself, who was clearly possessed of a fortune. She distrusted all politicians on principle, she said. Even the ones who had been guests in her house.

The news over, Gerry would put on a pleasant smile the way another woman might put on fresh lipstick.

"There now! I feel much better. Let's go eat."

For the most part, of course, she kept her temper in check and Lee had never seen her out of control.

Until today.

For the first time in their months of friendship, Lee was granted a taste of the O'Neal fury unabated. She was its witness, fortunately, not its victim; nonetheless the outburst was terrifying.

Gerry had asked her to come around at five and Lee was seated in the reception room, thumbing through a magazine when BOOM! Vesuvius exploded. Even with doors closed, it was impossible to ignore the ruckus emanating from the inner office.

"Idiot!" Gerry was screaming at some poor wretch. "Asshole! And you talk about a career in PR? You've fucked up everything, you stupid bitch. . . ."

Her voice rose, became shriller, angrier. Every other word was an obscenity. Then a crash and the sound of breaking glass. What had set off such a storm of invective, Lee couldn't imagine, but the sound was that of a crazy lady. God pity the poor soul on the receiving end.

Lee was embarrassed. For herself. For Gerry. Even for Brett, the combination receptionist-security man, who pretended to be absorbed in the mail. At last, she caught his attention with a quizzical glance.

"New girl," Brett said, as though that explained everything.

Gerry was constantly hiring fledgeling associates and trainees. "It's my duty to give bright young kids a break," she said, although Lee suspected the policy had as much to do with money as with merit. Gerry, so lavish in her personal expenditure, could be notoriously tight when it came to the payroll. Perhaps she felt the privilege of working for her was compensation enough. Unsurprisingly, trainees came and went with regularity.

Lee endured the barrage a while longer.

"I'll come back at a more convenient time," she whispered to Brett, although the lowered voice was redundant. Given the din inside, Gerry was in no position to overhear.

"Stick around," Brett said with a shrug, making Lee wonder if such fireworks were a frequent event. "It'll blow over, a couple of more minutes. Anyhow the boss is expecting you, and if you're not here, she'll wind up dumping on me."

True to Brett's prediction, the inner office door swung open a minute later and out flew a woman in her twenties looking like a fugitive from hell. She was gone before Lee could divine what had happened. Then the office door slammed shut once again.

Ten minutes passed before Lee was buzzed in to find a pale but composed Geraldine O'Neal seated, hands folded, at her desk amidst shards of shattered crystal. She had been weeping.

"You know why I never parlayed this into a multinational firm?" she asked with great bitterness. "How come I never made millions like every other schmuck in the business? Because I don't delegate. That's the secret of my failure, Lee. And the reason I don't delegate is that the world is full of congenital idiots. You want something done, you have to do it yourself." She blew her nose in a tissue.

"You going to fire her?"

"Who?"

"The gal who just left?"

"Who . . . what's-her-name? Oh, yeah. Leslie Balsam. I suppose not. She's only been here a week. She's bright and reasonably cheap. Anyhow they're interchangeable, these young college grads. Just out for what they can get. I'm nothing but a line on a résumé to them. Why do I hang in there, I ask myself. For my staff? For my clients? Fucking ingrates, the lot of them! If I had any sense, I'd be leading a life of self-indulgence instead of trying to maintain professional standards."

Her mood softened. She almost managed a smile.

184

" 'Alas! What boots it with uncessant care
To tend the homely, slighted, shepherd's trade?. . . .
Were it not better done, as others use,
to sport with Amaryllis in the shade?' "

"Milton," she added. " 'Lycidas'."

But Lee wasn't a poet's daughter for nothing.

"Yes, but then Milton goes on to say 'Fame is the spur . . .' Fame. Glory. The reason you hang in there is because you're a winner, an achiever. Me too, Gerry. Our work is our identity. It's what sets us apart. My bet is even if you tried, you couldn't join the ladies-who-lunch bunch. You'd go nuts in a week."

"Thanks. . . . I think."

"And by the way, congratulations! I saw the story in the papers, about how fare-beaters are cheating the New York subway system out of five million bucks a year. You planted it on behalf of that Japanese client of yours, the turnstile guy. Right?"

Gerry grimaced. "Right. Only the figure was wrong. It should have been fifty million dollars a year! Barely less than the cost of new turnstiles! A beautiful story, till Miss Leslie Bollocks-up Balsam sent it out with a typo. So much for trainees! However, I've issued a correction and made the proper grovelling noises. The right stuff should appear in tomorrow's edition. But I'm sick of the topic. Talk to me about something else."

For the third time that week, Lee launched into a paean to the talents of Michael Avesian. They'd had dinner last night, she was privy to all of his plans. It had shaped up into a fabulous story.

Secretly, she wished Gerry might meet him, wondering what would happen when two such enormous egos collided. She squelched a smile.

"Well, I finished the draft this morning, showed it to Fletch . . ."

"And?" Gerry asked.

"That spec writing paid off. You're looking at a bylined reporter!"

She didn't add (it would only diminish her accomplishment) that Fletch, finding much of it fulsome, had wielded a liberal blue-pencil through the most glowing accolades. "High-school crush stuff," he declared. Nonetheless, he liked the piece well enough to run it in the next issue of *Trend*. Gerry seemed suitably impressed.

"So," she commented, "opportunity knocked and you answered."

Like almost every occasion in life, Gerry saw this as cause for celebration. Champagne at the office. Cassoulet at La Côte Basque. And for dessert, one of those marvellous anecdotes culled from her own long history of triumphs.

"There's nothing sweeter than first success," Gerry said. "Especially when you've your own initiative to thank. Did I ever tell you how I became a columnist? Actually, I was saving that story for my memoirs, but what the hell, if I don't get around to writing them, you can hand this on to Albert Goldman after my death! Jesus, those biographers put a new fear into dying," she added parenthetically. "Anyhow, let me tell you how I got my job on the *Globe* . . ."

In the wake of the briefcase fiasco, Gerry found herself out of a job. She was twenty-four and broke: no references, no resources, no rent money, even. A Seventh Avenue garment manufacturer had stopped her in the street and offered her a job as a runway model at good wages, but on this point her will was unbudging.

"You had to give your measurements," she told Lee, "your hips, bust, waist, to see if you measured up. To me the idea was hateful. The only thing they didn't measure was your IQ. To this day, I'd rather starve than be judged as meat on the rack."

But having been fired from one job for "flagrant misbehaviour" (the unspeakable Frankie had threatened to sue), a second position was even harder to come by. At her mother's insistence, she agreed to take the Civil Service exam.

"It may not be exciting work," Mimi O'Neal cautioned, "but you'll have job security for the rest of your life. You can retire with a pension at sixty-two."

A reluctant Gerry made her way downtown on the day

of the exam, arrived early, then sat down in the little park outside City Hall for a last breath of "free air" before entering the ranks of Civil Servanthood.

She was pondering the misery of fate, feeling very sorry for herself, when a taxi pulled up a few feet away, disgorging a stunning if somewhat tipsy couple. The woman had tossed a sable boa over a pink Chanel suit with luxurious abandon and Gerry thought her the embodiment of chic. She had the cabbie in tow.

"You there!" The glamorous creature called to Gerry, then giggled. She wasn't drunk, Gerry realized, just blissfully happy. "How'd you like to be second witness at a wedding? We're eloping. Running away. Please don't say no. Our entire future depends on it."

Maybe it was the prospect of missing the Civil Service exam. Or maybe it was just the fun of brushing elbows with glamour, for Gerry had recognized the bride-to-be as the columnist, Suzie Slade. Either way, she didn't think about it twice. "I'd love to!"

Fifteen minutes later, the fugitives were standing in an overheated chapel in the Municipal Building while a short squat judge tied the knot. Ceremony over, the groom kissed the bride. The bride kissed both Gerry and the cabbie, handing them each a fifty dollar bill. Then she thrust a letter in Gerry's hand.

"Be a lamb, will you, darling? Take this over to Robert Obermayer at the *Globe*. You'll get good marks in heaven, I promise."

Once in the taxi Gerry opened the note. Why not? It wasn't sealed. In it, Suzie breezily informed her publisher that she was quitting the paper, giving up her column on the Woman's Page and taking out a first mortgage on a rose-covered cottage in paradise.

"All for love, or the *Globe* well lost," Suzie signed it, adding a smear of lipstick for good measure.

Which meant – Gerry realized – that there would an opening at the paper. Not that she had any qualifications as a journalist, aside from that ancient item in the *Herald Trib*. On the professional level, no one at the *Globe* would even look at her.

Yet in her bones she knew a chance like this might never arise again. Forget the Civil Service! Forget being pensioned off at sixty-two! The morning's extraordinary chain of events had been no accident. It was Providence. Fate knocking at the door. She buried the note in the depths of her purse, freshened her make-up and strode into the *Globe* building as though she owned it.

Once inside, she quickly bluffed her way into Suzie's cubbyhole, sat down at the typewriter and began banging out copy.

The Features Editor came by. "Who the hell are you?"

"I'm Gerry O'Neal and I've been assigned to fill in for Suzie Slade all this week. Suzie's been called away on an emergency."

"Nobody around here tells me anything," he growled. "Yeah . . . well you got an hour to turn out a column for this afternoon. Six hundred words. What's it on, by the way?"

Gerry smiled her sweetest smile. "Getting fired."

An hour later it was complete.

"One of the best things I ever wrote," Gerry said. In her own brisk punchy style, she recounted the story of her last day at Winterbourne's, briefcase and all.

"Only the names were changed to protect the guilty. But it didn't matter. Believe me, every working woman around identified with my situation. One way or another, they'd all been dumped on, taken crap from dumb male bosses. The big difference is, they were supposed to suffer in silence. I didn't. The piece went over like gangbusters."

It was a milestone for the paper as well as herself. At the time, she explained, the Women's Pages contained little more than fluff and household hints: food, fashions and cutesy tips on how to get rid of grass stains on a white dress or unblock your kitchen sink. "Getting Fired" was the first column to address itself to the working girl.

Gerry managed to squeeze out two more columns before the imposture was discovered. At the end of the week, Obermayer's private secretary, a formidable personage known throughout the company as the Dragon Lady, appeared at Gerry's door with a summons from the great man himself.

"Is he mad?" Gerry asked.

"Spitting!" the older woman said. "He asked that I bring your head on a tray." But as they neared the executive suite, the Dragon Lady allowed herself a small tight smile.

"Good luck," she whispered. "I read your column every day."

America's Master of Media, as Obermayer has since been styled, had not yet scaled the Valhallan heights of fame and power, but even at forty, he reeked the zesty confidence that bespoke the future billionaire.

"Short, bald, ugly as sin," Gerry described him. "That is, assuming that sin is truly ugly. And the manners of a longshoreman. An ill-bred longshoreman at that. Needless to say, I found him attractive."

Instinct proclaimed that this was a man she could deal with.

"What have you done with Suzie Slade?" he asked.

Gerry gave him the crumpled note and an explanation.

"You needed a columnist, I needed a job. It was simple."

"Simple!" he roared. "In twenty years of newspapering, I never heard of such chutzpah! Missy, you're fired."

"You can't fire me," Gerry shot back. "I'm not on the payroll. But if I were and you did, I'd write an absolutely wicked column about getting canned from the *Globe*. Then I'd take a cab crosstown and sell it and me to the *Daily News*. Believe me, Mr Obeymayer, getting rid of me will be a huge mistake. I've done your paper a favour."

Without giving him a chance to interrupt, she launched into the biggest selling job of her life. The old column was full of pap, she declared, articles that were an insult to intelligent women. Every day the female workforce was growing larger, more articulate. And even that vast army of housewives and homemakers resented being talked down to as mere cleaning-and-cooking machines. It was high time someone addressed women's real needs, spoke to them without getting swallowed up in the cute and the coy. Gerry was that someone. The response had proved it.

"If you're smart," she finished her lecture, "and I know

you are, you'll put me on staff, give me a byline and a chance to speak my mind. With a picture. Why not? I'm good-looking."

She wanted to call the column 'On My Own', "because there are a lot of women in this country who are on their own too, worrying about the rent, the boss, how to survive in a man's world. They can identify with me – and they will. Well!" She suddenly ran out of steam, as Obermayer shook his head in awed amusement. "I guess I've said it all and then some. By the way, Mr Obermayer, what's chutzpah?"

He was quiet for a moment.

"You are quite likely the most outrageous young woman I've ever come across. I ought to take you over my knee and spank you."

"Mmmm. . . . ." Gerry hummed. "Sounds interesting."

They talked terms for a while, reached a meeting of minds, then spent the rest of the afternoon in more intimate configurations.

"You still haven't told me what chutzpah means," Gerry said afterwards, pulling on her stockings.

Bobby laughed. "Chutzpah, my dear, means balls. And lady – you have 'em!"

After that, she told Lee, "We were close as paint."

"You mean you went to bed with him," Lee exclaimed.

"To couch with him, would be more accurate. It was strictly an office-furniture fling. Which isn't how I got the job, mind you," Gerry was quick to add, sensitive to any implication that she'd slept her way up. "The business end of it had already been settled. I went to bed with Bobby because I found him attractive. It had nothing to do with the column or gratitude or anything else."

"Speaking of gratitude, what about Suzie Slade?" Lee asked. "Suppose she'd wanted her old job back?"

"Dear Suzie." Gerry beamed. "Or Mrs Ben Klugman, to be more precise. Happily married to this day, thank God. Every year on their anniversary, I send her a hundred long-stemmed roses."

"Like the income tax forms to Frankie Cavallo?"

"I honour my debts," Gerry said.

And the birds? For it was on the tip of Lee's tongue to ask about the gifts her mother received each Christmas. Were they, too, some suitable form of debt repayment? Inconceivable. For what on earth could Gerry O'Neal owe her mother? In any event, it seemed tactless to ask.

The conversation veered to other topics. Lee's first byline. Her apartment hunt. Her new American Express card. And the ever-enigmatic Michael Avesian.

"I'd really like you to meet him," she said. "Maybe help him."

"From what you say, he seems quite adept at helping himself. Is this going to be a big romantic attachment, Lee?"

"I don't know," came the honest answer. "That's why I want you to meet him, look him over, get a feel for the situation. I think I need advice on this one."

"Very well," Gerry sighed. "Although I can't say I'm particularly equipped to act *in loco parentis*. But have him call my secretary and she'll set up a date for lunch."

They spent another amiable hour chatting and eating cassoulet. By ten, Gerry was feeling marginally better. For a moment, she forgot the miseries of the day.

That was the virtue of having young people around you, she decided. Their optimism was contagious. She almost envied the girl.

When the bill came, Lee reached for it.

"Are you sure?" Gerry asked. "This place is bloody expensive!"

"Positive!"

Gerry protested no further. Let Lee pay for once, she thought. Let her learn how to pick up a check. It was good experience. Besides, a hundred bucks saved was . . . well, a hundred bucks to squander on something else.

Yet she was touched by Lee's gesture. It was most generous and, warmed by good food and brandy, Gerry was momentarily inclined to take Lee into her confidence and reveal her engagement to Sir Campbell.

I've a bit of a surprise for you (that would be one way of putting it). *Or Lee, my friend, you're the first to know. . . .* (at least on this side of the Atlantic . . .)

Lee would be thrilled and flattered to be the recipient of such a secret. If it was still a secret. By now, Campbell would have told his children. So what was the big deal?

Yet the words stuck in her throat. Somehow, it was easier to talk of the past than the present. And almost impossible to talk of the future. Least of all, when the future entailed a major change in status.

Besides, Gerry might be hit by a truck tonight, in which case the whole conversation would be academic.

Then again, she might not.

She drew a deep breath.

Clearly, the only way to say it was to come right out and say it.

"Lee," she mumbled, "I'm going to get m . . . m . . . m . . ."

Lee, who was checking the bill, looked up briefly. "Yes?"

Gerry paused.

"I'm going to get a m..m . . . move on home. My god," she gave a sharp laugh, "I'm so tired I can't talk straight."

"Then I guess I'll go back to the office." Lee had signed the check, kept the tab. "Get a jump on tomorrow. I've got a big story in the hopper. Potentially cover stuff. Gonna dash!"

Such energy, Gerry sighed getting into a cab. Her own plans called for nothing more than a long hot soak in the tub.

Alone, worse luck!

Yet her recollections of the *Globe* had induced a state of nostalgia. In her mind it would always be the Martini Era: dry, bracing, urbane. "Drive me through the park," she ordered, then leaned back in the cab remembering when . . .

She'd gone into the job a raw kid, as the saying went, and come out, if not a star, at least a glamour girl. Now there was an expression that was obsolete. Hell – it was extinct!

From the start, Gerry had determined to make everyone around her aware that she was possessed of a special glitter. The dreary space allotted her in the city room was soon transformed into an island of elegance. Amidst the shabby grey lino and battered desks, she'd installed a Louis Quatorze chair and a six-foot ficus tree. "Just because I'm one of the boys," she told Lou Snyder at the next desk, "doesn't mean I have to live like a cave man."

Colleagues loved her or hated her, but everybody knew her, from the mighty Obermayer to the kid who emptied the ashtrays.

Sprightly and sassy, 'On My Own' quickly found a national audience, becoming syndicated in newspapers across the country. The following year saw Gerry in an office of her own, with a secretary and a lavish expense account.

Her secret was simple: she wrote about whatever struck her fancy on the premise that what interested her was guaranteed to intrigue other women. Her favourite topic was herself.

Five days a week, thirty million women were privy to Gerry's inmost thoughts on politics, pop culture, business, literature, men, marriage, social issues ranging from racial segregation in the South to sexual segregation in Afghanistan, from the birth of Sputnik to the death of the Edsel. Her style was forthright and chatty, as if she'd grabbed you by the shoulder and hollered "Listen!" Women did.

And though she never committed herself to any one cause above others (her major commitment being the promotion of Gerry O'Neal), she managed to address the burning questions of the late fifties.

With her first big raise, Gerry shipped her mother and crazy Eva off to Florida. They were immensely grateful. She was relieved to have them out of sight. With her second, she rented a penthouse on Central Park West. She then set about turning herself into the kind of woman who was born to live in such luxe.

Over the next four years, she learned how to dress, how to flirt with celebrities, how to tell the difference between mink and coney, between a Rolls and a Bentley, between a Gibson and a dry Martini. She even learned how to talk.

"You speak French without a New York accent," the *Globe*'s drama critic twitted. "How about English?" He sent her to a coach and after six months of tutelage, all trace of her origins had been banished. Except in those moments when she was angry and sometimes in the act of love, her speech might have fooled even Professor Higgins.

By the time she was thirty, her face was famous. Total strangers stopped her on the street. Letters poured in from all over, seeking advice or tendering it. "How come a nice girl like you isn't married?" wrote *Bronx Mother of Four*. It was a frequent question.

Gerry's answer was to look in her mirror and smile. The creature who smiled back was far more glamorous than Suzie Klugman née Slade.

Marry? What on earth for, when every moment was crammed with friends, lovers, travel, money, fame and acclaim?

Gerry worked ten hours a day, socialized another ten, begrudging the miserable four required for sleeping, then awoke the next morning raring to go. Marriage could hardly compare with such an existence. And the thought of settling down with one person appalled her.

She loved the ambiance at the *Globe*, with its overwhelmingly male population. Men were more fun than women. Being a columnist was more fun than work. To air your opinions on matters great and small and get paid for it into the bargain! Could there be anything better? She often felt herself personally blessed by a benign deity, a woman incapable of putting a foot wrong.

With each passing month, 'On My Own' kept getting bolder, sharper, less concerned with middle class mores. In fact, in the area of feminist advocacy, nothing like it would appear for over a decade, when Women's Lib was in full swing.

Had she played her cards right, Gerry brooded, she might still have a column. Be a respected pundit, with a pension plan, a hefty chunk of stock and a seat on the Board of Enterprise Publications. Instead, she blew it. The Greeks had a word for it: hubris.

The occasion had been a column, simple yet feelingly written, entitled "My Abortion". In her allotted six hundred words, she talked about going through a back-room procedure with the attendant secrecy and expense. *The conventional wisdom is*, Gerry wrote, *that having an abortion will scar you forever. Untrue! Don't feel ashamed. Don't let yourself be bullied. Remember, it's your body and your life.*

As a rule, no higher-ups passed on her copy unless there was a legal problem. She was Geraldine O'Neal after all. She enjoyed freedom of speech and a devoted following.

That particular day, however, a copy editor saw the text and panicked. Within an hour it was on Obermayer's desk. Thirty minutes later, Gerry was in there with it.

"You can't write this," Obermayer said.

"What do you mean I can't. I just did."

"Then I can't run it."

"Why not?"

"This is a family newspaper."

"Abortion is a family matter."

"That word has never appeared in print in my paper and it ain't about to. Period! Case closed."

Thus began a violent argument, with Gerry reminding him that "This is 1960 for Chrissakes. Not the Middle Ages."

"Smarten up, Gerry. We'll have the Church at our throats. The whole fucking Moral Brigade. I have no intention of getting the *Globe* involved in that kind of shit."

"You hypocrite!" Gerry gave him a filthy look. "How dare you deny me my say! As you well know, it was your child I aborted."

"So is this paper my child, Gerry. And I'm not going to throw it to the wolves to soothe your ego."

She stalked out without a word and went directly to the composing room where she collared Mark Kepinski, an elderly typesetter and particular pal. Mark was a Socialist from the days of the Wobblies, still feisty and unabashed. He was also retiring at the end of the month.

"Set it, Mark. It's my last column for the *Globe*."

"It'll be mine too." he said. "A privilege."

As Obermayer had predicted, the outcry had been horrendous, every right-wing organization in the country hollering for her scalp. In California, a branch of the John Birch Society burned her in effigy.

"I'm flattered," Gerry said gleefully. "With enemies like these, who needs friends?"

Even her high-school beau and fellow-jitterbugger Andy Novak called to lodge a complaint. Except he was no longer cute little Andy, the boy next door. He was Father Novak, SJ, and, like Gerry herself, a careerist on the rise.

Fifteen years had passed since she and Andy had destroyed his mother's living room furniture to the tune of *The Woodchoppers' Ball*. Fifteen years that turned Gerry from an awkward schoolgirl to a national figure.

For the young priest, the interval had also been productive. After being ordained, he had gone to Rome and earned a brilliant doctorate in Church Law, traditionally the first step in a long upward climb. Now, scarcely thirty, he was auxiliary bishop in a populous diocese upstate. Father Novak considered himself a centrist in most social questions. He also considered himself a good friend of Geraldine O'Neal's. As such, he felt honour-bound to bring her to task. This once, Gerry had trespassed beyond the pale.

He came down to New York and they had lunch at Giambelli's. As always, she was pleased to see him. They ordered Martinis and reminisced about the old days. Then ordered another round.

"Are you aware," she remarked, "that you and I are well on our way to becoming legends in the neighbourhood? Who would have figured it back in high school? There must have been something in the Yorkville air that's driving the both of us so hard."

"Poverty?" he suggested.

"Or the smell of Mohawk Beer. The old brewery's come down, did you hear? Gone the way of the big bands and nickel hot dogs. No great loss. They're building luxury housing on the site. Pretty soon it'll be fashionable to say you're from the East 80s. You know," she said thoughtfully, "you're about the only person who knew me when . . ."

He folded his hands and looked suddenly sacerdotal.

"And it's because I knew you when that I can talk to you."

With that, he got down to business. He wanted Gerry to print a retraction.

"And say what, Andy?"

"That you sincerely regret your abortion. That you realize it was a crime against state and church both. That you urge other women in your situation to avoid your example. You're surely aware of the enormous influence your column exerts . . ."

"I am," she said. "That's why I wrote it. It's very warm in here. I could do with another martini."

They wound up getting rather drunk, with neither party budging an inch.

"At least take confession," he pleaded.

"Why should I? I don't feel the least bit guilty."

"One of these days," Andy predicted, "you'll see the error of your ways."

"And one of these days you're going to be a cardinal."

He smiled. "I hope we're both right."

She winced at the memory as the cab pulled up to her townhouse. A quarter-century had passed since that conversation, and at least half the predictions had come true. Andy had made cardinal. But for herself, she was as impenitent as ever.

Even with all that anguish and turmoil, life was finer when she was young. Funnier. Braver. More meaningful. By and large, "then" was better than "now".

The day just ended, for instance, if not technically qualifying as a nightmare, was surely a series of ominous defeats. That asshole intern! Those fucking turnstiles! Now there was a cause for you – right up there with civil rights and the Viet Nam War.

Nonetheless, if she were to salvage the account, she'd have to take drastic measures. Her Mr Yoshimura was one very unhappy camper.

Not that losing the business would mark the end of the world. She could close shop tomorrow, call it quits, marry Campbell and live comfortably ever after.

But she had wanted to leave New York on a high note. As the undefeated Champion of the World. *In this corner and still swinging. . . .*

Thirty years ago, she'd written a column blasting women who took refuge in marriage.

Marriage, she had confidently proclaimed, *can be an enticing prospect when the competitive world gets too tough. But you won't respect yourself the morning after.*

The Career Cop-outs she designated the breed. The coinage had since become a cliché.

Cliché or not, Gerry still believed the truth of it. If her own career was coming to an end after a long and brilliant run, she yet desired a professional coup to polish it off. A grand finale. A great last act. Then. . . . *then!* she could – would marry Campbell with joy.

Regarding him, her intentions were honourable. She was not – repeat – *not* weaselling out! It was simply a matter of timing. She would make her engagement public when she was ready and not before.

However, as a measure of her commitment, she decided to call up Jake Matthews first thing tomorrow and break the news. She felt guilty about not having confided in Jake before. After all, he knew more about her than any man alive. He was not just a lawyer, but a friend whose discretion was absolute. They had shared far weightier secrets in the past. By rights, he should be the first to know.

Jake would doubtless insist upon drawing up a prenuptial agreement, one of those long boring documents full of quibbles and quiddities.

Party of the First Part . . . Party of the Second Part.

Gerry presumed she would be the Party of the First Part. She'd always hated playing second fiddle.

The next day she phoned to discover Jake had gone out of town.

"If it's urgent . . ." his secretary said, but Gerry broke in with, "Nothing important. It can wait."

Then she hung up with an odd feeling of relief, as though simply placing the call was a dramatic demonstration of good faith. Her intentions were indeed honourable. And,

though no further proof was required, she actually pro-
pelled herself into Martha's that afternoon (better than
Bergdorf's or Austrian's where the staff knew her well)
and asked to see something "suitable for a wedding".

"The mother of the bride?" the saleswoman said
brightly.

Gerry skewered her with a look, then spent the better
part of an hour trying on five thousand dollar concoctions
in ivory, satin and lace. "Crazy," she muttered, "for something you can only wear once."

She left without making a choice.

eighteen

For Michael Avesian, life in Manhattan was approaching the schizophrenic.

His days whirred by in an unrelenting battery of contacts and phone calls, perhaps a hundred in all, packed between a seven-in-the-morning breakfast meeting and seven-in-the-evening business drink.

By eight o'clock it was over and he had settled into his rented suite at Trump Tower with a briefcase full of papers and a sandwich. As a rule he called home at this hour, spoke to the kids, reported the day's battles to his wife (*Did she listen?* he wondered. *Did she care?*), then launched a familiar complaint.

"I wish you'd come up, Sandy," he'd say wistfully. "I could do with some company and a bit of home cooking."

She always had an answer and the answer was always no. Reasons varied. She must have drawn them from a large stockpile assembled in off hours just for this purpose. She couldn't take the kids out of school. The Labrador was going into heat. Natasha had a cold. Amy had a piano lesson. They were coming tomorrow to fix the garage door.

At first Michael pressed her hard, figuring if he could get to the end of the alibis, push her to the wall, Sandy would have no choice but succumb. She would have to do her conjugal duty. That's what marriage was all about. And conjugal duty meant more than just sex.

But Sandy's fortitude was proving greater than his own. For a self-effacing woman, one who shunned arguments and scenes, she could be remarkably stubborn. Having attached herself, limpet-like, to the house in suburban Baltimore, she refused to be dislodged. This far, her attitude said, and no further.

Pretty Sandy! The cutest, cuddliest, most popular girl in Teddy Roosevelt High School. Not a mean bone in that adorable body. The girl "most likely to succeed . . . Raquel

Welch" the Yearbook had quipped. Lucky Michael had been the envy of his classmates.

They had made a stunning couple in those days, the lovebirds of the Senior Class. And though they waited four years to marry, everyone agreed they were a perfect match.

Yet from the start Sandy had never really believed in him, never taken him at his word. The promises he'd made her in high school ("I'm going to make a mint, Sandy, you wait and see. Someday I'll deck you out in diamonds.") she had seen as just that: promises. Youthful ramblings. She didn't expect them to come true. Hadn't wanted them to. To Sandy, his success would always be a fluke.

Well before he made his first million, it became apparent that they had different growth rates, different values. Sandy couldn't handle change. The idea of moving up in the world intimidated her. She feared risk, hated uncertainty. At first, Michael used to ask her to entertain his colleagues, but on those occasions she had suffered such agonies of insecurity that he soon stopped asking.

It would have been better, he realized, better for their marriage if not for him, had he entered the dry cleaning business with his father. In that environment, measured and unthreatening, Sandy would have been content.

And Michael would have gone bananas!

There could be no question of Michael drawing in his reins. He was born to the fast track. In a different century he might have been a Mississippi Riverboat gambler. In this one, he was an entrepreneur. The more heart-stopping the undertaking, the more he loved it. And he loved the money that was the proof of success.

Being *nouveau riche* was terrific as far as Michael was concerned. In fact, the *nouveau* was the very best part of it. To step into a stretch limo (especially one that had been kept waiting for an hour), to shoot the breeze with the white-bread boys down at Morgan, to lunch with a judge at the University Club – that was pure bliss! Never once did Michael Avesian forget that he was the son of an Armenian dry cleaner. It was that knowledge that intensified the pleasure.

If only Sandy could have shared it! He would have

draped her in sables, indulged her every whim; for he was an open-handed man, free-spending to the point of extravagance. Or would have been, given a woman with similar tastes.

One time, shortly after their marriage, Michael had scored a quick coup on the market. He had taken his profit in cash and gone home early to find Sandy in the kitchen.

"How'd you like to wallow in money?" he asked his bride, then flung the contents of his briefcase in the air. The bills rained down like confetti. On Sandy. Over the pots and pans. Into the sink.

"What'll I do with it?" she cried.

"Spend it! Eat it! Burn it! Do whatever you want, honey. I don't care." He picked her up off her feet and swirled her around.

She looked at him as if he were crazy, then burst into tears.

"I'll put it in the bank," she snuffled.

That was a dozen years ago.

Since then, nothing had changed except the distance between them. The greater his success, the more profound her withdrawal from his world. Yet he clung to the belief that his was a viable marriage and continued to see himself as a reasonably good, though not always faithful husband, and Sandy as a devoted wife. And when he was unfaithful, he was always discreet.

Family meant a great deal to Michael Avesian. It was part of his culture, his Armenian heritage. For centuries, his people had been persecuted, massacred, driven from their homes. They owed their very survival to family life. Michael accepted that as he accepted the fact that he was a married man with two children he adored. His solution was to split his life in unequal halves. He could find no way to reconcile them.

Although at heart he knew Sandy would never join him in Manhattan, he never stopped trying. Sooner or later, he'd have to face the truth: she wasn't born to be the wife of a tycoon.

No use Michael telling her that meeting people could be "fun", that she would soon learn the knack of running with the rich. No use telling her that he needed a hostess and chatelaine. Both the duties and the pleasures of her station eluded her. She had little self esteem and less small talk.

Now, with Michael moving into an international framework, her panic was growing apace. New York! London! Whatever next!

"Come on, hon," he'd urged the preceding week. "We'll take the Concorde, go to London, then bop around Paris for a couple of days."

How could he ask this of her? Sandy – who was scared even to step on a plane!

"You know I don't like to fly."

"With a few belts of champagne, you'll hardly know you're off the ground."

"I'll know. Anyhow, I can get just as tiddly drinking beer as sipping champagne."

"Conceivably," Michael replied. "But why should you?"

Tonight's conversation proved equally fruitless.

"I'm all tied up. Can't you just come for the weekend?"

"What'll I wear, Michael? Everyone in New York is so smart, so fashion crazy!"

"You'll go into Bergdorf's and get a personal shopper. She'll see to it you're properly turned out. My God, sweetie. It's not as if we don't have the money . . ."

But Sandy's anxieties ran deeper. Not, *what will I wear?* but *what will I say? how will I do? will I be a credit to my husband? or a humiliation?* Those questions paralysed her will.

"Maybe next weekend," she tried to put him off.

"Liar!"

"Michael! What a mean thing to say!"

He hung up furious.

He loved his wife. She was a kind woman, good mother, prudent manager. Nonetheless, he felt swindled. He deserved more: socially, sexually, emotionally. A man who worked this hard shouldn't have to come home to an empty bed. He was entitled to laughter, companionship. To a woman who shared his spirit of adventure.

For several weeks he'd toyed with the idea of having an

affair with Lee Whitfield. She found him attractive. Most women did. Time and again, Lee had indicated her willingness. One needn't be a psychic to read the signs. Michael had seen them many times in the eyes of many women. On occasions he had responded.

But this time, some self-protective instinct warned him off. Michael trusted his instincts rather more than he trusted her. She was too needy. Too driven. Who needed that!

Nonetheless he was grateful for her efforts on his behalf. When she called to say the piece had grown into a full-fledged story, he was delighted. When she sent him the galleys, ecstatic.

The timing couldn't have been better. Michael immediately went to his bank, showed them the galleys and came back with a larger line of credit. The week of publication, he would send out reprints to every top retailer in America. From the funding point of view, Lee had been worth her weight in gold.

For despite what he had led her to believe, the Hailsham project was a house of cards erected atop a mountain of "ifs".

If he raised enough capital. *If* he found enough backers. *If* the conservationists in Britain kept their cool. *If* his nerve and cunning held out. The gambling man in him knew it was a long shot. Lee's story had made it seem a sure thing.

His first reaction was to express his gratitude by giving her something smashing – a Rolex, perhaps, or a fur coat. His second thoughts were warier. A gift of that ilk was likely to be misinterpreted as the next step in a courtship. He settled instead, on a case of Dom Perignon and a graceful yet impersonal note.

That, he felt, pretty much concluded his association with Lee Whitfield except for this business of Geraldine O'Neal.

The first time Michael had met Lee, she had talked of her friendship with the O'Neal woman.

"We're very close," she boasted, "and as you know, Gerry is a powerhouse. If you're looking for connections in New York or anywhere, she's the person to see. I'll introduce you."

The name meant nothing. Michael construed this as an effort to impress him. But Lee continued to harp on the matter, always in the context that Michael would be doing himself a favour by meeting her.

"She was a very special friend of the late Henry Winterbourne's," Lee pointed out. "She controls his entire estate. I doubt there's a more influential woman in all New York. You must call her."

Intrigued – who could not be intrigued by a woman who controlled a billion-dollar estate? – Michael asked his secretary to do a little checking. Sally's findings lent weight to Lee's claims. The O'Neal woman apparently did have entrée to every office and dinner table from Wall Street to Fifth Avenue. A former Ambassador, no less, with infinite connections. It was impressive. Very big-league.

As Michael well knew (his father had an Armenian adage on the subject) it never hurt to have friends in high places. Or friends who have friends in high places.

He lingered for a moment over an ancient file photo of the great woman seated at a table next to Henry Winterbourne, her fingers entwined around the stem of a martini glass. Then without further ado, called her office and made a date for lunch.

"The pow! treatment," he told his secretary, "and you can tell the caterer to lay on a pitcher of dry martinis."

An hour with Lawrence Winterbourne was like a day with Lawrence Winterbourne. Endless. First the usual diatribe about the State of the Nation. Then the whines about his own "penniless" state. This morning he'd sought Gerry's permission to sell his mother's emeralds.

Permission denied. But Gerry couldn't leave it at that.

"Why don't you go out and make something of yourself, Lawrence. Get a job. Find the right girl . . ." (Briefly, she toyed with the idea of fixing him up with Lee. Except why wish a lifetime of Larry on a friend!) ". . . and I'd give her the goddam emeralds. Otherwise, wait till you're forty."

Predictably Lawrence rose to the bait. He pushed back the chair with an angry scrape.

"Stop trying to run my life," he snarled. "All I want is what's mine. Remember, Gerry, I'm asking you nicely."

"Asking me nicely," she mocked. "Honestly, Larry, that's Mafia talk. You've been watching too much junk on TV."

He slammed the door as he left. She kicked the wastebasket. Another long boring stupid morning, unproductive as hell. And the afternoon promised a long boring stupid meeting with Yoshimura. Shit!

Sharon buzzed her on the intercom.

"Yeah. . . . what is it?"

"Your lunch date is here. A Mr Avesian?"

Oh yes. That promoter Lee had the hots for. Gerry freshened her lipstick and checked her watch. Right on time.

"OK," she sighed. "Send him in."

nineteen

In his dreams she was a constant.

No matter how strenuously he sought to rid himself of the memory, the image recurred night after night, poisoning his sleep, leaking into his waking hours. It was clear and fixed as a picture in a gallery. No detail ever changed.

In the foreground, Geraldine O'Neal stood over the body of his father. She wore a sable coat over a sweater and jeans. Her hair was loose. His father had no socks. At the far corner of the room, Margaret Winterbourne sat in a wheelchair, weeping. Hovering near the edge of the picture was a priest.

In memory, he could observe himself in the third person, a sleepy twelve-year-old peering through a crack in the door, mesmerized by the sight of his father's blue-white ankles.

"How does it happen," he asked Risha many years later, "that a man wears shoes and no socks? It was midwinter."

Risha smiled her inscrutable smile.

But Lawrence Winterbourne knew the answer.

"Because he was already dead when she dressed him. Bizarre! The pervading fear of my childhood was that she would somehow get rid of my mother and marry him. It never occurred to me that she would get rid of him first!"

Risha hummed sympathetically.

"How did your father meet her," she asked, "since they seemed to occupy such different worlds?"

"In the Men's Room of the Opera House, would you believe!"

Lawrence proceeded to tell the story of that legendary encounter.

Götterdämmerung was being performed that evening with a first act running over two hours. At the intermission Henry Winterbourne went to the Men's Room to relieve himself.

As he emerged from the stall, a woman came out of the adjacent one almost in lock step.

"Young lady!" he spluttered – for she was young, early thirties against Winterbourne's fifty-eight – "Are you blind? This is the Men's Room."

"I know," she smiled sweetly, "but it's impossible to get into the Ladies'. Are you aware, sir, that about three-quarters of all opera goers are women, yet the facilities here are divided half and half? The work of a male architect, no doubt, as ignorant of opera fans as he is of female anatomy. I didn't mean to alarm you," – for Henry's hand had automatically reached down to check that his fly was done up; it was – "but it was a question of either missing the second act, using the Men's Room or disgracing myself in public. You're Henry Winterbourne, aren't you? I recognized your face. I used to see it every morning on my way to work."

By now, Lawrence's father was sufficiently intrigued to suggest that he and the intruder forego the second act and repair to the bar for a drink. The woman was lovely and in any case, he never cared much for Wagner.

Over cocktails, his new acquaintance spoke of her "career" in an outpost of the Winterbourne empire and its ignominious conclusion.

"When it comes to women, Winterbourne's is in the Stone Age, like the architect who designed the plumbing at the Met. And I expect women make up three quarters of your customers too."

By now Gerry's name had rung a bell.

"So you're the gal who used to take potshots at me in the *Globe!* 'Henry Winterbourne, the Clown Prince of Catalogues . . .' "

"Oh dear!" Gerry had the decency to blush. Then she put an elegant hand on his sleeve. He recoiled. He was not used to being touched. She kept her hand there. "But of course it wasn't personal. Personally I find you a most attractive man and a delightful companion, to boot. I was referring to your policies."

The firm's attitude towards women was not only archaic, she went on, but suicidal. There was a movement underway in America, as yet rumbling and unfocused, yet its thrust was ineluctable. She was referring to the growing economic power of her sex.

"I was down south last month, with Martin Luther King. And you know what's proving the most effective weapon in the civil rights movement? The power of boycott! Why should Negroes shop in stores that won't hire them or pay full fare to ride in the back of a bus? And the merchants down there are hurting. Believe me, Mr Winterbourne . . ."

"Henry . . ." he insisted.

"Hank," she one-upped. "I think I shall call you Hank. It's cosier. As I was saying, American women are on the move, too."

Henry Winterbourne sucked in his breath. No mere female had ever spoken to him so disrespectfully. So candidly. And no one had ever called him Hank! Not his devoted fleet of secretaries. Not his well-bred thin-blooded wife. They wouldn't have dared.

For that matter, few men would have taken on Winterbourne either. He was a formidable figure, a rock-ribbed conservative who ruled his underlings with a granite face and an iron hand, as had his father and grandfather before him.

Was she aware that he was one of the hundred most powerful men in America? One of the ten richest?

Aware, he concluded, but not impressed, for she continued her lecture unabashed.

"The day will come, mark my word, when women will be everywhere. In Wall Street, in industry, on the Supreme Court, I daresay. Even in the Metropolitan Club! And when that happens, firms that have maintained a men-only policy through the years will pay the price. Fines, boycotts, law suits. Women are smartening up, demanding their rights. Comes the revolution, Hank, I wouldn't want to be in your shoes." She lowered her voice. "I tell you this in confidence, but I was in Washington last week and such legislation is already being bruited about. It's a matter of time, ten years at most."

"As little as that . . . !"

He listened spellbound as Gerry unrolled a nightmare scenario of boycott, demonstrations, bankruptcy. Then another one placing Winterbourne's in the forefront of progress, esteemed as much for the quality of its chairman as for the quality of its goods. Alternately, she appealed to his self-interest, his common sense, to an idealism that had been buried since childhood.

She appealed to him as only a pretty woman can appeal to an aging gentleman.

"You're too clever to turn your back on the twentieth century. And there's no need to. You can serve both God and Mammon, Hank. Not every man is afforded such a chance."

Thoroughly captivated, Winterbourne asked for suggestions. Gerry provided them by the gross.

"But," she cautioned, "it's not enough simply to effect change. You have to let the outside world know it's taking place. What you need is a spokesman . . ."

". . . or a spokeswoman . . ." he brooded.

". . . or a spokeswoman. Someone dynamic, exciting, forward-looking. Someone who symbolizes Winterbourne's at its best."

But one look at Henry Winterbourne's face was all it took to recognize who, in his mind, was the most exciting, most dynamic creature in the world. At that moment, even his own wife wouldn't have recognized him: for his expression was as foolish as a schoolboy's.

By the end of Act Three, the deal was set. Geraldine O'Neal would enter the company as Vice President of Public Relations.

Did they become lovers that very night or did this epic union take place with as much fanfare as the coupling of Siegfried and Brunhilde?

Did the union ever take place at all? Lawrence never learned the exact details, but the gossip was pervasive. And confusing.

There were those who said she kept Winterbourne in a sexual stupor, others who claimed that her power over him had a supernatural base. She had bewitched him. Whatever its source, Gerry's hold on the tycoon was swift and total. Lawrence himself could testify to that.

Years later, he heard the story of her introduction to the firm's senior staff. The occasion was a high-level meeting in the large conference room. All the vice presidents attended. The only absentee was Winterbourne himself, off on a tour of his properties.

Amidst a sea of blue serge and rep ties, Gerry appeared in a red Chanel suit and satin blouse. She smiled, looked about her, then seated herself to the right of Henry Winterbourne's vacant chair.

That act, as much as anything, was seen as a declaration of war, particularly by Richard C. Diedrich, the firm's second in command. When Diedrich didn't ignore her, he sniped at her. Whenever she made a suggestion he cut her down with a frosty smile and a "Mr Winterbourne this . . . Mr Winterbourne that. . . . Mr Winterbourne would never agree to such nonsense."

Halfway through the meeting, Gerry's secretary appeared.

"Excuse me," she said in a stage whisper, "but Mr Winterbourne is on the phone from Chicago."

The room was suddenly all ears. Gerry alone appeared unimpressed. Dismissing her secretary with an airy wave, she said, "Tell Hank I'm busy. I'll get back to him later."

Then, in the ensuing hush, she folded her arms, turned and smiled at her adversary. The blood drained from Richard C. Diedrich's face.

"As you were saying, Dickie. . . ."

The battle was over, the new champion declared. She had been at Winterbourne's less than a month.

"Diedrich confirmed that story himself," Lawrence told Risha. "He didn't realize until afterwards that he'd been out-manouevred. It was a set up, of course. Gerry faked that call. What a phony she is!"

"But a smart one," Risha added. "It worked."

Over the next several years, Gerry managed to reshape the public image of Winterbourne into a firm that suited her vision. She wrote, lectured, went on talk shows, set up scholarships, bought art, sponsored seminars on social issues, advanced the cause of women, all under the corporate name. Nothing was too grand or too trivial to escape her notice.

"We were the first company to stop trading with South Africa," she boasted, receiving her umpteenth public service award. And the only company with a lobby designed by Andy Warhol.

There was a bullshit element to much of her work, as Gerry would be the first to admit – in private.

"Public relations is ninety-nine per cent hogwash," she once said to Lawrence. "It's the other one per cent that makes it worthwhile."

Gerry-watchers (and the company housed an army of them) argued as to whether she was motivated by money, power, idealism or simply a puckish sense of fun. The more observant ones noted that despite her vocal feminism, she preferred to surround herself with the company of men. Winterbourne's was only big enough for one Queen Bee, Gerry made it clear, and she was it!

But if her own department was hardly exemplary in the matter of female advancement, elsewhere in the firm her policies were enforced with a vengeance. Today, largely due to the efforts of Geraldine O'Neal, business schools throughout the nation point to Winterbourne's as a textbook case of corporate enlightenment and vision.

"The details are in the company history," Lawrence said, "if you want to bone up on them." (Risha already had.) But what was not there inscribed was Gerry's impact on his family life.

"My mother was an invalid, you know. Not a terribly assertive woman, I'm afraid. We were very close. But Gerry came in and just took over."

She fired the cook, bossed the servants, and periodically reprimanded Henry Winterbourne for the way he was bringing up his son.

"Why are you having the boy tutored privately?" Lawrence once overheard her saying. "He should go to school, play baseball, maybe even have a paper route. Learn to cope with life like everyone else."

"He's all Margaret has," Henry Winterbourne replied.

Gerry had snorted. "Yes, well, he's going to wind up leading the same kind of narrow cloistered life as his mother. If you're not careful, Hank, you'll turn him into a nothing. A namby pamby."

But Winterbourne remained protective of the boy. He had married late in life and fatherhood was an unfamiliar experience.

Eventually, Gerry did prevail, at least to the extent of inducing Henry to revise his will.

"Ironic," Lawrence now told Risha. "She tried so hard to run my life while the old man was alive and couldn't. Now she's trying to run it from his grave. Well, we'll see." His voice took on an edge. "We'll see who's the namby pamby here!"

twenty

"The thing is . . ." Lee kept shifting from foot to foot, in an agony of indecision. "The thing is . . ."

"Do you have to go to the bathroom, Lee? If you do, then go. If you don't, then sit down, stop fidgeting and talk rationally."

Lee scrunched down in a wing chair and bit her lips.

"The thing is, Gerry, if I take this assignment I'll be out of circulation for the next two weeks. May as well be in Katmandu. Which means I won't be able to see Michael. And the way I'll look, I wouldn't want him to see me!"

"And if you don't take the assignment . . ."

"Then I should have my head examined!"

It was a major concept, everyone agreed. Conceivably, *the* story on New York's homeless. Who were they – these panhandlers, these drifters and grifters who had transformed the city's parks and terminals into a vision of Third World horror? Were they the needy or the greedy? Were they truly homeless or simply unscrupulous hustlers, playing on the sympathy of decent folk? Should you give or should you run like hell?

Granted, the subject had been written up, written about in practically every publication except *Jack and Jill*. By now the reading public was almost as exhausted as the poor, because no one had fresh answers, new insights.

That's where Lee's slant differed. Where other journalists had covered the territory from the outside looking in, Lee proposed to go underground. Not simply to befriend members of this nomadic underclass, but to become one of their number. To live the life.

She was slight. Skinny. With second-hand clothes and no make-up, she would look hardly different from any of the runaway teenagers, junkies usually, who haunted the Port Authority Bus Terminal, hustling commuters, scavenging trash cans, sleeping rough on the steps, taking "baths" in the dripping sinks of the public washrooms.

214

"If I do it," she told Gerry, "it'll be all the way. I won't cop out and come home each night to sleep on clean sheets."

"Bravo!" Gerry clapped her hands. "A simply brilliant idea. I can even see it as a book proposal. You're to be congratulated."

For a moment, she thought Gerry was being fulsome in her praise, but the older woman appeared genuinely enthralled. Uncharacteristically, Lee blushed.

"The thing is, I'm afraid if I don't see Michael for two weeks running. . . ."

"He'll get away?" Gerry interposed.

"Something like that. You still haven't told me your impression of him. What do you think? Should I go ahead and get involved?"

Gerry shut her eyes for a moment and brooded.

"Let me ask you this, Lee. What did you come to New York for? I understood it was to have a career. Let's put aside the suitability of your Mr Avesian for a moment – I promise you I'll get back to it – and explore what happens if you turn this assignment down. I see three possible outcomes. One: you'll lose the respect of your editor. Two: you'll miss what could be the break of your career. And three: even if I'm wrong about the other two points, even if there are no serious consequences, you still come out a loser. Because in your position, Lee, if you're not moving up on the escalator, you're falling behind. And it is an escalator, sweetie. There's up and there's down, but there's no standing still. Consider that. Consider too that an opportunity of this calibre may not come your way again for a long time.

"Of course," she continued, "if you feel it's too danger-ous, that's another story. I'm talking real physical threat. Two weeks living like a bum in the Port Authority is not exactly a country outing. That place ought to carry a sur-geon general's warning: this terminal can be dangerous to your health. If you're having second thoughts, well – no wonder! Frankly I'm surprised Fletch would allow a girl to – "

"I'm not scared!" Lee burst out hotly, her sense of macho

touched to the quick. "Jesus, you talk just like Bill Frazier. He says he'll sneak me pâté sandwiches and a can of MACE. Well, fuck that. I'm a reporter, a professional. Gender doesn't enter into it. If breaking this story requires personal risks, I'm willing to take them. I've even decided to cut my hair to avoid lice . . ."

"OK . . . OK . . ." Gerry raised her hands in surrender. "I was just saying that if you did chicken out, most people would understand."

"Would *you* turn it down because of the risk?"

"Me personally? No. But that doesn't mean . . ."

"Enough! I'll tell Fletch yes in the morning. But you've dodged my other question. What's your opinion of Michael Avesian?"

Gerry leaned over and patted Lee on the cheek. It was a tender, comforting gesture, but her smile was sad.

"He's good looking. Charming. I can see why you find him attractive. If I were to point out to you that he's married with a family or that he's a good deal older than you, you'd be within your rights to call me a hypocrite. As you know, I'm no moralist when it comes to sex. Consenting adults and all that jazz . . . That said, I'd strongly advise you to run like hell."

Lee's spirits sank. "You didn't like him, did you?"

"I didn't say that," Gerry looked troubled. "It's just that I know that type and he's all wrong for you, sweetie . . ."

"You didn't like him," Lee stated flatly. "May I know why?"

Gerry hesitated. Lee could see she wanted to be tactful.

"Go ahead, Gerry, I can take it."

"I hate to say it, Lee but the man's, well – a bit of a hustler, to put it bluntly. Maybe sleazeball is too strong a word, but one thing's clear: your Mr Avesian is out for what he can get. A real manipulator. I don't deny he's quite sexy in a pushy sort of way, but who needs that! The man's a user." Gerry sighed and shook her head. "He already got free publicity out of you, didn't he? Believe me, toots, a guy like that could break your heart. And probably would. Let it go, Lee. You're better off channelling that marvellous emotional energy of yours into truly

216

productive areas. Your career. Your new apartment. Your cover story. Go get 'em, tiger! You can do it!"

Lee sat for a while in silence. Then she nodded and acquiesced. As always, Gerry's word was gospel.

"I'm sorry. . . ." she said finally.

"So am I, darling."

"I meant sorry you wasted your valuable time on my behalf."

Gerry managed a brave face. "Oh, have no regrets on that score. Actually, your Mr Avesian threw a little business my way. He's retained me to throw a party on his behalf, introduce him to some biggies. You know, love, the usual do. Lots of food, lots of bodies. I hope you don't mind. Business is business, after all. We've set a date for the tenth, by which time you'll have completed grubbing your way out of the bowels of the Port Authority. It'll be a good way to re-enter civilization. You will come, won't you? But," she added playfully, "not before you've changed your clothes."

Lee was blinking back tears, then suddenly she rose and flung her arms around Gerry.

"Thank you!" she blubbered.

"For what?"

"For your advice . . . your friendship. For everything! And to think I was ready to throw myself at the man! Oh Gerry! Whatever would I do without you?"

twenty-one

"You shit!"

Gerry collapsed on her bed.

"You total shit!"

Suddenly she giggled. No point in repressing it. She didn't feel guilty. She felt happy. Why pretend otherwise? Sisterhood had never figured highly in her life, least of all when it came to men.

Besides, much of her counsel had been excellent. Lee was *not* the kind of girl who could handle a Michael Avesian. She was better off concentrating on the job. Looked at in that perspective, Gerry had done her a favour.

And come to think of it, Lee had never once mentioned the word *love*. Not that it would have made much difference if she had.

Still, Gerry was amazed at how easy it had been. A little flim-flam, a little flattery and presto! Lee had signed up for a two-week stretch in the Port Authority! The masterstroke had been when she'd challenged Lee's pride. *Of course if you feel it's dangerous . . .*

With someone else, that approach might have spelled disaster. What woman in her right mind wouldn't have flinched? The place was a fucking zoo! But not Lee. Not Miss Galahad. She'd mounted her white charger and galloped off.

Gerry had been certain she would. In some ways, Lee was not unlike herself at that age: gutsy, defiant, always having to prove herself and too stubborn to admit when she was scared.

But in her place, Geraldine O'Neal would have managed it all. She would have done the story *and* won the man. You may be sure that no mere woman would have euchred her out of an affair with Michael Avesian once she'd set her mind to it.

God! Just thinking of him made her pulse beat faster.

Gerry couldn't recall when she'd felt so full of life, so

eager for adventure. She intended to relish every second of it. After all, she told herself wryly, you're only old once. A man like Michael might never come her way again.

Except she wasn't old. Not where it counted. Not in the mind or the heart. Should she live to be a hundred, there would always be that other Geraldine inside her: young, foolish, full of hopes and dreams, ready to respond to the smile of a handsome man, to the promise of a rollicking love affair.

For years that youthful Geraldine had lain dormant, quiescent, and the other Gerry, hard-working responsible Gerry, as was meet for a woman of her years, had presumed that those emotional tidal waves had gone the way of mini-skirts and three-inch heels. She was at the time of life that called for sensible shoes.

But now she knew she would never grow up, never grow old. Not as long as she could feel this way.

A crush? An infatuation? A mad mad passion? Who gave a damn about the semantics? The sensation was all that mattered. And the sensation was like breathing pure ozone.

Nothing in the world beats falling in love, she'd written years ago in her column. *I should know. I do it at least once a month.*

What a wise young soul she had been! And what a fool to have put these pleasures behind her. Why, it had been years since she had done anything reckless, at least where her heart was concerned.

When this affair was all over (a month, maybe two?), she would do the sensible thing and marry Campbell. But in the *meanwhile*. . . . oh! that marvellous meanwhile!

She adored the whole heady sequence of falling in love at least as much as she relished the act itself. Their courtship would be a pavane, she decided, measured and sensuous and elegant. Over the next two weeks she and Michael would play out the elaborate dance step by step, savouring each moment. Not too fast, not too slow. And certainly nothing so crude as a roll in the hay. She yearned for romance, not mindless coupling. And in love, as in most other aspects of life, anticipation was everything.

The dance had already begun. She and Michael would enjoy it all. The first exquisite moments of discovery. The little gifts, the tiny flutters of the heart. A kiss. A swift touching of the fingers. The midnight calls. Then a startled retreat (did we touch? could it be?) only to draw closer in the next encounter. Until at last, when the alternatives became unbearable, they would arrive at that sweet moment of mutual surrender.

She rested for a while, bathed in delicious fantasies, then got up and waltzed over to the mirror, full of energy.

Gerry stripped and took a good hard look. In the soft light of her bedroom, her body still looked youthful and athletic. Better with clothes on though. She put on a slithery satin peignoir.

Not bad! At least in this light. She tossed her head. Turned. Peered seductively over her shoulder, then smiled.

My God, she looked terrific! Already she could feel the years falling away. Love was better than a face lift and much more fun!

Next . . ! She flung open the closet and began sweeping through its contents, tossing rejects on the floor.

Boring boring boring. Even the classic Chanel suits. They marked her as a woman of a certain age. She would buy some kicky new clothes. Have a makeover at Private World. Treat herself to glamorous lingerie. Get the TV set out of the bedroom.

And all new sheets. She'd buy lovely Porthault sheets, creamy and beautiful. *For him! For us!*

She fell back on the bed in a cloud of happiness, remembering how he looked when he first walked through the door.

To believe that there were still thunderbolts!

Or maybe God had simply saved the best for last!

part two

one

He swept into her office like a blast of oxygen.

"Mr Michael Avesian," her secretary announced; and Gerry's first thought was, Thank God I had my hair done this morning.

"Miss O'Neal!" He strode across the office as though to embrace her. Happy to be alive, his body language said; and even happier to be in your company. The room lit up with his thousand-watt smile.

"A great pleasure to meet you!" He wrung her hand vigorously. "Lee has told me so much about you. . . ."

"Not too much, I hope!" a near breathless Gerry returned. For the record, it was the last time that day either of them mentioned Lee's name. Gerry swiftly recovered her balance. "Won't you sit down, Mr . . ."

"No time," he broke in. "I've planned something very special and if you're ready, my car is waiting right downstairs."

"A surprise?" Gerry laughed. "I adore surprises."

But Michael – he insisted she call him Michael – was already helping her into her jacket. "You may need it where we're going." He steered her out of the office almost at a trot. "I guarantee it's some place you've never been before."

Lunch at the zoo? At the Water Club? In the garden of an "undiscovered" little French cafe? The insistence on a coat implied they would be eating al fresco on this glorious late-summer day.

But as far as surprises went, there weren't any left. Over the years, Gerry had been taken to lunch at every "undiscovered" eatery in town. Armenian food was her guess. Maybe Brooklyn for a lark.

"I have to be back by three," she said.

Michael's answer was to hustle her into a chauffeured Mercedes and they headed down town.

She took the opportunity to inspect him more closely. He

really was as handsome as Lee had implied. Handsomer! A magnificent creature: lithe, athletic, bursting with animal vitality that had been improbably confined within a dark pin-stripe suit. She resisted an impulse to straighten his tie. The off-kilter tie suited him admirably. Like the man, it was brash and a little bit vulgar.

For a minute or two they sat taking silent inventories. The young man must have liked what he saw because his eyes smiled. Hers smiled back. She was the first to speak.

"Are you an ex-boxer by any chance?"

Instinctively, Michael touched the bridge of his nose.

"Lightweight champ until I was five," he said. "Lost the title in a dispute over baseball cards and laid down my gloves the next day. Anyhow, she was bigger than I was. People keep telling me I should get the nose fixed, but I keep it as a reminder of the power of women. Ah! Here we are."

They pulled in at the East Side Heliport. Once out of the car, he grabbed her elbow and began running across the tarmac, where a Bell four-seater was warming up. Gerry, high-heels clattering, could barely keep pace. Didn't he know that running was undignified for a woman her age? But he wasn't treating her like "a woman her age". More like a partner in a getaway. No respector of persons, this Michael!

"Are the cops on our tail or is this how you usually spend your lunch hour?" she asked as he bundled her into the helicopter. "And where's the pilot, by the way?"

"You're looking at him." Michael climbed in beside her. "I love flying this contraption. I like the mobility. Even the noise."

She was silent, watching him at the controls. The moment they were aloft, the idea struck him. "You're not afraid to fly, are you? I never thought to ask!"

"Good heavens, no. I adore it. Although the truth is, I haven't flown in . . . ye gods! at least a dozen years."

"As long ago as that?" He looked puzzled.

Gerry smiled and delivered the cruncher. "And then only single-engine planes. I'm not licensed for rotorcraft, you see. Although this little number looks like fun."

"You mean – you actually have a pilot's licence?"

"One of my most treasured possessions."

"I don't think I've ever met a woman pilot before."

"There are a few of us around. In fact, I used to belong to something called The Powder Puff Derby back in the sixties. We were a bunch of women recreational pilots – copywriters, secretaries, academics, a very motley crew indeed – but we all were crazy about aviation. Fun-flying only. We held our own meets, and every now and then we entered air shows to show the guys what we were made of."

Michael gave a roar of approval. "Absolutely marvellous! Well, Gerry, if you want to try your hand on the controls once we're out in the countryside . . ."

"Thanks, but for the moment, I'll just relax and enjoy. Besides, I don't know if I have the eyes for it any more."

"You have perfectly magnificent eyes."

They exchanged a quick smile.

"Remember," she chided. "Back by three!"

"We'll see about that."

The truth was, she couldn't care less. She was thrilled to be here, delighted to have impressed him with one of her more offbeat accomplishments. She loved surprising people. So, apparently, did Michael. Moreover, the day was beautiful, the foliage superb and she hadn't a clue as to where they were going. Who could ask for anything more?

Twenty minutes later, he put down in a broad meadow surrounded by rolling hills.

The helicopter coughed and came to a stop.

Then Gerry stepped out into a hundred acres of farm-land. There wasn't a soul in sight, not a road, not a car, although there were vehicle tracks. The land was empty, except for an occasional copse of trees. Yet here in this rustic isolation, surrealistic by contrast, stood a Queen Anne table groaning with delicacies. It had been set for two, with a full flourish of china and crystal. There were tiny pots of beluga caviare, gravlax, baby chèvres, lobster salad, silver chafing dishes filled with mysterious goodies: enough for a small but discerning army. And in the centre of each place setting was a stemware glass. Michael poured the drinks from a pitcher.

"Dry martinis." Gerry clapped her hands. "And with a twist. My God, man, you're psychic."

"I hope so. Here's to."

They clinked glasses and Gerry took a long brisk gulp of her favourite tipple. The liquid was so cold it made her teeth chatter.

"Perfect!" she breathed, then looked around. "I gather that we're in New Jersey on the site of Hailsham Castle."

Michael nodded. "At the moment, we're smack in the middle of the banqueting hall. The historic North Tower is over to your right. To your left, there is a duplicate of the maze at Hampton Court. And over by those oak trees . . ." Just as he was veering off into the pompous, Michael caught himself and did a swift about-face. "Over there is the shoe department, housewares and women's lingerie. I'll show you around after lunch. Meanwhile, let's fall to. I'm starving."

He began loading her plate as Gerry poured herself another martini. The second drink homed in on her brain with the impact of an ICBM.

"What have we here?" she asked as he ladled a spoonful of stew.

"*Patlijan silkme*. It's an Armenian dish, made with egg-plant and lamb with lots of herbs and spices. You are a meat eater, I hope? I never thought to ask."

"A dedicated carnivore. People have been known to throw me raw haunches of large animals." Then she giggled, pleased with herself. "Something told me we were going to an out-of-the-way place and eat unpronounceable Armenian food. See? I was right."

She was rewarded with a buccaneer grin. "Then you're psychic too," Michael said. "Eat! You'll love it."

It was a splendid lunch full of good food and laughter and a lusty but treacherous red wine. The conversation touched upon a number of things, not one of which had to do with business. They traded views on Broadway shows, Tom Wolfe, the relative merits of the various Virgin Islands, the disgraceful performance of the Baltimore Ori-

226

oles. But mostly they talked about themselves: their likes, dislikes, greatest pleasures, silliest defeats. During the course of a leisurely meal, they managed to learn a good deal about each other.

By the time the last of the pastries had been polished off, a distinctly light-headed Gerry felt herself falling in love. It was closer to three o'clock than she cared to think about, so she didn't think about it.

"Now!" she said, removing her shoes for the ground was soft and the grass felt good beneath her feet, "you're going to treat me to the grand tour of the Hailsham site including the sales spiel you give prospective backers."

Michael took her arm in the crook of his elbow. "OK, here we go."

As they strolled, he proceeded to deliver a set presentation much like the one Lee Whitfield had enjoyed. The phrases rolled off his tongue ("A showcase for America's finest products . . . a link between the great English-speaking nations . . . a landmark in creative merchandising") but behind those visionary words Gerry detected something Lee had missed: a sense of playfulness. The man was having fun.

She listened, nodded, hummed from time to time. Michael concluded his pitch then looked to her like a schoolboy hoping to discover he'd earned good grades.

"Outrageous!" Gerry said, then shook her head. "Outrageous! Outlandish. Just like you. In fact, it's the daffiest scheme since the South Sea Bubble . . ." Michael looked crestfallen. "Or Disneyland," she continued, "depending how you look at it. In short, Michael, the entire project is looney toons. It's also dazzling, sensational and I adore it. But, lacking Disney's resources, how can you hope to pull it off?"

Her wristwatch alarm went off with a tiny but insistent beep. It was 2:30. Late! But the idea of playing hookey was irresistible. Pretending not to hear it, she turned and smiled.

"I could do with some coffee," she said.

A light suddenly danced in Michael's eyes and she knew he had heard the alarm. "Coffee sounds wonderful."

They started walking back leisurely, arm in arm, while he mulled over her comments.

"Your reaction was funny," he said finally. "About my pitch, I mean. I've made that presentation to a lot of people. Some of them find the idea ridiculous. Some think it's terrific. But you're the first person who ever voiced both sentiments simultaneously."

Suddenly, he burst into laughter.

"What's the old saying? Never try to con a conner. I should have known better. But what the hell, Gerry, you asked for the full treatment, so I gave it to you. Most of the time my spiel goes over like gangbusters. It's only later they have second thoughts. In fact, I had intended to seek your professional opinion, pick your brains. But no matter. Anyhow, here we are and the coffee's still hot."

"You said 'intended'," Gerry seized upon his use of the past tense. "What service exactly did you want me to perform? Are you looking to hire a PR firm? In which case I should be taking you to lunch. Why did you want to meet me, Michael? Why such elaborate arrangements? I'm impressed, but curious too."

Black eyes met green eyes in a long devouring glance.

"To charm you," he said softly. "You're well-connected, influential. I hoped you'd provide me with the entrée to significant people."

"You were trying to hustle me." She sounded neither surprised nor offended. "I guessed as much."

"Absolutely. But I've shelved that idea, at least temporarily. We're too much alike, you know."

"Both charmers?" she asked.

"Both adventurers. Free spirits. You're a woman after my own heart, Geraldine."

"And are you hustling me now?"

Michael laughed. "I'm not sure. Yes . . . no . . . probably, given my nature. The truth is, you're not at all what I'd expected."

"What had you expected?"

"I'll tell you some other time when I know you better."

"And when will that be?" Her heart skipped.

"How about dinner tomorrow at eight? That is, if you're free."

She was flying to Mexico City tomorrow night where Sir Campbell was attending a conference. On second thought – no, she was not!

"I'll make myself free."

Michael glowed.

"Now, my turn to ask a loaded question. Knowing that I invited you to lunch just to hustle you, I wonder – why did you accept?"

For a moment, Lee's name hovered in the air. But instead, Gerry broke into a wicked grin.

"I saw your picture in *Trend*. I liked your looks."

He laughed.

"And am I what you expected?"

"Oh, Michael!" she breathed. "Even more!"

Three o'clock came and went and still they sat there, lost in each other.

The following morning, Gerry arrived at the office late, having made an expensive detour to Bergdorf's.

Her secretary fell upon her the second she walked through the door.

"What happened to you yesterday? All hell's been breaking loose. Mr Yoshimura practically called out the National Guard."

"Oh shit!"

"And these are your phone calls."

Sharon handed her a stack of pink chits an inch thick. Gerry thumbed through them swiftly. Lee Whitfield. Jake Matthews. Eli Landau. Rosenthal of *The Times*. A Mr Karl Wummer of the IRS. . . ."

"Oh double shit!"

"And then this package came for you by messenger just ten minutes ago. No return address. I didn't know what to do. I thought maybe it was a bomb."

Gerry put her ear to the box. There was a definite tick. Then she looked at the address. No matter that she'd never seen his handwriting. She instantly divined its source.

"I'll take it into my office. Hold my calls, will you, sweetie?"

She shut the door and practically tore open the wrapper. Inside was a cheap pink alarm clock, the kind you buy in a drugstore for five dollars and that can be heard a country mile away. The alarm had been set for 8 p.m.

She unrolled the accompanying note.

VANILLA ICE CREAM
WOODSMOKE
THE ROLLS ROYCE SILVER CLOUD
MOZART
INDIAN SUMMER
THE ELGIN MARBLES
MACY'S THANKSGIVING DAY PARADE
IRISES
GERALDINE O'NEAL

two

Immediately upon receipt of the story in *Trend* (Lee had rushed it out Federal Express), Nancy Whitfield headed straight for Kopy Korner.

"I couldn't be prouder," she told the kid behind the counter. "My daughter's first big byline. I thought I'd have some copies run off for our friends. How many, d'you think?"

"You limiting it to close friends?" Nick inquired.

Nancy nodded.

"Then I guess a hundred fifty will do."

"Oh Nick!" She tapped him playfully. "You're such a tease."

They settled on a hundred instead.

On Saturday morning, she set off in the Honda with a stack of photocopies and a list a yard long. Making house calls, David said. It was a familiar routine. This week it was Lee's story going the rounds. Last Saturday, a petition against toxic waste in Cottonwood Creek. The week before, tickets to the Harvester's Ball.

"Back by three," she assured him. "I'll just drop 'em in the letter box, or maybe pop in a few places and say a quick hello."

But her husband knew better. "You'll be back when you get back, with an acute case of coffee-itis. Enjoy! And don't worry about dinner, love. I'll throw a pizza in the microwave."

"Throw in two." She blew him a kiss. "And make a salad. I promise I'll be back by seven."

"You have time for a coffee, don't you honey?"

"Thanks, Nell. No sugar. Looks like you're doing up the house. What's the occasion?"

"My sister's son is coming to stay for a bit."

"Really? How nice."

"I just hope the bed is long enough. Stanley's six foot seven. He played basketball for Penn State. He just graduated engineering."

"Uh huh," Nancy hummed. "So what brings him to Cedar City?"

Nell lowered her voice. "It's very hush hush but I can whisper it to you. He's going to work on a new missile base."

"The one over by Wolverton?"

"Honestly, Nancy," Nell clucked. "I can't tell you anything. You get all the low-down before any one else. It's a good thing you're not an enemy agent."

Nancy finished her coffee and left muttering: *Stanley . . . silos. . . . six foot seven.*

"Coffee?" Dr Goldman asked. "It's decaffeinated."

"Thanks, Ed. Just a quickie. I've got a million calls to make."

"Well, now that you're here, Nancy, I've been wanting to talk to you about the Andricek girl."

"She's pregnant, isn't she?"

"And scared to death. Do me a favour and speak to the mother."

"Oh, c'mon, Ed. The woman's a religious nut. She'll go bananas."

"Please, Nan. As a personal favour. You handle that sort of thing so tactfully. Besides, Mrs Andricek respects you."

"Gee doc. You sure save all the goodies for me."

"Thanks, love. I owe you one."

"Coffee, Nan?"

"Half a cup, then I've gotta run. Listen, Linda, I got news for you. Our pals at the Pentagon are back in business."

"You mean the missile silos over at Wolverton?"

"Yup."

"I thought that programme was dead."

"It's come alive again."

"How do you know?"

"I've got sources."

"Oh shit! Forgive my French. What do we do now?"

"What we did before, toots. Make a nuisance of ourselves. I'll get on the senator's back first thing Monday."

"How about a cuppa?"
"No thanks, Mr Mayor. Well, just a small one. And
while I'm here, I want to ask you what the hell is going on
over in the Third Ward. Nobody's collecting the garbage."
"Third Ward! Third World is more like it."
"Don't give me that, Arthur. We had the same problem
with snow removal last winter. Stuff sat on the streets till
May. If you want that neighbourhood to come up, you
have to start treating it right."
"I'll think about it."
"Do more than think about it, Art. Act on it. Besides,
you owe me one."
"For what?"
"For getting out the vote last November."

"Espresso, Nancy? Just made it fresh."
"A demi-tasse. Listen, Carole, something interesting's
come up. How's Stephanie, by the way. She get a date for
the dance yet?"
Carole shook her head.
"What did I ever do to deserve a six foot daughter?"
"Same thing I did to get a five foot two one. Let's get
down to cases. How'd she like to meet a terrific engineer,
recent graduate of Penn State, basketball star . . . ?"
"Are you kidding? Who is this paragon, by the way?
And how could we have overlooked him?"
"His name is Stanley, he arrives next week and doesn't
know a soul in town. I'll fix it."

"Good day?" David asked.
"Busy, that's for sure. How 'bout you? You do anything
interesting?"
"Pottered in the workshop. Napped a bit. Repotted the
hyacinths."
"Sounds like bliss to me." Nancy mixed a pitcher of dry
martinis. "I was reading in *Trend* that they're coming back
again."

"Hyacinths?"

"Martinis, dopey!" She handed him his.

"I didn't know they'd ever been away."

"Me neither," Nancy giggled. "Just shows how benighted we are. Driving home I was thinking about Gerry wheeling and dealing in what do they call it? . . . the corridors of power."

"You're not so bad in that department yourself."

"Yeah, only somehow my corridors keep looking like the front yards of Podunk. Oh well, at least Lee's enjoying the scene. I wonder what she's doing right now? Catching a show, going to some smart restaurant? Dancing all night with some fabulous guy? I hope! He was cute, that fella in her story. Too bad he's married. Still, she doesn't seem to lack for company. God knows she's never home when we call. Let me see, it's what . . . 9 p.m. in Manhattan? Betcha at this very moment she's swilling French cuisine at Le Cirque."

The one thing she refused to do was eat out of the garbage bins. If she couldn't pan-handle enough for a sandwich and coffee at Zaro's, then she'd damn well starve.

After a rocky start, business was beginning to pick up. Any day now, she'd hit subsistence level, especially now that she'd staked her territory.

For a start, she tried working the rush hour commuters on the Red-and-White lines, but her first evening there, a beady-eyed grifter wearing a greasy baseball cap and a tee shirt emblazoned MORGAN GUARANTY TRUST approached her with blood in his eyes.

"Move, motherfucker. You're standing in my face."

"I beg your pardon?"

"I said, listen, motherfucker. Get off my turf."

For a moment, Lee considered pointing out to him that the Port Authority was a public facility wherein no one might stake a private claim, but a second look made her rethink the proposition. A mean pulse had begun throbbing on his forehead.

"You got it, mister. Have a nice day."

The following morning, fortunately, she found an undis-

234

puted stretch of terminal between the coffee shop and the Montclair-Caldwell lines. By then, she'd perfected her pitch.

"Excuse me sir," (or madam as the case might be) "but I'm a stranger in New York. I was mugged and they took all my money. Could you help me with the fare back to Cleveland?"

The fact that hardly anyone believed her seemed to have no effect on her earnings, although one guy asked her which part of Cleveland she came from.

"The nice part," she answered.

"Yeah?" He looked sceptical. "Well you shoulda stayed there."

"Smartass," she muttered under her breath.

Every few hours, Lee would repair to the Ladies' Room to scribble quick notes in a steno pad. Not that she needed these *aides memoires*, she felt, for the experience promised to be unforgettable.

Before long, she began to see patterns among the panhandlers: cliques, clans, certain types that recurred time and again. She divided her fellow mendicants into three basic categories.

There were the Nodders: mostly older, usually horizontal, thoroughly out of it, scarred, scabby, plastic-bagged, having given up on a life which had long since given up on them. World War III might have broken out without commanding their attention. Some of them formed little cities. Others lay where they fell.

The Prowlers: young, tough, roaming the terminal in packs, stealing suitcases, hassling commuters, dealing drugs. Sly and fly, at their individual best they could charm. But in fact they were every bit as dangerous as –

The Crazies. Enough of them to fill two of Lee's notebooks. There was Flash Gordon who was in constant contact with Mars. Rex the Wonder Dog, known to burst into sudden paroxysms of barking. Twinkle-Toes, a grotesque old doll in tatty finery who sidled up to young Wall Street types and startled them with lewd propositions. There were screamers, scratchers, mutterers, God-fearers, droolers, twitchers and one wild-eyed crack head who roamed through the terminal shouting "I'm gonna kill 'em all . . . I'm gonna kill 'em all!"

Lee never tried to discover the object of his wrath. For all she knew, it could be five foot two blondes.

At the start of her ordeal, sleeping presented the biggest problem. Those areas of the terminal that were dark and quiet – the back halls and staircases – were to be avoided at all costs. There had been gang rapes there, muggings and murders. Even the cops gave those places a wide berth.

First choice would be the top floor with its plastic benches. But they were pathetically few. In their eagerness to discourage transients, the powers-that-be had penalized the weary commuter as well. Lee noted the irony. And even when she did land one, it was a limited treat. Every hour or so the cops came by, rapping the back of the seats with their billies as a cue to move along. Towards midnight the cleaners would come and move everyone again. Still it was better than sleeping on the floor. (She wished she'd been smart enough to wangle a wheel chair like the old guy who lived next to the Tropica juice stand. Now that was foresight!)

Usually, she wound up camping on the main floor near the ticket counters. The lights were merciless, the din non-stop, the traffic heavy, the vinyl filthy and cold, but if nothing else the area was well patrolled and relatively safe.

Lee would open her plastic shopping bag, take out an old Army blanket (her one concession to comfort), place an empty styrofoam cup by her side on the off chance that some passerby might have a charitable urge, and then bed down for the night. At first, she worried about being robbed as she slept. It took a while to realize that except for her notes, she possessed nothing worth stealing. She slept with her notebooks under her head.

One morning she awoke to find that someone had left a doggie bag for her. Overcoming an instinctive repugnance (was she an animal, after all?) and beguiled by the smell, she opened it. Inside were fresh rolls, a piece of Brie, a half pound of prosciutto, a jar of Grey Poupon mustard, paper napkins and a cake of Roger et Gallet soap wrapped in lavender tissue.

Lee stared at the booty for an uncomprehending moment, then held the soap to her nose. Carnations. The scent was so fresh, so clean, so piercingly lovely – so everything the Port Authority was *not* that it brought tears to her eyes.

Gerry! she thought. Gerry had come like a fairy godmother and touched Lee with her wand as she slept. Bless her!

This windfall, however, posed a dilemma. Her fellow hustlers and homeless had no guardian angel to transport delicacies to their bedside. No outside allies and loving friends. In this wise, as in so many others (after all, Lee never forgot, she could go home at any time), her experience was tainted. For authenticity's sake, she ought to forego Gerry's indulgences. The decent thing would be to dump the food into the trash cans for one of the grubbers to find. That was only fair. To the scroungers belong the spoils.

Lee explored the moral implications of this for a full thirty seconds before falling onto the bag like a ravening wolf. It was the most succulent meal in her life.

Several more such packages were to come.

But if bed and board were manageable problems, keeping clean was a greater predicament. She could not bring herself to strip and take a sponge bath in the Ladies' Room, the way the hookers did, drying themselves in front of the tiny hot-air blowers. Logistics aside, the thought of standing half-naked and vulnerable in such a place filled her with horror. She didn't bathe. Instead, she washed her hands and face a dozen times a day, with the precious cake of Carnation.

Her favourite fantasy (dinner at Côte Basque) was soon replaced with images of herself standing in a tall shower of her new apartment amidst a cloud of fragrant steam. Once this nightmare was over, that would be her first act as a free woman. In her dreams she could smell it, feel it, imagine the whole delicious sequence, the paraphernalia. The French-milled soaps. The luxurious lashings of Lancôme's Après Bain. Then yards of spotless Turkish towelling. And to top it off, whole powderpuffs-full of Estee Lauder's White Linen talc.

How many hours would it take to wash this filth, this accumulated stench and decay out of her system? She dared not think, but it was an image that sustained her during the last difficult days.

As for Michael, she was determined to put him out of her mind. He refused to stay put. Time and again his image, handsome and sexy, would catch her off guard. What was he doing now? Was he thinking of her? Wouldn't it be marvellous if. . . . ?

Then, briefly, deliciously, she'd succumb to perilous daydreams, only to come to her senses with a wrench.

Yet Gerry had doubtless been right and wise in her judgement. An affair with Michael would be a drag on her career. Giving him up was a necessary sacrifice if she were to follow her star. What was required here was self-discipline. Total control.

She made a bargain with herself. Each time she thought of him she would replace that vision with an imaginary cover of *Trend Magazine*.

HEARTBREAK HOTEL
My two weeks living underground:
by LEE WHITFIELD

Maybe even a picture of her in an insert.

For whatever one might say about the physical indignities that Lee endured in the process of getting this story, the potential for reward was infinite. At the least, a place in Journalist's Heaven. At the most – who knows – a Pulitzer Prize.

And what mere man, what mere love affair, could successfully compete against that! She must never let that vision go.

At noon sharp, on Wednesday the tenth, two weeks to the minute since -Lee had begun her assignment, she washed, she packed up her notes, put her blanket into a trash bin for the next bum to salvage and took a taxi home to her new apartment.

"87th Street and Third," she gave the uptown address with pride.

"Whew, lady!" the driver said. "Where ya been – the slaughterhouse?"

three

Michael Avesian was ridiculously happy.

At odd moments, he would catch himself humming, whistling, actually singing out loud. Even snatches of Verdi, would you believe! Twice this week, he'd forgotten appointments. Once, he'd left the keys in the car. Sometimes, he laughed for no reason at all.

A more reflective person might have recognized the symptoms of a man newly fallen in love. However, Michael was a doer, not a theorist. Rather than analyse and anatomize the source of his happiness, he simply reached out and grabbed it with both hands.

Never before had life been so intense, so brimming with the new. Not just his work, which never failed to engross him, but his leisure hours as well. Suddenly the days were filled to overflowing.

Gerry O'Neal had made the difference. Of that there could be no question. It was a difference, Michael perceived, comparable to that between a black-and-white home movie and a Technicolor extravaganza.

In a matter of weeks, she had turned his world upside down and sent him spinning.

Was this Michael Avesian, the renowned workaholic, playing the thoroughbreds at Belmont? Dancing all night at S.O.B's? Driving to Montauk to see the sun come up? It surely was.

No one had ever fussed over him in such affectionate and savvy detail. She bawled out his cleaning woman. She selected his ties. She turned the most routine events into a spree.

Charity affairs, for instance. Michael subscribed as a matter of course. They were deductible and made good business sense. But now he actually attended the damn things, enjoying himself to the hilt. For the first time since his arrival in New York, Michael felt like something more than an aggressive upstart. He was the good friend of Ms

Geraldine O'Neal. Ambassador O'Neal, as it often appeared on the place cards. Elderly Europeans kissed her hand.

Nothing gave Michael more pride than to arrive at an elegant ball with this magnificent creature on his arm: so vibrant, so witty, so beautifully gowned. He adored showing her off to his acquaintances. There were times when Gerry literally glittered, and Michael felt himself the luckiest man alive. He loved her sense of fun, her buoyancy, and had he stopped to consider, it might have occurred to him that he loved the woman as well.

Now and then, amidst the sparkling chatter and tinkle of wine glasses, he would have a swift vision of his wife, followed by a stab of guilt. Sandy's shadow fell across the table like a pall.

In theory, it was she who ought to be here, sequinned and bubbly at his side. Yet the very image was a contradiction in terms. Poor Sandy. In Gerry's place, she would be sitting silent and lumpish as a stone, spreading her misery till it rubbed off on him.

Then Gerry's effervescent laughter would soar above the crowd and his guilt would vanish as swiftly as it had come. Thank God it was Gerry, not Sandy sitting next to him! Gerry with her boundless zest for life. Who wouldn't be proud to know such a woman? Or flattered to share her secrets?

She gave him not just her time, but her trust, welcoming his own in return. Often, at evening's end, the two of them would nestle down in her den to "take coffee" as she put it and rehash the events of the day in a way he could never have done with his wife.

They shared an irreverence for all things bloated and pompous. Look! she would say, the Emperor has no clothes! Nor does the mayor! Nor even the Cardinal!

In Gerry's view, nothing was sacred and while she maintained exquisite tact in social settings, she could break loose in these late night tête-à-têtes. Well, so could he. Irreverence was how you cut the mighty down to size.

"What did you think of so-and-so?" she'd probe Michael

for first impressions. He would oblige with a thumbnail sketch.

She giggled when he described the head of an investment bank as the kind of guy who secretly watched Roller Derby on TV while drinking beer out of a six-pack. "You're a wicked wicked man. But intuitive," she added. "You're right. Old Merriman is a hopeless klutz."

Not all her judgments were so harsh. There were good guys and bad guys, as Michael well knew. The eternal problem was figuring out which was which. Only Gerry had managed to turn the sorting process into a game. A wonderful game. "Us-versus-them." An entertainment just big enough for two. You have just become a member, Gerry's smile implied, of the smallest most exclusive club in the world: the club of you and me. Michael basked in the privilege.

At first the difference in their ages didn't bother him. Why should it? There was nothing sexual between them. They were friends, allies, confidantes. She was wonderful to be with. That was all.

Then, briefly, the matter caused him concern. Was he using Gerry? Was she using him? He didn't want to look foolish, responding to overtures that were all in his head. Gerry was not some young sexy piece, after all; she was a person of stature. Yet now and again, to his embarrassment, he reacted to something she said or did with a sharp nip of desire.

Could she be coming on to him? At her age? Damn it! the woman was a mystery.

Two days ago, however, they had gone to the opera with an outcome that resolved the relationship once and for all.

It was a benefit performance and they both arrived looking their spiffiest, Michael in a new Dunhill tuxedo, Gerry resplendent in a streak of gold lamé. She had taken a box for the occasion, filling it with influential friends. The curtain rose before Michael had a chance to read the programme.

The production was a lavish affair with much dramatic toing-and-froing. At various points in the action, there was

242

a party of sorts, some curses were hurled, then a girl with a yellow wig was carried off down a ladder while a misshapen fellow in a blindfold staggered about the stage.

"Who's the old walrus with the hump?" he whispered to Gerry.

"Her father," Gerry mouthed.

Michael was puzzled, but Gerry brushed his ear with her lips.

"I'll explain later," she murmured.

Obediently, Michael sat through the rest of the opera which, happily, featured some catchy tunes, a couple of which were vaguely familiar. He enjoyed the music, but never did get the hang of the story. Towards the end there was a storm. The little blonde had been murdered then dumped in a sack, which didn't prevent her from singing some more. It was all very confusing.

Afterwards he and Gerry joined a supper party at the Café Luxembourg and it wasn't till midnight, over brandy in the den, that he had a chance to ask her what the hell had been taking place on stage.

"Did you enjoy it?" Gerry asked. "Did you like Pavarotti?"

"Well yes," Michael said, and suddenly began bellowing one of the tunes in pidgin Italian. He had a pleasant voice and a quick sly talent for mimicry.

"*E molto sillio . . . e molto foolisho . . .*"

Gerry laughed. "For the record, the name of that aria's *La donna é mobile.*" Then it dawned on her. "Why Michael! You've never been to the opera before, have you?"

Michael flushed. For a man who liked to appear unflappable, he was nonetheless keenly aware that in a world full of gentlefolk with Ivy League educations, he lacked the finishing gloss.

"You know me, Ger," he said diffidently. "Mike Avesian, college drop-out. You're dealing with a genuine peasant-type here. Where I came from, we didn't go to the opera for a night on the town. We went to Kentucky Fried and played Stevie Wonder on the juke box."

She was watching him, absorbed, and it struck him that she didn't know who Stevie Wonder was. Had probably never eaten Kentucky Fried chicken, either. Maybe they *were* both street-smart hustlers at bottom, as he had stated, but with Gerry, the seams no longer showed. He envied her the achievement.

She placed her hand on his knee.

"Gee, Michael, I feel as if I've robbed you of your musical virginity. I hope it was a good experience. You have a lovely voice, by the way. And a terrific ear. Better than a lot of professionals. I'm perfectly serious. You ought to take singing lessons."

Flattered, Michael felt obliged to protest.

"Now, there's a screwball idea! What would happen to my toughest-kid-on-the-block image?"

"You might want to polish it up," Gerry said.

Michael grew thoughtful. "I do, actually. You know, I've never really cultivated tastes like opera and ballet. Never had the time, And as for . . ." he started to say *my wife* then caught himself up short. "As for my life, I've been too busy grubbing money to look up. Tonight, for instance. I enjoyed the opera but I didn't really understand or appreciate it. Hell, I didn't even know when to applaud. Which one was Rigoletto, anyhow?"

Gerry looked touched. Then she smiled.

"OK. Talk about screwball, this is a real screwball plot. Rigoletto is a court jester to the Duke of Mantua and has a daughter named Gilda. Only nobody knows about the daughter. Don't ask me why. Now . . ."

She was off and running and as the tale unfolded in all of its convolutions, Michael felt his credulity being strained.

"In other words, he kidnaps his daughter by mistake?"

"You got it!"

"He couldn't possibly!"

"He could," Gerry insisted.

"He'd know her in the dark."

"How?"

"Her touch, her smell, her feel."

"They're father and daughter, Michael, not lovers." Her voice had grown low and thrilling. "How would he know her from any other woman?"

244

Michael paused, acutely aware of the warm scented flesh beneath its slithery lamé. The room was very silent.

"We're not lovers, Gerry, but I'd know you in the dark."

"Would you, Michael?"

She drew in her breath as though he had said something absolutely wondrous. The green eyes glittered. And then he knew. She desired him. Incredible! Michael felt his mouth go dry.

Could it be? Could it be that this unique, rare, utterly remarkable woman wanted to make love to him? And that he wanted to make love to her?

His penis stiffened in immediate response. God knows he hadn't planned this moment. Hadn't even envisioned it. Yet the rightness, the inevitability of their becoming lovers now struck him with the force of revelation.

He tensed for a moment, like a cat about to spring, then walked quietly across the room and dowsed the lights.

Gerry sighed. It was a sigh full of promise.

"I would know you in the dark," Michael murmured, moving toward her blind yet sure-footed, drawn by the sense of her presence. "I would know the scent of your perfume. It's very sweet and tart all at once, like you. I could sense the warmth of your skin through my fingertips. I'd know the rustle of your dress, the sound of your foot-steps. If it were silent enough, I'd recognize the rise and fall of your breath."

Then he heard her rise and brush past him with a swish of silk, a cloud of Sortilege.

"Find me," she murmured almost inaudibly.

She was there. She was gone.

Michael shivered with delight. Hide and Seek. The notion aroused him almost unbearably.

For a moment he stood there, adjusting his eyes to the darkness, all his senses keyed to a peak. From the passage-way came the click of her golden sandals. Two small thuds and silence. She must be barefoot now. Breath held. Waiting.

In his mind he recreated the geography of the floor. It was a large house. There were half a dozen doorways off the hall, but which of them led to her bedroom, he didn't know. Except for the den they were usually shut.

Gathering his bearings he began to feel his way across the hall, moving slowly, quietly, desire sharpening with every step. Behind him, a phone rang. The noise startled him.

"This is Gerry O''Neal . . ." the recorded answer crooned intimately. "I'm unable to come to the phone at this time . . ."

Michael smiled and inched forward, feeling his way. His fingers caressed the cool marble of the hall table with its China vase. Traced the gilt edge of the Sargent portrait. Glided over the light switch and moved on. No. He would find her in the dark. That was the given.

Something soft caught at the hem of his trousers. He bent down and picked it up, puzzled for a moment. It was the lamé gown, still warm from the heat of her body.

He continued his progress past closed doors and featureless walls, moving toward her by instinct. By automatic pilot. Then he sensed her presence, exactly as he foretold. In the hush, he could even hear her breathe.

Heart pounding, Michael stepped across the threshold into her bedroom and a moment later, drunk with sensation, engulfed her naked body. Mouth sought mouth. Arms enfolded into arms. Flesh dissolved into lubricious flesh.

They made love once – urgently, swiftly, with a kind of first-time desperation. Then once again, leisurely, sensually, as though the morning would never come. Then once more for fun and good luck.

Toward dawn he fell back content, happy to talk, to just be.

Gerry kept fruit by the bedside which Michael decided was a very good thing. They nibbled on grapes and made small foolish talk. Being with her was so pleasing on every count. It catered to his sense of luxury. Even the sheets felt like cream.

"Where'd you learn to move about in the dark like that?" he asked at one point. "You're a regular cat."

"In Paris, when I was young."

"I never realized . . ." he began, but she put her finger to his lips and shook her head as if to say, don't tell me.

I never realized, he'd wanted to say, that you really were so young. You've made all the calendars lie.

For in her way, Gerry was. Younger, freer, fresher, fuller of life than Sandy ever was or would be. So much for chronology. He could scarcely credit his luck.

Michael left before breakfast, light-hearted, light-headed, taking the steps two at a time. He sang Verdi as he went.

Life is magnifico . . . You are fantastico!

Gerry had stood at the top of the stairs, roaring with laughter.

That was two days ago and he had yet to come down to earth.

This evening as he dressed for what he knew would be one of the seminal engagements of his life, he could only feel relief that Sandy had decided not to come. He had assumed she wouldn't. In fact, the more he inflated the importance of the occasion, the more surely he could count on her absence. This once, he gilded the lily.

"It will be," he'd told her, "the most significant gathering I've attended since I came to New York. Eli Austrian will be there. Leveque-Brun, the jewellers. People from Dior, Bloomingdales, Rolls Royce. Practically every top merchant in the north-east. Plus celebrities. Bankers. The whole infrastructure. I'll be operating at the highest level."

Predictably Sandy had panicked out.

It wasn't his fault, Michael assured himself. He had done his duty and requested her presence. Staying in "Baw-lamer" had been her decision.

He straightened his tie, brushed down the elegant Cardin suit Gerry had chosen for him and left the apartment with good conscience.

He was in the mood to deal.

Gerry had outdone herself, everyone agreed.

"This must have cost a pretty penny," Eli Austrian remarked to his latest mistress.

Yvonne, a smart pricey blonde to whom all pennies were pretty (and dollar bills even lovelier), agreed that such indeed was the case.

"Look at that cake!" She pointed to an elaborate confection in the shape of a castle. "Wow! Never saw anything like it. One million calories is my bet."

"Marzipan," Eli smiled in fond recognition. "It was my favourite childhood treat in Utrecht."

"Something for everyone." Gerry came over to greet him. "And the marzipan was especially for you. And now, Eli, I'd like you to meet my guest of honour. I suspect you two are going to be doing a lot of wonderful creative things together."

The evening's theme was the Glory of Tudor England, and it was echoed in the food, the floral arrangements, the period costumes of the waiters. For those in quest of authenticity, a great serving bowl of mead had been set out, though most of the guests passed it up in favour of the Veuve Clicquot.

"One can only be authentic to a point," she told a freshly scrubbed and smartly clad Lee Whitfield. "You look terrific, by the way. Survived your ordeal, I see."

"And you . . . !" But Lee was at a loss for words. Gerry looked slim, radiant, twenty years younger. It was miraculous. And she was wearing one of the sexiest dresses imaginable. Lee couldn't help but seek an explanation. "Were you at a health farm while I was gone?"

"Good lord, no," Gerry laughed. "Been eating and drinking to beat the band."

Lee shook her head in admiration. "Fantastic. And

before I forget, Gerry, I want to thank you for the doggie bags. They saved my life – especially the Carnation soap."

But Gerry apparently hadn't heard her for she had turned away, in a hurry to do her duty to other guests. "Oh Jake," she collared her lawyer. "You remember Lee Whitfield. Lee wrote that wonderful story in *Trend Magazine*. Do get her some mead, darling, or I'll be bathing in the stuff for a month . . ."

"*Plus ça change,*" Jake said while Gerry skittered off. "Which is French for – back at the same old stand. How've you been?"

"Busy," she replied.

As they chatted it struck her that tonight she didn't need a Jake to show her the ropes as she had on the night of her debut. Or even a Michael Avesian. In a room packed with celebrities, Lee could honestly claim to have arrived with her own credentials. She was the rising star of *Trend Magazine*, sophisticated and newly chic. No more scratchy black dresses from the Bismarck Bon Ton, thank the Lord. Reflexively Lee smoothed down the skirt of her Perry Ellis (two weeks' salary but worth it) and surveyed the crowd with approval. Gerry had hit the jackpot with her guest list.

"Some do!" she commented.

"And some do not," Jake returned. "Personally, I find the mead disgusting. Can I get you something else?"

But Lee was tuned in on a different frequency.

"That's Phil Donahue over there, isn't it?" she mused. "Excuse me, Jake. I want to talk to him about an idea for his show."

She zigzagged through the crush, earmarking people for later conversations, getting her act together as Gerry might say.

From the corner of her eye she caught a glimpse of Michael deep in conversation with an elderly gentleman. Her heart did a flip-flop. Sleazeball or not, (perhaps Gerry had been too harsh), Michael was far and away the most exciting man present. Maybe she needn't have forfeited him. Maybe there still was hope.

249

He waved to her, a friendly casual wave, then turned back to his interlocutor. Lee mustered a painful smile.

Later, she decided. She would catch up with him later. Right now, Michael was on the job and she should be too.

"Hi, Mr Donahue," she introduced herself. "I'm Lee Whitfield of *Trend* . . ."

"A hand across the sea between America and the old world," Michael was saying while Eli Austrian nibbled on marzipan.

"Of course, I envision Hailsham as more than just an extraordinary retail opportunity. My hope is that it will be a cultural beacon for the area."

(He adores the ballet, Gerry had mentioned.)

"It's a personal weakness, I admit," Michael said. "But I've already initiated talks with the New Jersey Ballet." (He would do that tomorrow.) "An excellent little company. I think it's high time they had a permanent home. You must come and have lunch with me one day next week and I'll show you the site."

(The picnic-in-the-park routine. He and Gerry had sharpened it up considerably. Was Eli kosher? He'd have to check it out.)

"Perhaps next Thursday," the older man said, then he smiled. "You're a very personable young fella with some interesting ideas. Tell me, do you prefer classic or modern ballet?"

Michael smiled. "Thursday would be perfect," he replied. "I'll check your office in the morning."

"How's my favourite sinner?" The Cardinal clapped a hand on Gerry's bared shoulder.

"Welcome, your Eminence. Delighted you could come."

"That's a remarkable dress you haven't got on."

"You like it, Andy? It's Christian La Croix." She swirled. "You could do the church an enormous service, I suspect, by commissioning him to design nuns' habits. It would do wonders for recruitment."

The Cardinal shrugged. "We're committed to Dior. What is that revolting brew the waiters keeping passing around?"

250

"It's mead, darling. You should love it. It figures in the Bible somewhere. You know, I've just had a very interesting idea . . ."

"Madonna records for altar boys?"

"Nothing so obvious. This has to do with Mr Avesian. I was thinking that Church might want to have a presence in the Hailsham Castle project."

"You're not serious, Gerry!"

"Absolutely. The place comes with a chapel, I imagine. All good castles do, and I do believe it might be useful for you to have a representative on hand. A priest, if you will. Someone to forgive shoppers their sins, conduct services now and then and maybe hustle some money into the bargain. It's been my experience that when people have spent an indecent amount of money on luxury goods, their conscience makes 'em ripe for fund raising. Just think about it, Your Eminence."

"I will," he said.

"And stick around," she whispered. "I've got a jazz group coming at midnight. We could dance . . ."

"A link between America and the UK," Michael told the head of Sotheby's. "As Churchill pointed out, our nations have always enjoyed a special relationship."

"It's a helluva long drive out of New York."

"But sales tax wise it makes sense. Eli's already very interested. I could see you people adjacent to him . . ."

"Eli Austrian?"

"He's coming down Thursday. Perhaps we might arrange something the following week . . ."

"A book proposal. At the moment, it's pretty sure to be a cover story in *Trend*, but I see it as a bigger story than that, Steve. Tentative title, *Heartbreak Hotel*."

"Sounds like a bit of a downer . . ."

"Or," she broke in, "something with a bit more hustle in it. How about . . . um, *Beg, Borrow and Steal*. The sensational story of New York's Third World."

"It's a possible . . ."

"Or," she quipped, "how about *Oh! Calcutta!* the story that takes the top off New York."

He laughed appreciatively.

"When you've got your proposal up, send it around. We might be interested."

"Thanks, Steve. I surely will."

"How come hizzoner didn't come tonight, Jake?"

"I guess he knew Donald would be here."

"Or else he's pissed off this development has gone to Jersey instead of New York. How come Jersey, though? What's your read on it? Gambling laws? Avesian gonna put a casino in this castle? Figures! That why Donald came?"

"Could be . . ."

"Me personally, I'd go condos with it. Luxury condos at a million a pop. With a pool, a health club. Call it 'The Palace'. I hear Eli's in for a piece of the action."

"I wouldn't be a bit surprised."

"Who's handling the legal shit in this development?"

"We are, actually."

"Should be a nice piece of business for your firm."

Jake smiled. "Not bad. Have some mead."

"Señor Oliveira." Yvonne approached the stout little man in the elevator shoes. "I hear you're in copper and divinely rich."

He smiled and stared down her cleavage.

"You don't speak English, do you?" she asked.

"A leetle."

"Myself, I've always had a weakness for Latin Americans," she said, leaning forward to maximize his view. "You people are so passionate, so virile. You quite make my heart palpitate. See? Beat beat beat."

The Señor nodded happily.

"Beat beat beat," he echoed.

"Very good, Señor. Excellent. And don't you worry your pretty little moustache about not speaking the lingo. We'll get along just fine. Who needs words, huh? Anyhow, it so happens Harpo is my favourite Marx Brother."

The Latin eyes suddenly kindled in recognition.

252

"Si, Marx Brothers. You like? I like, too."

"Bless you, lambchop. I knew we'd hit on something in common. And I'll tell you one thing, Ollie baby. At least the Marx Brothers are better than that fuckin' ballet."

She gave him her card.

The crowd had begun to thin. In the drawing room, a jazz trio was setting up. The business end of the evening was largely over, the social part had begun.

Lee had done her duty, having chatted up everyone of consequence and a number of marginal people as well, even extending to Gerry's bitsy tenant from Bolivia. Funny bird. Not that you could really carry on a conversation with Señor Whatsis, although that half-naked blonde seemed to be doing okay.

The one person she hadn't spoken to was Michael.

Everything Gerry had said came winging back to her: Michael was pushy, manipulative, the lot. Lee ought to steer clear.

Still it would be downright rude to leave without speaking to the guest of honour. They had worked together so closely, exerted such an influence upon each other's careers. She couldn't let it go so completely. Not yet. Even despite Gerry's injunction . . .

Downing a glass of mead for courage – the stuff was sweet but potent – Lee cast a glance about her. Michael was nowhere to be seen. Then she spotted him silhouetted in the doorway, slim-hipped and elegant, his back to the room. He was talking to someone in the hall beyond her line in vision. Not his wife, Lee knew, for the retiring Sandy had never showed up. She couldn't help but feel glad of that.

She swallowed her drink, then sidled up to the doorway. If he was talking business, she'd wait till he finished. This was Michael's big night. Then she saw it was only good old Gerry, after all. She was fiddling with Michael's tie.

"I can't take you anywhere," Gerry murmured as she adjusted the knot to her satisfaction.

Lee was about to speak up when some instinct stopped her.

"There you are, darling." Gerry had done fussing. "Good as new." She patted his tie flat.

It was such an intimate gesture. So proprietary. So domestic. For a moment Lee watched, numb and mute. They were engrossed in each other, utterly oblivious of her presence. Michael had taken Gerry's hand and brought her fingers to his lips. Then slowly, lovingly, he kissed each fingertip in turn.

The blood drained from Lee's face. She turned and fled.

five

Betrayed!

The most devastating word in the English language.

Betrayed and humiliated.

That Michael Avesian had cheated on his wife was to be expected. But that Gerry had made a mockery of Lee's trust, her friendship – that was the unendurable crunch.

For the last half hour, Lee had been circling Central Park in a taxi, unable to face the thought of going home. Home to what? An unfurnished apartment. An empty bed. And the memory of Michael kissing that woman's fingers in a gesture as explicit as sex.

What a fool Lee had been, to swallow Gerry's lies, kowtow in gratitude, and then return like a good little puppy for seconds.

Were they already lovers, Lee wondered, that night when Gerry had filled her full of "good advice"? Had Gerry schemed for Michael from the start? Why? To prove herself sexier, more desirable than Lee?

Like the mead, that woman was! Sweet and cloying and golden. And stomach-turning.

"Pull over." Lee thumped the plastic divider, her whole body in revolt. She began gasping for air.

"Quick," she cried. "I'm going to throw up."

She got out and vomited into a clump of shrubbery, while the cabbie, a sad-eyed Pakistani, watched her with an expression of dismay.

The night had turned cool. She had left her coat at the party. Lee shivered, feeling suddenly more lost, more homeless than at any time during those dreadful weeks in the Port Authority.

Because then, even when the situation was at its worst, she had something wonderful to return to. She had Gerry's friendship and respect.

She stood for a while by the side of the road with her

head in her hands. Tonight had been the worst night of her life.

The driver poked his head out the window. "You get in the cab, missie. This a bad place full of bad people. You'll get mugged."

Lee sighed and stepped back inside. "I've been mugged once already tonight!" Then she gave him the address of *Trend Magazine*.

There was no one in the office except some poor slavey doing pasteups in the art department in a little pool of light. She headed for the Ladies' Room, bathed her face in icy water, then put on fresh lipstick and went to her desk.

Two weeks' worth of unorganized notes lay were piled up with the stench of Port Authority still on them. Plus a stack of memos, phone calls, press releases, galleys. Time had not stopped while she was away. She sat down and routinely began thumbing through the contents of her In Box. It was better than thinking. Feeling.

She liked the office at this time of night. Its emptiness endowed her with a sense of ownership. My kingdom, she thought. My fortress. The place where you go when you've no place else to go.

She recalled one of Gerry's *mots* concerning work and love.

"I sublimate my career drive into sex," her idol had said, "and my sex drive into career. It works out admirably all around."

Right now, Lee presumed, Gerry and Michael were busy sublimating their careers in the sack.

She conjured up a swift vision of the lovers in Gerry's perfumed bedroom. It boggled the mind. How could she! And how could he – that gorgeous young man – climb into bed with someone her age! Dear God! Gerry was old enough to be his . . .

Lee choked down the bile.

Better not to think about it or she'd be spewing her guts out all night. Work! That's what. Better than a Pepto-Bismol.

First thing she had to do was organize her notes. That

was real. That was vital. She switched on the word processor and began transcribing her notes. Numbing work, but at least it helped dull the pain.

"Hey Lee!" The bank of overhead lights blazed into action, drowning her in its glare. "What are you doing here at this hour? You ought to be home wallowing in clean sheets. Jesus, you look like death warmed over. Port Authority finally got to you, huh?"

"You could say." Lee swivelled around to face Bill Frazier. He looked very natty, as though he'd just come from dining at Lutèce. She tried to focus. "What are you doing here, Bill?"

"I forgot my housekeys." He grabbed a typing chair and pulled up level to her. His expression was troubled.

"Are you OK, Lee? You look almost ready to pass out. Can I get you a glass of water? Coffee from the machine?"

She bit her lips and muttered, "I'm fine. Just leave me be."

But Bill had come to his own conclusion.

"It's that fucking assignment, isn't it! I warned Fletch. I told him absolutely not to let you spend two weeks in that snake pit. For a sensitive person, it had to be a total nightmare. You're still in a state of shock, I can see that. You want to talk about it, Lee? Maybe talking will help."

His voice rang with affection, honest concern. He took her hand in his. The combination was too much for Lee. At his touch, the misery of the evening, the depth of Gerry's betrayal, of Michael's indifference overwhelmed her. She burst into tears and fell into Bill's arms.

"Oh, life is so awful, Bill. I never knew it could be so bad. I've been through such hell."

"There there, sweetheart." he crooned while she sobbed uncontrollably onto the shoulder of his best grey suit. After a few minutes she pulled away and wiped her eyes.

"I'm so embarrassed."

"Why embarrassed? Because you're compassionate? Because you have feelings just like everyone else? That's nothing to be ashamed of. You drive yourself too hard, Lee. And if you want to cry some more, just go ahead."

257

She shook her head. "A glass of water, please," and when he'd returned with three Dixie-cupsful, she almost mustered a smile.

"You won't say anything, will you . . . about my breaking down and slobbering tonight."

"Of course not, Lee! What do you take me for?"

"A gentleman," she said softly. "I'm sorry I asked."

It was Bill's turn to be embarrassed.

"Forget it," he said. "I'll run you home."

Lee looked at him with renewed interest. He was sweet, especially when he wasn't teasing, and fairly sexy in his Ivy League way. At that moment, the thing she needed most was acceptance, approval. Bill could provide.

The thought of Michael and Gerry making love, laughing – perhaps even laughing at her! – charged through Lee like an electric current.

It was unfair! Why should Lee continue to live like a nun? Why deny herself one of life's most basic pleasures? She was lonely. She had feelings, just as Bill had said, though not necessarily the ones he'd ascribed to her.

Lee lifted her face to Bill.

"I don't want to be by myself tonight. I don't want to sleep alone. Spend the night with me."

Bill's face grew grave.

"You once said, Bill, you wanted us to become lovers. Well, I think maybe I do too. Let's give it a try, at least this once. Don't say no, Bill. I couldn't bear it," she added truthfully.

He leaned forward and kissed her.

"I'll get your coat."

"I lost it."

"Take mine."

"All I've got at home is a mattress on the floor," she said.

He smiled. "Who could ask for anything more."

When it was over, she dozed off instantly. The act of love had drained away much of the tension and she enjoyed the first decent night's sleep in weeks.

She woke in an uncurtained dawn to find Bill propped up on one arm gazing at her with a bemused expression.

"I wish you wouldn't do that," she said.

"Do what?"

"Watch me while I sleep. It makes me feel very vulnerable."

"You're pretty when you sleep, and I enjoy looking at you. Besides, I've seen you sleeping before."

She sat up abruptly. "Where?"

"Curled up on the floor of the Port Authority."

"You!" Her jaw dropped. "You brought the doggie bags!"

"I remember your saying you liked the smell of carnations."

Lee was speechless. What a fool she had been. A double fool! It wasn't Gerry who'd come looking for her after all. She had been mistaken on every count.

"How did you find me?" she asked. "The place is so vast."

"I looked hard."

Bill got up and went into the kitchen to make coffee.

"This is a cute place you've got here," he called out from the tiny galley. "Small but cute. You could sure do with some furniture though. Like a chair, maybe. A table if you want to go whole hog. You can pick up stuff reasonably at the Door Store."

"I just moved in, Bill. Give me a break."

He appeared with two mugs of steaming brew and knelt to place one on the bare parquet floor beside her. Room service, as he had provided at the Port Authority while she slept.

In retrospect Lee was uncertain as to whether she resented his kindness or welcomed it. Already he was furnishing the apartment in his mind. Settling in. Playing house.

"You're no cream, one sugar, if I remember aright, Lee. And I'm the reverse should you care to keep that in mind. Taste it and see if it's OK. Personally, I like my coffee full industrial strength, but that's negotiable. Given incentives, I can be housebroken."

259

"I'm sure it's fine," she said without tasting it. "I have other things than coffee on my mind. About last night . . ." She faltered.

"You're not having second thoughts, I hope!"

"No no, Bill. It's simply that . . . well, I don't want us to plunge into some sort of premature domesticity. I'm not ready for any kind of heavy going. I've just come out of a very difficult period. No reason at all we can't continue to be friends. Lovers too, provided we both keep it cool. But I need time. I need space. Please don't crowd me."

"I understand. Now drink your coffee."

He perched beside her on the mattress, long gangly legs folded under him, naked and somehow vulnerable. In the thin morning light, his body was a near-translucent white beneath the remnants of a fading Hampton tan. He was skinny, yet graceful too. Almost like a dancer. Soft brown hair fell loosely over his forehead, giving him the look of a schoolboy.

She thought of Michael with his vibrant olive skin and buccaneer eyes, the palpable virility. The contrast could not be more complete. Still, Michael had proved to be a fantasy, whereas Bill . . . Bill was here and now.

Lee sipped her coffee thoughtfully. It was excellent. There was this to be said of Bill, she brooded. He was good in the kitchen. Good in bed too, for that matter. She studied him with heightened interest. For all their easy familiarity, their months of friendship, she had never seriously considered him as a person, someone to be analysed and explored.

How little she knew him!

Beneath that sophisticated chatter there lay a heart – of what? Of slush? Of sentimentality? Of honest-to-god feeling? Would Bill be good for her or bad for her? As yet, she couldn't determine. But it certainly didn't pay to trust to instinct.

Instincts betrayed. Trust invited treachery. Her experience of Gerry confirmed that much! Suddenly, she had a swift vision, of Michael kissing Gerry's fingertips. The memory of the previous night's humiliation returned full force. Her stomach knotted, her eyes welled with hot tears. Embarrassed, Lee turned her head to the wall.

"Poor baby!" Bill had put down his coffee and pulled her towards him, enfolding her with those long lanky arms. "I feel for you."

She loathed being the object of pity, yet the warmth of his touch was soothing. His lips brushed her red-rimmed eyes. Lee felt herself go limp.

"You've been through a terrible ordeal these past two weeks," he was crooning, "but it's over now, Lee. You're back here with me in the safe world, the good world, where people are kind and loving to each other. Try to put all that ugliness behind you. It was only a story. A clever story for a cheap magazine."

Lee wanted to weep. He hadn't a clue as to the source of her misery. He must think her a bleeding heart. The ultimate soft touch.

How little they knew each other! It was ironic. Two strangers sharing a bed.

And yet, she was glad of his presence. Not to be alone in this painful juncture – that was what mattered. His constancy would see her through these hours.

She shut her eyes, sank backwards against the pillow, let her mind go blank.

"Hold me," she murmured. "Take me. Help me to forget."

He began stroking her gently, lithe firm fingers describing the curve of her breasts, the flat of her belly. His thumb played a soft tattoo amid the tangles of her pubic hair. And as he caressed her, he feathered her face with kisses. Her body responded with a violent surge of pleasure. Eyes shut, she felt herself falling through a darkness, while his warm mouth explored her heavy lids, her cheeks, the little hollows of her throat. He was very sensual, an artist at foreplay.

In a white lubricious haze, nipples taut, she could pretend it was Michael stroking her, savouring her, erasing the past with sly tongue and nimble fingers. But what difference did it make – Bill or Michael, Michael or Bill?

The press of tumescent flesh against her loins held the promise of pleasure.

Somewhere in the distance her clock radio switched on, reminding her that it was late and getting later. They didn't have all day. This kind of leisured love was OK for Sunday mornings. Right now, she had a need for swift no-nonsense sex.

"I want you," she whispered.

Easily, he slid on top of her, light yet muscular, pressing mouth to mouth, thigh to thigh. She began to move to his rhythm, engrossed, forgetful, writhing, legs wide, pulse racing, greedy for the moment of consummation.

Michael . . . Bill . . . Bill . . . Michael . . . What did it matter! As long as the flesh was willing. She placed her hands on his buttocks and plunged him into her with all the force she could muster.

"Now!" she gasped. "For God's sakes . . . now!"

She could hear her heart pound as he entered her. Hear her voice cry out in a mindless climax, ecstatic, out of control. The intensity of the moment frightened her. Seconds later, she fell back, spent.

The clock radio droned on, seeping into her consciousness, bringing the real world in its wake. Weather reports. Traffic conditions. At the tone, the time will be eight o'clock. God! Already!

But Bill, deaf to outside influences, seemed possessed of a limitless sexual energy. She felt him stir within her, quickening, ready to embark on the cycle yet again.

Enough, a voice within her cautioned. Enough for this morning. Bill had propped himself up on his elbows, his eyes focused on her own, and had begun weaving in and out of her with a lazy rhythm. With each successive stroke, her body grew tenser, less responsive. Enough! She clenched her fists, anxious, angry, afraid of letting time and emotion slip beyond her grasp.

"Enough, Bill," she groaned. "I'm wiped out."

He halted, gave a long sweated shudder and rolled off her. For several minutes they lay panting side by side, then Lee sat up briskly.

"We ought to get cracking. You know the time?"

Bill pushed the hair out of his eyes and stretched like a cat. He was disinclined to hurry. "Yeah . . . it's the nicest time. Après sexe . . . like après ski, only cosier. Let's relax for a bit, enjoy the glow. Then I'll put on fresh coffee."

"We can get coffee at the office."

He scanned her face carefully, then sighed. "I'm sorry."

"What for?"

"For not giving you greater satisfaction."

Lee smothered a tremor of impatience. What did men want – total surrender? Total possession?

"You were fine, Bill. Just terrific."

"Was I? I wonder. You seemed so. . . ." He was at an uncharacteristic loss for words.

"So . . . tense?" she completed his thought.

He nodded.

Impulsively, she leaned over and kissed him, afraid that she'd stomped on his pride. He really was sweet, if perhaps a bit touchy. Helpful, too, she appreciated. Lee was not an ingrate.

"I'm still pretty edgy," she apologized. "Recent events and all that jazz. Besides, I don't like making love against the clock."

"OK," he said good-naturedly. "You win. I'm up. I think I'll go home and change. When will I see you, Lee?"

"See me? I'll be at the office all day."

"I mean, really see you. How about an early dinner tonight?"

"Not tonight, Bill. I've got too much work."

"Tomorrow then? We could go to this new Afghan place."

Already he was trying to move in, take over.

She put her robe on, pulled it tight.

"As I told you before, Bill, I need space. Don't crowd me."

They finally settled on Saturday night.

six

"It was a triumph!" Michael declared.

"Unconditionally," Gerry concurred.

"All except the mead."

"Lovely for bathing, though, don't you agree?"

"For fucking too. Whose idea was this, anyhow?"

"Yours!"

He stretched out in the tub and contemplated their naked bodies in the huge gilt mirror, his sense of well-being nigh complete.

Gerry nuzzled him. "Soap my back, will you darling?"

Michael soaped and smiled. No one but his mother had ever called him darling, and she only said it in Armenian.

"What d'you think, Gerry? Will Eli Austrian really come through? Jesus, if he does, I'm half-way home."

"He certainly seemed interested, Michael, and if there's any manner in which I can help . . . Eli and I go back a long way. He was one of my indulgences."

Michael looked at her with interest.

"You were lovers, in other words."

"Once upon a time. He was madly in love with me for a while, wanted us to get married."

"My God, Gerry, the man's a mountain of blubber. How could you even consider it? Beauty and the Beast."

"Well, looks aren't everything," Gerry said, delighted with the compliment, "and he used to write the most romantic love letters, full of Continental schmaltz. He once told me he wanted to drink my bath water, would you believe, speaking of which, should I run some more hot?"

"Please, but easy on the bath oil. That stuff's slippery."

"I still have them somewhere . . ."

"What?"

"Eli's letters."

"Don't you ever throw anything out?"

"I threw Eli out – at least as a prospective husband.

Anyhow that was a zillion years ago. You're not jealous, Michael, are you?"

"Would you like me to be?" He began soaping between her legs.

"Of course!"

Michael laughed. "I'm not the jealous type, although I do admit to a raging curiosity. For instance, who's this guy who keeps leaving urgent messages every night on your answering machine? British accent, very tony sort of voice."

"Aaaah . . ." Gerry exhaled slowly. "Campbell. Why, have you spoken to him?"

"I don't pick up your phone, Gerry, although I'm sometimes tempted. This Campbell fellow . . . is he one of your indulgences, too?"

Gerry didn't look amused.

"Sir Campbell," she said strictly, "happens to be a prominent diplomat and a friend of many years' standing. Look, do I ask you about your wife?"

"Would you like to?"

"That's not the point. The point is, I respect your privacy. We're two very sophisticated people having a sophisticated affair. Let's just relax and enjoy it. Besides, I don't feel like getting into a serious discussion. Not this morning, at any rate. We're here. . . . we're happy . . . we're up to our ass in mead. That's all that counts."

"Well, about my wife . . ." Michael shifted uncomfortably. "I'm going to have to go down there this weekend. I haven't been home in nearly a month."

"Go go!" Gerry urged. "I don't want to have your guilt on my conscience. "Go!" She slithered on top of him, toes touching. "But not quite yet."

Silently, they began wrestling in a broth of bubbles, hot water and honey wine, their bodies sleek and primed, playing a wordless game of desire and withdrawal.

It was delicious lying there, his teasing hands idling over her flesh, entering into her, retreating and returning. Gradually she tensed, wanting more of him inside her.

"Take me," Gerry said, locking her thighs about him.

"Make me," he replied, then ducked his head beneath

the surface and held his breath for what seemed an unconscionable time.

"Michael!" Gerry was momentarily alarmed, but after a
few seconds he swallowed and emerged spewing out a
mouth full of bubbles.

"Well, I've done it." He laughed and pulled her to him.
"I drank your goddam bathwater."

Gerry kissed him. "For a moment there, I thought you
were in over your head."

"I probably am," he said. "So let's make love."

That night he took her out to dinner at Le Bernardin.

"Avesian," he told the maître d.' "We have a reservation.
I've ordered our dinner in advance."

They were led to table where two martinis awaited, crisp
and cold. Hers was in a tumbler.

"I don't take ice in mine," she remarked, but Michael
smiled. "This happens to be a very special martini. Take a
sip, darling. I guarantee you'll enjoy it."

She tilted her drink, touched it to her lips, then put it
down with a squeal of delight.

"Why Michael! What on earth have you done!"

Gerry reached into the tumbler and fished out the "ice".
It was a bracelet of *pavé* diamonds.

"My God!" She examined the plunder. "It's absolutely
gorgeous. But I couldn't take it. Honestly, darling. I never
accept expensive presents from men, nothing more expensive than a small memento. It's a life-long policy. I'm sorry."
Reluctantly she put it down. Michael picked it up.

"This one you'll accept," he said.

"It's much too pricey," she protested. "I'm frightfully
touched, Michael, but I couldn't keep it. Please, darling,
take it back to Cartier's or wherever."

"I can't. I had it custom-made. Look, Gerry." He twisted
the bracelet until it caught the light. Then she saw that
both their initials had been worked into the *pavé* surface
with tiny rounded chips of white diamonds. It was craft-
manship of an exquisite, painstaking order.

"Accept it," Michael urged in a low voice, "or else I'll
leave it for the waiter as a tip."

266

"Would you really?" she started to ask, then checked herself for she knew he would. That was what fascinated her about Michael. His recklessness, his feeling for the grand gesture.

Gerry closed her eyes and nodded her consent.

"But first," Michael said, "I want you to take off all those silver bangles of yours. Take them and stow them out of my sight. Because I don't want you mixing me up with any of your other lovers. We're like no one else, you and I. And what we have must be absolutely unique."

"Which doesn't mean you own me," Gerry said with her last vestige of caution. "No one has ever owned me, Michael."

"It means I love you, that's all."

"On that condition . . ."

One by one she worked off the line of silver bracelets and with them, their memories. Then she dropped the lot into her bag and snapped it shut.

Michael took the diamond circlet and fitted it about her wrist.

It shone there, solitary, dazzling, commanding, as Gerry flooded with joy.

It scarcely occurred to her that Michael Avesian wasn't the only one in over his head.

seven

Like her own mother before her, Sandra McKay Avesian was thrifty, loyal, sober, selfless. Her family's comfort was her sole concern.

Sandy came by these attitudes naturally. In her parents' home, Father knew best. Harry McKay was a pharmacist, a man of strong if eccentric opinions, accustomed to being treated with deference by those near and dear. His wife believed it her duty to oblige, reminding one and all that her husband was "a professional man".

"Never contradict your husband," Hilda McKay instructed her daughter. "It's the first law of a successful marriage."

Her second precept for marital bliss was "always be cheerful".

Her third was to have a hot meal on the table every night.

Sandy had absorbed this wisdom early and struggled to live up to its lofty demands. It wasn't easy. A complaisant wife in most matters, she displayed a stubborn streak when her security was threatened. And Michael's latest venture was the most serious threat so far.

She had stuck with him through the mongoose farm, the Spanish galleon nightmare, had dragged from one unwholesome place to another. But with Hailsham Castle he had overstepped the bounds. Sandy was convinced he was headed for bankruptcy. Easy come, easy go. Any day now, they could be out on the street. The prospect filled her with terror.

Why couldn't Michael settle down like other men? Get a nine-to-five job in an office? If God had meant her husband to own a castle, He would have made him a duke.

For her part, Sandy had no wish to play the duchess, cut a swath. The boldest act of her life thus far had been her decision to marry Michael, whom her father insisted on calling "the greenhorn's son" and "that college drop-out of yours".

"You're marrying down," he warned her, but Sandra couldn't be budged. She worshipped the ground Michael walked on.

Over the years, an uneasy truce had grown up between the two men. Occasionally they went to ball games together. Yet though the "greenhorn's son" could now buy his father-in-law twenty times over, the pharmacist continued to view Michael with disdain.

"Your husband should be here with you instead of 'hooring' around New York," Harry McKay had announced the previous week at dinner and Sandy had quailed. He was only voicing her worst fears.

"Mikey doesn't fool around," she reflexively flew to his defence.

"Three weeks a man doesn't come see his children . . ." her father grumbled, then shrugged as though to say: Immigrants, what can you expect?

Sandy's eyes welled and she looked to her mother for some sort of moral support, but Hilda McKay just shook her head and echoed her husband's sentiments. "Three weeks is an awfully long time . . ."

And Sandy bowed her head in shame.

It never dawned on her that her father was a petty tyrant or her mother a dishrag. She believed in the natural superiority of men.

And if Michael was really "hooring around", then it behoved Sandy to triple her efforts to please. She was a good wife, a wonderful wife. Two beautiful babies and she still kept her figure, "the best little bod in Roosevelt High". She knew her duty. Make your home and person attractive enough and a husband has no reason to stray.

The house looked terrific: two million dollars' worth of centrehall colonial in the nicest suburb. Immaculate. Comfortable. With a heated swimming pool out back and a wet-bar in the basement. And a "media room". And a helicopter pad. What sensible person wouldn't prefer these amenities to a claustrophobic high rise in Manhattan?

She had but to make herself as appealing as her surroundings.

When Michael announced he was coming for the weekend, she headed first to the hair-dresser, then to Hecht's
department store.

"*Trend Magazine* says Lace is the Latest,"she quoted a
fashion spread, "so I guess that's what I want." But where
Trend had decreed see-through lace coupled with spicy
black-leather minis, Sandy deemed it unnecessary to go so
far. Nothing drastic. She preferred a look in keeping with
suburban mores.

"Now that's pretty!" She seized upon a pristine white
blouse with a huge lace jabot. "What d'you think?" she
asked the saleswoman.

"Very youthful," was the reply.

Sandy nodded and allowed herself a moment's vanity.
"You know I look almost the same as the day I graduated
high school. You wouldn't guess I'm the mother of two."

She was wearing the blouse tonight over a tartan skirt, in
honour of her husband's return.

Thus far, all had gone well. In the afternoon, Michael
had taken the girls to a movie, treated them to waffles at
Friendly's, played a rousing game of Monopoly in which
he'd actually let Natasha win, then tucked them into bed.

Now Sandy and her husband could sit down to that
hot dinner that constituted her mother's Precept Number
Three.

"Brunswick stew, baking powder biscuits, green beans
with almonds and butternut squash. I thought it would be
nice if we ate in the dining room by candlelight. Real
romantic, Mikey, don't you think?"

He gazed at her pensively.

"You know, you're the only one who still calls me Mikey.
I'm Michael to everyone in New York. It's a bit more dignified."

She smiled. "To me, you'll always be that cute Mikey
Avesian . . ."

". . . the dry cleaner's son," he finished the sentence.

She giggled and led the way to the dining room, feeling

270

festive, but Michael's mood refused to catch fire. The table looked lovely.

"I made the squash just the way you like it, Mikey, drizzled with honey and brown sugar on top. And I bet you don't get Brunswick stew in New York."

She served him a helping of everything and then sat down and waited for him to eat. He was staring down at the honey-glazed squash. Poor man, she thought. He radiated tension. It must have been a very hard week.

"Eat, eat," she urged, for he was pushing the food around on his plate with a fork. Their eyes met briefly.

"Have you ever had honey wine?" he asked.

"I didn't know there was such a thing," she said. "Is that what you want? If you like, I can call up the liquor store and send for some. Bernie's delivers up to nine o'clock. Or maybe Pierlucci's over in Glen Ridge. They have a bigger variety, especially in fancy wines. You want me to call . . . ?"

"I just mentioned it, Sandy. I didn't say I liked the stuff."

Michael reached for a roll. She watched him with anxious eyes.

"Oh Lordy!" she suddenly leaped up. "I forgot the butter. Forgive me, sweetie. I'll get it right away."

"For Chrissakes, Sandy, will you stop jumping up and down? It makes me nervous."

"But I never forget the butter . . ."

"Fuck the butter!" he shouted, then suddenly quietened. "I'm sorry. I didn't mean to yell."

At that moment, Sandy blinked back tears and tried to to observe Precept Number Two. Be cheerful. But how the hell could she be cheerful when her husband was so tense?

She forced a smile. "Anyhow, butter's supposed to be bad for you, isn't it?"

They ate for a while in silence.

"You're still the greatest cook in the whole Chesapeake Bay area, Sandy," he said politely, but she could see his thoughts were elsewhere. For all that talk of honey, he hadn't touched his squash.

Then he folded his hands on the table and studied her thoughtfully. "Is that a new blouse?" he asked.

"You like it?"

"Jesus, it must have ten square miles of lace."

Her face fell. "You don't like it!"

"I like it, Sandy. It's pretty. A little on the girlish side, but pretty. I'm glad to see you buying clothes. Enjoy the money. That's what it's there for. If you don't mind, I'll take coffee in the den. I have a lot of work to catch up on."

"Take coffee." What an odd phrase. To Sandy's ears, it sounded like an affectation. Where they came from, you didn't "take" coffee. You "took" medicine. Coffee you drank or you had. Maybe they spoke the language differently in New York.

He worked till two and when he came up to bed, it was on tiptoes. He didn't even switch on the light.

"Honey lamb?" she snuggled up to him the moment he hit the sheets, but Michael yawned and pecked her cheek.

"Not tonight, Sandy. Do you mind? I'm totally wiped out."

He stayed until Sunday night, making an effort to be chatty and interested, but she had the feeling he was aching to get away. It wasn't until he got into the helicopter and waved goodbye that she managed to put her finger on what was wrong.

Not once – for the first time since he set up in New York – did Michael plead with her to come and join him.

Should she be relieved, she wondered; or panic-stricken?

eight

"I really must go down there once a week," Michael told Gerry. "My kids hardly hardly recognize me."

Gerry was all sympathy.

"No explanations necessary, darling. We're both grown ups. And I'm not the possessive type, as you well know."

Yet despite her insistence that they were responsible, worldly, intelligent people, she hated every moment away from him.

It wasn't as though they had forever. Gerry recognized the transient nature of such affairs. Soon the music would end, and at the back of her mind was her impending marriage. What to do?

Campbell's retirement was only a few months off and he was busy with plans, ranging from guest lists to a "honeymoon in paradise".

Only yesterday, he had called her at the office to tell her that he had rented a villa and chartered a yacht. "No, I won't say where. It'll be a surprise. Now about the wedding invitations, I'm waiting for your list. And when can I put the announcement in *The Times*?"

November, she began – then corrected herself. November was unbearably close. Well, at any rate by year's end, this madness with Michael would have run its course.

"Let's wait till Christmas and send out the invitations along with the usual greetings. You have my word, Campbell. Everything will be settled by Christmas."

Logic dictated that she begin making plans of her own, at least concerning her business. It ought to be put on the block, although outside of some bits of office furniture, all she had to sell was "goodwill". Such a vague commodity, so hard to put a price tag on. For all she knew it might be worthless. Could there be, after all, an O'Neal Associates without a Geraldine O'Neal?

And vice versa?

The question made her pause.

For try as she might, it was nigh impossible to picture life without a job, an office, a place to go each morning. Without money of her own to jingle. She had never been dependent on any man and, with due respect to Campbell's largesse, couldn't envision herself asking for handouts. How other women did it, she'd never know.

Financial independence had always meant so much.

At least, Gerry consoled herself, she would continue to enjoy her trusteeship of Larry Winterbourne's inheritance. True, the fee was less than handsome. But if she could hardly endow universities with the proceeds, it was sufficient for buying *chotchkes* at Harrods. She could survive.

The following weekend, when Michael returned to Maryland, Gerry found herself with time on her hands. She spent the morning culling her closets. By late afternoon she had sorted the no-longer-wearables into separate piles on her bed. The good things would go to Encore on consignment for resale. The not-so-good to Irvington Thrift Shop for the tax deduction. Some sensible knitwear for her cleaning woman, Ida. Then a separate stack she couldn't make up her mind about. Save or scrap?

The Perry Ellis coat, for instance – a slouchy beige cashmere with gilt buttons. Gerry couldn't recall why she'd bought it in the first place. Beguiled by a fashion spread, no doubt, or was it wishful thinking? The style was far too youthful, the colour more suited to a perky blonde.

It would look terrific on Lee Whitfield.

Gerry felt a swift stab of conscience. These past weeks she'd been so wrapped up in her affairs, she'd scarcely given her protégée a thought. By now, Gerry presumed, Lee would have recovered from her crush on Michael and be back to business as usual.

So! Lee would have the coat. Plus all the right accessories. It would be a wonderful way to make up for these weeks of inattention. With gusto, Gerry began plundering her dressing room for the perfect scarf, costume jewellery, a rakish Italian felt hat. She arranged the ensemble on a chair and surveyed it with satisfaction. Stunning. Then she reached for the phone, feeling good.

"Hello stranger," she said. "Will you accept an abject apology from someone who's been neglecting you woefully and come around for dinner? Anyhow, I've got a whole evening clear and I'm dying to hear what you've been up to. So drop everything and head right over. I'll send out to Pig Heaven for Chinese. And by the way, Lee, don't let me forget – I've got a special surprise for you."

From the moment Lee walked in the door, Gerry sensed the shift in mood. Gone was Lee's usual ebullience, her cheerful trusting chatter. In its place was a sullen reluctance to be forthcoming about anything other than the weather.

While Lee picked at her ribs, Gerry asked the expected questions to be rewarded with monosyllabic answers.

How was the Port Authority? The pits.

The big story? OK.

The new apartment? Not bad.

Your parents? Fine.

Could it be, Gerry wondered, that Lee was still hurting over the "loss" of Michael? But that was ridiculous. There had been nothing between them, *ergo* there had been no loss. It was unlike Lee to be so petulant.

"How's your love life these days?" Gerry prodded, her antenna on alert.

Lee shrugged.

"You seeing anyone special?"

"No one you know."

"Perhaps someone I'd like to know," Gerry said. "You might want to bring your young man around some evening and I'll look him over."

Lee shot her a baleful glance.

"What's this wonderful surprise you have for me?" she asked.

"It's in my bedroom."

"Where else!" Lee muttered which struck Gerry as a snide remark, but she didn't care to make an issue of it. Life was too short, too happy to waste time in needless confrontations. She would cajole Lee into a cheerier mood.

Dinner over, the two woman trooped upstairs to the bedroom and Gerry held up the coat with a flourish.

"Gorgeous, *n'est-ce pas*? Perry Ellis. From the days when Perry Ellis was Perry Ellis. I don't think I've ever worn it. Now slip it on while we consider the effect. Ah! scrumptious. Casual, but sexy. I'm green with envy."

"It's too long."

"That's what tailors are for, darling. The important thing is it fits beautifully through the shoulders. And you look terrific in that slouchy cut. Now . . ."

Gerry began fiddling with the scarf ("that's a Hermes, I'll have you know!"), adjusting the collar to the proper roguish angle, expressing second thoughts about the hat. Then she stood back to admire her handiwork.

"Like a page out of *Vogue!*" she said approvingly. "Come, look at yourself in the pier glass mirror. You need to see it full length to really appreciate it. There, darling! What you think?"

But in the mirror, Lee's cool eyes were on Gerry, not the coat. Her face was expressionless.

"Feel the fabric," Gerry insisted. "A hundred per cent pure cashmere." She stroked the silky sleeve with her thumb, a tender fondling gesture, but Lee might have been made of stone.

Exasperated, Gerry turned away.

"Take it or don't take it, as you please. I have no intention of forcing it on you. It happens to be a three thousand dollar designer coat and it suits you to a T. However, if you don't want it, I'm sure I can find somebody who does. Someone whose vocabulary includes the word 'Thanks'."

Lee took off the coat, folded it and replaced it on the chair.

"I don't wear cast-offs, Gerry."

"Cast-offs!" The older woman sat down on the bed and crossed her arms. "What gall! You've been boorish all evening, Lee. I think I'm entitled to an explanation. Probably an apology as well. That crack, for instance, about my bedroom. What was that supposed to mean? What the hell did you expect to find?"

Lee bit her lips. She was making a visible effort to maintain control.

"Michael Avesian," she said.

"You're kidding!"

"I thought Michael was your big surprise."

"Oh for God's sakes!" Gerry flushed. "What a ridiculous notion. Michael indeed! He's a client. We have dinner now and then . . ."

"He's a sleazeball. A man I should have nothing to do with, right? You shafted me, Gerry. You deliberately shipped me off to the Port Authority with a bunch of lies and half-truths just so you could have a clear field. How dumb do you think I am? Obviously, dumb enough to believe everything you said at the time. Why not? You were my ideal, my mentor. It never dawned on me that you had ulterior motives. I honestly thought it was for the good of my career."

"And so it was," Gerry broke in. "You seem to have some idiotic idea that I've – what? taken Michael away from you. Absolute rubbish. He was never yours in the first place. In the second place, even if he was, you ought to have enough sense to guard your own interests. And in the third place, you've jumped to an erroneous conclusion. Michael and I are friends . . ."

"Bullshit! I've seen you together."

"Where?" Gerry snapped.

"What does it matter where? I'm not blind. I've seen the way you look at him, the way you touch each other. It's disgusting. You're lovers. Do you deny it? Why can't you be honest, for once?"

Gerry rose and swept past Lee.

"I don't have to deny or confirm anything, thank you very much. I find your behaviour offensive."

Lee followed her down the staircase, yelling after her in grief and pain.

"Why did you do it, Gerry? What did you have to prove? That you were – what? prettier, sexier than I am? Jesus! Don't you ever stop being competitive? I worshipped you, Gerry. Was this my reward?"

At the foot of the stairs, Gerry whipped around to face this unexpected adversary. Then suddenly she melted. Perhaps it was the thought of losing what had hitherto been the Number One Member of her fan club, distaff side. Besides, she had a genuine affection for Lee.

"How quickly I've fallen from grace," she remarked wryly. "*Sic transit Geraldine*. Now, like it or not, I'm going to give you another lesson in the way of the world. If you're wise, you'll heed me. At the least, you'll hear me out."

Lee grimaced.

"Stop acting like an outraged wife," Gerry continued. "That's my advice. It's a waste of time and emotional energy. I'm sorry your ego got bruised along the way and I realize you feel you've been swindled. But you haven't been, not really. You had no claims on Michael. It's time you recognized that we don't always get what we want in this world. That, my dear, is part of the pain of growing up. Put it behind you and move on. Whatever relation exists between Michael and me is quite immaterial and I trust you'll be discreet enough to keep your suspicions to yourself . . ."

"Who would I tell?" Lee blurted.

"Precisely," Gerry replied, aware that what she had said was tantamount to an admission. In Lee's eyes, there was a flash of acknowledgement. The girl had a reporter's nose for facts.

But Gerry hadn't finished. "I want to assure you that everything I told you that day – about Michael, about the assignment – was absolutely in your best interests. I'd say the same thing again. Major careers don't come without a price tag. I should know. You'll do yourself a helluva lot more credit with the pan-handling story than you will mooning after Michael Avesian. When you're rich and famous, you'll probably thank me. Now why don't you pop into the kitchen and brew us some coffee and we'll forget this whole wretched conversation. About the coat, Lee . . . I have a little Polish woman who does marvellous alterations. That'll be my gift."

Gerry settled in the living room, nibbled her nails, and prayed Michael wouldn't call while Lee was there. The situation was patent; still, she had no desire to rub it in.

Lee took an unconscionable time about getting the coffee and when she returned, her mood was quixotic.

"I've been thinking . . ." she said.

"Always a bad idea," Gerry jollied.

"Don't try to deflect me. I have to say what I feel. Didn't you once say that was the curse of my generation, we didn't know when to shut up?"

"Good lord," Gerry groaned. "Give up on Michael already."

"I have given up," Lee returned. "It's not Michael who's hurt me so. It's you. You preach one thing and do another. Your advice was so terrific, but you didn't take it yourself. You were right, Gerry. Michael *is* a manipulator. A user. He used me. And now he's using you. And you're letting him do it. It sticks in my craw, Gerry. I can't bear to see the woman I admire most in the world making an utter fool of herself. Is that the so-called passion you once talked to me about? Bullshit! It's nothing but self-indulgence. You think you can get away with everything, don't you – including the most outrageous behaviour. Passion! for Chrissakes! – " the words ripped out of her " – You're behaving like a goddam teenager – at your age. Where's your dignity? Your judgement? For shame, Gerry! You're old enough to be his mother!"

"But I'm not his mother!" Gerry spat out. "And you're not mine! Who the fuck do you think you are, Lee? The Commissar of Public Morality? The Jerry Falwell of the Upper East Side? How dare you speak to me like that! However, for your information, this superannuated 'teen-ager' happens to be madly in love with Michael – an emotion you clearly have trouble grasping – just as he's in love with me. And if you don't like it, that's too damn bad."

"No, I don't like it," Lee retorted. Now that the flood-gates had broken, she could no longer contain the gush of words. She had been brooding on nothing but the past weeks. "Michael doesn't matter to me, not any more. It was an attraction, that's all. But you! You're the one I'm concerned about. Madly in love! How can you say such things? You're in your fifties, for Chrissakes. Don't you

279

care that you'll be a laughing-stock once this gets around? That is, presuming it's not common gossip already. Do you know what people will think when they see you hanging on his arm? 'No fool like an old fool.' That's what they'll think, that's what they'll say. I can't stand by and watch it. I respect you too much. Give him up, Gerry. Do the right thing for me, if not for yourself."

Gerry's eyes were blazing, her body tense with rage.

"You honestly think if it came to a choice between you and Michael, I'd choose you? No fool like a *young* fool, I daresay. Now that you've done what you consider your public duty, just go and leave me in peace. You've caused quite enough aggravation for one day."

But Lee wasn't done.

"He's using you," Lee burst out. "He's exploiting your fame, your connections. It's the oldest scenario in the world. Ambitious young man. Powerful older woman. Do you think he really cares for you? How blind can you be!"

There was a long, terrible hush, then Gerry pulled herself up to her full height. She loomed over Lee.

"So Michael Avesian is using me." Her voice was low, vitriolic. She was in full control. "My . . . my . . . my! How shocking! And what about you?"

Lee blanched. She sensed what was coming, but it was too late. There was no recourse as Gerry steamrollered over her.

"I wouldn't talk about exploitation if I were you, Lee. You've used me from the moment you first stepped into this house. You've eaten my food, enjoyed my hospitality, milked my contacts. I've given you everything from story ideas to jewellery to unlisted phone numbers. Tell me, when I offered you these goodies, did you ever once say no? Let's face it, Lee. You're at least as much a user as Michael." She snorted. "How the hell do you think you got the job on *Trend Magazine*? Because you were the hottest shottest writer that ever walked into Fletch Birnbaum's office? Balls! He could have had a dozen like you! The streets are teeming with so-called talent, and most of it interchangeable. Fletch was under orders. He would have hired you if you'd been a functional illiterate. You got that

280

job for one reason only: because I pulled strings with Bobby Obermayer. And don't you forget it. Why, if not for me, pal, you'd still be covering weddings for the society page of the *East Jeezus Gazette*, or whatever the fuck it was. Now you've had your say and I've had mine. I give you twenty seconds to get out."

Lee grabbed her bag and ran to the door. Then she turned.

"You'll regret this, Gerry. Mark my words."

"Get out," Gerry snarled, "before I call the police!"

Lee left with a slam of the door.

"Good riddance," Gerry yelled, but a scant minute later, she had burst into tears.

"I don't need this," she sobbed.

It had been one of the ugliest scenes in memory, all the nastier because, wittingly or not, Lee had given voice to her darkest fears. Maybe she was an old fool, reckless, romantic, wagering her last penny of emotional capital on a love as brief as it was incandescent.

Was it worth it? Yes . . . no . . . maybe. Edna St Vincent Millay's haunting quatrain came to mind.

My candle burns at both ends,
It will not last the night.
But ah, my foes and oh, my friends,
It gives a lovely light.

She thought of Michael – his smile, his warmth, his touch. Of the pleasures, no matter how fleeting, that marked their hours together. Yes, it was worth it.

She switched on the answering machine to screen out unwelcome callers, then went upstairs and waited for Michael to phone.

Sandy couldn't sleep. How could she sleep when her marriage was in jeopardy? Not that Michael had said a word, but his preoccupation was almost tangible. It differed from his usual absorption with business. When business problems troubled him, he had a distinctive pattern, marked by lip-chewing, frequent references to a pocket calculator

281

and a tendency to doodle on all writeable surfaces from wallpaper to cereal boxes.

But this recent mooniness was decidedly atypical. That very afternoon, she'd caught him singing to himself – something he hadn't done since they were engaged.

"What's that tune?" she asked.

He stopped abruptly. "It's from some opera or other."

"Since when are you an opera buff, Mikey?"

It was an innocent question, but Michael's response was to fold his arms and inspect her as though she were an insect under glass. Then he tugged at his ear, a sure sign of stress.

"There's more to life than Stevie Wonder, Sandy. Maybe you ought to subscribe to a few local cultural events. Go to a museum now and then. Enlarge your horizons. It would get you out of yourself."

But Sandy didn't want to get out of herself. All she wanted was her husband back home.

"Who's enlarging your horizons?" she was tempted to ask.

Throughout dinner, she brooded about confronting him point-blank, but couldn't muster up the nerve.

If he said yes, that he was having an affair, what could Sandy do without provoking a scene? And if he said no – well, what did that prove? To quote her mother: least said, soonest mended.

Although if *Dynasty* was any indication as to the behaviour of tycoons, they lied to their wives all the time. She decided not to put the axiom to the test. Besides her husband wasn't a "real" tycoon. He was her Mikey.

They had spent the evening in the old neighbourhood playing poker at her cousin Dedee's house. Sandy was an excellent card player and, even at nickel-dime stakes, had managed to clear over forty dollars.

"I think I'll retire," Michael kidded graciously while she cashed in her chips, "and let Sandy support me on her ill-gotten gains. The little lady's got a mind like a calculator."

Sandy flushed with pleasure. Tim and Dedee dutifully laughed, and by the time they got home, she was feeling more cheerful.

"Let's go to bed, Mikey. It's past midnight."

"You go, honey, I feel like watching *Saturday Night Live*."

Her eyes welled. "You can watch it in the bedroom. Please, sweetie pants. I don't want to go to bed alone."

"I didn't want to disturb you, that's all."

They got into bed. Michael pecked her on the cheek and put on ear-phones. "No point in keeping you up," he said.

It was a totally isolating act. With that one gesture, he had effectively shut her out, plugged himself into some other frequency. For all the intimacy between them, he might as well have stayed in the den. After a while, Sandy fell asleep.

She couldn't say what woke her. Second sight? Sixth sense? Something called "woman's intuition"?

Whatever, she awoke with a start to discover he was no longer by her side. She checked the clock. Almost three in the morning. Her heart began to race. Yet some innate caution restrained her from calling out. She tiptoed to the door.

The light was on in the the den and from the top of the stairs, she could just make out the hum of Michael's voice on the phone.

At three in the morning!

Sandy broke into a cold sweat. Suppose he should step out and find her spying on him? He would be furious. She wasn't ready for that kind of scene.

Instead, she scurried back to bed, pretending to sleep. It was another half hour before he returned. He crawled in beside her, taking the utmost pains to be stealthy. A minute later, he was sound asleep.

She waited in torment for what seemed to be an eternity. Ten minutes, twenty minutes, pulse pumping, mind whirring with possibilities.

At last she drummed up her nerve. "Mikey?" she whispered. There was no response. He was dead to the world.

Carefully, she made her way downstairs in the dark, silent as a ghost, then went into the den and picked up the phone.

At the bottom of the instrument was the REDIAL button.

One stroke and it would automatically ring up the last number called.

Sandy pressed the button. A dozen electronic beeps followed. Then the phone began ringing in some distant unknown room. Sandy wet her lips. What would she say if someone answered? Was it sufficient to know that there was another woman? Would she dare ask who it was?

Then a click, and a recorded voice came on, low and sexy.

"This is Geraldine O'Neal. I'm sorry I'm unable to take your call at this time but if you'll leave your name, number and the time that you phoned, I'll get back to you as soon as possible."

Sandy replaced the telephone cradle and crept back up as quietly as she had descended.

He was leaving early the next day. "Business," he claimed, too self-absorbed to notice Sandy's stricken face. As he was about to step into the 'copter, she ran out of the house after him.

"Wait! Don't go yet! I've been thinking, Mikey, and if that's what you really want I'll do it! I'll take the kids out of school and move to New York."

He wheeled around, his eyes flashing with annoyance.

"The supreme sacrifice, eh?"

"Please," she clutched at his jacket. "Don't be sarcastic. I don't know what more you want from me. I'm willing to uproot myself. To go where you go. I'll cook. I'll clean, I'll make a proper home for you. I'll be the best little wife in the world! We could have such great times together, just like when we were first married."

Michael looked at her thoughtfully.

"Did we have such great times together? I don't know any more, Sandy. We've grown into different kinds of people, we lead different kinds of lives. As far as your moving to New York, you were right all along. I very much doubt that you'd be happy there. The pace is too frantic. And even if you did come up, we wouldn't get to see much more of each other than we do now. I put in very long days . . ."

"And nights?" she broke in. "What about nights?"

He gazed at her evenly, perhaps waiting for her to bring the issue out into the open, then gently plucked her hand from his sleeve.

"I have to run, Sandy. Anyhow, this is neither the time nor the place. I'll call you from the city tonight."

Her voice trembled. "You can't wait to get out of here, can you! You begrudge every second you spend with your family."

She thought she saw a tear glisten in his eye.

"Mikey . . . stay!" If she could, she would have held him by force.

"I'm sorry, Sandra. It can't be done."

She spent the next several days wandering about the house in a state of shock. How could it be? Michael and this ancient glamour girl – this Geraldine O'Neal! Where was his judgement?

She would look at herself in the mirror. "I'm young," she assured her image. "And still cute."

How could Michael prefer an older woman's embraces to her own? It was incredible. Insulting.

He phoned later in the week to say he couldn't make it down on Friday. "Press of business," he said.

And something within her snapped.

The Monday after her showdown with Gerry, Lee approached Fletch in his office.

"I've an idea for a story that I want to run past you," she told him. "A personality feature. A sort of exposé."

"Yeah? Who?"

"Geraldine O'Neal. I know an awful lot of behind-the-scenes stuff about her. About her life as a show girl. How she conned her way into the newspaper business. Lovers . . . scandals . . . the real inside poop."

Fletch cocked his head. "How'd you get to know so much, Lee?"

"We're friends."

His lip curled. "If that's what you do for your friends, I won't even ask about your enemies."

"Would you consider it?"

"I already have, for about two seconds. Forget O'Neal. Who gives a damn what the old bird's been up to? She's history, hasn't made headlines in years. Now if she were to marry the Pope or do something funsy. . . . Meanwhile, when am I going to see the panhandling stuff?"

"Soon, Fletch. Soon. I'm working on it."

Lee went back to her desk in an emotional quandary.

That had been a trial balloon. But suppose Fletch had said yes. Could she have written the story, bared Gerry's flesh for all to see? Even after that ghastly scene on Saturday, she could scarcely picture life in New York without her. She wasn't ready to go out in the cold.

Gerry had a fierce quick temper, but she could be forgiving, too. Perhaps Lee had been too rash and when this all blew over, she'd be invited back to the inner sanctum.

On reflection, she felt relieved that Fletch had turned down her proposal. It had been a quick cheap shot, not even a major story. Not worth sacrificing the relationship for. Practically speaking, the relationship was worth more than the exclusive.

But suppose it had been the other way around? Did Lee have the requisite steel to deliver the stab in the back? She wasn't sure. A good journalist certainly would. Toughness was a virtue, not a vice.

And as Gerry was fond of saying, "the wonderful world of media" was no place for marshmallows.

That same morning, Gerry arrived in her office and informed her secretary that "under no circumstances" was she to put calls through from Miss Whitfield. "Ever ever ever!"

Sharon Lapidus nodded. She knew better than to ask for explanations, none of which would be forthcoming anyhow.

"Now get me Jake Matthews on the phone."

nine

Sir Campbell Simms had every reason to feel pleased. He had come to London for the weekend to inspect his flat in the Albert Mansions. Morag had done a splendid job with the decor.

Liberty silks in the drawing room, Laura Ashley in the bedrooms, the long dark halls now asparkle with fresh paint. In the library, his old leather sofa had mysteriously vanished to be replaced with a pair of graceful Sheraton chairs. The place positively glittered.

He posed, for a moment, before the new pier glass mirror in the dressing room, pulled himself erect, and ran a hand through his thinning hair.

Then he smothered a grin. "Do you think I'm 'a fine figure of a man'?" he asked his daughter, who laughed.

"Why, is that what she told you? Yes, you're a fine figure and I can see your fiancée has a way with compliments. More important – do you think she'll like the drapes?"

"How could she not? Although I must say, two thousand pounds for a few curtains does seem a bit dear."

"Now stop sounding so Scottish," she scolded. "Money spent on fine things is never wasted. Besides, you only get married once or twice."

"Miss my old sofa, though," he grumbled more for form's sake than out of discontent. "Where'll I take my afternoon nap?"

"From what I hear of your Geraldine O'Neal, you won't be napping in the afternoons. You'll be having the time of your life."

Campbell looked positively sheepish.

"You are happy about my remarrying, aren't you, darling?"

His daughter turned serious. "Almost as happy as you are. Everybody says you look like a schoolboy these days. I can hardly wait to meet the next Lady Simms. What should I call her, by the way?"

"Gerry. She's not the type who stands on formality."

Father and daughter spent the rest of the afternoon going through address books, drawing up lists, discussing caterers. Morag made an efficient major-domo.

"Well, that's the lot," he said, handing her the finished check-list, "if you don't mind handling the mechanics. One more thing, do you think it's too late to get a season's subscription to Covent Garden? Gerry's a fierce opera fan."

"I'll do my best," she promised.

He marched off to his elegant new dressing room to change for dinner at the Reform Club before returning to Bonn in the morning.

"A bit of an occasion," the Minister had said when he tendered the invitation. "Just a few old friends to help commiserate with you on the impending loss of your freedom. Thirty or forty of us at most. Unfortunately, the PM can't make it. It's what one might call a bachelor party!"

Sir Campbell adjusted his bow tie, brushed an invisible bit of lint from his dinner jacket and rechecked himself in the mirror. By God, if Gerry wasn't right. He did cut rather a fine figure.

He left the house whistling a tune from *Rigoletto*. There wasn't a happier man in London that night.

Anna Benson loved banking.

Let others paint pictures or write novels. As a lending officer of Mercantile Trust, she expressed her creativity by "making something out of nothing".

Which was not literally true of course. For while the "somethings" varied (they might be new businesses or new products), the "nothing" of which they were made was money. The bank's money, to be sure, but Anna was the channel that put Mercantile's funds to optimum use.

Tall and attractive, with soft honey-blonde hair and a Harvard MBA, she made an excellent spokeswoman both for Mercantile and for the community of women bankers in general.

"A banker is like a mother," she once addressed an assembly at Smith in a recruitment speech. "She brings the new-born enterprise into the world, feeds it, nurtures it, keep it out of mischief until at last it's a full-grown member of the business community. I think of each client as my baby. And like any other parent, I take enormous satisfaction in the growing health and wealth of my offspring. Besides," she added, "it's fun!"

And sometimes it was.

There was a belief in the upper echelons of Wall Street that men operated on facts whereas women trusted to instincts. In Anna's experience, the opposite was true. It was men, by and large, who embarked on flights of faith and risked failure, while women, ever mindful of being relative newcomers to the turf, relied on data and common sense.

Anna liked to think she trod a midway path.

She was, simultaneously, firm and feminine. Hard-nosed and daring. Practical and intuitive.

Any banker who had a hundred per cent success rate with loans, who never lost money, never made a doubtful guess, didn't belong in the business, she believed. That banker was taking too few chances. Banks didn't get rich that way. They got moribund. No pain, no gain was as true of lending as of body-building. To Anna, the thrill of banking consisted of seeing opportunity where others saw only risk.

Hailsham Castle, for example.

Several of her colleagues had turned the project down on the grounds of insufficient collateral. But Anna liked it from the start. She saw potential there, a way of turning a dull little corner of New Jersey into a vibrant, money-making attraction.

She liked Michael Avesian, too, and wasn't ashamed to acknowledge (at least to herself) that this liking had figured in her calculations. The man was a born salesman with a splendid track record. Compelling. Personable. Sexy too, which never hurt. And shrewd.

The first time they lunched, the waiter had brought a plate of sweet biscuits with the coffee.

"Madeleines," Michael announced. "I ordered them special."

"How did you know I like madeleines?" she inquired.

"Just a hunch," he grinned. "You seemed the type."

"And what type is that?"

"Extremely elegant, yet rather sweet."

Flattered, Anna laughed and bit into one of the little plump biscuits. It melted on her tongue.

The madeleines were more than a hunch, she realized. Michael had done his homework (or had it done for him, since she didn't think him the bookish type) and had learned that before entering B-school, Anna had been a Lit major with a passion for Proust.

It was a graceful gesture and far from feeling manipulated, Anna was gratified. In the business of selling, that kind of attention to detail never hurt.

And, of course, Michael Avesian had continually to sell himself to Mercantile Trust just as surely as he was selling Hailsham to a host of major merchants.

At each meeting, he pushed Anna to increase his line of credit. "It takes big money to fulfil big dreams," he said, and she agreed. But there was just so much commitment she could make without seeing tangible results. She had her limits, too, and lately Mercantile's Credit Committee had begun giving her flak.

"This guy defaults and what do we have for all our money?" Jack Stallings wanted to know. "A cow patch in Jersey and a fuckin' castle in Spain?"

"In England," she corrected.

"I was speaking metaphorically, Anna. In any case, a pile of crumbling bricks three thousand miles away. I don't like investments I can't drive to on a Saturday morning and see how they're progressing."

"When he moves Hailsham Castle to Jersey, you can see it as often as you wish."

"And when'll that be?"

"They expect to start shipping after the first of the year, and have the place ready for the first tenants by next June."

"Any takers yet?"

"He's working on it, Jack. It'll be a shot in the arm for the local economy. That's what the whole exercise is all about."

"The whole exercise, Anna, is about the bank making money."

Well, yes and no.

Anna had been almost as sanguine as Michael himself about the "vision" of Hailsham. It was a glorious idea. She had wanted to rename it Avalon for it appealed to the romantic in her. As did the man himself. (Why were the great ones always married? she occasionally wondered in an aside.)

But while the passing months had done little to dim Michael's personal lustre, she had begun to have doubts about the project. Progress had been so slow as to be imperceptible. Figures were not always forthcoming. Was it truly Avalon, or had smart sensible Anna Benson bought off on the century's biggest white elephant?

When Michael called on an October morning to ask her for lunch, she had the queasy feeling of a deal gone awry. She suggested the Harvard Club. If the news was bad, she could always go upstairs and cry.

He arrived on the stroke of one looking absurdly handsome. And more confident than ever. She suppressed a sigh of relief.

"This is a very pleasant dining room." Michael gazed about him at the rich wood panelling, the portrait of FDR. "I always think in my next reincarnation I'll go to an Ivy League college and join a decent club. I must say, you're looking marvellously well today, Annie."

She peered at him over her Perrier. He always called her Annie when he wanted something. And he always wanted something – money.

"Does this mean you're going to give me problems?" she asked.

"Nope," he replied with a smile. "I'm going to give you solutions. What would you say if I brought in Austrian's, Fifth Avenue as a primary tenant of the Hailsham development. Twenty thousand square feet leased to the finest name in retailing, practically the entire West Wing. What would you say, Annie?"

"I'd say—" she tried to restrain her excitement. Her

"baby" was taking its first steps "Yippee! Have you done it, Michael? Really locked him up? Simply fabulous."

"Eli's all but signed. Our lawyers have already started drawing up the papers. Of course it'll take a couple of months to iron out all the details, but I'm ironing, I'm ironing . . . !"

They both laughed.

"The thing is, Annie, Eli and I have shaken on it. You realize what this means? With a presence like Austrian's at Hailsham, there'll be a dozen other majors clambering to get aboard. I think it's what they called the domino theory in the Viet Nam War. Once the big one falls, everything else comes tumbling after. In the meanwhile . . ."

"Yes?"

"I want to institute improvements on the Jersey site before winter sets in. Work on the ornamental lake, get the plantings down for the maze, which means – "

"Money money money," Anna broke in.

"That's right," he said with a smile. "Back to the cookie jar. But I tell you, prospects have never looked so rosy. For both of us, Annie. I can't sufficiently stress the importance of Eli's commitment. It's his first venture out of New York."

Anna sighed.

"How much are we talking about?"

He named a figure.

"If it were up to me, Michael, I'd lend you on the come. I've every confidence. But once it's over three million I need blessings from above. And you know what sceptics the guys on the Credit Committee are. Oh they of little faith! They'll insist on seeing something concrete."

"Such as . . . ?"

"Such as Eli Austrian's name on the contract. With all the nice juicy figures filled in. As soon he signs on the dotted line, let me know. Then we can talk bigger bucks. But I have to protect myself too, you understand. Business is business."

Michael nodded sagely. "In the meanwhile, what do you suggest?"

"I'd suggest you keep a sharp eye on expenses . . ."

292

"I meant for lunch." He flashed his wonderful smile. "I'm absolutely starving."

She laughed, relieved that the awkward moment had been bypassed so gracefully.

"You might try the crab cakes. They can be very good here. And lunch is on me, by the way."

"Money money money," Gerry wailed to a sympathetic Jake Matthews. "Don't those leeches from IRS ever let up? I've been on their shit-list for years and once you get on, it's impossible to get off. They tell me I owe a bloody fortune in back taxes . . . Plus penalties, compound interest . . . the works! And they've disallowed practically everything – even my hair-dresser bills. How can I run a snappy PR firm without putting up a certain front, I ask you?"

"What does your accountant say?"

"He says I should see my lawyer. And what does my lawyer say?"

"You should see this Wummer fellow from IRS."

"In person?"

"In person you can be very compelling."

She sighed. "I did actually. A mark of my desperation. I invited him into my parlour. Our Mr Wummer turned out to be a pragmatic young man in a three piece suit with no interest at all in minor flirtations. 'Just the facts, Ma'am', like on that old TV show which you're probably too young to remember. That's all he wanted, love. Just the facts and the goddam figures. Well, Jake," she moaned, "you know how I am about mathematics – hopeless! When I went to school, innumeracy was a matter of pride, at least for girls. We wrote poetry, we didn't do logarithms. To this day, I can't balance a cheque book, with or without a calculator. That's how come I keep so many different accounts."

"How many?"

"Three, four. I forget. With each chequebook in a different colour. The idea is that when one account gets all fouled up, I let it lie fallow and start using another. Then onto a third and so on. That way I don't get overdrawn. The cycle takes about six months. As you can guess, my book-keeping method drove Mr Wummer bananas and I wasn't much help. I used to think it a very clever arrangement, but now I wonder. You see, I don't have the foggiest as to what I've spent or why."

"Gerry!" Jake reproved. "How can you run a business that way?"

"Obviously, not very well which is why I want you to handle this tax muck. I refuse to let it ruffle me. Life's too short. See what kind of deal you can cut and spare me the grizzly details. Leeches," she added gaily, "these auditors are, blood-thirsty leeches sucking you dry. You know my motto: Never trust a man in a three piece suit."

They exchanged affectionate glances, then he said, "You don't look as if anyone's been sucking you dry, Gerry. You look positively blooming. Tax worries aside, I gather life has been good."

She clasped her hands behind her head and beamed.

"Wonderful! Blissful! I can tell you this in confidence, darling. I'm expecting major changes in my life. Major major major . . ."

"You're in love," Jake said.

"Well, of course!"

"That hardly constitutes a major change." Then it dawned on him. "You're actually thinking of getting married."

Gerry, who never blushed, blushed.

"Possibly," she said, "and possibly not. Let's just say that everyone is entitled to one big folly in life. That's my second motto. And I'm enjoying mine. Now let's talk shop. Should I put the agency on the market? More to the point, can I? What d'you think, love?"

He ordered in coffee, dispensed some practical advice, mostly having to do with accounting procedures, after which they gossiped for a bit in the manner of old friends.

When she was ready to leave, Jake walked her to the elevator.

"Now promise me you'll mend your ways," he cautioned. "One personal chequebook. . . . receipts for everything . . . keep a lid on how much you spend on clothes . . ."

294

"OK, boss!" Then she rolled her eyes and laughed. "I sure have pissed away a lot of money in my time on one thing or another."

Jake paused. "Including a fortune on me."

"You've paid me back."

"I could never pay you back."

"Ah, Jake . . ." She looked at him with real love. "That wasn't money pissed away. But enough of this mush. See, you've made my eyes water. Anyhow, call me and let's have lunch one day soon."

He buzzed for the elevator when suddenly she turned to him with an equivocal expression.

"Was there some other matter you wanted to discuss, Gerry?"

For a moment she looked doubtful.

"It's about my Mr Yoshimura . . . You know, the Turnstile King?"

"Yes?"

The elevator door slid open. Inside, people were waiting.

"Some other time, lovey." She blew Jake a kiss and disappeared.

Bemused, Jake stood in the corridor for several minutes after she left. He felt uneasy. He had the distinct impression that Gerry O'Neal warranted some serious looking after – which made for an interesting reversal in their roles.

"Life couldn't be more perfect," she had said with a characteristic hubris, "except for this bloody tax stuff. And what the hell – it's only money."

Jake wished he could be so sanguine. When it came to spinning rose-coloured scenarios, he had the lawyer's scepticism, the black man's wariness. Whereas Gerry was the eternal optimist.

He remembered the time she had flown in from Togo to attend his college graduation. En route, she had stopped off in Paris to pick up an engraved Cartier watch. She handed it to him after the ceremony.

Jacob Matthews, (the engraving read): *Summa cum laude Harvard 1978*

He was touched but also baffled. They hadn't seen each other in nearly a year.

"Who told you I'd be graduating *summa cum laude*?"

"Nobody. No one had to. I know my Jake. I ordered it last Christmas, engraving and all."

"But you couldn't be sure," he argued.

"Stop being such a casuist. Of course I could be sure. You never disappoint." She smiled and linked her arm through his. "Anyhow, you'll always be *summa cum* with me."

Typical Gerry. So certain things were going to work out just as desired, always assuming fate was on her side.

Jake sighed and went back to his office.

He spent the afternoon at his desk, busy with other matters, yet she hovered on the edges of his mind. And when, towards five o'clock, Lee Whitfield phoned, he found himself unsurprised, even though she had never called his office before.

"I need to see you, Jake," she said. "Today if possible."

"Are you in some kind of legal trouble?"

She hesitated. "Not legal. Personal."

They made a date for drinks at the Parker Meridian.

"I'll have a Campari and soda," Lee told the waiter.

"I thought no one drank that stuff but Gerry," Jake remarked.

Lee laughed and made a face.

"On second thought," she said, "bring me a Jack Daniels on the rocks."

She looked leaner and marginally harder since Jake had last seen her the night of Michael Avesian's party. But perhaps, like everyone else in New York, Lee was merely over-worked.

They spent the best half of a drink bandying the requisite small talk before she launched into the matter at hand.

"It's Gerry," she confided. "We've had a rotten row and I'm afraid I'm in her bad books at the moment."

"Oh?" came Jake's non-committal response.

Lee sipped her drink moodily.

"You know about her and Michael Avesian, I presume. Incredible!"

His reply was an ambiguous "hmm".

Of course he knew. Everyone knew, with the possible exception of Mrs Michael Avesian. But Jake had no intention of raking over his client's private life, least of all with a reporter.

He listened patiently as Lee spewed out her version of what sounded like a dormitory cat-fight. Undignified, perhaps, but hardly tragic. Yet Lee was near tears.

"I'm being utterly sincere. What I said was for Gerry's own good. The result: she threw me out of the house!"

"And what exactly did you say."

"That she was making herself ridiculous. Which is true! Act your age, I said. Well, that blew it! Now she won't return my calls, answer my notes. I can't get through to her on any level."

Jake arched an eyebrow. "It sounds like you got through to her all right," he said. "Perhaps too well. But why take it so hard? It'll blow over before long and if it doesn't, I'm sure you have plenty of friends your own age to pick up the social slack."

But Lee, fists clenched, was in no mood to be pacified.

"I've invested a great deal of myself in Gerry," she exclaimed in a burst of rancour. "A very great deal! I thought she had done the same with me. Then boom! All of a sudden I'm a non-person. I don't exist. You don't know what it's like, being shut out! Excluded. What am I – a fucking leper?"

Her spleen startled him. She sounded more like a rejected lover than a leper. Jake refrained from the obvious comment – that he knew a good deal about being shut out. Instead, he tried to defuse her wrath.

"Don't be bitter, Lee," he soothed. "Bitterness is such a destructive emotion. Granted, you've had a bit of a blow to your ego, but you're young, you'll recover. And Gerry's been a very good friend to you. Look back upon the good times. . . ."

"They're precisely what make the bad times unendurable! I can't believe they're over."

Jake sighed. "In which case, I'd advise you to put the whole business behind you and get on with your life."

"That's what everyone says about everything," Lee said broodily. "Like a machine that can turn it on and off. And what about Gerry? Tell me, Jake, aren't you worried about her welfare? This thing with Michael . . . well, it's crazy!"

"You know how the old expression goes. Gerry O'Neal is free . . ." He paused. "White and twenty-one . . ."

"Over twenty-one," Lee broke in. "Way way over!"

". . . and perfectly capable of running her own life. What is it you want from me, anyhow?"

"I want back in the fold. Just put in a good word for me, Jake. Tell her I'm sorry, apologetic and hope to be friends. From you she'll listen."

Jake, thinking of his meeting that very morning full of unheeded advice, could only laugh.

"I'll do my best," he said. "But as for listening – Gerry never really listens to anyone. She'll come round when she's damn good and ready, not before."

Jake paid the bill and saw her into a cab. As far as he was concerned the incident was a tempest in a teapot. Lee didn't know what real heartbreak was.

He did. Gerry did. They had that in common.

As for Lee, her complaint was little more than wounded vanity.

Yet her remark about Gerry's welfare had struck a responsive cord. He was deeply worried about what was going on in Gerry's life. Between Michael Avesian and the IRS, she was steering a course fraught with hazards.

It never occurred to him that Lee herself might pose the ultimate threat.

ten

In the grand ballroom of the Waldorf, the Society of International Lawyers was holding its annual luncheon.

It was the kind of gathering Gerry loved best. Her fellow-diners were accomplished, intelligent, amusing – and predominantly male. She was seated at the head table. On her left was the SIL's incoming president, a distinguished figure fresh from his recent triumph at the Hague. On her right, a former US Attorney General of great age and note, Mr Blagden Geare.

They both agreed she had looked splendid that day. And so she should. Time and money had gone into the effort.

The suit she was wearing had cost a fortune. Armani at his best – a soft tender-to-the-touch woollen in a creamy off-white. White took years off one's face.

Had he known of the expenditure, Jake would have screamed. He was always preaching fiscal prudence. But Jake wasn't here, and far from regretting the purchase, Gerry believed that it was a fortune well spent. Few things gave greater pleasure than feeling beautiful.

Tonight, she'd wear it to the theatre with Michael. In the interim, she basked in her neighbours' praise. In a little while, the after-dinner speeches would begin. Gerry had been up till three in the morning perfecting hers. The press was here, she noted with pleasure. With luck, there might be a picture in the *Economist*.

The waiter came around with ruby port.

"Ah!" She watched him pour some into a crystal glass. "Doesn't that look lovely!"

"Almost as lovely as you," Blagden Geare remarked, pulling out a post-prandial cigar. Cuban, she noticed with a barely suppressed smile. Age not withstanding, the old war horse couldn't resist making a political statement.

"You don't mind my smoking, do you Gerry? People are so churlish nowadays." He began fumbling with a match.

"Quite the contrary, Blagden. Allow me." She lit the

Havana for him. "Personally, I've always found the aroma of cigar smoke delightfully masculine. Just be sure and blow some my way."

The old gentleman beamed.

"You still know how to turn a compliment, my dear. What's your secret, Gerry? Have you found the fountain of youth somewhere?"

She swirled her drink around in the crystal goblet. Such a beautiful colour.

"Ruby port," she said. "Taken after lunch with a friend."

"In that case, I'll have some too. I must say, Gerry, you've scarcely changed since . . . when did I first meet you? At Lyndon's inauguration, wasn't it? In any event, well before you went off to Africa, I believe. Now let me see . . . that was in . . ."

"No dates please, Blagden." She tapped him playfully. "We can't have the guests speculating about how truly ancient we both are. We'd be escorted out in wheelchairs and even worse – they'd take our drinks away."

"But at least we'd be kicking and screaming as they did."

In fact, it was only Blagden who was ancient. Eighty-five, eighty-six, give or take a decade. Still, Gerry was grateful to see that there was life in the old boy yet. Style too. And a healthy disrespect for convention. It made one sanguine about the future.

The waiter refilled her glass. It was an excellent port.

"Leave the decanter here," she said.

Then Blagden put a finger to his lips. "I believe the speechifying is about to begin."

". . . our distinguished Guest of Honour . . ." the master of ceremonies was winding down – "the well-known ambassador, civil libertarian, a national – nay, an international monument – The Honourable Geraldine O'Neal."

Gerry rose and smiled into a tidal wave of clapping hands and uplifted faces. A few feet away, a photographer's flash bulb popped.

She cleared her throat, waiting for the ovation to die down. "Ladies," she began, though there were damn few women present, "and gentlemen." She was vaguely conscious of some scuffling at the back of the hall. "It gives me enormous pleasure to address perhaps the ablest lawyers of the international community."

Her attention was momentarily diverted. A woman with flyaway hair was zig-zagging between the crowded tables with the speed and force of a steel pellet coursing through a pinball machine. She seemed to be moving in the direction of the main table, but with such urgency that Gerry presumed she was *en route* to the Ladies' Room. Some emergency or other, no doubt. Although the food hadn't been *that* bad.

Ignoring the distraction, Gerry continued. "It is a particular privilege for me to be here today since I understand this is the first time your Award for Public Service has been granted to someone outside the legal profession."

There was a clatter of silver, a generalized murmur nearby.

"Speaking to you as a lay person . . ."

But Gerry was not to complete her sentence, for suddenly she found herself confronted by a wild-eyed stranger.

"Bitch!" the disturbed woman screamed.

"Speaking as a lay person . . ." Gerry tried to proceed.

At which point the lunatic picked up the decanter (according to some observers precisely on the word "lay"), and hurled the contents into Gerry's face.

"You stole my husband!" she hissed.

Gerry gasped and reeled back just as the flashbulb popped again.

There was a shocked hush, a collective buzz, then an uproar.

"Stop that woman!" Blagden squeaked in his paper-thin thousand-year-old voice, but the intruder, mission complete, had staged a miraculous escape through the service door to be seen no more that day.

Gerry was the first to recoup her equilibrium.

She mopped her face with a napkin, then holding up her hand for attention, called out in an authoritative voice:

"Let her go! She's a crazy lady."

Gradually the crowd quietened. Gerry took a deep breath and raised her head high.

"Well, my friends. I do believe we've just been visited by an unravelled member of the lunatic fringe." There was a nervous titter. Gerry gathered strength. "However, as you yourselves know, those of us who spend our lives in the struggle for civil rights are bound to make some fairly flaky enemies along the way."

With that, she took off her wine-splattered jacket and examined it ruefully. The stains looked like blood. She draped the jacket over her chair, then, rolling up the sleeves of her blouse, faced the audience full of confidence and good humour.

"This isn't the first time I've shed blood in a righteous cause. I'm gonna send the cleaning bill to the Ku Klux Klan."

This time, the laughter was general, and she delivered the rest of her speech without a glitch.

"It was your wife," she told Michael on the phone the moment the luncheon was over. "And some photographer caught the whole fucking thing. Don't be surprised if we wind up in the afternoon papers."

Michael was incredulous.

"Are you sure?" he whispered. She had caught him at a meeting. "I can't believe she'd do such a thing. Not Sandy. She's the world's meekest female. Describe her . . ."

Gerry obliged. Short. Cute. Teased hair. A bit on the plump side. "And wearing this weird blouse with a gigantic lace jabot."

"It was Sandy all right," he conceded. His voice sounded as though it came through clenched teeth. "How idiotic! I feel I should apologize for her. The important thing is – are you OK, darling? You're sure you weren't hurt? Well, you must be terribly shaken up, poor babe."

"You know me, Michael. I'm a . . .' she started to say *tough old bird* but thought better of it. "I'm a survivor. Anyhow, I'm going back to the office and change. I've got a three-thirty meeting."

"The hell you do! You're going straight home. I'm sending a car over and I want you to take it easy for the rest
of the day. That's an order. I'll get there as soon as I can."

"Really darling, no need to fret. I'm perfectly capable of
going back to work."

But he sent a car, and it was comforting being fussed
over *in absentia*, being treated like a frail little creature. She
went off meek as a lamb. She would simply wash the
experience away.

An hour later, she was soaking in a bubble bath, biting
her nails, wiping away the occasional tear. She refused to
cry. Michael mustn't see her looking weepy.

But every time she shut her eyes, a vision of Sandy
Avesian rose before her. Such hatred had been in that
woman's face, such rage. Gerry shuddered. In all, an ugly,
unsettling afternoon.

When she was younger, the angry emotions aroused in
various corners hadn't fazed her. She had always been able
to slough them off with a quip and a boast, priding herself
on being "one tough broad".

And while it was all very well being what the toastmaster
today had fulsomely called "a national monument", that
was a relatively recent development. For as much as Gerry
had been loved in her day, she had also been hated.

By some who knew her. By many who did not.

At the peak of her influence, the "national monument"
had been hanged in effigy by right-to-lifers; stoned by
racists in Selma. Anathametized by Bible Belters. Picketed,
persecuted and reviled by groups ranging from the DAR
to the KKK. When she'd run for congress from a hide-
bound district upstate, she'd been the recipient of rotten
eggs and ripe tomatoes and death threats, to say nothing
of endless demands that she go back to where she came
from. Presumably Russia, not the Upper East Side.

"I have not fared well," she once commented on a foot-
high pile of hate mail, "with organizations that feature
grown men in sheets or little old ladies in tennis shoes."

She had also been hated by select individuals. By competitors she'd bested in business. By women she'd bested
in love. Margaret Winterbourne, Gerry had it from a

303

reliable source, kept a voodoo doll that bore a remarkable likeness to her hated rival – with a five-inch hatpin stuck through its heart.

Poor Maggie. For all the good it had done her!

These days, however, hardly any one hated her with vigour. Was it simply that times had mellowed? Or that nobody cared any more?

There was always Lawrence Winterbourne, to be sure. But though he certainly loathed her, she doubted that it was with the same ardour as his mother. He was probably a second-class hater as he was second-class in all his endeavours.

Cranky but sexless. Passionless. Cursed by a lack of deep feeling. Like most of his generation, she thought.

Lee Whitfield, for example, charting her way to the top as if she were following an engineer's blueprint.

"I modelled myself after you," she had said, but Gerry thought not. Lee was driven, yes. But passionate? No. She left no margin for error or instinct. That recent display was nothing more than bruised ego. Lee was essentially a planner, a mechanic.

No passion there.

Michael was passionate.

At least she wanted to think so. That was the difference between him and all those other young men in three-piece suits. He was the exception to the generational rule. Her love was predicated on that conviction.

And it appeared his wife was passionate too. A first class hater, was Gerry's bet.

She shivered and got out of the tub.

By three o'clock the phone was ringing off the hook.

"Some reporter from the *Post*," her housekeeper called out from downstairs.

"What does he want, Ida?"

"It's a she and she wants to know about someone called the 'mysterious marauder'."

"I'm not home to anyone," Gerry snapped. "Except Mr Avesian. Show him upstairs the second he arrives. And bring me up a brandy."

Michael didn't get there until late afternoon by which time Gerry was a nervous wreck.

"Have you seen the papers?" he asked.

"Do I want to?"

"Nope," he snapped. He began flexing his fingers, knuckles white with tension.

"Jesus, I could kill that woman. I told her if she ever pulls another stunt like that again . . ."

"You mean you've already spoken to your wife?" Gerry was aghast.

"She called the office an hour ago. She's back home."

He shook his head in disbelief. "Sweet little Sandy who would – to use her own words – 'rather die than fly' managed to charter a private jet this morning just so she could pull that little hit-and-run number at lunch. How did she find out about us, I wonder? You haven't been in touch with her, have you, Gerry? No of course not. Forgive me for even thinking that, darling. One of the things I love about you – you're not the sort of woman who makes scenes. Although," he added, "I didn't think Sandy was either. Dependent yes, but melodramatic? That's hardly her style. Still, I suppose I'll have to go down there and straighten this out."

"Straighten what out?" Gerry reared up in alarm.

"You, me, Sandy, the kids, arrangements . . . the lot!"

Briefly, Gerry's spirits soared. That sounded like divorce talk.

"Does that mean . . ." she wanted to ask, but Michael was so tense, she dared not pursue it. What he said next afforded her scant comfort.

"We've never talked much about my family. Under the circumstances, it didn't seem particularly appropriate. Up until today, I've been able to keep my life in tidy little compartments. But now Sandy seems to have brought matters to a head. You understand, darling, I love my children very much. I can't simply walk away. Don't ask me to. My entire adult life is invested in that marriage."

Gerry felt a frisson of terror.

"Oh, God, Michael," she began to tremble. "Are you telling me it's over already? I don't think I could bear it."

"Trust me." He put his arms around her. "All I ask is that you trust me, darling. I wouldn't hurt you for the world."

When he left, Gerry got stinking drunk for the first time in years. For all Michael's promises, she didn't know if he'd ever come back.

eleven

There was a staff party for Samantha Loring that Friday afternoon. She was leaving *Trend* and going to *Elle* as Beauty Editor.

With my ideas in her portfolio, Lee thought bitterly. The theft of her "freebies" story still rankled. She wasn't sure that she wanted to attend.

It had been an unbelievably rotten week, as she'd told Bill Frazier. "I suspect God has personally put me on some kind of hit list. Although I can't fathom what I've done wrong."

Monday, she'd had her wallet lifted at Bendel's. Wednesday, the dentist told her she needed a root canal. But the hardest blow had come yesterday morning, when Fletch called her into his office.

"You might want this for your files," he said, handing her back the Port Authority story. "I've decided not to run it."

Lee felt as if she'd been punched in the solar plexus. She'd expected some quibbles but this rejection was completely unforeseen.

"I don't believe my ears! What's the matter with it?"

His face was purposefully bland. "I just don't like it."

"What d'ya mean you just don't like it?" She was too outraged to play the respectful employee any longer. "Christ, Fletch. I busted my ass for that story. I lived with those fucking creeps for two solid weeks eating garbage, sleeping on floors. A war correspondent couldn't have done more. And all you've got to say is you don't like it? What do you want, Fletch? You want rewrites, I'll give you rewrites. You want statistics, I'll get you statistics. You want additional research – I'll even go back into that hell-hole! But give me a chance. I counted on that story running. You can't dump on me like that."

"Sorry," he said.

"Sorry means zilch. Where'd I go wrong? I demand an explanation."

'Something's missing."

"What?" she pressed him. "I have to know."

Fletch's answer was to raise his arms by his side and flap his hands like a newly-hatched bird.

Lee stared at him, confounded.

"Is that your cute way of saying 'It'll never fly, Orville'?"

"You got it, Lee. It doesn't have wings."

A few minutes later, Bill found her in the supply room crying her heart out. "Close the door," she said. A little coaxing was all it took for the tale to emerge.

"Wings, for Chrissakes! What kind of crap is that! I worked so hard on that story. I was in this office every night till midnight, polishing each little word."

"Maybe you worked too hard."

"What do you mean?"

"It's only a story."

"It's only my life!" she groaned.

He handed her a tissue. She blew her nose.

"I've got half a mind to take this job and chuck it."

"Would that be wise?"

"I don't know. I don't know anything anymore."

In a sane world, she would have applied to Gerry for comfort and counsel, but the Great Ms O'Neal still refused to take her calls.

"Touch me," she said to Bill. "Please!"

He placed a tentative hand on her cheek.

"Thanks. I just wanted to assure myself I don't have leprosy." She tried to summon a bold face through the tears, but she was trembling still. "Ah, what the hell . . . fuck 'em all!"

"Poor baby . . ."

Bill locked the door, then took her into his arms. And there, amid the boxes of steno pads and paper clips, comforted her in the way that men have been comforting women since time began.

By Friday, Lee had regained her cool. She turned up at work as though nothing had happened. And while instinct demanded that she boycott Samantha's party ("that bitch!"), prudence decreed otherwise. Bitch or no, a contact at *Elle* might prove useful. Besides, Samantha Loring owed her one.

Accordingly at five o'clock, she pasted a smile on her face and headed over to the second floor at Casa España, where there was an open bar and enough tapas for a year's worth of garlic breath. With a few drinks in her, life began to look almost tolerable. These were her colleagues, her age-mates. This was where she belonged. She flirted furiously with Ollie Dichter, hustled Teddy Goodman for stock tips, got the name of the hot new hairdresser from Bea Jones.

"Kevin Kaplan. He's very forties, very Hollywood. He makes you look like – oh, who's that old movie star, the one with all the hair?"

"Lassie?"

"No, but that's a thought. Tell Kevin you know me, he'll give you a break on a cut."

"Will do."

"Hey chica!" *Trend*'s Travel Editor cornered her, back from an assignment entitled 'Romantic Rendezvous'.

"Hey Marvin! Seen any good islands lately?"

"St Helena's."

"Where Napoleon died? That's a place for a Romantic Rendezvous?"

"Unspoiled. Historic. Windswept. Wild. And completely off the beaten track. I plan to 'discover' it in the Christmas issue."

Out of the corner of her eye, she saw Wilson Cortland III sneak off to the Gents with a waiter. To do coke and God knows what else. Another Romantic Rendezvous.

"Oh ducky." Samantha Loring pecked her cheek. "I heard about the Port Authority disaster, Fletch killing your story and all."

Lee didn't turn a hair. She checked to make sure Fletch wasn't in the room.

"Oh, have you got your facts wrong! Fletch loved it. Said it was the best piece he'd seen in years. He wants desperately to run it but *they* won't let him . . ."

"They?"

"The big boys at the top. It's too strong, too disturbing. Some crap about 'tearing the social fabric and revealing the open wounds.' Well, you know *Trend*'s readership – who better? They're not up to anything more substantive than, say, a haircut at Kevin Kaplan's."

"Kevin who?"

Lee fought down a smile. Then she lowered her voice.

"Actually, I've been invited to submit a book proposal on my experiences. By a very major house. But that's strictly confidential."

"Lips are sealed, pet. We must have lunch as soon as I'm settled in at *Elle*. Where's the Constant Companion by the way?"

"You mean Bill Frazier?"

"The same. No send-off would be complete without him."

"Bill's holed up at home, poor thing, under the weather and absolutely convinced he's developing a terminal ulcer or gout or some such. Indigestion is my bet. He gets it all the time." Lee giggled. "Honestly, to hear him talk, you'd think he was engaged in a hazardous occupation, like toxic waste disposal. Men are such hypochondriacs."

"Well, even hypochondriacs get sick sometimes, I suppose," Sam said cheerfully. "Give him my love."

Lee had popped in to visit Bill an hour before the party in the hopes of getting him to attend.

He lived alone in a high-ceilinged apartment on East End Avenue that boasted a tiny terrace and a panoramic view. He sublet from his mother. It had been her New York pied-à-terre and though small, the place retained an air of pre-war opulence.

Lee had found him sitting up in bed reading an outsized book and nibbling on French *biscotte*. He was wearing faded striped pajamas.

"How are you feeling?"

He sighed. "Surprisingly delicate. I should have passed up those desserts last night. Killer stuff. Or maybe I should switch to sports reporting. Or war! War could be enjoyable. At least it helps you cut down on calories."

He patted a place for her alongside him. Lee took off her shoes and stretched out.

They admired the view for a peaceful minute or two.

"What're you reading?" She picked up his book. It was in French.

"Escoffier. My mentor and model. It's kind of fun, actually. He has a way of placing food in a social context. I came across this recipe for lamb chops as prepared for the royal table by a chef of Louis XVI. You take three prime loin lamb chops, stack 'em up like a sandwich, grill the stack on both sides so all the juices from the outer lamb chops run into the middle one. Then you throw the two outer lamp chops away. Now there you have as complete a recipe for revolution as one can desire."

Lee smiled. "Actually it sounds delicious. The sort of thing they'd do at a Malcolm Forbes shindig. And speaking of shindigs, since you seem on the road to recovery, how about throwing some clothes on and coming with me to Samantha's party?"

"Better idea," Bill said. "How about you taking some clothes off and climbing into bed with me. We could play lamb chops," he added. "Rub up against each other. Get all those juices running, mingling. Now that's a much nicer way to spend the evening."

He began undoing the buttons of her blouse.

It was tempting, but Lee shook her head.

"Do come," she urged. "Make the effort. Everyone in the office will be there. It's a good chance to score some Brownie points."

But Bill had slid his hand beneath her bra and was playing with her nipples. He seemed very intent. His face had taken on a healthy glow.

"Wouldn't you rather make love? Your nipples say yes. They're quite emphatic. Stay, sweetie. To hell with the party. It's no big deal. You see those guys every day. And it's not as if you like Samantha Loring."

"Like has nothing to do with it. It's a company affair." She stood up and straightened her clothes. "We'll make love later. Now get dressed, Bill. If it's boring we can leave early."

He retreated under the covers with his box of *biscottes*.

"I don't feel up to going," he said flatly.

"I see," she said. "You only feel up to fucking."

For a moment she thought he'd taken offence.

Instead, he laughed. "Exactly right. At almost any given time. I guess I never get enough of you."

She leaned over and pecked him.

"I'll come over after," she promised.

"I'll save you a place. And bring some chicken soup, will you, darling? Man does not live by *pain grillé* alone."

By eight o'clock, the party had turned drunk and raucous. Lee decided to slip out and spend the night with Bill.

She was retrieving her coat just as Fletch put in an appearance. She hesitated, undecided whether to speak to him or not. She wouldn't know what to say. Then she noticed he was crooking his finger at her.

An apology! her heart leapt. Maybe even restitution of her story. She made her way across the room.

"You looking for me, Fletch?"

He nodded. "Have you seen the afternoon papers?"

She shook her head.

"The *Post*, Page Six," he continued. "Some caption like MYSTERY MARAUDER MAKES CELEB SEE RED. Complete with a picture of your pal."

"Fletch, I'm mystified."

'Geraldine O'Neal," he said. "Looks like there could be a story in the old gal after all. See what you can dig up."

She didn't go to Bill Frazier's apartment that night. She ran.

A long punishing run, across 86th Street into the park, around the reservoir, then doubling back, pace never slackening. Running until her hamstrings ached and her heart slammed against her ribcage, running through the pain and fatigue and mortal agony until she reached that euphoric, oxygenated consciousness that admitted nothing but the abstraction of self.

312

She liked running in the dark. There was nothing to see nothing to hear except the sound of her breathing and occasional footsteps of others running, pursuing their own nirvana. She liked the isolation of it. The sense of control. Of apartness. Of beating down her weakness, marshalling her strength.

When she ran she had freedom of the city.

twelve

That evening, Michael took the Metroliner to Baltimore. He needed the train time to consider his situation.

Despite the photo in the *Post* (and it was Sandy all right. He'd recognize that hair-do anywhere!) Michael had difficulty grappling with the reality. In this case, a picture was not worth a thousand words. It explained nothing. His wife had acted totally out of character, betraying a melodramatic flair he could never have foreseen. The mouse turned killer shark, so to speak. He didn't know whether to be angry or respectful. This was a new Sandy surfacing.

For the next several hours, he tried to evaluate the predicament logically, listing the various alternatives, as if it were a business problem. They boiled down to three.

He could deny everything, try to tough it out.

He could confess everything and beg her indulgence.

Or he could end the marriage once and for all.

The one thing he didn't consider, at this juncture, was giving up Gerry. She had become essential to his life in New York.

By journey's end, he was no closer to a decision than when he'd boarded. He would have to play it by ear and trust that his instincts wouldn't betray him. They never had yet.

Only one thing was clear. Whatever the outcome, he would try to spare his wife further injury. Poor Sandy! She'd suffered enough. This must have come as a terrible shock.

Such a trusting soul she was! But so dependent. Utterly without inner reserves. Killer shark? Hardly. More like a fish out of water.

By the time the cab pulled up to his house, Michael's mood was positively benign. He would be kind. Fair. Sympathetic. He would have his cake and eat it too.

"If it had been a model or a movie star," she began scream-

314

ing even before he had his foot in the door, "some beautiful young girl, I could understand. But my God, Mikey, for you to cat around with . . . with that ancient old hag! She must be a hundred at least. How could you! It's obscene! Kinky! I've never been so insulted in my life!"

She flung herself upon him like a woman unhinged, pummelling his chest with clenched fists. The blows were as futile as they were pathetic. A moment later, she burst into tears of frustration.

"Sandy, Sandy." Michael tried to stem the tide. "Calm down. We've had enough violence for one day. Let me come in, get my coat off. Then we'll sit down and talk this through like sensible adults. We've both been under terrific strain lately. No point adding to the hysteria. Where are the kids?"

"At my folks'. I didn't want them witnessing any scenes."

However, the thought of the children apparently had a mollifying effect for Sandy wiped her eyes and let him into the hallway.

"That's better, hon. Now suppose we go into the kitchen, have some coffee and sort things out. There's a good girl. "

"You want coffee, make it yourself."

He was glad of the occupation. It gave him time to gather his thoughts. Her outburst had puzzled him. "If it had been a model . . ."

What an extraordinary thing to say! It was not the adultery itself his wife found intolerable, only the humiliation. She had lost face, and for such a conventional woman, face was everything. Perhaps if he took another tack, tried to brazen it out, that would afford her an avenue of escape.

By the time coffee was on the kitchen table, Sandy had regained her composure, even managed to fluff up her hair.

He sat across from her and rested his head on his chin.

"If I were to tell you honestly that there was nothing between Gerry O'Neal and me . . ."

"You'd be lying."

"What makes you so sure?"

Sandy fortified herself with a jolt of coffee.

"I've had my suspicions since you started making those middle-of-the-night phone calls."

"That's silly!" His mind was clicking on the double. "And completely unwarranted. I've always been a round-the-clock workaholic. You know that. Those 3 a.m. calls were strictly business. To London as it happens. It's eight in the morning there."

But Sandy shook her head. She'd seen the phone bills. Besides – "I've got more than suspicions. I've got proof. I hired a detective last week and had you followed. I know where you spend your nights, Mikey. In an East Side brownstone with that . . ." her lower lip began trembling, "that relic!"

"A detective!" He blinked, and a pulse in his temple began to throb. How little he knew his wife. How profoundly he had misread her. Absurdly enough, he began to think of himself as the one betrayed. But Sandy had merely gathered second wind.

"You think I'm stupid, don't you? Sweet dumb little Sandy. But I know all about you, Michael Avesian. I know about the black girl down in St Thomas. And the weekend you spent with the advertising copywriter in Key West."

"They were nothing," he protested. "Passing fancies."

"And I let them pass, didn't I? I never uttered a word, because at least you had the decency to be discreet. But this thing with O'Neal!" Her voice began rising to hysterical pitch. "Disgusting! What is it you see in that old bag?"

Michael felt his heart harden.

"Well, for one thing, she doesn't make vulgar scenes. If you think I'm going to sit here while you badmouth someone I care very deeply about, you picked the wrong guy. And maybe I've picked the wrong wife. You amaze me, Sandy. I never laid claim to being the ideal husband, but I'm not the Don Juan you make me out to be either. One hundred per cent fidelity is a very big order – especially considering that you were never around when I needed you."

"You were never home when I needed you!" she yelled back.

"Bullshit! My welfare means less to you than bricks and mortar and Sunday dinner with your folks. You've spent years trying to tie me down, cut off my balls, lock me into some lousy nine-to-five job. You never took a flier, never gave me moral support. What you did was run a household – that was all. But that's not enough. I wanted a lover, a companion, someone to share my aspirations."

"Like that little tramp in St Thomas?"

"She was there, you weren't. Did it ever occur to you that I might get lonely? For the record, as occasional flutters go, Sandy, they were quick and meaningless. Why didn't you say something back then? We might have cleared the air. But no! you deliberately shut your eyes and pretended ignorance. There's a kind of screwball logic in this, I suppose. You let me sow the occasional wild oat and bingo! you're off the hook."

"I don't know what you're talking about!" she snapped.

"I think you do. I was getting mine, you were getting yours. Big bad naughty Michael. You didn't have to be a wife to him. You didn't have to grow, change, expand your circle, share his life. You could just stay home and play Earth Mother. It was the easy way out."

"I wanted to save our marriage!" she cried.

"Well, so do I!" Michael drummed on the table. "Why the hell do you think I dragged down here? Which brings us to that charade at the Waldorf! For someone who's so eager to turn a blind eye, you certainly made a spectacle of yourself today. What possessed you?"

"Because what's happening now is different. And you're different. This time you're besotted, behaving like a fool. I could forgive the one night stands, but not this . . . this sordid affair. How do you think that makes me feel, to be passed over for a woman her age? It makes me feel like shit! Dirty and humiliated. I haven't slept for a week. Then this morning, I knew I couldn't stand it any more. I had to do something, anything, no matter how crazy! I had to get your attention."

He snorted. "Well, lady, you sure have got it."

They sat for a while in silence, then Sandy blew her nose

into a napkin. Then she spoke as though an inner struggle had been resolved. There was steel in her voice.

"You'll give her up, won't you? All will be forgiven and forgotten. Please, Mikey. Be sensible, I beg of you! No, I've stopped begging. I order you. You'll do it for me . . . for the children. And in return, I'll do anything you want. Come to New York, whatever. Attend all those stupid dinners, wear the clothes, play the role. I love you, Mikey, and I'll do the right thing. But you have to do the right thing first. If our marriage means anything, if I mean anything. . . ."

She darted out of the room to return a minute later clutching a cordless phone.

"Do it now, Mikey!" She brandished the phone. "Quick and clean. End all this craziness tonight. What's the area code for New York? Oh yes, 212. I should know by now . . ."

"Are you mad?"

Sandy began dialling. "I'm calling her. I know the number by heart and when she answers the phone, you'll pick it up and tell her it's over. For ever and ever. That you never wish to see or speak to her again. I'll be on the other extension listening in."

"Put the fucking thing down!"

"It's ringing . . ."

But Michael didn't wait. He grabbed the phone and hurled it through the kitchen window. A gush of cold air rushed in.

"Nobody gives me orders, do you understand?" he shouted. "Nobody – in business or anywhere else! If you think you can work me over with emotional blackmail, you couldn't be more mistaken. I've had it with your spying, your conniving, your melodrama. When you've come to your senses we can talk."

He spent a sleepless night at the airport hotel and took the first flight out in the morning.

Gerry woke before eight to discover him looming in the door of her bedroom, pale and excited.

"Michael!" She clasped her hands in prayer. "Oh my

318

God. I was terrified you were never coming back. What happened in Baltimore? Was it awful?"

"Awful!" He remained in the doorway as though undecided. "And over, I suspect. So if you'll have me, I'm here to stay."

She opened her arms wide.

"Oh darling, will I ever have you! I just may decide that I'll never give you up!"

Michael Avesian hesitated a fraction of a second, then swept into the room, conscious that a threshold had been crossed.

Lee couldn't help gloating.

"Will you look at that!" She handed Bill Frazier the *Post* photo. "Page six, no less! Up there with the hookers and homicides. Or should I say down there! 'The Ex-Ambassador made a splash at the Waldorf.' Jesus! How tacky can you get!"

"You mean your pal or the *Post*?"

"Both!"

"You seem to be taking it personally," Bill observed.

Lee stiffened. Maybe she was, but weeks of being frozen out of Gerry's company had hardened her emotional arteries.

"Only to a point, Bill. To think – that woman was once my role model! I'm talking prehistory, of course, before I got smart. Personal or not, this could be a major opportunity and it's time I scored some Brownie points with Fletch. Especially after that Port Authority fiasco. What a waste! As far as I'm concerned, Geraldine O'Neal is a subject like anything else, and I'm going to treat her as such. Coolly. Professionally. Dispassionately." She smiled suddenly. "Like a certain restaurant reviewer I know!"

"With a touch of dyspepsia thrown in."

"Well, better dyspepsia than a bleeding heart. It makes for racier reading. Besides, interpretive journalism is not my cup of tea," she said thoughtfully. "That's what was wrong with that Port Authority story. I didn't have a handle on it. I know my strength, Bill. I'm an investigative reporter, essentially, better with facts than with feelings.

So this assignment is tailor-made. I've got the background colour, the connections, the sources . . ."

"What about the ultimate source?"

"Gerry herself, you mean? I'll just have to worm my way back in her good books, at least till the story's complete. Funny, when you come to think of it. The last time I saw her, Gerry kept bleating about how much she's done for my career. If only she knew," – the idea amused her – "how right she was!"

"Don't be bitter." Bill looked faintly shocked. "It's unbecoming."

His remark brought her up short. Jake Matthews had said the same thing. Perhaps the wisest course would be not to confide in Bill so openly. She liked him too much to incur his disfavour.

"I'm not bitter at all," she lied. "Simply professional."

thirteen

Among the Indian tribes of the Pacific North-west, there is a winter ritual known as potlatch. It is marked by gift-giving of a stupendous order, each gift leading to an even more elaborate present being offered in return in a reciprocal show of respect and abundance. The ceremony escalates continually until, as sometimes happens, one or the other tribe is impoverished. It is a cultural phenomenon.

Potlatch is accompanied with much feasting, dancing and singing.

With the advent of the first snowflake, Michael and Gerry went to Revillon and bought each other matching lynx coats.

"Don't you dare scold," she said as she swirled into Jake's office eye-deep in furs. "Be happy for me. I'm having the time of my life."

"But Gerry . . . !"

"And next week," she continued unabashed, "Michael and I are off to England. I want to see Hailsham before they pull it all down. Plus, catch some theatre, make contacts. We've booked a suite at Claridge's for a couple of weeks, after which we're going to rent a Rolls – or maybe an Alfa Romeo, it's sportier – and tour France. I want to hit all the four-star restaurants . . . get a few rags in Paris. I plan to indulge myself totally, darling. It's been ages . . ."

"And who'll be running the shop while you play hookey?"

"Herman. The kids. All the panting little interns and associates. What the hell, the place can run itself for a while." She pulled a wry face. "I've already done my best for Mr Yoshimura. Jesus! more than my best! Nothing else in the pipeline is that hot. Honestly, Jake, you're the one who's always after me to delegate. Let the next generation sweat for a change, take responsibility. I'm out of here!"

She laughed, very pleased with herself. "Look Ma, no hands!"

"Look Ma, no brakes!" Jake replied.

"Now don't begrudge your poor old Gerry a bit of fun. I've earned it. As a matter of fact, I might hand over the business to the kids outright one day soon. Then retire. It's an attractive idea."

"You always did have a weakness for grand gestures, Gerry."

"Well, grand passions call for grand gestures. Although I don't see why I have to rationalize. Hell! For the last million years – at least it seems like a million! – I've been such a sober citizen. Nose to the grindstone, shoulder to the wheel. I've met the deadlines, kept the appointments, put in the hours. Enough already! I deserve to kick up my heels. *Pourquoi pas?*"

"*Parce que* you're gonna maybe wind up broke? Be sensible."

"No, Jake. This time I am making sense. Like that Massachusetts Senator said, when it comes to the final roll call, no one ever looks back and says 'Gee I wish I'd spent more time at the office.' "

"He made that statement when he learned he'd been smitten with cancer," Jake reminded her. "Whereas you . . ."

"Have been smitten with a handsome young man." Gerry giggled. "What can I tell you? It may be just as fatal, but it's a helluva lot more fun and you're not going to talk me out of it. Jake, darling, I leave everything in your capable hands. Don't call. Don't telex. Don't even try to bring me down to earth."

In the past month, her entire existence had undergone a transformation. It had begun the morning Michael had returned from Baltimore, his marriage in ashes.

They had spent the day making love, and half the night making plans. Bermuda. Barbados. London. Paris. Rome. Parties and palaces. Little luxuries and grand treats.

"Have you ever skied Kitzbühel, Michael?"

"No."

322

"We'll go in the spring. You'll love it."

"Only if I can find an emerald the size and colour of your eyes."

"But won't that be terribly expensive?"

"I certainly hope so."

She would take up flying again. He would take up riding. They would rent in Southampton next summer.

The future had never looked brighter. Secretly, Gerry couldn't thank Sandy Avesian enough for that scene at the Waldorf. She had lost an Armani suit – and gained a foothold in paradise.

To Michael's amazement, Gerry had been able to laugh off the picture in the *Post*. "At least the photographer got my good side," she said with equanimity, and tossed it into her "memory box". Michael murmured something about "grace under pressure", which she found enormously gratifying.

For if he had crossed a Rubicon of sorts that day, so had she. The last mingy vestige of restraint, the last scrap of half-hearted caution and mealy-mouthed discretion could now be thrown to the winds. She felt personally blessed, as though Michael's love would make her immune to all pettiness, all miseries, even the ineluctable assault of the years. Indeed, "blessed" was hardly the word. She felt immortal.

That same night, while Michael slept, she wrote a letter breaking off her engagement.

My dearest Campbell,

She penned the words with difficulty. Though it was nearly impossible to stifle her joy, she could scarcely expect Campbell to share it.

You will always occupy a special place in my heart, a place reserved for those few for whom I care deeply. I have always known you to be a kind and generous man. Now I ask you to be an understanding one as well. I have fallen in love with someone else. I am certain you would not wish to deny me life's greatest happiness . . .

Was that too fulsome? she wondered. Probably. One couldn't write such a letter without drowning in clichés.

Was it too cruel? Undoubtedly.

Why rub Campbell's nose into the fact that he was being passed over (or, to be more accurate, unceremoniously dumped) for a man half his age. She dropped all reference to love and began again.

My dearest Campbell,
Some part of me has always quailed at the prospect of marriage (now that was certainly true!), *even to someone as marvellous as you. I fear it's too late for me to change my ways and that I could not be the sort of wife you deserve. I beg your forgiveness and I'm sure you agree that at least for the present it is best we not see each other. It would be too painful for me.*

There was more in this vein, with Gerry indulging in a bit of self-flagellation ("not worthy of your love . . . too set in my ways") but ultimately, the phrasing was irrelevant; Campbell's ego was bound to be bruised.

But only his ego, Gerry assured herself. Other vital parts would remain intact. Though Campbell and she had been friends and lovers for many years, this proposed marriage, even at its optimum, was less a union born in a primal outburst of passion than a treaty between two neighbouring states.

She wished there were some way to compensate the dear fellow for all the trouble he'd gone to, boat charters and such. But Campbell was not the kind to exact tribute, bear a grudge. On the contrary, he might actually feel relieved.

The idea appealed to her, as did the notion of introducing him to Michael at some future date, when this transient unpleasantness had passed. She liked the people she liked to like each other.

Who knows! The two men might even share a hearty laugh about his "escape". Sir Campbell was a gentleman after all, who prided himself on his unflappable demeanour. Her guess was that he and Michael would enjoy each other's company. The thought made her smile.

She concluded the letter with a half dozen pat phrases, then sent it to Bonn by courier next day.

And that, she told herself, was that. At last, she and Michael were free to lead their own lives.

324

From then on, they'd spent every conceivable moment together – and a few inconceivable ones as well. "I just can't get enough of you," he said as they made ferocious love on the partner's desk in her office one rainy afternoon. It was mere chance that no one walked in.

When apart, they were on the phone constantly, checking in, chattering away. No incident was deemed too trivial to s are.

Now that the need for discretion was past, Gerry plunged into every area of his life, including Hailsham. Within a week, she had become its unofficial spokesman, courting the press, entertaining Michael's clients. Her presence added fresh lustre to the enterprise. "It's as much my baby as his," she explained to a sceptical Bobby Obermayer. And when accused of talking with her heart, not her head, she answered with a quote from Pascal, "The heart has its reasons, which reason knows not of."

Michael felt the same way.

The night before departing for London, he took her to the theatre. On their way out, he dismissed the limousine and insisted they walk part of the way. They passed Number One Times Square.

"Look!" Michael pointed to the dazzling electronic billboard that dominated the Broadway scene.

She looked up and saw a bright red heart a hundred feet high, composed of a thousand flashing lights. Scrolled across the top, in a perpetual band, ran the message for all the world to see:

MICHAEL LOVES GERRY . . . MICHAEL LOVES GERRY . . . MICHAEL LOVES GERRY . . . MICHAEL . . .

fourteen

David Whitfield died on a clear winter morning.

He was in his studio, reaching for a high note – that final piercing E flat of Bunny Berrigan's *Can't Get Started* – when a blood vessel burst in his brain.

Only the night before he had remarked to Nancy that "the chops" were going, then made a small joke about it, "along with everything else". She had tried to jolly him along with the comment that he never looked or sounded better. "I'm no music critic, but . . ." she'd said, to which David had shaken his head in mute despair. He had found old age ungrateful, retirement odious.

He was buried, along with his beloved Conn trumpet, the following Sunday in a church filled to overflowing. The Cedar City Wolverines played a commemorative programme of Sousa marches. The St Mark's brass choir followed with a rendition of Carl Ruggles' *Angels*. Mayor Arthur P. Blound delivered the eulogy.

"He died," said the Mayor, "doing what he loved best. May such a peaceful end be granted all of us."

For the next several days, Nancy scarcely had a free moment to grieve. Company streamed in and out of the house in a continuous flow, a communal out-pouring of respect and affection. Lee rented a coffee urn from Solomon Caterers, capable of brewing fifty cups at a time. It barely sufficed.

"I guess the idea is if they keep Mom busy enough," said her brother Drew, "she won't have time to fall apart."

By midweek, the callers had dwindled to a trickle and Nancy Whitfield was left to face a dubious future.

"Don't leave," she pleaded with Lee after Drew and the others had gone. "I see little enough of you as it is. A few more days won't make any difference."

Lee, guilty about the neglect of previous months, agreed to stay.

For the rest of the week, she put her own worries aside and was the dutiful daughter while her mother roamed through the house in a state of bewilderment. Nancy seemed to be looking for something to do with her hands. Repeatedly she would pick up objects and put them down with a comment that this had been David's favourite sweater or ash tray or photograph. Her talk was bounded by memory.

"I just can't get used to waking up and not finding David there," she said one morning while Lee fetched breakfast. "He always made the coffee. Your father made the best coffee in the world."

"Wait'll you taste this!" Lee tried to lighten her mood. "Guaranteed to be industrial strength, the way we like it in New York. The finest Colombian beans from the Gourmet Deli."

Nancy took a sip and made a face.

"Too bitter! If you don't mind, I'll make another pot." She got up and began puttering. "Although how you can go wrong with a Mr Coffee machine beats me. I thought your generation was so comfortable with gadgets."

"I guess I wasn't cut out to be a homebody."

Nancy looked at her with a painful smile.

"Your father was so proud of you darling. And I am too. Well, at least you'll amount to the something I never was. I'll tell you a secret, Lee. The day you were born, and I knew there'd be no more babies, I made a solemn pledge. I swore that you were going to lead the life I never had, the one I only dreamed about. That when you grew up, you'd go out into the world and make the name Whitfield count for something. After all, you were my baby. My last chance to make good." Nancy turned her face away, pretending to be very busy with the coffee. "All I ask is that you keep in touch."

Lee felt her throat tighten. It was one more burden to bear. The obligation to succeed for her mother's sake, as well as her own. She lowered her eyes. "I'll do my best not to disappoint you."

"Disappoint! Why, darling, you're halfway there already. Whereas I . . . I'm nowhere at all. I haven't a clue what I'm going to do with the rest of my life. Everything was so wrapped up in family, now there's nothing left. First Drew went away, then the girls got married, then you moved to New York. Your dad was all I had remaining."

"Oh Momma!" Lee started to weep. "Don't you dare say such a thing. Everybody loves you. You've got a million friends . . ."

But at heart, she felt the horror of her mother's predicament: the lack of resources, the empty years ahead. So much for the life spent in dedication to one man's happiness. It was a cautionary tale.

Nancy returned to the table with a fresh pot of coffee, far tastier than Lee had brewed. "Now tell me, darling, about life in New York."

Lee wiped her eyes and made an attempt to sound gay, aware of a responsibility to provide comfort and cheer. She told her mother about her job, her new apartment, her jogging, her friends. She talked about Bill Frazier, in rather warmer terms than Bill had ever been privileged to hear. To her astonishment, she discovered she missed him.

"An awfully sweet guy," she said. "We have a lot of laughs."

Nancy listened, engrossed. "You think he's serious, honey?"

"If you mean about marriage . . ." Lee paused. "Well, I don't know if *he* is – I doubt it – but I sure as hell am not."

Nancy nodded. "Quite right, darling. There's no rush."

Inevitably the conversation turned to Gerry O'Neal. Her mother was avid for intimate details, with Lee uncertain how to respond.

More than two months had passed since she had last seen her nemesis. Two months of unanswered letters and unreturned calls. Jake Matthews' intervention had been to no avail. He mentioned that she had gone to London, leaving Lee to despair of getting the lowdown for her magazine. Her fabled "source" had become as remote as though they'd never met.

Lee had said nothing to her mother about the breach. Why add to Nancy's misery by piling on sordid details?

But now, facing a barrage of eager questions, she had trouble controlling her bile.

"What's her house like?" Nancy wanted to know and wasn't satisfied until Lee had supplied every specific. The size of the drawing room, the Chippendale sofas, the fresh flowers on daily order, the Wedgwood service, the refrigerator empty of everything but champagne.

Nancy devoured each luxurious titbit in turn, all the while running her forefinger over the top of the chipped formica counter. No further comment was necessary.

"And at the head of the stairs, there's a full-length Sargent portrait of an English noblewoman. It's called Lady L." Suddenly, Lee's bitterness brimmed over. "Gerry fancies there's a resemblance. In fact, she lets people think it's a portrait of her grandmother."

"You're kidding!" Nancy was astounded. "Why, her granny was a crazy old Hungarian who wore a fright wig! I don't recall that the woman even spoke English!"

Lee's ears perked up. She had not hitherto considered her mother as a source of material, but in fact, few knew Gerry's background more intimately. Mentally, Lee began taking notes.

"Now about Gerry's wardrobe . . ." Nancy was asking, like a child demanding the next installment of a fairy tale. "I bet she has fabulous clothes."

Lee obliged with a description. The Chanel suits. The sequinned ball gowns. The huge closet packed with furs.

"Of course she doesn't pay for a lot of this stuff, you realize. Her Blackglama mink, for instance. It's yea long, absolutely stunning, but she got it free by posing for an ad."

". . . what becomes a legend most," Nancy mused. "I remember the campaign. Still, it must be marvellous having a closet full of fur coats. Me, I'd settle for one. 'Dripping fur' – isn't that the expression?"

Did Lee imagine it, or was there a hint of resentment in her mother's voice? Of envy?

"Now tell me," Nancy geared herself up to the ultimate question, "how does she look after all these years? Really! Close up! She still so slim?"

Lee rubbed the bridge of her nose. She wished passionately to spare her mother's ego, to say that Gerry O'Neal was "fat, faded and nowhere near as pretty as you!" The reporter in her won the day.

"Gorgeous!" she blurted out. "Glamorous! Lord knows how she does it! Maybe she sold her soul to the devil, which wouldn't surprise me a bit. Believe it or not, she has a lover even younger than Drew."

"My God! How gross!" Nancy shuddered with revulsion, then recanted. "I'm sorry for that outburst. I was being unfair. Although I suppose it's easy to stay youthful-looking if you've never borne children. Never raised a family. Never had anything to worry about other than your own well-being."

Instinctively, Nancy touched her hand to her salt-and-pepper hair, her wind-weathered cheek. The gesture – so sad, so futile – wrenched Lee's heart.

"The hell with Gerry!" she cried. "You've let her dominate your life long enough. It beats me why she should mean so much to you – a woman you haven't laid eyes on in over thirty-five years!"

Nancy stood up, face ashen, eyes brimming. For a moment her mouth worked but nothing came out. Then –

"It should have been me!"

"What do you mean?" Lee felt a chill go through her.

"Everything Gerry's had could have been mine – instead of which I'm left to live my days out in this backwater, with nothing to show. Nothing," she added bitterly, "but a little bird every Christmas."

The birds! They had puzzled Lee for months. "I always repay my debts," Gerry had boasted. So she did. The tax returns mailed to the hated Frankie Cavallo. The flowers sent to the former Suzie Slade.

She took her mother's hand and led her into the living room where the precious collection was on permanent display, the birds that Nancy always called "the trophies of a friendship".

"Beautiful precious things," her mother murmured.

"Yes, but why birds?" Lee repeated. "We're going to sit down and you're going to tell me all about them."

When she got up a half-hour later, another piece of the puzzle that was Gerry had fallen in place.

"I see," she said softly. "Not trophies. Tribute."

She flew back the following Sunday, having extracted a pledge from Nancy to visit her in New York when the weather turned nice.

In the meanwhile, both women had a lot to chew on.

Over recent weeks, Sandy Avesian had done more than chew on the hard fact of her husband's desertion. She had had ample leisure to digest it.

Being the centre of a scandal was a novel sensation. There was, she discovered, a certain thrill in seeing her picture in the papers. The photographer had mostly caught her back (too busy focusing on "that woman", Sandy presumed), but enough of her profile was visible to be recognized by those who knew her well.

"I spotted you right away," her cousin Dedee phoned when the photo turned up in *People* magazine. "I think it was the hair-do."

Thus far, the reading public knew her only as the Mystery Marauder and while Sandy wasn't about to hold a press conference to add to their fund of information, she nonetheless enjoyed the brief bright light of neighbourhood celebrity.

"Welcome to the Singles Club," Iris Daniels commiserated. Except that her tone was more congratulatory than sad. "You sure have spunk. Only while I was about it, I would have socked *him* one, too!"

Iris was the most glamorous mother at Country Day School. Soignée and wealthy, the head of her own real estate firm, she flitted in and out of PTA meetings in a cloud of perfume and mink, leaving an intimidated staff in her wake. Sandy felt flattered to be singled out for her approval.

"Thank you, Iris. I must say, it's so hard being on my own after all these years."

Iris shrugged. "It's easier than living with those assholes!" – that being her generic term for ex- and about-to-be-ex-husbands. "Now why don't you and the girls come over for dinner one evening? And in the meanwhile, if you need a good lawyer, just holler."

"Well, I don't think it's time for lawyers yet."

Iris gave her throaty low laugh. "Honeybunch, it's always time for lawyers."

Her father gave Sandy the same advice.

"I always knew that fella was a low-life," he gloated. "Didn't I tell you that, Hilda?"

"Your father always said Michael was a low-life," came the echo.

"Your mother's right. As a professional man myself, I advise you to see an *at-tor-ney*." The word rolled out with a stentorian flair – the homage of one lofty professional to another.

"Did he ever hit you?" Natasha's teacher asked, when Sandy called at school to explain a change in domestic circumstances.

"Michael hit me?" Sandy's jaw dropped. "Never!"

"It doesn't have to be physical." Ms Finneman adjusted her tie and went on, "To be a woman is to be a victim. We're all of us battered wives in this society, Ms Avesian. I trust and hope you're taking appropriate legal steps to protect yourself and the children before that brute returns."

Sandy's cleaning woman voiced it differently.

"Stick it to 'im!" Mrs Prohaska said, waving a Johnny-Mop. 'Take the bastard for all he's got. If I'da done the same to Mr Prohaska, I wouldn't be scrubbing toilets today."

The passion which Michael's desertion aroused in others left Sandy reeling, as did the responsibility of running the household alone. Michael had always paid the bills, sitting at the leather-topped desk in his study. It was a man's job. But when the first of the month rolled around she viewed the accumulating pile with dismay. Just as "life had to go on" – which everyone kept telling her, surely bills had to be paid.

She could either forward the lot to New York or have her father handle them or – she squared her shoulders – take charge herself.

Why not? She was the Mystery Marauder, after all. The feared and fearless Phantom of the Waldorf Astoria. Iris Daniels had called her "spunky". What were a few chits of paper alongside of that?

Accordingly, one night in mid-December, Sandy sat herself down at Michael's huge desk and began hunting for his chequebook. At the bottom of the desk was a locked double drawer. He kept the key beneath the lamp base. Its location had never been secret. In any case, Sandy was neither breaking nor entering. This was her house, no one would disturb her. Moreover, Michael was in London with that woman. "The lovebirds," she thought with a quiver of disgust.

The drawer unlocked to reveal a treasure trove. Stock holdings. CD's. Brokerage slips. Chequebooks and bank statements galore. Her husband had bank accounts in Baltimore, Washington, New York. Even one in the Cayman Islands (wherever that was!) And everything – her heart skipped a beat – right down to a $50 Savings Bond from the first year of their marriage was registered in both their names.

For years, Michael had always sought her signature on one boring document or another. "Communal property," he'd say. "I only wish you'd take an interest. It's your future too."

Sandy was taking an interest now.

By midnight, she had the contents of the bottom drawer in a semblance of order. Then, beginning with the mortgage, she attacked the pile of bills.

Cautiously first, later with increasing confidence, she worked her way through the lot. There was a physical pleasure in the process, a sense of accomplishment. By the time the last cheque was written, she felt heady with power. Even her signature had taken on an undeniable swagger. Alexandra McKay Avesian – she used her full legal name. It certainly looked impressive. She straightened out the stack, then balanced the chequebook to the penny before going up to bed.

Bed didn't seen quite so empty that night.

She spent most of the following weeks at the Public

Library, reading up on everything from options to REIT's to Ginny Mae's. It was fascinating stuff.

When the holidays were over, Sandy presented herself to the firm of Moore, O'Sullivan and Mintz.

"You've been recommended by Iris Daniels," she told the twinkly-eyed Mr Mintz. "Iris says you're terrific."

"I like to think of myself as firm but fair."

Sandy had a brief image of the lovebirds in London.

"Forget the fair. I'm interested in the firm."

It was a full hour later before she was ready to leave.

"Have I omitted anything?" She straightened out the pile of documents. "I did include that little parcel of land in Key West?"

Mr Mintz shook his head in awe. "Admirable!" he exclaimed. "How can you say you're 'just a housewife'? That was one of the best, most lucid expositions I've ever seen. You have a superb grasp of financial detail, young lady."

"Thank you. Oh yes . . . one more question. If a bank account is in both our names, do I need Michael's OK to make withdrawals?"

"Not in the US you don't."

Sandy chewed her lip.

"Then I could close out all our joint accounts and put them in my name only?"

Mr Mintz stared at her with heightened respect.

"Just for the time being," she explained. "I think it might help in the negotiations."

"My dear Mrs Avesian! You're a marvel! I dare say you've missed your *métier*."

"Nooooo," Sandy drawled thoughtfully. "I think I just found it."

fifteen

"Style."

It was the key word in Michael Avesian's vocabulary.

The Concorde had style. The Daimler that met them at Heathrow had style. As did the chauffeur. As did the liveried doorman at Claridge's. Claridge's had style to burn.

The public rooms were fitted out in Art Deco that reminded Gerry of a thirties ocean liner, lacking only a waltzing Fred and Ginger. Ginger would have been wearing bias-cut silk.

In the lobby, a logfire crackled and a Hungarian quartet played perfumed music above the tinkle of tea-cups.

"Style," Michael murmured. "Bliss!" Gerry amended when she saw their suite.

Spacious and handsome, full of priceless antiques and elaborate mouldings, this very set of rooms, according to the hall porter, was where the Empress Eugenie had once entertained Queen Victoria.

"Don't you feel regal?" Gerry said. Michael's response was to fling himself on the outsized bed with a thump that said "not bad for a kid from Baltimore".

The following morning they made a pilgrimage to Hailsham Castle amidst an entourage of nearly a hundred. The cavalcade of Rolls Royces included journalists, personal assistants and British businessmen and public officials. Also present was the Earl of Haslemere, a shy, amorphous young man who reminded Gerry in attitude if not in accent of Larry Winterbourne.

His only aim in life, as far as she could ascertain, was to outsmart the roulette wheels at Monte Carlo. Privately, she didn't think him capable of out-smarting a trained monkey (so much for twenty generations of breeding!), but Michael had nonetheless given the youthful peer a seat on his Board of Directors.

"A title looks good on the letterhead," he said.

As the party drew near Hailsham, Gerry felt a thrill of anticipation.

"The less there is standing," Michael had warned her, "the further along we are. We've had an army of workmen at it hammer and tongs – and bulldozers too! The progress has been tremendous."

Already, the interior fittings had been stripped, labelled, packed into container cars and sent off to Southampton, awaiting shipment to America. Only the shell and the battlements were left.

But for Gerry, who had thus far seen Hailsham in clay models and marzipan, even the bare outlines sufficed to propagate the dream. The place was as romantic as a fairy tale. What a castle to be queen of!

For the occasion Michael had put the demolition crews on hold, and in place of wreckers and crane operators, a band of pipers welcomed the guests from the parapet of the Great North Tower.

"Style," Gerry said.

"A bloody fortune," Michael murmured. "But worth it!"

The grounds, too – at least those that had been spared the ravages of the dismantling process – were splendid beyond words. Beyond the acres of tyre tracks were other acres of velvet lawns, green despite the winter chill. Fish ponds teeming with golden carp. Lordly avenues of beech and oak. An Elizabethan maze, shamefully overgrown, yet still clinging to the secrets of some four hundred years. A topiary garden of sculpted unicorns.

The tour of the grounds was followed by a buffet luncheon in the remnants of the main hall where Fortnum & Mason delicacies mingled with hot pastrami flown in specially from New York. After which, Michael made his presentation.

". . . link between our two great English-speaking nations, a unique opportunity for British retailers to extend into a limitless new market. At Hailsham USA, we welcome British participation and I assure you, you'll be in good company alongside such American merchants as Austrian's of Fifth Avenue, Gumps of San Francisco . . ."

Gumps was highly iffy, Gerry knew, as were half a

dozen "participants" he'd mentioned in his pitch. But exaggeration was par for any sales spiel. In all, Gerry had never seen him in more confident form.

They returned to London at dusk, happy but tired.

"Asprey's was interested," Michael gloated. "What a coup that would be!" However, Gerry's mind was elsewhere. The castle grounds had captured her imagination.

"Let's find out if there's a way of importing the trees," she urged. "They add such a sense of nobility. And those topiary unicorns! They're to die from! Absolutely tops on my 'must-have' list."

"Darling!" Michael burst out laughing. "There are some things even I can't do."

But Gerry had been bitten by the authenticity bug and nothing would suffice except that Hailsham USA be ultimately more English than the Union Jack.

"The whole thing – grounds, gardens, interior decor – simply cries out to be done by British designers," she insisted. "After all, darling, if people are going to schlepp out to New Jersey, they deserve to find something distinctive, beyond what can be had in Manhattan."

To that end, Gerry got on the phone (she still had excellent connections in London, thank God!) and rounded up the names of the top practitioners in every field. For the next two weeks, a stream of landscape architects, decorators, museum curators, clothing designers and shipping agents fluxed through their suite at Claridge's.

"No no," Michael would step up the pressure, unused to the more leisurely pace of British business. "Not next month. Not tomorrow. Not even today. I need answers yesterday! If you can't give me an estimate, give me a guesstimate. Then maybe we can do a deal."

Most suppliers were happy to oblige.

Before long, every available surface in the suite was piled high with sketches and plans and six-figure proposals. Hailsham would boast a "white garden" to rival Sissinghurst and a rose garden to match Queen Mary's in Regent's Park. British birds would sing amidst the British bushes. British blossoms would loose their scent in Jersey air.

Even the parking lot attendants, Gerry determined, would be kitted out in the spectacular dress of the Household Cavalry.

"How do you feel about deer roaming the grounds?" she asked.

But there Michael drew the line.

"Uh – unh! We'll wind up with sozzled hunters taking pot shots at the customers."

It was enormous fun, this creation of a fantasy world, and many a night Gerry and Michael would sit up in bed ploughing through reams of proposals, approving this one, booting out that, feeling semi-divine. Amazing what money could buy, Gerry speculated. And what it couldn't.

Those hundred-foot oaks, for example, had proved impossible. "Joyce Kilmer was right," she sighed. "Only God can make a tree."

The out-of-doors now theoretically conquered, they focused attention on the castle interior. A visit to Bath with its elegant Assembly Rooms ("Now that's style!" Michael said) sold them both on the merits of Georgian decor.

Back in London, they summoned the experts for advice.

"Ah! The renowned Mrs Goldenbloom," Gerry greeted her visitor early one bright Sunday morning. "So kind of you to come. I know it's terribly American of us to conduct business seven days a week but as you realize we're pressed for time and you have been so highly recommended. Michael, darling," for he had just emerged from the bedroom doing up his tie, "this is the decorator Betsy Rothschild told us about. Michael will explain what it is we have in mind."

But Mrs Goldenbloom's attention seemed fixed on the adjacent room. Gerry followed her gaze to the tousled double bed and snippets of lingerie strewn on the floor.

"Sorry about that." She got up to shut the door. "The maid hasn't come yet. I was going to order breakfast. Can I get you something?"

"No thank you."

"Not even coffee?"

"Nothing." The woman scanned Gerry with an enigmatic expression.

"In that case, let's get down to it," Michael said. He went on to explain his wishes while Mrs Goldenbloom listened patiently without uttering a word. At the end of a half hour, she reached for her coat.

"I'm afraid you'd find me most unsuitable, Mr Avesian."

"If it's a question of price," Michael said, eager to talk her around, "I'm sure we can arrive at a mutually agreeable arrangement."

"I'm sorry." The voice was frosty but polite. "Under no circumstances could I accept your commission. Do I make myself clear?"

"Perfectly," Gerry shot back, annoyed. "I regret that we wasted your time."

"Not at all," Morag Goldenbloom said with a peculiar smile. "It's been a most instructive morning."

Reluctantly, Michael decided to postpone their Continental holiday. "In the spring, darling," he promised. "Paris, Rome, the works."

The sojourn in London, although bracing in every other way, had temporarily wreaked havoc with his finances. The best place to repair that damage was New York. The best method, getting Eli Austrian's name on the dotted line. "Quick, before he melts," Michael said.

"You know what would be perfect?" Gerry speculated. "If Princess Di were to cut the ribbon at the official opening. My God, what a press release that would make!"

She promised to work on it through the Ambassador.

They spent a final week mixing business with pleasure, in a round of dinners and theatre and topped off with a shopping splurge that ranged from Sotheby's to the Portobello Road. Gerry insisted Michael be fitted for a dozen Turnbull and Asser shirts. He reciprocated with a pair of crystal decanters that had been the property of the Windsors. She went mad in Janet Reger's.

Back at the hotel she could only look at all their purchases and groan. "We'll never fit all this into our luggage."

Michael's answer was to order two huge Vuitton trunks,

lined with French watered silk, and leave them for the porter to ship.

"Now that," he said, "is style."

The day before departure, they gave a lunch at Inigo Jones for the press corps, which Gerry deemed a necessary expense.

"Happy journalists are the essence of public relations," she declared. "And nothing makes them happier than free food and booze."

Thus far, their progress through London had elicited mixed reaction in the papers. The "Michael and Gerry Show", as some called it, had cut a wide swath, but not always a welcome one. And while much of the coverage had been good-natured, now and then a rumble was heard deploring the loss of a national treasure.

First the Brain Drain, a columnist in the *Guardian* had noted, *then the Sterling Exodus. Now Hailsham Castle is on its way to America. What next – Buckingham Palace on the Hudson?*

"First, let me assure you," Gerry told their guests at lunch. "At present, we have no designs on Buckingham Palace. Further, despite all my efforts, the Archbishop absolutely refuses to relinquish the Abbey."

There was an amused titter while the waiter handed round canapés and champagne. Gerry proposed a toast. "To the ladies and gentlemen of the press. My fondest hope is that when Hailsham is rebuilt on the other side of the Atlantic, you'll come visit. Among its amenities, I promise to have an open bar for members of the working press. As a former journalist, I know how much it means."

She made a short graceful speech containing a little hard news – Mr Avesian planned to open a London office – and the announcement that several British retailers had joined the project, after which the group got down to serious eating and drinking and joshing.

"What do we get in return for Hailsham?" one reporter wanted to know. "You already have McDonalds," Gerry said. "What more can you ask for – Times Square?"

A pretty girl from *Harpers & Queen* began making goo-goo eyes at Michael who had the good sense to flirt back. A staffer from Channel 4 suggested to Gerry that as long as she was in the business of importing ancient monuments, how about the House of Lords next? "Not the building," he amended. "The occupants." A chap from the FT got dreadfully drunk and the young man from *Private Eye* nicked an ashtray. In short, a lovely time was had by all.

It was almost dusk when Michael and Gerry tumbled out into the street, happy and more than a little tipsy. They walked through Berkeley Square in a fine grey rain.

"I love this town," Michael said. "Someday I want to live here."

"I almost did," Gerry replied, thinking of Campbell. Her letter to him had never been answered. She shivered slightly and changed the subject. "What would you like to do on our last night, darling? Go to the theatre . . . dancing?"

"Let's go home and make love."

"Home?" Gerry looked up.

"Claridge's," he said. "It's almost like home. It's the first place we've ever really lived together like . . ."

Like man and wife – the words hung in the air.

She stopped to kiss him, there in the middle of the square, with the rain dripping down her collar.

"Let's not go back," she murmured.

"Not go back to the hotel?"

"Not go back to America. Let's pool our credit cards and run away forever and ever . . . Tashkent . . . Samarkand . . . all the perfumed places."

"And when the credit cards run out . . . ?"

"We'll live on love for the next hundred years."

Michael pulled her to him and clasped her tight.

"I wish . . . !" he said dreamily. "I wish."

They wandered back to the hotel in a haze compounded of love and longing and the soft London mist. The quartet in the lobby was playing Cole Porter, gay and nostalgic all at once.

". . . no kick from champagne . . ." Michael sang along in his light musical baritone. Then, encircling her waist, he began dancing her through the lobby – a swirl here, a dip there, like a pair of old-timers at Roseland – as their fellow guests watched in benign amusement.

"Michael!" Gerry didn't know whether to be pleased or embarrassed.

Pleased, on the whole.

Then into the lift –

". . . doesn't thrill me at all . . ."

Then booting open the door of their suite with a flourish – "

". . . but I get a kick . . ."

The moment the door shut, their bodies, still damp from the rain, converged in a seamless embrace. He had stopped singing. Yet as they kissed, the melody, imagined and unheard, played on to its close.

". . . out of you."

The hush that followed was profound.

Then Michael pulled back and held her at arms' length, his dark eyes filled with admiration. He looked very handsome. Very grave. A connoisseur considering a brilliant acquisition.

"I love you," he mouthed silently.

Gerry felt her heart brim over.

For a moment they stood motionless in the fading winter light listening to the hum of distant traffic. Then he took her hand and led her to the bedroom.

"I'll draw the curtains," she said.

He shook his head. "I want to see you," he said. "I'll always want to see your lovely face. Your smile."

The bedroom was a chaos of half-packed luggage, boxes, cartons, long dresses wrapped in tissue, gaping trunks, shoes strewn around like confetti: the signs of imminent departure, lending a poignance to the room.

They undressed, swiftly, deftly, letting clothes lie where they fell, then moved to the bed, with the consciousness of a chapter drawing to its end.

The coverlet was hidden by a welter of gifts. Of souvenirs. Sweet remembrances of a stay in paradise. Michael swept the stack aside with a casual hand. For the ultimate gift was each other.

By now the months of love had taught them all of each

other's touch points. Where flesh was hard, where it was tender. Where pleasure might be pushed to the edge of pain. What depths were to be searched. Yet tonight there was a first-time freshness in their caresses.

Like new and shiny honeymooners, she thought.

For a moment, they lay embraced. Imagining. Fingers intertwined. She looked up into his eyes with a mixture of solemnity and anticipation, then she shut her own and felt her skin go liquid beneath his smooth dark hands and eager tongue.

He was defining her body for her, committing it to memory. The hollows of her throat. The pulse beneath her ear. The roundness of her breasts. The curve of her thighs. The gathering river of moistness between her legs.

Time stopped. Light faded. Nothing existed except the consummation of their love.

Then hard and rhythmic and magnificently male, he invaded the portals of her body. They rolled together breathlessly, like animals in heat. Now he was above her, now under her, always deep within her until she could no longer tell what was hers, what was his. Hair tangled with hair, h art beat against heart, sweat mingled with tears mingled with semen.

Till at last she gave a sharp bright cry of joy.

And in that moment of fulfillment, Michael Avesian had become something transcendent. Almost divine.

He had become all the men she had ever loved. The only man she ever loved. He had become the embodiment of Love and Youth and Beauty.

Flying home the next day in Concorde, they sat side by side, contented, fingers interlaced. She looked out of the window as the coastline began to take shape some 60,000 feet below.

Wordlessly, she turned to him and smiled.

Gerry O'Neal was on top of the world.

part three

one

"First the good news!" Sharon Lapidus greeted Gerry on her return to New York. "Looks like the Transit Authority is going to buy off on the new turnstiles. Mr Yoshimura is delirious with joy."

Gerry nodded. "About time! And the bad news?"

"Well, not bad news exactly. More of a mystery. That trainee of yours, Leslie Balsam? She's gone."

This information elicited a state-of-the-art shrug.

"I should care, Sharon. We'll hire another trainee, that's all."

"Well, Leslie didn't just quit," Sharon expanded. "She walked out without a word – and never came back. With half a month's salary due."

"Oh dear, not the victim of violence, I hope."

"Not a victim at all, as far as I know. In fact, we may have been the victims of a hoax. It seems she gave us a fake address and home telephone number."

"Probably living with a guy, that's my bet. Well, as long as she didn't steal anything, no harm done. What else do you have for me?"

"Mostly the usual – and this." Sharon handed her a letter. "You said I should open your personal mail. I think you should read it."

Dear Gerry (Lee's letter began)
I know you'll be sorry to hear about my father's death. It's been a devastating experience for Mom . . .

She went on to describe David's funeral and Nancy's bereavement in evocative terms, with an indirect tribute to Gerry.

Mom would want you to be informed. She loves you so. Your friendship meant so much to both my parents. As it still does to me.

Gerry brushed back a tear.

347

I can't begin to apologize for the awfulness of my behaviour that afternoon last autumn. I can only implore your forgiveness.

Not a day goes by but that I think of you fondly. If only I could turn back the clock and unsay the words. Dear Gerry – can't we make it up? I miss your wit, your wisdom. I miss you! Please, let's be friends again – if not for my sake, then for my mother's. . . .

Gerry didn't even finish before she was on the phone to *Trend*.

"Poor baby," she consoled Lee, who sounded genuinely thrilled to hear from her. "How sad about your father! Such a dear man. And I'm the one requiring absolution. I should have got back to you ages ago. But better late than later. How about lunch next Friday, if you're free?"

"I'll make myself free," Lee's voice crackled with excitement.

"Terrific! I missed you, you crazy kid."

They chatted for a while, and Gerry hung up the phone with a lump in her throat.

David Whitfield's death had touched her. He was her generation, a contemporary. In her mind, still young and golden.

As for Nancy, Gerry's heart went out. Impossible not to grieve for the poor woman, lost and lonely in widowhood, the one man she loved gone forever. In Cedar City no less! And what a contrast between Nancy's bleak prospects and the blissful direction her own life had taken these past few months.

Gerry squeezed her eyes shut in gratitude.

Thank heaven for Michael Avesian!

No, not heaven – she corrected herself. The party to be thanked was Lee Whitfield. If not for Lee, she and Michael might never have met, never have fallen in love. One more reason to end this foolish feud. Life was too brief for recriminations.

"Forgive and forget," she murmured when Sharon arrived with coffee.

"Are you referring to Leslie Balsam?"

But Gerry, whose thoughts were elsewhere, was feeling

positively benign. She winked at Sharon. "Leslie who? I've already forgotten."

"My my," Sharon clucked. "Aren't we mellow!"

Back in the fold!
Lee could scarcely help gloating.

Not only had Gerry treated her to a fabulous lunch, but the great woman seemed chattier, more forthcoming than ever. Perhaps it was those martinis she'd become enamoured of these days. They loosened her tongue.

"No Campari?" Lee had asked when Gerry placed her order.

"Campari is for little old ladies."

From the opening Judas kiss to the request for wardrobe advice, Lee had played her cards exactly right.

As soon as the condolences were over ("Yes, I think your mother should come to New York, too!"), Lee had let it be known that she and Bill Frazier were "a couple".

"He's the sweetest guy, Gerry. I . . . well, in retrospect I can only thank you for not letting me fling myself at Michael Avesian. What a fool I made of myself!"

It was an awkward moment, but one Lee deemed necessary. It must be clear she had no designs on the master of Hailsham.

Gerry leaned over and patted her hand.

" 'Nuff said, Lee. I understand perfectly. Now tell me all about your young Lochinvar . . ."

It was easy to speak well of Bill Frazier. Only the night before she had confessed to being "genuinely fond" of him. Now she sang his praises to Gerry.

". . . writing a novel about his prep school experiences. We're hoping it'll be finished by the end of next year."

"How nice! I'm happy for you, darling. I always did have a sentimental weakness for writers. And they're usually pretty good in bed . . ."

"You think so?" Lee begged for reminiscences, and predictably, Gerry set off on one of her name-dropping excursions. The ghosts of former literary lions were duly invoked – men, Lee observed, who were either dead or a million years old. Lee took the opportunity to appraise her subject with a cold and analytic eye.

In the unsparing winter light, Gerry looked wearier than before. The lines about her eyes and mouth were deeper, more numerous. She had also put on weight. Love had gone to Gerry's hips as well as her head. How long, Lee wondered, before Michael Avesian sobered up? All it would take was one good strong dose of reality.

Lee let her ramble on for another round of drinks, then shifted the conversation to more recent events.

"I was horrified when that picture ran in the *Post!*" she said. "I presume that ghastly woman with the hair-do was Mrs Avesian."

"You presume correctly. I'm probably speaking out of school, but confidentially, his about-to-be-ex- is behaving like a crazy lady. Greedy. Spiteful. Resorting to every low tactic her lawyers can think of. She's even asked for sole custody of the children. Poor Michael's devastated! He adores those kids. Called them every day from London, picked out scads of marvellous toys at Hamley's. She sent them all back. Hell hath no fury – well, you know the rest. And just when everything was going so well!"

"Poor Michael," Lee echoed. "So he's filed for divorce?"

"*She* did, actually," Gerry replied. "Divorce I wouldn't mind. Michael will be well out of it. She's crimped his style long enough. But now she's determined to make both our lives miserable!"

"Disgusting!"

"It certainly is. And this happens to be a very difficult period for Michael, with all those balls he's juggling in the air. Well, you know how hard he works! The last thing he needs at this juncture is to have his assets tied up in litigation. If you ask me, she's cutting off her nose to spite her face." Gerry shook her head. "I just can't understand that type."

"What type?" Lee asked.

"Vengeful women!"

Lee gave a sympathetic smile. "Neither can I."

She left with the sense of having played Gerry like a fish.

The woman hadn't had a clue that Lee was after a story. Which went to prove that the old cliché about love being blind was true. Go figure!

"Blind!" Morag Goldenbloom told her father. "Blind to everything but him. I had the notion it was all she could do to keep her hands off . . . off the toy boy. I know it's a hateful term, Daddy, but when you consider the difference in age . . ."

"Actually living together in Claridge's?"

She nodded. "I'm sorry, Daddy. I don't want to wound you further, but the moment I realized who she was, I felt my heart turn to stone."

"She didn't realize who you were, I gather," Sir Campbell mused.

"Obviously not. As I said, she was blind."

He had come back to London to find that Geraldine O'Neal had left her footprints everywhere. She had tapped his connections, called mutual friends, even tried to engage his daughter in this fatuous project.

"I say, Campbell," one of his clubmates at the Reform inquired. "This O'Neal person . . . isn't she the woman you were . . ?"

Sir Campbell beat a hasty retreat.

For the next several days, he sequestered himself in his newly furnished flat in Albert Mansions, like a male version of Miss Havisham contemplating her mouldy wedding cake. Of his own Great Expectations there was nothing left except a bill for expensive draperies. But unlike his Dickensian counterpart, Sir Campbell found the solitary life distasteful. He was a man of action and when he emerged, on what ought to have been his own wedding day, it was with a sense of fierce purpose.

"A bloody outrage," he told a governor of the National Trust. "These Yanks come over here and plunder our national treasures. Hailsham Castle! Imagine! An integral part of Britain's heritage being turned into a row of suburban shops. Although we can't blame them entirely, can we, Adrian? I regret to say that the profit motive seems to have replaced traditional values in this country as well.

Better that 'fast buck' those Americans are always talking about than the slow stately tread of history. What next? The Crown Jewels? The Stone of Scone? Why not sell the Tower of London to Disneyland? After all, the Americans have already acquired London Bridge. One wonders if all of Britain is up for sale these days. It's shameful – and it must be stopped – beginning with Hailsham."

"I agree," the governor said sadly. "But how? Hailsham is a done deal, so to speak, and as far as the National Trust goes, our cash resources are finite."

"What can't be effected with money," Sir Campbell replied, "can often be achieved through a combination of public awareness and private pressure. We must influence views, beginning with the opinion-makers. The rest will follow.

"I haven't spent forty years in the foreign service without learning that there is more than one way to skin the proverbial cat. What's called for here is suasion. Making one's case to the right people and seeking their co-operation. Yourself, for example, and those others who combine a deep concern for the integrity of British life with the ability to act. These are the people I hope to reach. Prince Charles . . . Lord Snowdon . . . the Home Secretary . . . the Minister for Trade . . . the Director of the V & A . . . the Saatchi brothers . . ."

Sir Campbell ran down his list winding up with the Headmistress of St Paul's School for Girls. "Have all those children writing letters to *The Times*. It couldn't hurt."

"Good Lord!" the governor said. "You seem to have covered the entire British establishment. An extraordinary list, but where will you find the energy, the time?"

"Don't worry, Adrian." Sir Campbell gave a thin-lipped smile. "I'll find it. As it happens, I have an unexpected amount of leisure time on my hands these days."

two

"Forecasting would be easy," Eli Austrian told Michael, "if it didn't involve reading the future."

To which Michael might have added: reading Eli Austrian was damn near impossible.

Eli was deceptive. Round, bubbly, wreathed in fat, he cultivated a persona that derived more from the musical-comedy stage than from real life: that of the lovable, bumbling, but ever-gracious Mittel-European innkeeper with a crust like strudel and a heart of marzipan. Despite the name, he wasn't Mittel-European at all, but a Dutch Jew, a member of the Resistance who had spent the war years hiding in a vegetable cellar, living on subsistence rations, a fugitive from the Gestapo. Only at nightfall, a knife strapped to his calf, did the hunted emerge to become the hunter. Never expecting to survive the occupation himself, the erstwhile philosophy student had determined to take as many of "them" with him as possible.

His genius consisted of staging each death in such a way as to prevent civilian reprisals. A car crash. A drunken brawl. A wrong turn that plunged an unwary bicyclist into a canal.

His final "accident" victim was well chosen. An SS-Colonel with a passion for jingling uncut diamonds in his tunic, Erich von Stiele became the unwitting founder of Eli's fortune. One bibulous evening shortly before the Liberation, Eli had "assisted" the officer down a flight of stone steps, searched the body and kept the diamonds. They were his stake when he arrived in America.

The years of deprivation had left Austrian with an unappeasable sweet tooth and an appreciation of beauty in all its forms: particularly the beauty of elegant women. Beginning with a small dress shop on the Upper West Side, Eli managed, within a remarkably short period, to parlay Austrian's into a formidable contender for the Bergdorf-Goodman throne.

Women's Wear Daily dubbed him the "High-flying Dutchman" for his instinct in predicting fashion trends. And though he never referred to his wartime exploits (one generation's hero being another generation's assassin), the experience stayed with him. "I bear no grudges," he once told an inquiring reporter, adding that among the employees at his store might be found the daughter of a Prussian officer. What Eli didn't mention was the capacity in which the former aristocrat was employed: as an assistant in the shoe department. It gave Eli pleasure to see Elsa von Stiele stoop before American feet.

Michael, who knew nothing of his past, was nonetheless astute enough to realize that Eli loved the exercise of power as much as he eschewed exercise in all its other forms. He was the toughest customer Avesian had ever dealt with, always pushing for the competitive edge.

"Dear boy!" he would say, clasping a heavy arm across Michael's well-tailored shoulders. "We're all pedlars at heart, eh?"

He seemed to derive a peculiar pleasure from keeping Michael off balance. In the matter of the Hailsham contracts, Eli ran hot, cold, lukewarm, ran off to Palm Beach or Paris or Rome, continually slithering in and out of Michael's grasp. He reminded Michael of the carp in the pond of Hailsham Castle: plump, golden and elusive. Probably indigestible into the bargain. Michael began to weary of the chase.

"If I could only get the fucker to settle in one place long enough to put a pen in his hand," he grumbled to Gerry. "Or a gun to his head! Christ! Every time I see him, he changes the terms. A reduction in rent, an increase in services – one damn thing after another. The bastard figures he's got me by the short hairs."

"I hope you don't use that tone with Eli," she reproved.

"I practically go in there on all fours – and usually leave with even less than I came in. But there's a limit as to how long we can keep waltzing around."

"What are the alternatives?" Gerry asked.

"I go bust," he said grimly.

"Surely not!"

The negotiating sessions took place in Austrian's office overlooking Central Park, a dazzling monument to its owner's exquisite taste, furnished with African masks, modern paintings and a magnificent Steuben bowl filled to the brim with Perugino chocolates.

"We have to set a date, Eli, and get the contract signed."

Michael had determined to be firm. The bank was already breathing down his neck. "I can't keep the site available indefinitely. I have other prospects."

"Of course, dear boy," Austrian replied with a shrewd smile, then went on to admire Michael's tailoring, his haircut, the cuff links Gerry had given him for Christmas. "If you're ever interested in a modelling career . . ." Eventually he returned to the matter in hand.

"You know, Michael," Eli popped a chocolate into his mouth, "you really ought to let me have the premises gratis, as a kind of loss leader. Or at most, a purely nominal fee. It would be worth it to you, considering all the related business I bring in. I'd save money. You'd get prestige and other tenants. A mutually profitable arrangement, don't you think?"

Michael sat very still for several seconds, then got up with great dignity and walked to the door.

"Thank you, Eli. It's been a most interesting acquaintanceship."

He was at the elevator when Austrian's secretary came tearing down the hall.

"Mr Avesian," she panted. "Could you please step back into the office. Mr Austrian hasn't finished . . ."

"But I have," Michael snapped. "If he wants me, he knows where to find me." He spent the next two hours contemplating bankruptcy.

That afternoon, a draft of the contract between Austrian's Fifth Avenue and Hailsham Castle USA arrived at Michael's desk by messenger. The terms were a mix of favourable and sharp, but there were no differences that couldn't be resolved. Michael was studying it when Eli Austrian effected an entrance in person, beaming as though the morning's events had never occurred.

Sally ushered the great man in with an awed expression. Michael refused to rise. He was still simmering.

"Well, dear boy, you've seen the contract . . ."

"What was the purpose of that charade this morning?" he asked between clenched teeth. "Did you want to see if I was capable of playing hardball?"

"Something like that," Eli said with an avuncular smile. "I had to know how far I could push you. Now I know. Not too far. Come come, my boy. You would have done the same in my position, tried for maximum advantage. We're businessmen, not pantywaists. All out there with our pushcarts, jockeying for space. Now let's shake and be friends."

But Michael wouldn't take the proffered hand.

"It's in or out, Eli. I'm tired of fucking around."

Austrian hesitated a fraction of a second.

"In. I'll sign the papers now if you like."

Michael smothered a triumphant hoot. Let Eli turn gently in the wind for a bit. Let him see that two could play the waiting game.

"Not so fast. I'll have to have my lawyers vet it first."

They set a date for March fifteenth.

"The Ides," Gerry commented. "Beware the Ides of March."

"Now who's superstitious! One day is pretty much like another."

"I don't see why you made Eli wait, Michael. You could have had the money up front."

"I don't like being pushed around," came the reply. "Anyhow, another week or so won't make much difference."

To Gerry, however, the days were not all alike. There were days when Michael called a dozen times full of news, others when she didn't hear from him until the evening. Not that he was less affectionate, she told herself; simply that he was under a great deal of pressure.

Today, for instance, was her birthday, an event that would come and go unremarked. She had decided against mentioning it to Michael. Birthdays were such a graphic reminder not only of *her* age, but of *his*. The cards that poured in from all over were stashed away in a lingerie drawer and she forbade her employees to send flowers.

As it happened, Michael planned to go to Baltimore.

"Must you?" Gerry had asked the night before.

"They're my children," he said with a touch of asperity. "Of course I have to see them. Besides, I can't make much of a case for shared custody if I don't even bother to visit."

"It's just that, well, last week you were in San Francisco . . ."

". . . for a whole two days!"

". . . and Wednesday night you stayed over in Chicago . . ."

"Gerry!" he pleaded. "Be reasonable. I have a business to run. Surely you can manage without me for a day now and then. You know a million people. Call 'em. Do something something constructive with your time. Look." He picked a pile of mail on the night table. "The Andy Warhol show . . . a party at the Brookmayers . . . a benefit for the Save the Children Fund . . ."

"I don't want to go without you, darling. It wouldn't be fun. And I certainly wouldn't go with some other man."

Michael looked perplexed. "Then take a girl friend and catch a show. Or spend an evening at home – what's the harm? You know, you've gotten so damn used to having people around you all the time, you've become rather spoiled."

"Don't be sharp, Michael," Gerry said glumly. "I just hoped we could spend tomorrow together."

"Why? Is tomorrow something special?"

She shook her head, then put a brave face on it.

"Every day that I know you is special."

He went to Baltimore and Gerry, despite excellent intentions of spending a fruitful evening with the new Rushdie novel, felt listless and bored. Michael's suggestion that she "take a girl friend and catch a show" had touched a nerve.

Thirty-five years of living in a man's world had furnished

her with no close women friends and few confidantes. In desperation, she rang up Lee Whitfield.

Lee trotted over obediently, bearing a cake from Eclair.

"Twenty-one candles. I thought that was sufficient."

Gerry's eyes welled. "But how did you know it was my birthday?"

"How could I forget?" Lee replied. "No Michael on hand to help you celebrate?"

Gerry made a face.

"He's doing the dutiful with his kids. That bitch of a wife! You wouldn't believe what's going on, Lee! He's not even allowed into the house, she's got a restraining order. Seems he broke a window last time he was down there, and Sandra now claims he's violent. Michael violent! Of all the rubbish. I'm the one who's feeling homicidal. Now his lawyers tell him to be on the safe side, he should have a chaperon along when he visits the girls."

"I don't get it."

"The latest wrinkle in divorce cases," Gerry said. "Wife accuses hubby of child molestation, not on any factual basis but out of sheer cussedness. Happens all the time and very tough to disprove. Not that Sandra has made those charges yet, but we wouldn't put it past her. She's hit Michael with just about everything else in the book."

Gerry poured them both martinis from a silver pitcher.

"Here's to Alexandra McKay Avesian, may she rot in hell! Although personally I don't begrudge her the children. It would make life easier for Michael. Hell, for me too. I'm all for anything that puts a distance between us and that crazy lady. God! I hate women who make scenes! You know what I've always admired about you, Lee? You're the non-hysterical type. Very controlled."

Lee laughed. "My boyfriend says the same thing. So tell me, you think you and Michael will get married when all this is over . . . ?"

They spent a long clubby evening, with Gerry tossing back drinks, but Lee observed that booze did little to quell her edginess.

"Was that the phone?" she would jump up at the slightest noise.

"Some guy honking a horn."

And when the phone did ring, it turned out to be a telemarketer soliciting a donation.

"How dare you tie up this line!" Gerry barked into the mouth-piece. "You people are a public nuisance."

Lee filed the details away. And though she stayed till after midnight, Michael never did call.

"Oh, I forgot to tell you, my Mom's coming in next month. She's dying to see you."

"Splendid," Gerry slurred. "We'll have a class reunion."

How could you go from heaven to hell so swiftly? Gerry asked herself lying in bed at one in the morning.

Sleep was impossible. So was peace of mind.

She had been trying Michael's hotel room for the past half-hour without response. Where could he be at this time of night? With whom?

Once, early on in their affair, he admitted that Gerry had not been his first extra-marital fling.

"I would have been surprised if I were," she replied. "You're a very handsome and sexual man. Besides, fidelity has never struck me as a cardinal virtue, except in spaniels."

At the time it had seemed an amusing remark, indicative of her urbanity and a contempt for *petit bourgeois* mores.

They were free spirits then, she and Michael. Free to come and go, to give or take love, with no holds barred and no questions asked. What less could be expected in a romance between a street-smart hustler and a woman-of-the-world?

Those were the days – easy and delicious. And controlled.

But those days were now gone, for somewhere along the road, the balance of power had shifted. She was careering down the precipice without brakes.

Like it or no, Michael Avesian had become the centre of her life, the sun around which all else revolved. For him, she had broken her engagement, let her business go to hell, written off those friends who frowned on her infatuation.

359

"Come on, Gerry," Bobby Obermayer had coaxed. "Act your age."

"I do." She was furious. "I subscribe to *Lear's*. Whereas you seem to look to *Seventeen* for inspiration."

The publisher turned successive shades of purple, walked away and never spoke to her again. Three decades of friendship out the window!

Still, Gerry felt justified. Who was Obermayer to preach gospel? That dirty old man! Into his seventies and still getting serviced by teenage tootsies who squatted underneath his desk. The inequity of it all! The inequity! Like Eli Austrian, showing up to her party with a *Playboy* centrefold.

"Lucky bastard!" a mutual acquaintance had said with an envious nudge. "Got himself the best that money can buy."

The message was clear. Men were smart, virile, admirable to avail themselves of young love in firm bodies. Women who did so were a joke.

So much for the feminist revolution!

A wave of indignation swept through her. The idea of comparing her feeling, her passions for Michael with the sleazy couplings of those old men and their tarts! It was demeaning.

What passed between Michael and her went beyond sex, transcended the nigglings of the social code. They loved each other – birthdays be damned! In their case, age was meaningless, she felt. Meaningless!

Michael's wife was thirty-three.

Lee Whitfield was twenty-four.

That banker Michael talked about at Mercantile Trust . . .

"Is she young, this Anna Benson?" Gerry had asked.

"She's no kid," Michael replied.

"What do you mean by that?"

"Thirty, maybe . . ."

By Gerry's lights, a kid.

But age was meaningless. And birthdays were bunk.

As a matter of principle, Gerry had never lied about her age. Her life was too well documented in any event. But bald statistics were inconsequential. Were she twenty or sixty, she was still Geraldine O'Neal, ardent and vulnerable, loving Michael with as much fervour, as much selflessness as she had ever loved any man. She needed him, ached for him. Michael!

She rang the hotel again. Still no answer. Where the hell was he at two in the morning! Where could he be!

Gerry poured herself another drink and brooded.

Lord knows she didn't want to appear possessive, grasping, hysterical. That kind of treatment he could get from his wife! Still, how could Michael be so callous, not phoning her goodnight? Didn't he know how lonely she was? How much she suffered when he was gone?

Perhaps he knew and it scared him. They weren't in London any more; that particular fantasy could never be recaptured. This was the real world of wives and children and mortgages and dogs and in-laws. Of prior ties and ancient affections.

Even now – it struck her – he might be making overtures to go back home. Gerry had a swift unbidden recollection of Michael's wife that day at the Waldorf. Not chic; but pretty, rosy, with velvet skin, vibrant with the bloom and resilience of youth. Thirty-three years old! How beautiful Gerry had been at thirty-three! The memory ached.

Gingerly, she put her hand beneath her chin and pinched the skin gently. A fold of flesh bunched between her fingers.

Age was meaningless?

Suddenly, intuitively, she knew where Michael was. With his wife! What else could explain his silence, his cruelty?

Why, at this very moment, they might be sitting at the kitchen table, drinking coffee, making small talk, healing the wounds.

Worse! They might be in bed, making love. Gerry could envision it with an immediacy that made her stomach turn: that woman's young flesh, tender and firm beneath Michael's caresses, legs entwined, mouths locked, bodies joined. Sweet, sweated love.

Trembling, she grabbed the phone and managed to get the number from information.

The phone rang and rang in some distant room.

"Michael?" she could barely control her anxiety. "I want to speak to Michael."

"Who is this?" The woman's voice was fuzzy with sleep.

Suddenly Gerry tumbled out of control. "You bitch! You greedy little bitch! I want you to leave him alone. He doesn't love you, you foolish bitch. He loves me . . . me . . . me . . !"

The woman on the other end hung up.

"OK," Gerry pushed the redial button. "You think you can hide from me? We'll try again, you fucking cunt!"

After the fifth call, her nemesis left the phone off the hook. Gerry made another thirty or forty attempts before dissolving into angry tears. She fell into an alcohol-induced sleep around dawn.

Michael rang up early next morning from his hotel.

"Where were you?" She started weeping. "I tried to get you all night. I was going crazy wondering what happened . . ."

"I'm sorry, darling." He sounded affectionate and reasonable. "I was so wiped out, I unplugged the phone. That's all. I didn't think you'd be worried."

"It was my birthday yesterday!" she blurted out, her good intentions forgotten.

"Why the hell didn't you tell me?" Michael was nonplussed. "I would have planned something special. Tell you what. I'll take the next plane out and we'll have a belated celebration."

"Oh god, Michael, I look a wreck and I have this terrible hangover. . . ."

"Well, get freshened up and I'll be there around lunch. I've got just the hangover remedy."

Revivified, she jumped out of bed and went down to the kitchen to bury her face in crushed ice. Then on with her best make-up, her sexiest Natori lingerie . . .

An hour later a bucket of white orchids arrived at her door. An hour after that, the man himself.

Gerry flung herself into his arms.

"Oh God! How I love you!"

From hell to heaven in twenty-four hours.

Sandy Avesian called in at her lawyer's office first thing that morning.

"My husband's 'girlfriend'—" She made a face. The term was thoroughly distasteful in reference to a woman of that age. "This O'Neal person," she continued, "has been harassing me with obscene phone calls in the middle of the night. See that you add that to the complaint."

three

"Welcome to The Apple," Lee announced with pride of place.

To which Nancy Whitfield said, "Might as well be Timbuctoo!"

Lee had met her at the airport, determined to pull out all stops and show Nancy a wonderful time. After thirty-odd years in the wilderness, the homecomer deserved a bit of a fling, for though Nancy was the born New Yorker, it was her daughter who understood the ins and outs.

"Don't you put your suitcase down for one minute," Lee cautioned her as they waited in the taxi line. "JFK is full of thieves."

Obediently, her mother clutched the handle of her bag as though assault were imminent. An SST screeched overhead.

"JFK." Nancy couldn't resist a moment's reminiscence. "It used to be Idlewild in my day. Idle . . . wild. Like in wild blue yonder. That's much more romantic sounding. Full of the poetry of flight."

"Yeah well . . ." Lee shrugged, absorbed in the competition for taxis. "And dinosaurs once walked the earth. Ah! Here we are!"

She stowed Nancy's suitcases into a battered Yellow Cab. "Eighty-seventh and Third. This time of day you're better off taking the Triborough and going down Second Avenue . . ."

Nancy leaned back impressed.

"You sound just like a genuine New Yorker."

"Well, you gotta watch it with these guys. If they figure you for an out-of-towner, they rip you off mercilessly."

Nancy coughed respectfully as the Manhattan skyline materialized in the distance. " I haven't decided whether I'm a space traveller or a time traveller. The Empire State I know and the World Trade Center I recognize from the movies, but what's that funny one that looks like an open cigarette box?"

"Citicorp," Lee said. "And there's AT&T with the fancy top. The idea was to model it after a piece of Chippendale furniture. Unlike the real Chippendale's, which happens to be a male strip club. Now if you look over there, you · an almost see my building . . ."

She enjoyed playing the sophisticated tour guide to the provincial visitor, thoroughly conscious of the reversal of roles. It was like being her mother's mother in a way.

"So what do you want to do while you're here, Mom? Go shopping . . . catch some shows? I can get tickets for anything you like through the magazine. You have but to say the word."

Nancy put in a request for *Cats*. "Though I suppose you've already seen it. And one thing I feel it's my duty to do is visit the house where I grew up . . ."

"The Bronx?" Lee broke in. "Are you kidding? Jeezus, Mom! Your old nabe is a war zone. Nobody goes up there any more without an armed guard. And if you're planning any other sentimental journeys, let me warn you – you can also write off Times Square, Grand Central Station, three quarters of Central Park, anything north of 96th Street. Ditto with the subway. Skip it. It's a sty at rush hours and a menace the rest of the time. If you don't see a bus, take a cab. But not a gypsy cab. Those guys aren't insured, besides which none of 'em speak English. I wouldn't lay all this on you if I didn't feel it was crucial, but there are certain things you have to know if you're going to survive. So listen to . . ." She almost stumbled into Gerry's locution, *Listen to Momma*, and smothered a grin. "Listen to your street-smart daughter 'cause she knows best. Now about grifters – you'll find 'em everywhere with their hands out, even on Park Avenue. Pass right on by. I know you're a sucker for a sob story, but these guys are mostly hustlers and freaks. The trick is, to avoid eye contact . . ."

Nancy looked at her daughter in dismay. "You make me wonder, Lee. If this city's such a garbage pile, why do you stay?'

"New York's marvellous, once you know the ropes. The point is, you've got to get it to work for you."

"Well, it's certainly working for you," Nancy commented when they pulled up in Lee's building. A doorman wearing gold epaulettes sprang into action, retrieving Nancy's bags. Compared to his splendour, to say nothing of the lobby's magnificence, even her brand-new luggage looked shabby. Meanwhile, Lee was paying off the cab driver with crisp ten dollar bills.

"Receipt please," she said, then got out and squired her mother through the lobby.

"Why did you need a receipt?" Nancy wondered as they rode up to the 26th floor.

"I'll write it off on the expense account," Lee said. "As far as the office is concerned, this is a working afternoon."

"Is that proper?' Nancy inquired.

"Proper-schmopper. Well, maybe not in Cedar City, Mom, but this is New York. Everybody does it all the time."

In contrast to the lobby with its twenty foot high mirrors and inch-thick carpeting, Lee's apartment was a distinct let-down.

"It's so tiny," Nancy said. "And there's no kitchen."

"It's a galley kitchen."

"I've seen bigger galleys in trailers. It seems to me that for eighteen hundred dollars a month, they could put in a decent kitchen. You ought to complain to the landlord. That's disgraceful."

Lee laughed.

"Nobody cooks here, Mom. Who has the time? I eat out every night along with the rest of humanity. And speaking of food, as it happens, we're smack in the middle of one of the city's finest restaurant districts. Japanese, Indonesian, Szechuan. You name it. I thought if you like, we could try Afghan tonight. Now there's something I bet you've never had! Or if you're too tired to go out, there are plenty of terrific take-away places that deliver. Remember, you're not in Cedar City any more. This is . . ."

"I know," a bemused Nancy concurred. " 'This is New York.' "

366

"And tomorrow night we're eating with Bill at Sign of the Dove."

"Well, do with me what you like, Lee. I place myself in your hands completely. Especially since I'm no longer allowed to go to the Bronx," she added sharply. "Or any of my other ancient haunts. The one thing I'm determined to do before I go back is see Gerry O'Neal."

Lee nodded enthusiastically.

"It's all taken care of. I've spoken to Gerry. You and she have a date for lunch on Thursday."

"Really! As soon as that!"

Nancy sat down suddenly. The imminence of their reunion had taken the wind out of her.

"My God, Thursday. Aren't you kind of jumping the gun? I'm not ready. What'll I wear? Maybe I should get my hair done first. I thought another week or so when I'm more oriented . . ."

"Relax, Mom. Be yourself. It's going to be an informal lunch in her house. Just the two of you. There's nothing to worry about. You make it sound like a trip to the dentist. For heaven's sakes, you've known the woman one zillion years."

But Nancy, now that this momentous occasion was looming large on the horizon, had a case of the jitters. "I know it sounds stupid, Lee, but after all these years, the thought of seeing her in the flesh makes me nervous."

Gerry O'Neal was nervous too.

Or, if "nervous" was too potent a word, then apprehensive. Gerry, who had met heads of state and film stars and titans of industry, who had addressed the entire Democratic Convention on national TV – that same Geraldine O'Neal felt a knot in the pit of her stomach at the prospect of spending a couple of hours with her oldest friend.

Finding exactly the right tone was difficult. She didn't want to lord her success over Nancy: that was crude in the extreme. On the other hand, she was proud of her accomplishments. She'd come a long way, baby, from her Hunter College days.

Even the question of venue proved troublesome. A "cel-

367

ebrity" restaurant usually afforded the best treat an out-of-towner could wish. The Russian Tea Room sprang to mind. But would Nancy appreciate the clout required to commandeer the first banquette on the right? And if she did, would it make her self-conscious?

She discarded the Côte Basque as too dressy. The Metropolitan Club, too male. The Cafe Maurice, too *too*! And God forbid Nancy should reach for the check!

She booked a table at 21, then cancelled five minutes later. She knew too many of the lunch-time regulars, a factor to be considered should Nancy turn out to be an embarrassment. Despite her democratic leanings, Gerry held outlanders in low esteem.

Ultimately, she opted for a catered lunch in the brownstone, elegant but unfussy. Gravlax. *Blanquette de veau.* And some of that divine chocolate cake from Four Seasons. A pitcher of martinis. A nice dry Puligny-Montrachet. Espresso to close. Her housekeeper could serve. Simplicity itself!

She decided to take the afternoon off and play the scenario by ear. Her secretary was instructed to phone at two-thirty. If Nancy proved tiresome, Gerry could engineer an escape. If not – well, the experience would be interesting, to say the least.

"What does your mother look like?" she grilled Lee in advance. "I have this ghastly feeling I won't recognize her."

"Pepper-and-salt hair," Lee replied, "which she wears clipped short. A little on the chunky side, but not what you'd call heavy. Far from it! Mom's a very attractive woman for her age."

The description sent Gerry's competitive instincts surging. "Attractive" was a loaded word. On the day she dressed and made up with meticulous care, then fortified herself with a double martini.

When the door bell rang at precisely 12:30, Gerry practically knocked Ida down in the rush.

"I'll get it myself," she hollered.

"Nancy!"

"Gerry!"

Five second freeze.

"Let me look at you!"

Nancy was as Lee had described. Crisp short hair. Thickish waistline. Bright clever eyes. And a perfectly dreary tweed suit with a hemline well below the knees. But then, Cedar City wasn't noted for its tailoring.

The two women exchanged self-conscious hugs.

"Come in, come in!" Gerry drew her into the house, while Nancy's eyes grew wider with every step.

"Oh, isn't this gorgeous!" she gasped. "Boy, what a change from your grandma's apartment. And that painting at the top of the stairs. A genuine Sargent, Lee said. Reminds me of that big billboard across the street where you used to live? The Indian squaw? Remember!"

Gerry rolled her eyes heavenward.

"I've been trying to forget it for forty years. How about a drink, Nan? A nice dry martini? To be perfectly honest, I'm just a wee bit nervous about seeing you after all this time, I expect you are too. A spot of lubrication will relax us both."

She suddenly had an alarmed second thought. Nancy had been living in the boonies, practically the Bible Belt.

". . . unless you have views about alcohol."

"My views," Nancy said, "are 'hold the olive, twist of lemon'!"

"What a relief!"

The martinis turned out to be exactly the right prescription. Within twenty minutes, the two women were cackling merrily, exchanging the expected rounds of "whatever-happened-to".

"Though you're in a better position than I to keep up, Gerry."

"Not really, although I do see a few of our old classmates now and then . . ."

Carole Wolff had become a literary agent. Marian Maltese was an editor on *Fortune*. Irma Zaplinski ("Remember her, she was the captain of the softball team?") had been elected a senior partner at Cravath Swaine.

"Wow! We were one terrific class, weren't we?" Nancy marvelled. "I guess I'm the only non-achiever."

"Far from it!" By now, Gerry was suffused with *bonhomie*. "I think three-quarters of us wound up with hubby and kids in the suburbs. Irma, Carole, Marian, me . . . we're the exceptions."

When her secretary rang, they were just finishing dessert.

"Cancel my calendar," Gerry said. "I'm with a dear old friend."

"More coffee?" she turned to her guest. "More anything?" but Nancy rubbed her belly with a guilty sigh.

"No thanks. That was a splendid meal. I won't eat for a week. You know what I'd really like. I'd love to take a tour of your house. Lee's always raving about it and if it's not an imposition . . ."

"No problem!" Gerry rose. "One grand tour coming up!"

Nancy found everything fascinating. The furniture. The bibelots. The Sèvres tea service. The African rugs. Every item carried its own anecdote concerning provenance. "I got that at the bazaar in Marrakesh . . . the Shah of Iran gave me this cigarette box . . . that Lalique vase was a birthday present from Malcolm Forbes . . . now these Ashanti goldweights are interesting . . ."

They wandered upstairs into the den, the guest rooms and finally into Gerry's own bedroom.

"My Lord!" Nancy fell back at the sight of an open closet. "I've never seen so many clothes. May I . . . ?"

"Be my guest."

"Just a little poke through."

It amused Gerry to see the impression her wardrobe made on Nancy, who appeared momentarily blinded by massed silks and sequins.

"This is so thrilling!" Nancy gasped. "I know you're going to think I'm nosy, but I've only seen clothes like this in the movies. They're fantasies!" She pointed to a beaded Geoffrey Beene sheath that practically glowed in the dark. "Stunning! What does something like this cost, dare I ask? Five, six hundred dollars?"

370

"Times ten," Gerry said with a swell of pride.

Nancy withdrew her hand as if burned.

"That's practically what we paid for our Honda! Imagine that! Six thousand dollars! I'd be petrified to wear it. And Lee tells me you have the most fabulous collection of furs."

"That closet on your left."

Gerry curled up on the bed, while Nancy inspected the contents one by one.

"Seven fur coats!" she marvelled. "One for every day in the week."

Gerry, suddenly made self-conscious by what must have struck her guest as an indecent display of wealth, felt called upon to apologize.

"Of course some of them go back to the dawn of time, Nancy. That beaver, for instance, is so old it's flea-bitten. It should have gone to the thrift shop ages ago. Along with that corny mink stole . . . shades of those old Doris Day movies." Gerry rolled her eyes. "You know, the ones where she always got Rock Hudson – lucky girl!"

But the irony was lost on Nancy. She looked dazed.

"And this? What do you call this fur, Gerry?"

It was the coat Michael had given her a few months back.

"That's Canadian lynx."

"Lynx," Nancy echoed as if in a trance. The garment had hypnotized her. Gerry sat up, half-expecting to be charged with endangering a species. But when Nancy turned, her eyes were glowing with desire.

"I don't think I've ever seen anything so beautiful. Could I ask a favour?"

"You want to try it on?" Gerry intuited. "Go right ahead, Nan. And there's a matching hat on the second shelf."

It was a fur for a much taller woman, she was tempted to add, but why spoil Nancy's pleasure? One thrill-of-a-lifetime coming up, she thought and smothered a smile.

As foreseen, the great lynx came almost to the floor on Nancy. What couldn't have been anticipated was the total effect. It was astonishing. The colour of the fur exactly complemented the silver highlights of Nancy's hair, illuminated her skin, brightened her eyes. Nancy fluffed up the collar until it framed her like a nimbus. As she did, her face took on an alabaster glow.

Good furs did that, as Gerry had long ago observed. They endowed the wearer with glamour, magic. Enhanced such beauty as you possessed. Fur made you feel rich, elegant, desirable, pampered, powerful. And sexy! Few things in life offered greater sensual pleasure than the intimate caress of fur against flesh.

Gerry remembered her very first fur coat, purchased when she was twenty-six. It was a silky nutria, then the height of fashion, and its acquisition had been a landmark of sorts. Her column, "On My Own", had just been syndicated and she decided to celebrate, as she told Bobby Obermayer, "by wrapping myself in the skins of dead animals."

After a happy two hours of trying on everything in Russek's fur salon, she settled on the nutria.

"That'll be charged to *Mr* O'Neal?" the salesman had asked, for those were the days when young women didn't buy such things for themselves. When credit cards and bank loans required a male guarantor.

"There isn't one, I'm happy to say," Gerry had retorted, and paid for the coat in cash.

She could still remember how luxurious she had felt standing in front of the three-way mirror in the fur salon, posing for all she was worth. Swirling. Preening. Even mugging a bit. Just as Nancy was doing now.

Gerry watched her with interest.

Nancy took a few tentative steps, did a half-turn and nodded at her reflection in approval. Then she began stroking the fur with a dreamy narcissistic air. At first her movements were delicate, almost fearful, palms open, skimming lightly across the surface of the fur. Then splaying her fingers, she ran her hands slowly down the length of the sleeves, going with the grain, watching the silky hairs spring up in the wake of her touch. She looked like a woman in love. Her self-absorption was absolute.

"That's your colour," Gerry said softly. "If you ever buy a fur coat, look for those beigy, silvery shadings."

For a long time Nancy said nothing, too smitten by the

image before her. Then she hugged herself and uttered a soul-felt sigh.

"David always wanted me to have a fur coat," she said at last, and Gerry caught an undercurrent of bitterness. "Winters are very hard in Cedar City. But of course it was out of the question. We had four children to put through college."

Disturbed at what she was hearing, Gerry seized upon a conciliatory tone.

"And now," she said graciously. "instead of a couple of moth-eaten furs, you have four terrific children to be proud of. They have to be terrific, if Lee is any example. Such a marvellous girl. Plus all those grandchildren! Well, you've got the jump on me there. Honestly, Nan, I envy you."

Suddenly Nancy whipped around, her face contorted with rage.

"That's hot! You envy me! Well, thank you very much, Lady Bountiful! It happens that I'm sick and tired of being patronized, which is what you've done from the moment I set foot in this house."

"Come on, Nancy!" Gerry struggled to maintain a reasonable pitch. "It's been a pleasant afternoon. Let's not ruin it by behaving like children. You talk as though I've had a free ride all these years. I worked for everything I've got – and damn hard! Remember, we made choices, you and I. You chose marriage, David. That was your prerogative. Don't belittle it. Think of all those years of love and companionship with a wonderful man . . ."

"One man! As against how many? Dozens? Hundreds?"

"So that's it!" an exasperated Gerry lashed out. "My sex life doesn't get the Good Housekeeping Seal. Tough! Although I'm not sure what your message is, Nancy. Do you disapprove of my so-called hundreds of lovers or simply envy me the amount?"

"I'm sorry!" Nancy drew back from the precipice, but only just. "That was a stupid and offensive remark on my part. Forget I said it. But it doesn't alter events. The point is, Gerry, that you wound up with everything – this house, clothes, lovers, fame. The jackpot! And I have zilch! It's not fair!"

Gerry didn't know what to make of Nancy's outburst, except to recognize that thirty-odd years of accumulated resentment lay behind it. But what, precisely, did the woman want from her? Was Nancy angling for her to make a present of the lynx coat? No doubt Lee had titillated her mother with tales of Gerry's largesse.

Well, that largesse did not extend to a $30,000 fur. Aside from its being a gift from Michael, Gerry adored the coat and had no intention of giving it away. Yet some gesture seemed appropriate, some bit of noblesse oblige. She considered giving her the pastel mink stole (much more in keeping with Nancy's style) and would have done so on the spot, but for that disparaging "Doris Day" crack made earlier.

She now scrutinized Nancy with sceptical eyes, less shocked than profoundly disappointed. It wasn't that unusual for acquaintances to ask about her cast-offs. Gerry's wardrobe was superb and the list of takers was long. The girls at the office, her housekeeper, cleaning woman, personal trainer: at one time or another they had all expressed an interest in Gerry's out-dated numbers. Gerry often obliged, viewing it as a form of tipping. She was only sorry to add Nancy to the list of "tippees".

"What do you want? Not the lynx, I'm afraid," she said coolly, "but if there's something else you'd like from my wardrobe, something a bit more suitable . . ."

"How dare you!" Nancy's eyes blazed. "You think I came here for a hand-out? A beaded dress? A bit of fur? So you could add it to the birds and write me off as paid in full? I'll never be paid in full. Never! Because if not for me, none of this would exist. How can you ever compensate me for what I gave you! It would take more than a fur coat, Gerry. I gave you the biggest break of your life. I gave you your career! You said part of it would always belong to me, remember?"

The two women faced each other, across a sea of turbulent years.

"Or maybe you'd rather forget," Nancy said in a low angry voice. "It was so very long ago."

374

"Of course I'd rather forget – but I *can't!*"

I can't!

The words echoed down the corridors of time.

I can't!

Memory surged. The decades fell away to that long-ago moment when they were young, when life was full of dreams and hopes. When the fate of two best friends was settled in a little coffee shop across the street from Hunter College.

"I *can't!*" A twenty-year-old Nancy began twisting her engagement ring in distress. It was a genuine half-carat diamond in a Sweetheart setting, still new enough to feel quite strange. "Don't ask me, Gerry. I couldn't possibly."

"But I am asking. Please . . . please give it to me, I beg you, I beseech you . . ."

"Implore? Importune? Petition? Adjure? Really, Gerry, you sound like Roget's *Thesaurus!*"

"I wish I did, but I leave the literary stuff to you, Nan. You're the one who's so terrific with words. And that's precisely why I'm asking. For heaven's sakes, you're marrying David in another couple of months, heading west. What difference can it make?"

Nancy drew a deep breath. "I *can't*," she repeated. "That's cheating."

"It's not cheating," Gerry pleaded, "it's sharing."

"Don't fudge with semantics!" Nancy shot her a rueful look. "You and I both know it's immoral. I sweated over that essay. It's mine! You wouldn't want to win the Goldman scholarship on false premises . . ."

"The hell I wouldn't!"

"With somebody else's written work. It would be – well, a tainted honour. You'd feel guilty forever."

"Let me worry about that," Gerry said, then turned almost kittenish. "Oh Nan! Wonderful brilliant kind supersensitive Nancy whom I love beyond all else in the world. You're my best friend – now and forever. Save my life! Only you can do it. If I don't win that damn scholarship and get out of here, I'll wind up as a secretary or a file clerk. God forbid! I'd rather die. I may never have a chance like this again. Believe me, I wouldn't ask if I had your flair for writing, your literary cachet. But I don't. This once, bend your ethical code. For me. Who will know? Who will care?"

"Suppose they find out it's my essay?"

"How?" Gerry pounced, for she scented victory. "They're gonna run a typewriter check? Who are we – Whittaker Chambers and Alger Hiss? I'll retype the whole thing, if that's what you're worried about. No one will ever know."

"But . . . but . . ."

"Look at it this way," Gerry pursued the advantage. "If I win the scholarship . . . better yet, when I win, you'll know in your heart that you're the real champion. Nancy Schroeder – excuse me, Nancy Schroeder Whitfield, the best that Hunter College has to offer. And whatever success comes to me from then on out, well, part of that will always belong to you."

A week later, she submitted an essay entitled "The Future Of Women," by Geraldine O'Neal.

"Brilliant," said the head of the English department. "Teeming with ideas. Literate. Full of style. One of the best pieces ever written by an undergraduate."

The essay was reprinted in that year's edition, *Best of American College Writing* and still turns up in anthologies now and then. Some people, noting that she dropped her "literary style" soon after, claim that it's the finest piece Gerry has ever written.

"It should have been me!" Nancy cried. "It should have been me on the *Queen Mary* sailing to France. Everything else stemmed from that."

There was a terrible silence, then Nancy took off the lynx coat and hung it up carefully in the closet.

"The eagle and the wren, you called us once, even though we started at par. You've soared, I've twittered. There you have it."

"Oh Nancy!" The tears were streaming down Gerry's face. "No one can change the past. I can barely handle the present any more. If it's any consolation – and it probably isn't – I can't even say my life has been happier than yours, on balance. More varied, perhaps, but not necessarily happier. I've had crazy ups and downs, along with those 'accomplishments' everyone talks about. Plenty of misery to dampen the joy. Nothing comes without a price, least of all success. Believe me, I've done many things I'm not terribly proud of, including the use of your essay. The one thing I've never regretted is our friendship. No one else has ever been so close to me as you have, Nancy. In my heart, you'll always be what you were that day in the coffee shop. My best buddy."

She put out her hand. Nancy took a step forward. Suddenly they fell into each other's arms, crying, clinging. Like lovers reunited at the end of a war.

"Still friends?" Nancy blubbered.

"Best of friends," came the reply.

After which they went downstairs and had a stiff brandy.

"And what will you do now?" Gerry asked gently. "Stay in New York or go back to Cedar City?"

Nancy shook her head.

"I don't know. The future's even more problematic than the past."

They kissed, the immediate damage repaired. But the afternoon's events had left both women shaken to the core.

four

Sandy Avesian too was involved with a "best friend", though hers was of more recent vintage.

Lately, she and Iris Daniels had become close as paint. They were an odd couple, the abandoned wife and the powerhouse realtor, and Sandy suspected the friendship had been launched on false premises. Iris admired her. She introduced her to Baltimore's movers and shakers as "Tiger Lady" in the belief that the wine-throwing incident at the Waldorf had been a sign, not of desperation, but of liberation. "This woman," Iris would amplify, "doesn't take shit from anybody."

The announcement was followed by a respectful hum.

Sandy didn't argue. Better a tiger than a mouse. She determined to live up to her notices. In the course of becoming the woman she was purported to be, she began to dress differently. Talk differently. Even to think in unfamiliar patterns, for there was more to toughness, she realized, than out-sized shoulder pads and the use of four-letter words. Toughness took practice. And what better medium for the sharpening of claws than the mechanics of a multi-million-dollar divorce!

In the intricacies of the legal process, she discovered the perfect outlet for her frustration. She supervised, refined, perfected, manipulated columns of figures, invested assets, handled cash flow, balanced claims and counter claims until Mr Mintz himself was limp with admiration. It was a full-time job, but the rewards went far beyond money. They could be assessed in terms of power and respect and self-esteem.

On occasion, she was struck by the notion that Michael had done her an inadvertent favour. If not for his desertion, she never would have developed her talents, never tasted the heady wine of autonomy. She would have ambled through life in the same old way. Even her father was impressed by the change.

"Well, Sandy, you sure are giving that low-life a taste of his own medicine," Harry McKay said. "My little girl is turning out to be one smart cookie."

"I'm not so little," she replied, adding that henceforth she preferred to be known as Alexandra.

Why not? It was her given name. Moreover it carried a significant heft and weight. Queens were named Alexandra. Conquerors. Alexandra the Great. Whereas Sandy was for baton-twirlers and short-order cooks.

By winter's end, she felt deserving of a break. Thus, when Iris suggested they spend a week at a spa in Virginia ("Let's stash the kiddies and indulge ourselves for a bit") Sandy concurred.

The experience was novel. Not since she began going steady with Michael at the age of sixteen had any hands other than his touched her body in a pleasurable capacity. After a few initially awkward moments, (well, it was odd having total strangers pummel one's buttocks), Sandy learned to shut her eyes and concentrate on end results. Alexandra the Great – and the Glamorous.

With that image before her, she submitted happily to the ministrations of masseurs and herbalists and shiatsu practitioners and aerobics instructors and dietitians and manicurists and the other adepts of beauty-cum-fitness. After years of fussing over others, she relished having others fuss over her.

She went to bed each night half-starved and wholly content.

"You're turning into quite the hedonist," Iris remarked as they lay on adjacent tables in the steam room, covered in layers of fragrant Hawaiian seaweed.

"Better make that *she*donist," Sandy said, reluctant to admit that she didn't know what a hedonist was.

Iris hooted with laughter. *"Touché."*

The coinage made the rounds at the spa and before the week was out, the "shedonist" had not only shed eight pounds along with her high-school hairdo, but Alexandra Avesian had acquired a reputation as something of a wit.

"Michael won't recognize me," she said to Iris at dinner the night before their departure.

"Michael who!" Iris snorted. "I thought you were through with that two-timing bastard."

"Well of course I am. But he still wouldn't recognize me," Sandy added, almost wistfully.

Iris chewed for a minute on a naked shitake. "You're not having second thoughts, are you – about the divorce? You got the man on the ropes, honey. He's reeling. It's time for the knockout punch. Is he still with that woman, by the way?"

"Yeah . . . she's been driving me bananas. Midnight phone calls, obscenities. That's why I got an unlisted phone. But I think Michael's getting bored. Why else would she be making these scenes? I figure if she knew where he was every moment, she wouldn't have to bug me."

"Serves the old husband-snatcher right. But that's no reason for you to let up on the guy. He fucked you over once, he'll do it again. I know this is a sticky period for you, lovey. I've been through it twice myself and my advice is – don't be a sucker for sentiment. Stick to your guns."

"But I'm not used to living without a man."

"Who said anything about celibacy? You'll go back to Baltimore – looking gorgeous, may I add! – get some new duds, then go out and break a few hearts. There are men galore if you know where to look. Remember, you're coming on to the market as a desirable commodity, Alexandra. As a woman of independent means."

Sandy sighed. "It's just that, well – I always considered myself the type of person who mates for life."

"Penguins mate for life," Iris said cuttingly. "That doesn't make 'em praiseworthy. Don't back down now. When I think of the way you've grown the last few months, taking charge of everything, handling the investments, the way you've looked out for Number One: well, who wouldn't be impressed! You have a terrific head for business."

Sandy laughed. "That's what my lawyer says. It's been an interesting experience – the whole divorce procedure. I developed muscles I didn't even know I had."

"Tiger Lady!" Iris said.

Sandy accepted the tribute with a graceful nod. And all

380

the while she couldn't help thinking: Mikey would be so proud.

Michael Avesian was nibbling on a Perugino.

He didn't normally care for chocolates, but this chilly March afternoon, with the culmination of his dream but moments away, his system cried out for something sweet and comforting. Across the elaborate bombé desk (more appropriate to a museum, Michael thought, than an office), Eli Austrian was flipping through the last pages of the contract.

Michael chewed and assured himself that today's ritual was but a formality, each item having already been worked out in precise detail. It was a *fait accompli*. The lawyers had had their innings. Gerry had handled the press release. All that was wanting now was Eli's signature, followed by a pop of champagne. But as always, the wily old Dutchman tried to milk the situation for maximum suspense.

"What is our agreement concerning hurricane insurance . . . ?" He looked up inquiringly at Michael.

"In Hereford, Hertford and the heart of New Jersey," Michael volleyed with a smile, "hurricanes hardly ever happen."

"What's that, young man?"

Michael sighed. "I permitted myself a small joke, Eli. The clause about hurricane insurance is in subsection 14, next to floods."

"Ah! A joke. I see!" Eli returned to his perusal.

Both men were aware of the ruckus that had been brewing in England. A high-powered campaign was underway with the catch-phrase KEEP HAILSHAM BRITISH, and it had come as something of a shock that the prime mover was Sir Campbell Simms.

"Why the hell would he do such a thing?" Michael asked Gerry. "I thought the man was a friend of yours?"

"More than a friend, actually. A fiancé. We were supposed to be married round about now."

"Shit, Gerry!" Michael struggled to silence the alarm bells that had begun sounding inside his head. "Why didn't you tell me you were engaged?"

"I didn't want to upset you."

Michael chewed on this. The source of his difficulties was becoming apparent. "You certainly seem to have upset *him*. Tell me, how did you go about breaking the news that the wedding was off?"

"Not very tactfully, I'm afraid. Campbell never even replied. Please, Michael, don't press me on the sordid details. At the time I was just too happy to think straight." She burst into tears. "I'm sorry, darling. I seem to have fucked up terribly."

He wound up taking her in his arms and consoling her with love and kisses, which was odd considering that he was the injured party. The matter was dropped. It could only lead to further tears and recriminations. Privately, however, Michael was staggered at her lack of judgement. Brilliant as she was in broad strokes and grand design, Gerry was neglectful of basic details. In this case, certainly, she had led with her heart, not her head.

When a reporter from *Business Week* had called him on the story, Michael shrugged it off. "Just a bunch of well-meaning but confused environmentalists," he'd told the newsman, pointing out that their efforts were too little and too late. By now, Hailsham had been completely dismantled. Even as they spoke, the components were being loaded onto freighters at Southampton. The first shipment was to arrive in a matter of weeks.

"All the king's horses and all the king's men . . ." he concluded. The statement spoke for itself.

Then he'd crossed his fingers behind his back.

Unconsciously, he was crossing them now, as Eli checked over the contract. At last the old man seemed satisfied.

"So!" the retailer said with his Buddha smile. "Everything is in order. I can't tell you, dear boy, how much I'm looking forward to a long and profitable partnership."

"And I!"   -

With a flourish, Michael reached for his pen.

At that moment Austrian's secretary entered the office and whispered something in his ear. Eli frowned.

"Excuse me, my friend, I have to take an important call. Do you mind stepping out for a moment?"

Michael paced restlessly in the outer office, his heart in his throat, sensing disaster. When he was ushered back in, he had only to look at Eli's face.

"That was my London agent on the phone," Eli said grimly. "Disturbing news, I'm afraid. Your export license is being held up."

"But that's ridiculous!" Michael burst out. "The paperwork was taken care of months ago. There's been some mistake."

Eli shrugged. "Get in touch with your own office if you're in any doubt, but I assure you, my source is impeccable."

Michael grabbed the phone.

"In that case, I'll call the Minister of Trade direct. The Home Secretary! Lloyd's! This is outrageous!"

But it was already early evening in London. Offices were shut and nothing more could be accomplished that day.

Michael made a rapid assessment of the situation. The London mess could be sorted out. It had to be! Michael couldn't envision failure at this point.

His immediate concern was the man before him. Without Eli Austrian's signature on that contract, Michael was in serious trouble.

Mentally, he kicked himself. Nothing but his own macho pride had let time run out so far. He and Eli could have signed two weeks ago. Gerry might have been wrong about a number of things, but she was proving right about the Ides of March. Inwardly he cursed. Outwardly, he turned to the older man with his most confident smile.

"It's only a glitch, you know. Some bureaucratic bit of red tape. You're aware of how civil servants function – that is, when they function at all. The whole business will be sorted out within twenty-four hours, I guarantee you, and some petty clerk will be out of a job."

"Good!" Eli nodded, then slowly pushed the contract across the desk toward Michael with the reluctance of a dieter foregoing a succulent dessert. "You sort it out and then get back to me."

"Eli!" Michael clucked. "We're both busy men. Why waste valuable time? Let's get the signing over with as long as we're here."

But Eli Austrian couldn't be chivvied. When the difficulties were resolved, he made it clear, and no sooner.

Michael quelled a stab of panic. He had a loan payment falling due in a few days. He needed money desperately. Yet instinct warned him against making a direct appeal. Any hint of weakness would be suicide. Eli was a shark. Once the smell of blood was in the water, the old scavenger would tear him to shreds. If Michael were to survive this day in one piece, an unruffled image was essential.

He now got up with a show of grace, as though the problem were of no more consequence than a forgotten umbrella on a rainy day.

"Of course, Eli. I want you to be entirely comfortable. My bet is that a week from now, we'll both be laughing at this business."

He put the contracts back in his briefcase and left.

Only when he was out on Fifth Avenue did he realize that his shirt was soaked with sweat.

How could it happen? How could everything in his life go suddenly so wrong and sour? That wretched divorce suit. Sandy tying up his assets. Now this godawful nightmare brought about by Sir Campbell Simms. If there was a common thread to all his travails (and he tried to squelch the thought), surely that thread was Geraldine O'Neal.

The rest of the day was spent in his office making one furious phone call after another.

five

"I've never asked you for anything."

He was sitting in Gerry's den, clutching a brandy snifter in a white-knuckled grip.

"I've never asked any woman for anything," he went on. "It goes completely against my grain."

"Oh Michael!" Gerry dabbed her eyes. "This is all so dreadful. Tell me what I can do to help. Shall I speak to Eli, perhaps?"

Michael shook his head vehemently. God forbid! Gerry's ex-lovers had already caused mischief enough.

"I'm in search of rather more practical assistance, I'm afraid. I need a bridge loan of one million five. I know it's a helluva lot to ask," he rushed on, for her face had turned the colour of library paste. "And believe me, darling, I wouldn't approach you if I had any other resources. I spent the entire afternoon trying to scare up money, but no dice. I had hoped to get an equity loan on my house in Maryland, but Sandy's tied up everything. Anyhow, that property is in both our names. So you're it, Gerry. My last resort."

"A million five!" she echoed in alarm. "My God, that's a fortune! I don't understand . . . how did you get so deep in hock?"

"Are you serious! Do you have any idea of the kind of bills we ran up on that London trip, the size of the commitments I made?"

An awful hush descended on the room. Two minds sharing a single thought. It was Gerry who had pushed for the whopping outlays: the decorators, the landscapers, the lavish entertainments. Gerry, whose mishandling of Sir Campbell Simms had set the project on a disaster course. Not that Michael was so boorish as to voice these charges; there was no need to. The facts hung in the air, ugly and palpable.

Their eyes linked. Gerry was the first to lower her gaze.

"Money money money," she sighed. "I'm not a rich woman, you realize."

Michael's response was a sceptical smile. Then he looked about him in a pointed manner as if to say: this house, these furnishings, the paintings on the wall, the clothes on your back. His gesture spoke volumes. No one who lived on such a scale could plead hardship.

Dry-mouthed, Gerry followed his glance.

"It's not what it seems, Michael. I'll do what I can, of course. You're welcome to whatever funds I can raise, but I assure you, it's nowhere near a million dollars. If you would like your bracelet back, for starters . . ."

Michael exploded.

"For Chrissakes, Gerry. I don't want the goddam bracelet back! It was a gift. Something precious from me to you. Besides, it wouldn't fetch the kind of money I need. You have so many other assets. Just help me out this once. I'm up against the wall. All I need is security for a loan, enough to tide me over the next month or two. What's the problem? This house, for instance. Must be worth three, four million in the current equity market. You could get two mil on it tomorrow."

"No I couldn't," she said warily.

"Sure you could! I'll fix you up with a good mortgage banker . . ."

Gerry began fidgeting. "This house isn't mine."

"Not yours! But I thought . . . !"

"Everybody thought . . ." Gerry went on to explain.

She had sold the brownstone three years ago to settle back taxes. The present owner was kind enough to permit her stay on as a tenant at moderate rent.

"Actually, this place belongs to Señor Oliveira."

"Little guy with a moustache and bug eyes? Lives in the basement?"

Gerry nodded, but Michael was unsatisfied.

"Why the hell should the Señor be so benevolent? Don't tell me. Let me guess. Christ!" He gave an irritated shrug. "How could you go to bed with something that looks like it fell out of a spaceship!"

"For all I know, Señor Oliveira is fantastic in bed," Gerry

snapped. "But I don't know, since I'm his tenant not his mistress. The arrangement is, I invite him to my parties. He meets celebrities there. That's his thrill. You needn't be judgemental."

"I see," Michael said thoughtfully. He looked about him again, this time with more of an auctioneer's eye. If the house wasn't hers (Michael wondered if Gerry was being truthful), the contents indubitably were.

"What about that painting of yours? The Sargent. I don't know much about art, but I see pictures like that going every day at Sotheby's for a bundle. What's the appraisal on it?"

"Lady L.?" Gerry's voice trembled. "Oh, I couldn't possibly part with it! I cherish that painting."

"I know you do, darling. And I appreciate the enormous sentimental value, what with it being a legacy from Winterbourne. I'm not suggesting you sell it. Merely borrow against it."

Gerry grew increasingly agitated.

"That painting . . . Oh Michael, Michael! Can you keep a secret?"

He nodded grimly, doubting it was a secret he wanted to hear.

"Well, you see, darling, when I was named Ambassador to Togo . . . ! You simply have no idea how much it costs to assume that kind of post. The constant entertaining. The gifts. The staff. In other words, a fortune, not all of which is reimbursable. The State Department can be pretty chintzy at times. Which is why most Ambassadors to minor powers are people of independent means. I sold the Sargent when I took the appointment. After all, I was a representative of the United States. It behoved me to maintain a certain style. A Japanese investor bought Lady L. for his private collection. It's in Tokyo now."

"Then the picture hanging in the hall . . ?"

"Is a copy. I keep it there because the lighting is so lousy."

As she went on to chronicle her present financial condition – the IRS had a lien on the business, she'd lost a mint in the recent stock market crash – Michael gradually drank in the fact that no aid would be forthcoming in this quarter. Her revelations amounted simply to one more nasty surprise in a wretched day.

He wasn't sure he believed all her tales of woe. It jarred with the image he had of her: an image of savvy and wealth. He suspected she was crying poverty to protect herself. Gerry was getting on in years, close to retirement. She was probably husbanding her assets to insure a comfortable old age. Nobody could mismanage funds to that degree, least of all a woman as clever as Gerry. Swiss bank accounts was his bet.

Michael stifled a sigh.

For all her protestations of love, when it came to the crunch, Gerry O'Neal looked out for Number One. Just like everyone else.

He felt vaguely betrayed, yet curiosity egged him on.

"And what about the estate?" he asked at the end of her account.

"What estate?"

"Winterbourne's. Lee Whitfield told me you control it."

"Did she now!" Gerry tossed her head. "Well, I'm merely an executor, one of many. US Trust handles the actual investments. I do get a certain small income, enough for body and soul – and that only lasts until the son reaches forty. No, Michael. I didn't take on that burden for the cash benefits. I did it for Hank's memory. A labour of love, so to speak . . ."

Michael had folded his arms and was studying her with unabashed amazement. His picture of her had begun to reshape. How little they knew each other, even after all this time.

"When I was young," she recalled wistfully, "and my column was syndicated, I was earning more money than I could spend. So what did I do? I went right out and spent it. Squandered it, you might say, on all kinds of foolish things. But on fine things, as well. Friends. Causes. Love affairs. Ideals. The occasional tilt at the windmill. That time I ran for Congress on the peace platform – you wouldn't believe the kind of money I blew! OK, I lost, but it was worth it. You're scowling, Michael. I suspect you think I was the world's biggest sucker. But you're wrong. I knew exactly what I was doing."

"And what was that, Gerry? Redistributing the wealth?"

She ignored the sarcastic pitch of his voice.

"Saving my soul. A psychiatrist once told me I was self-destructive concerning money. Well, I showed him. I stiffed him for the bill. But the man was right. At gut level I distrust the stuff. I don't like what it does to people. Look around you. New York is full of rich shits. Shallow, vicious, self-obsessed. Grubbers with less social conscience than you could inscribe on a gnat's behind. Perhaps at some instinctive level, I took steps to insure against becoming one of their number. Anyhow, even if I'd wanted to wallow in wealth, I wouldn't have made it. I'm a lousy manager." She shrugged. "What the hell, Michael! I was born broke. I'll probably die broke."

Michael didn't know what to believe. In his life he had never heard such rubbish. Yet it hardly mattered whether she was telling the truth or not. One thing was clear. Despite all her talk about love and sacrifice, he could look for no help in this quarter.

One detail rankled in particular. The fake Sargent had left a bad taste. How did you care for a man so deeply and sell off his most precious bequest? Some bit of male solidarity was at stake.

"I thought Henry Winterbourne was the love of your life . . ."

"I never said that exactly."

"OK, then the love of a given decade."

This time, she couldn't miss the angry undertone.

"Why are you being so snide?"

"Well, I find it extraordinary that you would get rid of something that had such intense personal meaning. If I'm correct, that painting was the great memento of ten devoted years and Winterbourne chose it with special care. I should think you would rather have done anything rather than convert it to cash. Why that's like . . . like selling your wedding ring!"

Unthinkingly, Michael twisted the gold band on his finger. Gerry caught him at it.

389

"I've never owned a wedding ring," she said.

Michael flushed. "I can't fathom you, Gerry. You're so damn careless about everything. Careless with the truth. With me. With money. With Sir Campbell. Even with the ghost of Henry Winterbourne."

"Not with you, Michael," she burst out. "I adore you!"

"But you'd hock my bracelet the same way you did Winterbourne's painting. That's one helluva way of showing adoration! What's behind all the fine words, Gerry? Is there any real feeling, any sentiment?"

Gerry winced. "That's not fair, Michael. I am an extremely sentimental woman. Extremely! But about people. Not objects. Not things. In fact, right now, I'd swap everything I own for one of your smiles. Come on, darling. Don't be so glum."

"I don't much feel like smiling."

"You're disappointed in me, aren't you?" She looked ineffably sad. "Why? Because I don't show the proper sentiment? Or is there another reason? Have I disappointed you because I have no money? Tell me, Michael. Was that what attracted you in the first place – my so-called 'position' in the Winterbourne estate?"

Michael's eyes flashed fire.

"God damn, Gerry! I'm not a gigolo! Or a fortune-hunter! As it happens I'm pretty well-heeled myself. Or I was, until this whole deal went splat."

"But you assumed I was rich."

"Give me a break," he protested.

"Give me an honest answer!"

He waffled for a moment, then shrugged.

"To be honest – yes! I assumed that. And no question, it made you that much more of a prize. It was part of the glamour . . ."

"I see," she choked on the words.

"No you don't!" he yelled.

Then he shook his head, struggling to conjure up what he had felt the day they met. It seemed so long ago. Ancient history. Yet some of the magic resonated still.

"My God, Gerry, you were something! You swept me off my feet. I'd never met a woman with so much style before. You moved in an aura of . . . of taste, luxury, I was fascinated. Flattered, too, that you'd waste your time on me." A note of playfulness crept in his voice. "Yep – you were some woman! Beautiful . . . witty . . . elegant. And rich."

"Stop referring to me in the past tense. I'm not dead."

Unexpectedly, Michael laughed. "Let me amend that. You still are – beautiful, worldly, elegant. And piss poor!"

Gerry laughed too, and the tension eased. With relief, they turned to the matter at hand.

"Why don't you declare bankruptcy," she urged, "and get it over with? There are worse things in life than going bust. They say everyone should fail big at least once. It builds character."

But Michael, whose career had been an unbroken success story, was less interested in character production than in survival. Lee Whitfield had once called him "The Man with the Golden Touch". He relished the epithet.

"I've never failed," he told Gerry, "and I don't intend to start now. There's gotta be a way out! If only Eli had signed that fucking paper this morning! At least I could have rolled the loans over."

"Don't drive yourself crazy, Michael! It's only money. You're young . . . resilient!"

He stared at her in astonishment.

Only money? What on earth did she think the whole project was about if not money? He struggled to keep his temper.

"You know the joke, Gerry. These two pilgrims are aboard the *Mayflower* and as they near the New England coast, one says to the other 'Short term, I'm in search of religious freedom. But long term, I plan to make a killing in real estate.' "

She didn't laugh.

"I expected more of you, Michael."

"What? The shining City on the Hill?"

In astonishment, he realized that Gerry had come to believe the substance of her press releases, that Hailsham was about international relations or creative marketing or providing jobs for New Jersey's unemployed. It was almost as if she wanted him to go down in flames, fighting the good and noble fight.

"Unfortunately, Gerry, I don't share your cavalier attitude about spending my declining days in the poor house. I've put myself on the line and I have to keep afloat, at least, until I recoup my investment." He began pacing the room, thinking out loud. "Long term doesn't worry me. It'll all work out if I can get over the hump. Maybe I should sell the goddam castle back to the Brits." The idea intrigued him. "The National Trust might buy. Maybe one of the museums. Nooo . . . I can't see them rebuilding Hailsham stone by stone, can you? Anyhow, where would the financing come from? Donations? Private funds? Take forever. Unless the Government tried to appropriate it. But who wants to get bogged down in litigation! Total nightmare. Christ, I hate bureaucracy. My bet is they'll back off, grant me the licence. All the king's horses . . ." he found himself repeating the litany, wishing he could believe it more heartily. He scowled. "That fucking castle! If only I could unload the goddam thing!"

"I thought the project meant so much to you," Gerry interjected, but he scarcely heard her.

"It's the timing that stinks. If old Eli had done his bit today, it would have meant a terrific show of confidence. That's what banks lend money on – confidence." He shook his head, like a terrier shaking off water, then rubbed his eyes. "Well, nothing more I can do tonight. You got anything to eat in the house?"

"Macadamia nuts . . . Fritos."

"Terrific!" he said. "If you don't mind, I'm going home, get some sleep. I can grab a bite on the way. Then tomorrow I'll head down to Baltimore, try to soften up Sandy . . ."

"Michael!" Gerry shrilled. "You couldn't possibly go there! That woman is trying to ruin your life."

Michael was too tired to argue.

"Doubtless she says the same about you. Be realistic, pet. What else can I do at this juncture? Now just hold on . . ." Gerry looked as though she were either going to faint or throw up. "My seeing Sandy doesn't mean I'm moving back in. All I want is to get a loan on the house. She'll understand that much. She's a practical woman. Besides, it's in her own interest to keep me pumping money."

"No . . . no! I won't let you!" Gerry was suddenly plucking at his sleeve like a pan-handler. "I implore you, Michael. If you go down there, it'll be the end of us. I feel it in my bones. We have to stick together, you and I. You're my life, my light. I don't give a damn about Hailsham! What's money, compared to us . . . to our happiness? As long as we have each other, we'll survive."

"Geraldine! Please!" for she had flung her arms about him in a desperate embrace, her entire body heaving with sobs. "Take it easy. Please, no scenes. That's everything I tried to get away from. Damn! I hate it when a woman clings . . ."

The words came out more brutally than he'd intended.

She jumped back. Her cheeks were smeared with mascara.

"I didn't mean to cling, Michael. It's just that I have an awful premonition. I see us breaking down, falling apart. Promise me you won't go to Baltimore! Please. And I promise not to make any more scenes. Oh God!" She caught a glimpse of herself in the mirror. The blood drained from her face. "I'm a wreck! Don't leave!"

She tore out of the room and returned five minutes later with swollen eyes, fresh lipstick and a gallant smile, a smile that proclaimed: see, I am not a hysterical woman à la Sandy Avesian. I am the indomitable Geraldine O'Neal.

But her hands were trembling. She looked haggard, unaccountably old. At that moment, all Michael wanted was to defuse the drama and go home to bed. He had had a surfeit of emotion for one day.

"Forgive me, darling." He got up and pecked her cheek. "But I'm ready to collapse. I think we could both do with a night apart."

She laid her head against his shoulder for a long tense moment.

"Give me twenty-four hours," she whispered. "I'll think of something. You know me. I'm resourceful, quick. I'll either figure out a solution or scare up the money myself."

"How, Gerry?" he asked wearily. "Rob a bank?"

"I'll find a way, Michael, I swear."

six

Gerry's revelations had hit Michael like a bucket of ice water. And like ice water, it had jarred him awake.

It was not just her poverty, real or imagined, that had done the trick; by the small hours of morning, he had adjusted to this unpleasant truth. What truly hurt was the sense that he'd been hoodwinked. Smart, shrewd, canny Michael Avesian had been taken for an emotional ride at great expense.

For the last six months he had been in love with a myth. A sham. As fake as the Sargent portrait on the wall.

The knowledge that "Lady L." was a cheap copy had dealt the final blow. To him, the painting had always symbolized Gerry herself. Something rare and precious. A prize genuine beyond all dispute.

And while Michael didn't pretend to be an art critic, he did fancy himself a connoisseur of people.

Now he was doubly infuriated. With Gerry for having fooled him. With himself for having taken gilt for gold. If there was anything Michael found intolerable, it was being played for a sucker.

"Never hustle a hustler," he had teased the day they met. But she had hustled him left and right. In the matter of images, he had his own to protect: that of "one smart Armenian". At the moment, his ego was sore to the touch.

To be fair, Gerry hadn't set out to deceive him. Her lies were without malice and, he believed, she loved him sincerely.

What the hell! He loved her too. In a way.

She was a remarkable woman. In a way.

She was also a liability.

He might have laughed everything off, her dubious fortune included, but for this fiasco with Sir Campbell Simms. If only Gerry had exerted common sense, basic prudence, Michael wouldn't be in this fix.

But no. Whether out of vanity or cowardice, she had

juggled both men in her life for as long as possible (one might say, longer) with dire results. And despite her tear-fulness, it was Michael who was paying the price.

Still, he struggled to be fair. Impossible not to feel sorry for Gerry. It couldn't be fun, growing old and being broke. He didn't much fancy the idea of being broke himself. But he was young and resilient. Whereas Gerry . . . ! Far from the tower of strength he had admired, she had turned out to be a hopeless woolly-headed romantic. A woman with both feet planted firmly in mid-air.

He, on the other hand, he was a realist. Realist enough to know that feeling sorry for Gerry O'Neal was one thing. Throwing in his lot with her, quite another.

"As long as we have each other . . ." she had said.

As though banks took love as a collateral.

Dear Gerry. What a fool!

Michael sighed.

The sooner he got disentangled, the better for everyone involved. In retrospect, he could only wonder how it had ever begun. He must have been bewitched.

But no more. Today's events had broken the spell. Loving Gerry was too expensive, emotionally and pro-fessionally. She had cost him, not merely the greatest set-back of his career, but his marriage as well. Conceivably, even his beautiful children.

It was time to come down to earth. Back to the "real" world, where no room was allowed for romantics.

Yet as he planned his escape, he felt a simultaneous pang of sentiment. For all her crazies, Gerry had meant a great deal to him. He pledged to let her down as gently as possible.

And begin mending fences with his wife.

Michael shut his eyes. Images of Sandy sprang to mind. He wondered how she was doing. Was she happy? Lonely? Was she managing all right? It was a big house to run. A lot of responsibility. In another few weeks the magnolias would be in blossom. That big tree would have to be cut back . . .

He fell asleep on the sofa, fully dressed, and dreamt he was back home. It was summer. His girls were having a teddy bear's picnic on the lawn. He could hear their laughter through the open window.

All my fault, Gerry reviled herself after Michael left. She poured herself a double brandy and slumped into a chair, feeling old and battered. It was just as well he couldn't see her now.

All her fault. She had created this mess. Now she would have to clean it up, if she were to win her way back into his good graces.

Superwoman, he once called her in the days when their love was young. Then, she had been Gerry the Wise, the Savvy. Gerry, the prestidigitator who could pull rabbits out of hats. Well, she needed one more rabbit. And a damn big one at that!

She bolted down the drink and poured another. The booze was making her mawkish.

"I bring bad luck to those I love," she thought. "I live under a curse."

The notion was familiar, one that surfaced when she was drunk. But there was a core of truth to it. For love of her, two men had died. One violently. Both needlessly. And while her legal innocence was beyond a doubt, she held herself morally responsible.

Or irresponsible, as the case may be.

Of Lionel's death, she still could not bear to think. Despite the passage of years, it still weighed on her conscience.

And then, of course, there was Henry Winterbourne. Poor unhappy Hank. He had died in this very house. At about this time of night.

Michael had been incorrect in calling Winterbourne the love of her life. He was both more and less.

From the moment they'd met at the opera, a powerful chemistry came into play. Theirs was the attraction of opposites. "We're as different," he used to say, "as Wagner and Puccini."

Puccini and Wagner. Light and dark. No question which

was which. He saw in her a last desperate chance to experience the emotional life. She saw in him an opportunity.

For in Henry Winterbourne, Gerry had found the perfect instrument through which she could express the full range of her beliefs. A force for progress no less powerful than her column. If money was power, then it was potentially the power to do good. To effect change. And Winterbourne had money beyond avarice.

It was the challenge she had been waiting for: to shape the policies of one of America's greatest corporations. To shape the man as well.

For much as she loved Hank, she pitied him too.

For all his brilliance, he was a profoundly unhappy man. Product of generations of grasping Yankee traders, he had been raised to view the world through unforgiving eyes. Human beings were frail and faulty vessels, an image that his marriage did much to compound. A man had better put his trust into things. Paintings. Ivories. Porcelains. Property. And money. Above all, money.

The Wagnerian aspects were manifest in that marvellous mind, intricate and convoluted, full of hidden recesses and subtle motifs and grand designs, most which had to do with the acquisition of art and wealth.

To watch Hank put together a business deal or negotiate the purchase of a painting was a lesson in complexity. Brain and will worked in perfect tandem. Winterbourne always prevailed.

By contrast, he had little feel for the human dimension. Pleasure did not come easily. Few had ever heard him laugh. His subordinates called him "The Icebox".

Yet he yearned for more. To be loved as well as feared. To be jollied on occasion. It was a yearning Gerry sensed. She treated him with an unaccustomed flippancy, skirting very close to the edge of disrespect.

"What would it cost," she asked him early in their relationship, "to tell me that you love me?"

A great deal, apparently. For when he tried to frame the words, his lips were loath to obey. She suspected that he had never uttered them in his life.

Over time, she taught him how to speak those particular

words without stumbling, although he found it easier to do at a distance. Only in letters could he dispel the shadows and let a long-suppressed eloquence shine through.

By any calculation, they were an odd couple. And though she was hardly a green girl when they met, he was the only man in her life to play the role of mentor.

Winterbourne knew. Appreciated. He was an aesthete of the first water, a man of taste and cultivation. Moreover, he took a particular delight in passing on this knowledge to the brash young woman from Yorkville.

He taught her how to look at pictures, listen to chamber music, admire porcelain, study antiques, respond to beauty on a dozen levels. She accompanied him on his buying sprees through the great houses of Europe and treasure chests of the East. He was her higher education in a manner that surpassed the Sorbonne.

The one thing he couldn't teach her about was sex.

Nor, to her grief, could she teach him.

The day they met, she had thought him wildly attractive. A titan. With his proud carriage and granitic features, Hank Winterbourne did indeed offer a virile presence to the world. She had been to bed with worse and fared well.

But sex wasn't just about rippling muscles, as she well knew. It was also in the mind. In the mood. She had long since discovered that one could be bored stiff by Hollywood dreamboats and enjoy satisfying flings with utter toads. On the whole she preferred the toads. They had an eagerness to please.

She also knew that there was little connection between power and sex. If anything, it was a negative correlation. Men could be omnipotent in Wall Street or government and total wash-outs in bed. Autocrats, who couldn't make their bodies obey.

Perhaps, she speculated, the very size and sweep of their ambitions had drained off all other energies. Or that somewhere, during the long hard climb to the top, such men lost the gift of intimacy.

Sex was the great leveller, the one area in which a factory hand might out-perform a Henry Ford.

Or a Henry Winterbourne.

Hank was a terrible lover. Feeble. Repressed. Unsatisfying.

Never once in their years together had he brought her to orgasm. She didn't know if his inadequacy was the result of a rigid upbringing or a lack of hormones or primal fears or years of marriage to a semi-invalid. Whatever the cause, the results were woeful. With the best will in the world (and God knows he tried!) Hank could never for a moment forget who he was. Never lose himself in the act.

Even at the height of (what was for him) physical passion, even as he gasped and panted, he remained Henry Winterbourne IV. The man on the cover of *Fortune*. An unbending Puritan out of his time.

Before long, their lovemaking had become an ordeal. As often as he willed himself to fulfil Gerry, that was how often he failed. If anything, his eagerness added to the agony.

He was furious. With himself. Unconsciously with her.

At bottom, he could never grasp why it was that he, Henry Winterbourne, able to command whatever he damn pleased in this world, could never conquer Geraldine O'Neal.

"You can't own me, my darling," she would say, trying to make light of it. "Nobody ever owns anyone."

But Winterbourne, who was an owner by nature, whose homes and warehouses bulged with acquisitions, who had devoured whole businesses and looted the wealth of continents, had finally to admit defeat. They arrived at an unspoken truce. There would be denial on his part. Discretion on hers.

They continued to cherish one another in their separate ways, each finding a different reward.

Henry Winterbourne had brought a new dimension into her life. A broadening of scope, a range of opportunity such as few women have.

She brought warmth into his. Warmth and laughter and even a touch of humanity. On balance, he had the better of the bargain.

"I was numb," he once wrote. "You made me feel."

400

She suspected he loved her most dearly when they were apart. Then he could forget the physical humiliation and pour out his soul in letters. They revealed the man that might have been.

When they were together, they sparred.

"I'm too old for you," he once said with great bitterness. "You deserve some strapping Adonis."

"It doesn't matter," she said.

But it did. To them both.

She was unfaithful time and again. With actors, ball-players, cab-drivers, college students, with an army of cheerful and uncomplicated young men who didn't require much conversation in the morning. The affairs were usually brief and amiable, always discreet. She wished to spare Hank as much as possible.

Yet sometimes, after an extravagant night, she would turn up in the office with the unmistakable bloom of a woman who had been well and truly fucked. He knew. How could he not? There was no hiding the white rage behind his eyes.

On those occasions, he would say nothing to Gerry. Instead, he would lash out at the nearest subordinate with a savagery that was truly awful to behold. "Genghis rides again!" the word would whip around the building, and those who could kept a low profile while the storm raged. By day's end, at least one underling would have been fired, to be hired back quietly by Gerry at a later date.

Thus Henry Winterbourne proved his virility.

With age, his behaviour grew more eccentric and unpredictable. It sometimes occurred to her that he might be going insane, that it was but a matter of time until something snapped.

The end came on a chilly February evening.

Hank, so she believed, was safely stowed in San Francisco. She was lolling in bed with a French pastry chef, more precisely, the Winterbourne pastry chef, when suddenly the bedroom door flew open.

What had brought him back, she would never learn. Maybe he'd been lonely. Or jealous. Maybe Gerry had got her dates wrong.

He stood framed in the doorway, pale as a wraith out of hell. There was a moment's shocked silence. Then –

"Get out!" Winterbourne screamed in a murderous rage. "Get out before I kill you."

The young man grabbed his clothes and fled.

Gerry was horrified.

"You have no right . . ." she started to say, but the look on Hank's face defied rational argument. The man was beside himself with anger. Instinctively she reached to cover her nakedness.

He strode to the bed and loomed over her. Then he stripped off the sheet.

"With a cook!" At last Hank found his tongue. "You go to bed with kitchen boys!"

Gerry mustered what dignity she could, but her own long simmering resentment began to surface. What did he want from her? What did he expect?

And even if he had been the world's greatest lover, it would have made no difference. Nothing gave Hank, gave any man, the right to burst in on her as though she were a piece of property. His behaviour was outrageous. An affront to everything she prized.

"Yes, a kitchen boy," she jeered. "Would you have preferred a Head of State as more in keeping with your dignity? Well, I've fucked those too, Hank, and believe me the so-called kitchen boy was better. And now, I suppose, you're going to fire him, to show just how big a man you are."

"I'll show you how big a man I am!"

He began ripping off his clothes. To her surprise, he was fully aroused. The sight of her with someone else had succeeded in exciting him where her own skills had so often failed.

Suddenly he was on top of her. Plunging into her. Fuelled by rage.

"I'll give you what you want," he said between clenched teeth. "I'll make you cry for love and joy. You won't have to debase yourself with kitchen boys any more."

It was rape. And for all his unaccustomed virility, for all

the many times they had gone to bed together with good will, this assault was unforgivable.

She didn't scream. She didn't fight back. Her revenge would be in letting him know that she felt nothing. Absolutely nothing. Yet on that night of all nights, his sexual energy was inexhaustible.

Even in the half-light, she could see the cords standing out in his neck, the dark flush that suffused his features.

"Come, damn you!" he was roaring as he drove into her.

Had she wished, she might have faked pleasure, as royal mistresses had done throughout history. Faked pleasure and got rid of him.

She wouldn't give him the satisfaction.

She couldn't. It went against her grain.

His thrusts grew harder, more relentless as she lay beneath him dry and unmoving. Her lack of resistance only added to his frenzy. Eyes bulging, arms rigid, pouring sweat, pumping up and down with the mercilessness of a stamping machine, he continued to strain for an eternity. Her entire body ached from his abuse.

She shut her eyes. Wished herself dead. Wished him dead. The nightmare seemed to have no end.

At last, almost beyond the point of human endurance, Hank could hold back no more. With a mighty groan, he reached a shuddering climax. Then he fell on top of her, crushing her with his weight.

With a spasm of revulsion, Gerry pulled away. She was covered with sweat and semen.

"I'm going to take a bath," she said evenly, "and wash away all trace of you. Have the decency to be gone when I return."

She ran a bath, stretched out in the scented water, shut her eyes and soaked her aching bones. The water was warm and comforting. She dozed off.

By the time she woke, the bath was tepid. She threw on a robe and went into the bedroom. Hank was still there, naked, lying as she had left him. One hand was outflung, as though reaching toward her.

Instantly she knew he was dead.

She went over to the bed. Felt his heart. Placed a mirror to his lips. Already his flesh was beginning to cool.

He must have died at the very moment of orgasm. She hoped so. The image of him struggling for life while she lay dozing in her bath was too painful.

Terrified, she hurtled out of the room.

What to do? Phone an ambulance. Call the police.

Clearly, that was the right and proper thing. In her mind, she could hear the sirens screaming. The tramp of feet. The flash of photographers' bulbs.

But what purpose would it serve? Henry Winterbourne was dead. Beyond their ministrations. Nothing in the world could bring him back.

She sat in the den, glazed, unable to grieve. The shock was too fresh. But her mind was still functioning, thank God.

Hank was gone. What mattered now was the living. Herself. Margaret Winterbourne. Also, the boy Lawrence would have to be considered.

Already she could envision the scandal. The gutter press would have a field day. Henry Winterbourne, that titan of industry, would be a permanent joke. "The guy who died fucking Gerry O'Neal."

A lifetime's accomplishment reduced to the level of a dirty anecdote. With Gerry herself as the punchline.

She phoned neither the police nor the medics. Instead, in the small hours of the morning, she made an urgent call to Andy Novak. At that time, her old high school dancing partner and future cardinal had risen to the post of Secretary to the Archbishop. He was a man of the world. But he was also a priest. A keeper of secrets.

Andy arrived within the hour. Gerry confessed everything.

"Upstairs in the bedroom," she said.

He came down some minutes later, calm but ashen.

"What is it that you think I can do for the man," he asked, "other than pray for his soul? I've already done that."

"I want you to call his wife. I want it to look as if he died at home." She was pleading, trembling like a leaf. "It

404

was a natural death, Andy. I've done nothing criminal. Why compound the tragedy? Three lives would be ruined, to say nothing of Henry's memory. Even if you won't consider my welfare, at least consider his family."

Andy nodded. Slowly. Sadly.

It took both their efforts to get the corpse dressed.

A large man, Henry Winterbourne was heavier in death than in life. Shorts. Shirt. Trousers. Gerry tied his tie. She was better at it than Andy. She'd had years of experience in tying men's ties.

The socks were more difficult. They were a fine silk knit, crackling with static electricity. No matter how hard she tugged, they refused to slide into place. After half a dozen passes, Gerry was on the brink of hysteria.

"It's OK, Gerry," Andy assured her. "Socks don't matter."

They toted the body down the steps and out on the street, two old friends apparently propping up a drunk. Then into Gerry's car. Out of it. Through the service entrance of his Park Avenue residence. To the door of his apartment where Margaret Winterbourne was waiting. As was the Winterbourne family doctor. He would sign the death certificate.

The two women never exchanged a word.

The next day it was announced that Henry Winterbourne IV had died peacefully in his sleep. The press release was simple yet dignified. Gerry wrote it herself.

That was another love. Another lifetime. The only traces of Hank remaining in this house were his letters and a painful memory.

Gerry rubbed her eyes, shaking away the cobwebs.

Tonight her concern was not with the past but with the future. She had promised to save Michael from bankruptcy. A reckless promise, more than she could deliver. Only the thought of losing him could have driven her to make such a statement.

Tomorrow, she would see what she had left to sell.

It was past three. Wearily, she roused herself and put away the brandy. Time for bed. As she was heading upstairs, she noticed that Michael had left his briefcase in the hall, where anyone could find it. She went to close it and put it in the closet when the Austrian contract caught her eye.

"That fucking paper!" Michael's curse came back to her. "If only Eli had signed that fucking paper!"

In Gerry's head, something went click.

Suppose Eli *had* signed those papers, then Michael would be off the hook. At least he would have bought himself time.

Of course Eli hadn't signed. But who was to know? Who – other than the principals?

Gerry had sent out a press release that very morning announcing the Austrian deal to the trade.

What if she didn't follow through with a retraction? *What if . . . what if . . . ?*

What if? became *why not? Why not?* grew into *but how?*

Letters!

Letters had been in her thoughts all night, triggered by memories of Henry Winterbourne. But Eli had also written letters to Gerry. Scads of them. And she had kept them as souvenirs.

Pulse racing, she took the contracts out of the briefcase and ran upstairs to her dressing room.

Somewhere in that big carton in the closet, buried in among the rest, were love letters from the old pirate himself, written in the days when he had been in hot pursuit. Signed, to be sure. Signed in a continental hand with the Dutchman's distinctive flourish.

Eli v. Austrian.

She had asked him once if the *v* stood for *van*. He had teased her, saying the *v* stood for *victim*. He claimed to be the Victim of Geraldine O'Neal.

Well before dawn, she was in the lobby of Michael's building, demanding that the concierge buzz his apartment.

"It's an emergency," she said. "I've been unable to reach him on the phone."

At last, Michael's voice was on the other end of the intercom. He sounded half asleep.

"Yeah . . . what is it?"

Gerry squelched a smile of triumph.

"I robbed the bank," she said.

"So here they are darling: signed, sealed and delivered."
She held her breath as he thumbed them through.

"But how . . . ?"

"Don't ask. You don't want to know."

They exchanged fraught glances. Michael backed off,
momentarily hesitant. No, she didn't have to spell it out.

"This is crazy," he said after a pause, but already his
fingers were itching to close about the document. To pack
it away.

"Not so crazy," Gerry whispered. "No one's going to
question Eli's signature, especially with the press release
out. You told the bank you'd get the contract. Now you
have it. What'll they do, run a handwriting check? Not on
your life! Anyhow, once the export licence is in order, Eli
will be signing the real article and we'll both be out of the
woods."

He still looked doubtful.

"I don't want you taking that kind of chance for me."

"But Michael," she argued, "we're cool. Who will know?
Who will find out?"

She had uttered much the same sentiment years ago, in
a coffee shop across the street from Hunter College. It had
worked. This time, the stakes were higher, the act more
daring. Yet now, as then, she felt a flush of confidence.

"Only you and I, Michael," she said. "And you can rely
on my discretion absolutely."

He rubbed his nose pensively, then put the papers in
his desk drawer with an air of what's-done-is-done.

"It's still a helluva risk," he said.

"Life is risk. We both know that. We're adventurers,
remember? And if worst comes to worst, we tough it out.
Deny deny deny. The Nixon stonewall technique. But it'll
never happen, darling. I forbid you even to think such a
thing. You'll go to England and wow the lady in No. 10.
Total success. That's the scenario."

"Alternative scenario," he said, "we both go to jail."

Jail. It was an ugly word, one that made her stop short.

"I'm doing it for you," she said softly, then twisted her arms about him. "You once told me you'd like to make love at the edge of a precipice. That the danger would only add to the spice. This is the precipice, Michael. Let's seal it with a kiss."

She pressed her body against his and wearily, mechanically, they began making love. Afterwards, as dawn broke grey and cool, Gerry had a stunning perception.

She and Michael had committed a crime. Formed a conspiracy.

Like it or not, their fates were linked.

He could never be rid of her now. Or so she believed.

seven

Inside every great journalist, there's an even greater actor.

Lee Whitfield was becoming one of the best.

Her career at *Trend* was blossoming, thanks to a mix of investigative skills: a nose for journalism, an ear for scandal and a face as innocent as a new-born babe.

People talked to her, confiding extraordinary details as if she were nothing more than she appeared to be: a corn-fed girl from the boonies. She cultivated an air – if not of stupidity, then of a monumental *naïveté*. "I guess I'm a hick," she would confess to her quarry, blinking those wide blue eyes. "Could you explain this to me?"

They clarified. And clarified. Lee's glazed innocence remained. "I still don't get it!" She looked almost ready to cry.

Then out of irritation ("Why does *Trend* send me such a dumbo?") or the desire to edify ("Poor kid. She'll probably lose her job!"), her victims proceeded to deliver the most intimate details. Lee kept up the front until she had winkled out the one crunchy quote, the telling instance that made a story spring to life.

And oh! the topics she professed to know nothing about! Her "ignorance" extended from the stock market to the fish market, from city hall to the garment district, from public transport to certain private clubs that catered to highly peculiar and particular tastes.

In the matter of extracting nasty secrets, Lee was second to none on the staff. Routinely, the day *Trend* hit the news-stands, her latest targets would call in stunned disbelief.

"How could you do this to me?" she heard time and again. "I trusted you. I thought we were friends."

But Lee's conscience was clear. She had done nothing illegal or unethical. Besides, good journalists had no friends. At least none that might provoke a conflict of interest.

People in public life should know what to expect when

talking to reporters. As for those in private life, the so-called civilians unexpectedly catapulted into the limelight through no fault of their own, Lee had a ready reply. "I'm sorry, but life is tough all round."

If Lee drove her subjects hard, she drove herself even harder. Little was left of the bumptious young woman with the one "good black dress". Big stories took big tolls.

Her life had assumed a propulsive rhythm which she was reluctant to break.

Five hours of sleep, enough for anyone on the rise. Then up at 6:00, often leaving Bill ensconced under the covers. Twenty minutes of advanced Jane Fonda, followed by a thirty-minute jog with a Walkman plugged in. No point wasting a full half-hour running when she could be doing something productive as well. Right now, she was working through a series of tapes called *Se Habla Español*. Spanish was useful in covering New York. The bilingual reporter had an edge.

Back home by 7:00 for a breakfast of skimmed milk and oat-bran cereal with a dose of multivitamins. Check *The Times*. The *News*. Yesterday's *Post*. And maybe get in a quick nuzzle with Bill.

By 8:00, she was at the office. Early morning was peak time for writing, organizing, getting a start. By 9:00, the phones were going berserk. A few vital calls to check contacts, then Lee was out of the box like a rocket. Pure energy. Pure drive.

"It only looks unstructured," she told Bill who accused her of a gross mismanagement of time. It wasn't. One never knew where a story might take her. She trusted her instincts to lead the way. In and out of subways, grabbing cabs, in phone booths, on interviews, in newspaper morgues, sweat shops, office buildings, school yards, chasing down leads, following up hunches. If she had time, a quick sandwich. If not, an amphetamine would do.

Some people she cultivated, some she conned. Any approach that worked was justified. Like the time Lee just "happened" to pick up a guy in a bar who just "happened" to be the brother of a notorious insider trader. OK, the pickup didn't just "happen" and OK, his hands wandered

410

a bit, but the point was, Lee had come back to the office with the goods. She could still hear the howls!

There were occasions when the quarry couldn't be socialized. If the topic was potentially embarrassing, Lee knew better than to ask for an interview. Why give the guy time to get his story straight? Instead, she became a master of the ambush. It was worth standing outside an apartment house in a drenching rain to catch some hardnosed celebrity off balance. She'd been called "bitch" more times than she could count.

As a rule Lee took notes during interviews, but not always. Some people froze at the sight of a steno book. When that happened, Lee managed to keep the conversation informal, filing away data in her head. Then a retreat to the ladies' room to get it all down. With practice, she learned to retain hours of information without putting pencil to paper. Memory was like any other part of the body, she believed. It improved with exercise. Hers was phenomenal. Sometimes, she'd flex it just for fun.

At day's end, Lee would hop a cab back to the office, scraps of paper jammed in every pocket. Another couple of hours to transcribe her notes, separating wheat from chaff, catch up on unreturned calls.

Around eight, Lee would change into heels, fix her make-up and meet Bill at a restaurant for the one proper meal of the day. She liked Bill. He made her laugh. He was also good in bed. Apart from jogging, he was her sole relaxation. But that was all right. Plenty of time to relax when you're dead. Meanwhile, there were points to be scored.

Trouble was, the harder she worked, the tougher the work got. You couldn't top a great story with some little piece of fluff. The next feature had to be sharper, bigger. More demanding. More startling. She had her own reputation to contend with.

A seventy-hour week was rapidly becoming the norm. Punishing, but she could handle it. Like the Porsche of her dreams, Lee could cruise at eighty. Ninety in a pinch.

She had it down to a formula.

"A formula for a nervous breakdown," her mother had warned.

"For success," Lee replied.

One fact was indisputable. It was working.

With Fletch Birnbaum, she could do no wrong.

Each week, before putting the magazine to bed, he would spread the galleys side by side on the floor, starting with his own office and snaking down the corridor till the entire contents of the magazine were on display. Then he would prowl back and forth, moving some pieces, discarding others, orchestrating for tone and colour and variety, until the issue took its final shape.

With satisfaction, Lee saw her own features edge toward the front of the book. It was a chronicle of personal progress.

Among her colleagues, she had developed a reputation as a writer – and a competitor – who went straight for the jugular. Praise didn't come much higher than that!

Thus far the high point of her career had been an exposé of the dry cleaning business.

"Dry cleaners?" Fletch had arched an eyebrow. "Jesus, that's got to be the world's most boring topic."

"Trust me," she said. "It's as fundamental to life in this city as subways or bagels or crack."

Her idea was to explore a putative relationship between dry cleaning and disease. She knew that hypochondria sold magazines.

"Think of the possibilities," she told Bill Frazier at home one evening. "Your stuff being tossed around in that slimy brew alongside clothes from total strangers. Talk about insanitary! For all you know, your intimate garments could be rubbing up against pants belonging to some guy who has AIDS. Or maybe pick up a tick carrying Rocky Mountain spotted fever. Ticks can survive almost anything, you know."

Bill rolled his eyes. "Except my credulity," he said, and went back to work on his novel.

Unruffled, Lee spent the next week in quest of some "expert" to make her case. Eventually she unearthed a Mount Sinai intern, who – after repeated "dumb" questions – agreed that yes, ticks were pretty tough customers and such a relationship could not be ruled out as "totally absolutely inconceivable. I suppose anything can happen," he conceded with a weary shrug.

That was enough for Lee. The story (Are You Being Taken To The Cleaners?) ran with the intern's quote writ large and out of context (*Mt Sinai MD* – "Anything can happen!") in a boxed caption. Briefly, the New York dry cleaning business screeched almost to a halt.

The power of the press, Lee said. What she meant was, the power of one Lee Whitfield.

Her professional timetable was zipping along on schedule. She was bylined in most issues and enjoyed the prospect of being Feature Editor within a year. The one item still lacking in her portfolio was the elusive cover story. The Big Mac, was how she thought of it. That breakthrough piece that would rocket her into the front ranks. And the six figures.

Fletch had put the O'Neal story on the back burner, since its subject had been keeping a low profile of late. Like his reading public, Birnbaum had a short attention span.

Lee, however, kept on digging.

By now, her dossier on Geraldine O'Neal ran to several hundred pages. Not only was it plump with exclusive anecdotes from Gerry's own lips, but Lee had also gathered, more discreetly, deep background from outside sources. New York was awash with people who had brushed up against Gerry. Not all of them had found it a joyful experience. There were disgruntled ex-secretaries. Former lovers. Angry wives. Unsuccessful competitors. Resentful colleagues.

Nor were her inquiries limited to New York.

She took off one weekend to interview Alexandra Avesian in Baltimore, then on to Washington to meet Bill Frazier's father.

She had hoped that the old gentleman might let loose with something juicy. However, Austin Frazier, though cordial, was scrupulously bland in discussing Gerry. He was far more interested in Lee herself.

"My son speaks so highly of you," he said. "Very highly

indeed." She had the impression he was on a fishing expedition, waiting for Lee to reveal herself as a prospective daughter-in-law. Although where he got such notions, she couldn't imagine. She and Bill were lovers. Nothing more.

But if that interview was a waste, others weren't. As a comprehensive picture began to emerge, Lee was again struck by the gap between public image and private reality.

Illustrations abounded.

For openers, there was the theft (or "borrowing" as Lee's mother had charitably defined it) of the Goldman scholarship essay. That had set the pattern. Consider the way she faked her way into the job at the *Globe*. Or the bamboozling of Henry Winterbourne and Co. Even the snatching of Michael (from right under Lee's nose, it must be remembered) was consistent with the woman's duplicity.

For your own good, Gerry had implied at the time. Bullshit! For Gerry's personal whim!

Fame and honours notwithstanding, Ambassador Geraldine O'Neal was a fraud and a hypocrite. That would be the theme of her piece.

And a damn fool, into the bargain.

Months ago, Lee had been given a set of keys and invited to enjoy the freedom of the house. Did Lee want to borrow a book or a fur? Use the car for a spin in the country? "Help yourself," Gerry would say. When Michael was away, she would invite her over as in the bad old days – the days before Lee had seen the light.

"Bring pizzas," Gerry might say, "and let yourself in."

And though they never quite recouped their former intimacy, the arrangement remained loose. Lee was free to come and go. To ferret about for titbits. Manipulate her hostess with ease. As things stood, she could have walked off with the silver, unobserved.

Such *naïveté*! Lee marvelled at Gerry's stupidity, and chalked it up to the treacherous power of love.

That, to Lee, was the most remarkable aspect of the story. Bottom line, when it came to men, the great rôle model was every bit as much the fluttering romantic as – well, as Lee's own mother, for example.

All for love and the world well lost! Such crap!

In mitigation, Nancy had been twenty when she had chucked it all for the privilege of a life spent bending over a kitchen sink in Cedar City. Whereas Gerry was more than double that!

And though the former ambassador was not yet reduced to doing housework, love was turning her into a Number One Sucker. Where were Gerry's eyes? Her judgement? How could she miss Lee's grand design?

For months now, their "relationship" had been a farce, a piece of theatre, with Lee playing the role of disciple to the hilt. And Gerry hadn't twigged! Was there a special Academy Award, Lee wondered, for Best Journalist? If so, she had an Oscar due.

Right now her journalist's sense told her that Gerry was heading for a fall. She was looking blowsy of late, edgy and unsure, like a tattered old lion well beyond its prime. When it was time for the kill, Lee would be there.

Meanwhile, she continued to compile her dossier, always sunny in Gerry's presence, never once forgetting her purpose.

Never forgiving, either. Lee nursed a deeper wound than the mere seduction of Michael. A hurt that refused to heal.

It harked back to the day when she learned that her job had been landed not on merit, but on pull. Gerry's pull. The words still stung. "If not for me," Gerry sneered, "you'd be covering weddings for the *East Jeezus Gazette*."

That the charge was partly true didn't make it less galling.

Well, Lee had proved her professional worth a dozen times over since that night. She would do it again, with this cover story. And then – *then*! who would have the last laugh!

There was still a distance to go, however, before her piece was complete. It needed a kicker, the final turn of the screw.

"You're obsessed with that magazine," Bill said at dinner one night. He was doing a round-up of New York's ten most expensive new restaurants. The Albuquerque was high on the list.

"Like you're obsessed with your novel," she replied equably. "That's what makes you a creative writer. Now – what should we eat?"

"Talk about creative writing!" Bill scanned the menu with a jaundiced eye. "Filet of rabbit with pistachio crust . . . monkfish caviare on wholewheat tacos. Barbecued *foie gras* with cactus garnish. Jesus! I didn't know cactus was edible. I can see me at thirty, dead of multiple internal injuries. The epitaph would go: 'Here lies William Frazier. He gave his life for a restaurant column.' Only instead of a skull and crossbones on the tombstone, there'd be a knife and fork."

The waiter came. Bill did his duty, ordering such dishes as befit his function. "And a Pepto-Bismol for dessert."

Lee laughed. "You're funny."

"I'm serious," Bill said. "I just talk funny. You know what I really crave for dessert? Rice pudding."

"My mother makes a great rice pudding."

"Does she?" He liked Nancy. "Maybe she'll do me one."

"It won't be elaborate," Lee warned.

"Nor should it be. It should be comforting. Nursery food. When I was a kid, we lived in Rome for a while – my mother was married to an Italian businessman, he was Number Three on her list – and we had a cook from the Po Valley who made the best rice pudding in the world. Every Friday Serafina would whip up this huge batch in an earthenware dish. Just rice, milk, cinnamon and raisins baked in an oven. Simple. But one bite and all your troubles disappeared, all your aches and pains were forgotten. It was like being wrapped in angel's wings. Serafina means angel, you know."

Lee was watching him with an equivocal expression. "Maybe she used a secret ingredient."

Bill shook his head. "The secret was in the simplicity. I miss that simple life, sometimes, although God knows it didn't last long. A couple of years maybe, and then my mother moved on to Number Four. Geoffrey. Gallopin' Geoffrey, I used to call him. He was second in command

416

at World Bank. An authentic powerhouse. We bounced all over the place. Washington, Tokyo, Singapore, Rio, Benghazi – you name it. We put in hard time."

"Sounds exciting."

"It was awful."

The food arrived. The *foie gras* proved delicious, the cactus had been unilaterally disarmed. Bill picked and sampled and took notes. The rabbit impressed him.

"That little bunny went for forty bucks a quarter-pound," he remarked. "Which has got to make it about the most expensive slice of meat in New York."

"I know where you can pay ten times that for a piece of rubbery chicken," Lee volunteered.

"Oh yeah?" Bill was always on the lookout for fresh columns.

"Any charity ball," Lee said. "They have got to be the most expensive feeds in town."

Bill picked up the idea and ran with it.

"That would be fun, Lee. A piece on banquet food. Like the story I did on airline cuisine. *Mystery Meat Flies Again.* Thanks."

"I'm just full of bright ideas," she grinned.

Bill nodded. "You made quite an impression on my father, by the way. He called you a fireball."

Lee was flattered. "Thank him for me."

"I'm not sure Dad meant it as a compliment."

"Well, I was running hard that day. What did you tell him about me? He was very inquisitive."

Bill put down his fork and folded his hands.

"I said I was nuts about you. That you were the most exciting woman I know, full of the kind of vitality I envy. I told him that we live together more or less. My father replied that under those circumstances, 'more or less' was either too much or too little. I should commit or get off the pot. Maybe father knows best, like in the old TV show. What d'you say? It's crazy for us to keep two separate establishments. Separate typewriters OK, and I'll give you the extra drawer on the dresser. So how about it, Lee? We'll move in together and simplify things?"

"And complicate them, you mean." Her answer was as

familiar as his request. "I'm very fond of you, Bill. You're fun. You're sweet. You're marvellous in bed. One of the nicest guys I know. But you push me too hard. I don't love you in the way you need to be loved. And I won't be your rice pudding, so to speak. Anyhow, there are a million women who'll be delighted to share your dresser space. Why pick on me?"

"First of all, I don't want rice pudding in the sense that you mean. And as for why you," Bill chewed his lip for a moment, "I ask myself that all the time, Lee. You're the world's most frustrating woman. One of the coolest, least spontaneous. I get very little change out of this relation-ship, you know. And yet – I always keep hoping that deep inside you, if I can only hit the right chord, push the right button, there's something grand and wonderful waiting to be released. A great reservoir of love . . . passion . . . joy. I sense that potential, Lee, and it's something rare. If I didn't believe you have an immense capacity for happiness, both yours and mine, I wouldn't be here with you tonight. Give, Lee. Soften. All I ask for is a sign. Some symbol of commitment. A hint that we could really make it big. Why do you always hold back?"

Lee sat very still for a moment.

"Maybe I'm not holding back," she said quietly. "Maybe you're looking for something that isn't there."

"I can't believe that," he said, his eyes burning and intense.

She picked up the menu. "May we have our coffee now?"

eight

Michael Avesian was moving with the speed of a downhill racer. Moving fast and smart.

The days were hardly long enough for everything he had to do, but that simply added to the challenge. There was no stopping him now. He felt invincible. It was an exhilarating sensation.

With the Austrian "contract" in his pocket (he made every effort to perceive it as "authentic"), the Hailsham project had once again become viable. Given a few weeks' breather, Michael was convinced, he stood to make a fortune. All kinds of possibilities arose.

His first overture was to Anna Benson, at Mercantile Trust.

"I have something you'll want to see," he told her on the phone.

"I'm sure you do," she answered in a cryptic tone.

"How about lunch today?"

"Do you play squash?" she said. "Meet me at the Vertical Club."

They spent a vigorous hour, one on one, with Michael enjoying himself enormously. Not until he had worked up a full rolling sweat did he realize how much he had missed this sort of physical exertion. Gerry, bless her, was not one for active sports. At least this kind. She certainly could not have kept pace with him today.

Whereas Anna Benson: Michael had to hand it to her, the banker turned out to be a strong competitor. She had a good body, trim and firm with the satiny muscle tone of someone who worked out regularly. She looked terrific in shorts. Briefly he considered letting her win. Decided against it. She wouldn't respect him in the morning, so to speak.

"You play mean," he said when their hour was up.

She laughed. "Thank you. So do you."

They showered and changed, two healthy young animals, then he took her for pasta at Yellowfingers, informality being the order of the day.

She looked particularly fetching, he thought, in a short grey suit that managed to combine seriousness of purpose with a hint of frivolity. Her skin was still flushed from exercise.

"So. What is it you have to show me, Michael?"

She crossed her legs, the skirt riding up over her thigh. Apparently Anna Benson had something to show him too.

"The Austrian contract. Signed, sealed and faxed to your office. It'll be waiting for you when you get back. The terms are terrific. I think the time has come, Annie, for you guys to give me a bigger line of credit. Why don't we begin by rolling over the loan?"

For the record, she inquired about the situation in Britain, but without real concern. If Eli Austrian saw fit to display this kind of confidence in Avesian, Mercantile Trust had no reason to cavil.

They ate their pasta, talked a little business, and concluded the details by the time the espresso arrived.

"I'm so glad we've had a meeting of the minds," Michael said. "It's a pleasure doing business with you."

"Speaking of pleasure," she leaned over to straighten his tie with long tapered fingers, "you know us bankers. Now that you've got my ducats, I just might demand my pound of flesh."

The following morning, Michael flew to Baltimore with the Austrian contract in hand. On the strength of it, he negotiated a million dollar loan from a private investment group. In the afternoon, he visited a large bank in Washington, then doubled back to a small one in Philly. By day's end he had tapped three new sources for as many millions.

The dipsy doodle, the manoeuvre was called, and it was one of the classic ploys of money-raising. Not exactly legal, but who's to know? The trick was in spreading the loans all over the map.

He would use the Baltimore money to pay off Mercantile, Washington to pay off Baltimore and so on. Just keep the whole ball rolling over and over until he was out of the woods.

Michael had employed the technique before and if he played his cards right, there was no reason it wouldn't work again.

Banks were wonderfully slovenly in their procedures, he felt, fired more by greed than by prudence. He returned to New York that evening, tired but happy and presented himself at Gerry's apartment.

"Am I too late for dinner?"

"Where have you been?" She practically bowled him over. "You said you'd be here by seven and it's nearly ten."

"Busy busy busy," he replied. "And getting busier. Forgive me, darling." He poured himself a Scotch, and keeping his voice scrupulously neutral announced that he was off to England. "It looks like I'll have to straighten out this mess myself, but Nigel has hopes of getting me an interview at No. 10. I don't know how long I'll be away. As long as it takes, I suppose. Anyhow Sally's booked me on the Concorde day after tomorrow."

She jumped up. "I'd better start packing."

"Gerry, sweetie, I don't want to disrupt your life any more."

"But I want to go . . ."

"What for? To hang around a hotel room while I lobby politicians? This is not going to be a fun trip. Tell you what. Why don't you take advantage of my absence and have a little vacation, get some rest. You've been under tremendous pressure. You'll go down to the Caribbean. Relax, enjoy the sun, get sand in your toes. I prescribe a week in Barbados. My treat. And if you need to reach me, leave a message at my London office. I'm not quite sure where I'll be staying . . . Sally will know."

"But, Michael! I thought . . ."

"That we could go to London together? Not this time, love." He kissed the tip of her nose. "This trip, I plan to keep a low profile."

She glared at him. "You think I'm a liability, don't you?"

"I think you could use a nice vacation."

*

She didn't go to Barbados. Instead, she would put the separation to better use. Michael was growing indifferent. She was desperate to look good for his return. A week wasn't long enough for a face lift, but it was ample for shaping up at a spa. She'd heard of a place in Virginia with a Japanese seaweed treatment guaranteed to do wonders for skin tone. Youth for sale at $2,500 a pop. Booze not included. But lately she'd been hitting the bottle much too much. *Oh God, make me young!*

"So I'm off tomorrow," she told Lee on the phone, "to rid myself of this disgusting fat. I'm ashamed to step on the scale these days."

Lee sounded sympathetic, adding, "You always look good to me."

"You're sweet," Gerry said. "Gallant. And a lousy liar. Although I dread the prospect of existing on 900 calories a day. Think of me when you're pigging out at La Tulipe with Bill."

Which reminded Lee, she said. Bill was doing a food feature on the charity ball circuit.

"Nobody eats at those things," Gerry said.

"No, but they dress. To the nines and the tens. Saturday, we're going to the April in Paris ball and I was wondering.."

". . . if you could borrow a suitable schmatte?" Gerry broke in.

"Well, maybe an evening wrap."

"Help yourself, as long as you return it in one piece. And be sure and double lock the door when you leave. Ida has the week off."

Lee gave a squeal of delight.

"Thanks, Gerry. You've no idea how much this means!"

Lee had never been alone in the house before. During the day, Ida held watch, fussing, cleaning, a Cerberus alert to any impropriety. And Lee didn't come uninvited at night. The last thing she wanted was to stumble into Michael and Gerry in full nuzzle. The thought nauseated her.

But now, Gerry was in Virginia. Ida god-knows-where.

And Michael off to London, which Lee found intriguing. It smacked of trouble in paradise.

Empty, the house seemed even larger, almost spooky. It didn't even smell familiar. No flowers, Lee realized. When Gerry was home, there were fresh arrangements in the hall every day.

Lee arrived before ten, bringing a couple of large manila envelopes and a supply of coffee in a styrofoam cup. She had no precise idea of what she would find, more of a general plan and a conviction that she would score. Today was not an opportunity to be missed.

Once inside, she bolted the door for safety's sake, then set about her chores.

First the answering machine. Lee played back the messages on the off-chance of finding something interesting, but it was just the usual mix of old friends, wrong numbers and telemarketers. No message from Michael, she noted with satisfaction. She rewound the tape to its previous status, then picked up the mail.

To judge by return addresses, it was mostly junk. Bills, fliers, bank statement, a bunch of fund-raising mailers covering every "worthy" cause from Save the Condors to the Soweto Defence Fund. The only items that looked personal were a few thick envelopes that appeared to contain invitations. She was curious about Gerry's bank statement, but it was hardly worth breaking the law for.

Lee felt a mix of relief and disappointment. Poking through Gerry's possessions was one thing. *Help yourself.* Tampering with the mail might be a Federal offence. She placed the stack on the hall table and made her way upstairs.

Even before she entered the bedroom, her hands were sweating with anticipation. She knew exactly where to go.

In a storage closet of the dressing room was a large cardboard carton jam-packed with memorabilia, whatever scrap of life Gerry had a mind to save. Some papers were placed in manila envelopes, some in shoe-boxes. Most were unceremoniously dumped into the stew. It was about as organized as a trash can.

"My skeleton closet," Gerry called it, and several times

in Lee's presence, she had opened the box and rooted about for a specific item ("That letter from Orson is in here somewhere, I'm positive!") only to give up a little later in despair.

"The hell with it," she would curse, and promise Lee that one of these days, when she wasn't quite so rushed, she would go through the bits and pieces properly, cataloguing every precious scrap. "After which, I can write my memoirs."

In short, like Gerry herself, the contents were in total chaos.

Which was good, from Lee's point of view, and bad. Good, because nobody would notice if they'd been disturbed. Bad, because she could be here all day poking through junk.

Lee had specific treasures in mind.

Anything from Kennedy would be a godsend. Some little mash note scrawled on White House stationery with the magic letters JFK. And maybe an RFK in the bargain. Fabulous, if she could find such a document. Dead Kennedys were still hot stuff. She'd keep an eye out, too, for anything personal from Cardinal Novak – although that might prove a dilemma. Fletch didn't like to buck up against the Church.

Also on the wish list were any items connecting Gerry with (a) movie stars, (b) mobsters and (c) multi-millionaires, although (give or take some overlap), she didn't hold out much hope for category (b). And if the Good Fairy really chose to bless her quest – who knows what gem might spring to hand!

Inside the box, Lee might find proof of a secret marriage or an illegitimate child. Find the peg that had eluded her thus far. She could almost hear her heart pounding in the heavy silence.

"Here we go!"

With that, she dived in and retrieved an armful of papers, then settled down, cross-legged on the floor, to sift them through.

Junk, much of it. Curios. Stuff going back to the dawn of time.

A passenger list, crumbling and yellowed, for the SS *Queen Mary* sailing to Southampton and Cherbourg. And there was Gerry's name, way down in the Third Class. Well, she'd be travelling Third Class again before long. Lee passed it up but lingered over a cracked glossy photo, just as ancient.

"*Mlle Mohawk des Folies Bergère*." And there she was clad in a G-string and a couple of pasties, with practically everything hanging out. Still recognizable as Geraldine O'Neal though. Christ! You'd think the woman would have had sense enough to burn that picture long ago. Lee could see the picture running with the caption: *Madame Ambassador in an Early Incarnation*.

In fact, Follies, with its undertone of sex and extravagance, might be just the peg Lee had been looking for. In a way, Gerry had remained a Follies girl all her life. She put the photo to one side.

There were other photos too, dog-eared and unidentified, mostly souvenir shots taken in night clubs. Lee passed them up, except for one tête-à-tête with Howard Hughes. He was looking down her cleavage. She was looking bored. Nothing with Kennedy, dammit.

Lee began skimming through the smaller items, with a sense that she could waste a day in this manner without making a dent. She didn't know where to begin or where to stop.

At last, she picked up the box and upended it over the floor. It was a snowfall. Letters. Clippings. Old theatre programs. Menus. Matchbooks. Telegrams. Snapshots. Christmas cards.

No diaries, as far as Lee could see. Not in the literal sense. Yet before her was something better than a diary; it was the collage of a life..

Lee spent an hour organizing the material into a rough chronology. Over thirty years of O'Nealeana was here, with items dating back to her college days and up to a recent snapshot of Gerry and Michael in matching lynx coats. For clarity's sake, Lee sorted the material by year.

There was, she noticed, a gap of some months in the early sixties without a scrap of paper to indicate what Gerry had been up to. A nervous breakdown? Some scabrous love affair? A secret marriage?

Whatever it was, Gerry had covered her tracks well.

The hiatus only heightened Lee's sense of mystery. But there was plenty to compensate. Some of the contents were useless without a frame of reference. Others were merely odd.

From the *Miami Herald* of June 1956, a clipping reporting the demise of one Eva Kandrassy in a nursing home. The woman had ingested a clove of garlic while she slept and choked to death. Bizarre.

From Harry James, who had been David Whitfield's idol, a lacy Valentine. Lee wished her father were alive to see it.

From Salvador Dali, a birthday card that had a likeness of Gerry sketched on the back. He had given Gerry three tits.

From Truman Capote, a lock of pale hair in a lavender envelope.

And everywhere, everywhere letters.

In packets. In shoe boxes. In manila envelopes. In file folders. Here, at least, Gerry had made some sort of effort at organization.

Pay dirt. The Lovers' List. Lee sipped her cold coffee and began arranging the letters in priority piles.

There were a number in French, which she skipped over for lack of time, although one bore a letterhead from the Elysée Palace. Nothing from the White House, regrettably. Lee guessed that JFK had been too cautious to write. But she pounced on a note from Martin Luther King. Had Gerry carried on with him as well? If so, that would be newsworthy. Disappointingly, the text turned out to be a little more than a "thank you" for having joined him in some march or other. The tone was warm, but not sizzling. Too bad.

By contrast, one correspondent was so sexually explicit she could barely believe her eyes. He was a Rubi somebody. The name didn't ring a bell, but Lee would have given her soul to read Gerry's replies.

In among the papers were half a dozen missives from

Austin Frazier, literary and full of sweet sentiments. The last one requested that Gerry return his previous letters, which she had clearly not done. Lee wondered if she should stat the lot and give them to Bill. She put them aside, along with a brief, rather charming set of notes from Cary Grant. Extraordinary that Gerry had never boasted about that particular conquest. For all her gabbiness, the lady still had secrets.

And then, of course, there were the Winterbourne letters, packed tight in a Delman shoe box, written in a fine old-fashioned hand on hotel stationery from all over the world.

Lee sampled a few.

My own darling each one began.

But of course, he had been the romance of Gerry's life.

Lee thumbed through them with a bemused expression. They were full of shop talk and complaints, as befits the travelling businessman. But beneath the chronicle of daily events, there was a running theme of tenderness, of love and longing. He must have written every time he went on the road. Why write when he could have called?

"It's been a terrible day, my darling. As is every day we're apart. I miss you dreadfully."

She could picture the merchant prince in a distant hotel suite, pouring out his loneliness on page after page at the close of a pressure-laden day. The letters ached. Lee presumed he penned them as a kind of therapy, yet it surprised her that someone so strong could be so vulnerable. Lee was tempted to mock. This was the man the *Wall Street Journal* had called Old Iron Pants?

Yet despite herself, she felt moved.

Nobody had ever sent her a hand-written love letter. Nobody had sent her a love letter in any form. The people she knew weren't inclined to commit such sentiments to paper.

Who bothered to write letters these days anyhow? Who could spare the time? The effort? You phoned. You telexed. You sent a humorous card. At most, you faxed, always being careful to maintain an airy tongue-in-cheek tone. And one thing for certain. You sure as hell didn't sign your name to anything that could be used against you in the future.

My love . . . my lamb . . . my life . . .

My God! If Gerry had been in the blackmail racket, it struck Lee, she could have cleared a fortune. And not just the Winterbourne stuff. The packing carton was a museum of extinct passions, ancient follies. Distinguished people brought low. Emperors without any clothes – to say nothing of businessmen, artists and various public officials in a similar state of undress.

More than the silver bracelets, these papers were Gerry's souvenirs. Thirty years of love letters! One had to be impressed. Lee couldn't help wondering if whether, in the course of her own life, she would ever have anything like this to show. Some written proof, some tangible evidence, that love had passed her way.

Oh well! She shrugged and closed the shoe-box. Maybe Bill would dedicate his book to her.

At noon she took a break and went to a Lexington Avenue copy shop with the first batch of papers. It wasn't stealing, she assured herself. Merely borrowing. The originals would be returned.

Then she grabbed a tuna sandwich and went back to work.

By mid afternoon, she considered calling it a day. Already she had amassed a gold mine of data, far more than required. And though she'd come across no proof of secret marriages or drug use or Oval Office capers, she had enough to make a solid story. There was a limit as to how many old love letters one could read. Wearily, she opened yet another manila envelope to find yet another yellow batch – from Eli Austrian.

Or Eli v. Austrian, as he signed himself with a flourish in ultra marine ink.

How could Gerry go to bed with that toad? Lee wondered. Although maybe he hadn't been so grotesque back when.

She scanned them swiftly. They were highly erotic in tone – one might almost say smutty – and might even have been publishable, were it not for the fact that Austrian's

Fifth Avenue advertised regularly in *Trend*. So much for that.

She was replacing them in the envelope when a sheet of paper fluttered out. With an intuitive blip, Lee recognized Gerry's current stationery. It was crisp and fresh, and as out of place as a spring daisy in a bouquet of dried flowers. The sheet was covered with samples of the same signature over and over. Eli v. Austrian.

Lee examined the page. It didn't make sense. Then suddenly it did. Practice makes perfect. She compared. The copies at the bottom of the sheet were better executed.

But what the hell did it mean? Why should Gerry O'Neal copy Eli Austrian's signature? Was she forging cheques? Out of the question! Playing practical jokes? There had to be a rational explanation. Lee promised herself to think it through at leisure, but instinct told her she was on to something hot.

Carefully, she took the signature sheet along with the entire Austrian correspondence and added it to the duplicating pile.

By five o'clock and another trip to the photocopy shop, her task was complete. Gerry's original papers went back into the carton – not too neatly, as that in itself might be a clue. Then Lee swept up the area with a dustpan and brush. It had been a highly profitable day.

Halfway down the stairs, her arms full of documents, she remembered the promised wrap for Saturday night. Ostensibly that was why she had come. But she couldn't carry any more. In any case, it was better to forego that luxury. Under the circumstances, wearing Gerry's clothes could be considered an ethical lapse.

"You missed all the excitement," Ollie Dichter said when she got back to the office.

"Yeah?" Lee stashed the papers in her bottom desk drawer, then locked it. "What happened?"

"Some maniac tried to murder Bill Frazier."

Less than an hour ago, Ollie recounted, the head chef at Casa Cuba had managed to slip past security. Then finding his way to Bill's desk, he pulled a machete out from under his coat and started swinging.

"You roon my life . . . you roon my life!" the lunatic kept screaming and slashing while all hell broke loose, chairs turning over, Bill jumping on top of his desk. It had taken six people to wrestle the lunatic down. The cops had only just departed.

Lee put her hand to her heart. "Omigod! Where's Bill? He OK?"

"He's fine. Not a scratch. More shook up than anything else. I think he's at the station house, making a statement."

Lee tore out of the office to find him, pale but collected, coming down the steps of the Precinct house.

Wordlessly he took her hand and marched her into the nearest bar. They slid into a red plastic banquette.

"Two double Scotches," he told the waitress. "And I don't know what the lady will have."

They sat holding hands until the drinks came. Lee waited till he'd downed the first jolt.

"I remember the review," she said. " 'Casa Cuba is a restaurant of such consummate awfulness, I suspect it's Fidel Castro's revenge for Bay of Pigs!' I thought that was kind of cute. And you had a funny pay-off line as I recall. What was it?"

Bill stirred his swizzle stick. " *'In this joint, you don't send the food back. You send the chef back!'* Ha ha ha. Just the kind of *bon mot* that trips off my lips. Too bad Mr Valdez doesn't share our sense of humour. Poor bastard's facing charges for criminal assault."

Lee couldn't believe her ears.

"You sound like you're sorry for the guy. Jesus, Bill. The son of a bitch tried to kill you! He's gotta be insane. Who else would do a thing like that? All it was was a lousy review."

"I ruined his life," Bill said dourly.

"Bullshit! You simply lost him a few customers here and there. Hardly an excuse to go bananas. And it's ridiculous for you to feel guilty. You've done nothing wrong, nothing unprofessional. If Valdez can't stand the heat, he should literally get out of the kitchen."

430

But Bill was pursuing separate thoughts.

"The food wasn't that bad, you know. Not good, but not toxic. OK, it stunk by gourmet standards, but I didn't have to review it, Lee. Except that I just couldn't pass up making the wisecrack." He tossed off the second double in a gulp. "There are times when I hate the so-called power of the press. You write something, it gets into print, you take your pay cheque – and you forget that you're fucking around with people's lives. I'm gonna dream about Valdez tonight – those big dark eyes, full of panic. He'll probably get deported after all."

"In which case," Lee remarked, "your review will turn out to be a self-fulfilling prophecy. Now there's an interesting story for a piece in *Trend*. Life following art, so to speak."

Bill stared at her. "*You've* gotta be kidding! To change the subject, Fletch says I should take the rest of the week off, get over the shock. Let's go up to Saranac for a couple of days. Walk in the woods. Pick violets. Get the smell of garbage out of our noses."

But she couldn't. She was on a major story, lots of research. Briefly, Lee was tempted to tell him about her day of discovery, but given his present mood she held her tongue.

"How about dinner instead?" she proposed.

"Simple," Bill said. "Let's keep it simple."

They went to a McDonalds and had cheeseburgers and shakes.

Gerry came back from Virginia slimmed and trimmed.

It had been an exhausting week during which she had been systematically pummelled, pounded, stretched and starved. For a woman who had enjoyed the good life as a matter of routine, being deprived of food was the hardest. She went to bed every night ravenous, ready to kill for a candy bar, sustained only by one thought.

"I'm doing this for Michael," she would say.

By week's end, she had so far succeeded that she could examine herself without quailing. Her clothes looked good on her again. The puffiness around the eyes was gone. She resolved not to drink for at least another month. She was doing that for Michael, too.

The sudden weight loss, however, had slackened her facial muscles. Close up she looked older, but that could be concealed with careful make-up and soft lights.

Young. Young was what mattered. Or as close to the illusion as one could get.

"At my age," she told the masseur with a smile, "all that's left is legs and eyes."

It was a shameless fishing for compliments. But the masseur, a Japanese girl, reed slim and with the unthinking arrogance of youth, merely nodded and pounded away.

And bloody painful those poundings were. That sweet young thing could beat her bones to jelly. But Gerry was enduring all this misery for Michael, too. As forms of torture go, it wasn't half as bad as certain others. The unreturned phone call was far worse.

Once home, Gerry's first task was to buy something lovely – nay, breathtaking! to sweep him off his feet when he got back. Money was no object. Beauty was.

"What have you got for me in the drop-dead department?" she asked her saleswoman at Saks. "Something for a fabulous home-coming." One hour later, some three thousand dollars poorer, she left, the possessor of a silk organza fantasy. It was a magnificent confection, fragile as butterfly wings, sheer as clouds: a thousand tiny pleats that framed the face and showcased the now-lean body. "A dramatic statement," the saleswoman had called it. "A knockout," Gerry said.

The following morning, she presented herself at Kevin Kaplan's SoHo salon and gave herself over to the master. This was The Hot Place, according to *Elle*, and Kevin the High Priest of Hair.

It was certainly a change from the quiet elegance of Elizabeth Arden. The walls were covered with glamour shots of movie stars and hair hair hair. The Veronica Lake peekaboo. The Joan Crawford pompadour. The Betty Grable page boy. The Dietrich golden waves. In short, the very women Gerry had fashioned herself after as a schoolgirl were playing their rôles once again. Only now it was the second time around. She wasn't sure if the effect was camp or chic or slightly foolish. Could one really turn back the clock just like that?

However, a lot of the clients appeared to be models, which made her more secure. Models could be trusted in these matters.

"Black is so old-making," Kevin said, cupping her face in his hands. He was a pleasant fellow, with a crew cut and Brooklyn accent. He worked in blue jeans and chatted as he worked. "I think we want to go light, don't you?"

Gerry gave a cautious nod. General wisdom declared that lighter was younger. She should have had the courage years ago.

Kevin took a strand and rubbed it between his fingers, as though sampling a piece of particularly fine fabric. "Oh, lovely, sensual. I can do things with this. What colour is it naturally, Gerry? A little on the grey side?"

Gerry laughed. "Do I know? I haven't seen it in twenty years."

After due deliberation, she and Kevin settled on Rita Hayworth auburn ("Now *there* was a goddess!") inspired by a forties poster of the star in *Blood and Sand*.

"But a little shorter," Kevin warned. "Long is age-making." Once the details were agreed, he called the colourist over. "Give me a Hayworth, Shana," he told her, "to go with those big green eyes."

"*Olé!*" Gerry said.

The dye job turned out brighter than she expected, more red than auburn, but Kevin expressed his delight with a clap of the hands.

"Perfect! If I were only what's his name . . . Aga Khan!"

Aly Khan, Gerry made the correction. She had known the gentleman.

But at the moment, she was occupied with other matters.

"You don't think it's too . . . well, garish?"

He sat down opposite her, chin in hand. Rodin's thinker contemplating the universe. Then he exhaled slowly.

"No. You have Kevin's word it's perfect. You'll need a different colour lipstick is all."

Gerry bowed to his expertise. He proceeded to cut and style.

When Michael rang the bell that evening, fresh from London, a perfumed Gerry was waiting by the door.

She was nervous. Expectant too. In a way even proud.

Proud of her health farm body. Of the silk organza fantasy from Saks. Of the new make-up devised that very afternoon at Face Place. Of the Hayworth hair. He would love it. Michael loved surprises. Change.

She opened the door with a glorious smile.

"My God!" Michael switched on the light in the hall. "What have you done to your hair?"

Her hands flew to her head. "You don't like it?" But there was no need to wait for his answer. Shock was written all over his face.

And before Michael could say anything in mitigation, Gerry's heart skidded to a halt.

Looking in the hall mirror, she had a moment of epiphany. The red hair. The painted face. The clothes that made her a mockery of youth.

Gerry stared at the image, hypnotized. Horrified.

Before her stood Kiki – the ancient whore of Montparnasse.

nine

After due consideration, Nancy Whitfield decided to stay on in New York. Nothing urgent pulled her back to Cedar City, so she rented her house and took a small furnished apartment in Rego Park. Despite Lee's claim that "nobody lives in Queens", Nancy found the neighbourhood congenial, hardly different from the streets where she grew up. As she told Gerry on the phone, she was trying to pick up where she'd left off years ago.

"Doing what?" Gerry sounded puzzled.

"Well, I'm not sure exactly," Nancy dithered. "Get a job. Build a career. Go back to school. Maybe law school even."

In fact, she quite liked the sound of that. Why not law school? Or anthropology? Why not write a book on Eleanor of Aquitaine? Anything was possible. She found herself quoting something she'd read a while back: " 'Age is no barrier for today's woman. Dream the dream. Then go out and live it!' "

"Who said that?"

"Why you did, Gerry! In an article in *MS* magazine. I found it quite inspiring. And it's true, of course. Not that anything can ever replace David, but I personally don't subscribe to the practice of suttee. The way I see it, this is a second chance at life. A kind of turning back the clock. Anyhow, I've decided not to leave until I've exhausted New York – or vice versa."

Gerry laughed, and asked her how she was set for money.

It was the opportunity Nancy had been waiting for.

"Naturally, I'll have to find some kind of of work and I was hoping . . ."

Lee had thrilled her with tales of Gerry in her office, of watching her operate in high gear. Nancy couldn't help but be struck by the similarities.

"Between what and what?" Gerry asked.

"Between you and me. At different levels, of course. But

435

as Lee described you in action, I noticed definite similarities. How you get things rolling. Put the right people together. Curry influence here and there. Lee was terribly impressed by the specifics, as you can imagine, and it'll all be in that article of hers. But the point is, Gerry, in my own small way, that's pretty much what I did in Cedar City. Most definitely, public relations. I've got energy, tact and a certain life experience. Plus you know I can write. I suspect I may have missed my calling. So," she caught her breath, "would you consider taking me on as an apprentice?"

"*You* work for *me*?" Gerry asked. "Impossible! We've known each other too long. Besides, PR sucks. I wouldn't wish it on my own worst enemy. But I'll see if I can find you some kind of job in media. Proof-reading, maybe. Copy editing. Continuity. I'll get back to you later this week."

In fact, she was back on the phone within ten minutes.

"*What* article?" Gerry asked.

After two weeks on the banquet circuit, all Bill Frazier had to show for his efforts was a gravy spot on his best tux.

"I'd send it out to the cleaners," he bitched to Lee, "except I'm terrified of catching Rocky Mountain spotted fever. Or was it AIDS? I forget. Jesus, those charity dinners are a crashing bore, gourmet-wise. People-wise, too. Same old food. Same petty conversation. I've decided not to write the fucking article after all. The idea gives me heartburn." He turned to her, hands spread in appeal. "Help me, Lee. I'm drowning in shallowness."

They were in her apartment. It was late. Now, arms akimbo, she watched him with impatient eyes.

"You're so jaundiced about everything these days, Bill. I found those dinners fascinating. A wonderful place to network, get leads. By the way, I've been invited to take a tour of Trump's yacht. Not by Ivana herself, actually – one of her decorators. I met him at the Save the Children do. It's supposed to be fabulous – the boat, not the kiddies, I mean . . . and I was thinking. There might be a cute snob story in having the yacht take the same course around

Manhattan that the Circle Line cruise does. Only I'd call it 'The Inner Circle Line'."

Bill didn't respond.

"Don't you get it, Bill? The Inner Circle? I'm referring to the people close to Trump. Or . . ." she chewed her lip thoughtfully. She was in a creative mode. "Different slant! Say we fill up the boat with distinguished foreigners. Claus von Bulow . . . Rupert Murdoch . . . Anna Wintour – you get the drift. No, not Murdoch though. I understand Bobby Obermayer hates his guts. Well, there are plenty of others around. Then we photograph the lot of 'em at Ellis Island. *The New Immigrants*. Now that's one helluva title . . ." In the flush of ideas, she had quite forgotten Bill's presence. "We get Annie Leibowitz to do the pictures, strive for a museum look. Might be interesting to do a show in our lobby. Will Fletch go for the tab, though? Cost a fortune . . ."

"Stop babbling!" Bill cut in.

Lee wheeled about, startled by the spike in his voice.

Bill waited until he had her full attention.

"I quit the magazine today," he said.

She had trouble shifting gears. "Be serious!" she said.

"I am," he said. "I gave in my notice this morning, effective a week from Friday. That's it. *Finis*. I'm out of here."

She let the news sink in, then burst into smiles.

"Let me guess . . . You're going to *The Times*!" She took his silence for assent. "Fabulous! Well, I heard they were looking for a new reviewer but it never dawned on me . . . Oh wow! Congrats!"

"I'm going to Rome, Lee . . ."

"Rome?"

"As in Italy, leaving on the twentieth. I plan to rent a little studio in some pleasant residential area, live simply and finish my book. If you would care to join me, I'd be overjoyed. You'd like Rome. It's a beautiful city."

She stared at him, incredulous.

"You are serious! But why Rome? Do you have friends there? Have you lined up a job? Hell! You don't even speak decent Italian!"

"That's why I'm going, Lee. No distractions, no phone ringing off the hook. Remember I told you I wanted to finish my novel before I was thirty? I meant it. Well, I'll never do it under present circumstances. All I do here is piss away my life in fancy restaurants. It's stupid. I hate it. I'm sick of having head waiters fawn and tremble when I step through the door. Of reaching for my poison pen every time some *sommelier* brings the wrong Chardonnay. Who am I, Hitler?"

"You're a journalist," she said.

"Not any more," he said. "I've decided I'd rather be a member of the human race. What function do we serve; don't you ever wonder? It's not as if we were breaking serious news. We're trivia, footnotes, fashionable sleaze – as vital as panties on a lamb chop. And I don't like what we're becoming. Look at you, Lee. You're twenty-five and already you're getting these driven lines around your mouth. You never laugh any more either. Where's the fun? Let's start over. Build a real life in Rome. Tender. Kind. Make love in the afternoons. Stroll through the Pincio on summer evenings. We could keep each other sane."

"I am sane, thank you very much. You're the one who's talking crazy. I know you, Bill. You'd be bored out of your skull within a month. You'd miss the throb."

"I'm all throbbed out."

"And what'll we live on?" she asked. "On love and rice pudding?"

"I have a certain modest income."

" 'A certain modest income,' " she mocked. "A quiet part of town. Perfect! I know what brought this about. That fucking chef from the Casa Cuba! You haven't been the same since. But that was a one-off incident! It can't happen now. They've beefed up building security. Get real, Bill. You're on your way to becoming the hottest food writer in Manhattan. Don't blow it for a fantasy! The book can wait. Besides, who reads literary novels any more? Who needs 'em? They're a self-indulgence. And it's not as if you had a publisher lined up. Suppose it bombs. You'll have thrown away everything – for zilch!"

"What everything, Lee?"

"Status . . . influence . . . success." Suddenly, she clenched her fists, white with rage. "Me! You'll have thrown me away!"

She wanted to punch him, beat him, make him repent. How could he be so pig-headed? Hot angry tears coursed down her cheeks.

"Yes me! You can't do this to me, William Frazier. You have no right. I've depended on you. We were a power couple. We were going to do great things together. I don't need this kind of rejection, thank you very much, not now when I'm under the gun. A huge story. Something's come up so fantastic it's gonna blow a certain celebrity right out of the water! Real big! Very big! A career-maker! And I've got two other stories under development. Fletch is breathing down my neck. Don't cop out now, Bill. Not when I'm under such pressure!"

"All the more reason to run away," he pleaded. "Jesus! Who needs that stress? It's only a job, Lee. Take a chance that there's something better ahead. Maybe we could be happy, but we won't know till we try. Give it your best shot. That's all I ask. And if things work out, we'll get married . . ."

"Married!" she spat out the word. "What is that supposed to be, Bill? The offer I can't refuse? You men are all alike. You, the guy I lived with out in Bismarck, you think all a woman needs is to hear the sound of wedding bells and whammo! the brains turn to instant jelly. I care for you, Bill. Quite deeply in fact. But that doesn't mean I'm ready to trail around the world in your wake. It's absurd. I wouldn't expect you to do it for me. Maybe, just maybe, I'll come for a visit during the summer. If I can get away, that is. I've never been to Europe. Should be fun. But that's the extent of it. And as for chucking my job at *Trend*, I'm astonished you even suggested it."

He looked at her thoughtfully.

"You never give up anything for anyone, do you?" he asked. "Why? Is it against your religion?"

Lee paused, then dried her eyes.

"My mother gave up her career for so-called love," she replied. "Don't expect me to be the same kind of fool."

The moment the door closed behind him, Lee changed into sweatpants and Nikes, too angry to do anything but jog.

Twice around the reservoir, never pausing, never slackening her step. Running. Driving herself until her thighs ached and her sweat ran in rivers and her lungs were ready to burst.

Then around once more. Running so hard that Bill Frazier could never catch up with her.

Until at last she ran him out of her system.

ten

The newly rechristened Alexandra Avesian·was having the
time of her life. So everyone told her. It was compensation
for those "lost years" with Michael.

In her glitzy new wardrobe and her hair à la Cher, she
hardly recognized herself in the mirror. A new crop of
words came to mind. The "s" words, she called them.
Svelte. Sleek. Sophisticated. Sexy. Smart. The only thing
she wasn't, was "Sandy". That poor little lamb had been
laid to rest, and every Saturday night at the country club,
Alexandra would dance on her grave. Dance the latest
steps only, in the very highest heels. And finish the evening with a blast of champagne.

At Iris's urging, she had joined not just the country club,
but everything in sight that afforded a chance to meet
men. Monday was Parents without Partners. Tuesday, the
ballroom dancing class. Wednesday was reserved for a
singles group that called itself The Mate Market. And so
on through Saturday night.

It was a rare evening that found her at home.

"I haven't done this in years," she told her bosom
buddy.

"Fucking?"

"Dancing," Alexandra said. "Dating. It's weird. I'm
having fun but I suppose I should think of settling down,
getting married once my divorce becomes final."

"Why buy a bull," Iris asked, "when beefcake's so
cheap?"

For months, however, her behaviour remained impeccable.
Beneath the surface gloss dwelt a conventional woman.

Thus it was with some surprise that Alexandra Avesian
awoke one morning to find herself in bed with the assistant
tennis pro from the club. The progression of events was
unclear. She had a woozy recollection of some turns on

the dance floor. A few drinks. A lot of laughs. An offer to improve her backhand.

Extraordinary that the end result should be this blond head on her pillow at six o'clock of a Sunday morning.

"Donnie, is that you?"

His response was to fumble blindly for her breasts.

"Wake up. Wake up!" She shook him violently, till at last he opened one eye. "What are you doing here, Donnie?"

"What d'ya think I'm doin' here?" He looked genuinely puzzled.

"Omigod!" Alexandra's memory began to return. "Well, you've got to be out of here quick, before my kids wake up. Out out out!"

He got up, yawned and threw on his clothes without protest, making her suspect this wasn't the first such pre-dawn summons the young man had ever received. But Jesus! (she thought) little Donnie Belcher! The kid was barely twenty. Not even a full-time pro. Talk about robbing the cradle!

"Do I get coffee?" he asked.

"Try the diner over on 128." She handed him his jacket. "They're open round the clock. And don't put your shoes on till you're actually out of the house. *Capeesh?*"

She accompanied him to the front door to make sure he didn't get side-tracked. But all the time, she was burning up with curiosity.

"Listen, Donnie, before you go. Ummm . . . I gotta ask. How was it for you? I mean compared to other girls you've been with. Did the earth move?"

"Oh Ma'am!" he gave a wicked smirk. "Did it ever! Three times running. Gee, Mrs A., don't you remember? 'Woof-woof'?"

She remembered exactly, including the time they'd gone down on all fours. Alexandra blushed, but Donnie still had that shitty grin on his face. "You are some foxy lady, let me tell you! The best in the club."

"Thank you, Donnie," she whispered. "That's quite a compliment."

At nine o'clock, as she did every Sunday morning, she made a big breakfast, pancakes and bacon and sausages.

Then she piled the food on the table and let the children help themselves. Natasha noticed that her mother was preoccupied.

"You OK, Mom?" the older girl paused in mid-fork.

"Fine fine," Alexandra hummed, and drew figure-eights through the lake of maple syrup on her plate. She was fine indeed. One foxy lady!

One crazy lady.

She could scarcely credit how easily, how casually she had lapsed from grace. Sandy, who had always danced with the guy that brung her! Twelve years of fidelity right down the drain, woof-woof.

Extraordinary how little guilt she felt, now that she was what her father called a "hoor". Harry McKay was highly judgemental in these matters. She preferred Donnie's description.

"Some foxy lady." "The best in the club!"

That was more like it! Rampant flattery, of course, but the kind that did wonders for the ego. Even better than sex, when it came right down to it. Although the sex had been pretty good too.

If only Michael had been there – she suppressed a giggle. He never would have believed it of her! That foxy Alexandra Avesian!

Not that she forgave him his transgressions with that awful O'Neal person. But for the first time in months, she could sympathize the tiniest bit. Who could resist being buttered up by a member of the opposite sex, being told you were fabulous in bed? Hell, it made you feel nine feet high.

The foxy lady picked up her fork and speared her sausage with gusto. It looked delicious. She devoured it in a single gulp.

Natasha was watching her through Michael's black eyes.

"Wow, Mom! You're always telling *me* not to eat like an animal!"

"Woof-woof," came the cheerful reply.

That rat! That ingrate! Damn him to hell.

Two days already and not even a phone call. A postcard even.

Well, OK, nobody sent postcards. Nobody ever wrote any more.

Except for forged names on the bottom of contracts!

Gerry winced at the memory.

In the month since his return from England, her life had fallen apart. To say Michael was cooling would be an understatement. He was trying to wriggle out. Break free.

When they were together he was scrupulously polite. Even affectionate within bounds. The trouble was, they were so rarely together. Her calendar was full of X's for broken dates, each preceded by a plausible excuse.

"Business!" he would say. "Something's come up in San Francisco." Or Felixstowe. Or Chicago.

Or Baltimore, for all she knew.

Excuses excuses excuses.

When he was gone, she passed the days in a state of suspended animation. Waiting for Michael to call.

She began avoiding friends, especially close ones, not wanting to explain Michael's absence when he was away. Not wanting to waste a precious moment when he was present.

Jake particularly was to be avoided at all costs. Ever since the night of the forgery she had been ashamed to look him in the eye, as though he could read her mind in a single glance, uncover her disgrace. Jake Matthews, who represented all that was finest in her life, would come to despise her.

She was beginning to despise herself.

Work, too, was becoming a burden, an intrusion on the main event of her life. Gerry who had never been able to delegate, now delegated left and right. "You handle it, Herman." She would pass on the most important decisions. "I don't even want to know."

She had no patience to spend hours at the office pushing stupid papers around on her desk. Her client list dwindled. No effort was made to replace it.

Life had been reduced to one simple question: where was Michael?

Sometimes he returned her calls. Sometimes he didn't. The worst moments were when his secretary phoned in his stead.

"I'm sorry, Miss O'Neal," she would say in that cloying voice, "but Mr Avesian has been held up by . . ." whatever the alibi du jour turned out to be.

Gerry simmered. If he could call his office, he could just as easily call her! How transparent these manoeuvres were. How familiar!

She herself had ditched too many lovers not to recognize the vital signs. Only this time, she was the one being dismissed.

It hurt. Intolerably. And after all she had done for him! She had saved his ass, saved Hailsham, although they had never once discussed the particulars. "Don't ask," she had said when she handed over the contract. He never mentioned the matter again. For all Michael knew, technically speaking, Gerry might have obtained Austrian's signature on her back. She hadn't, and he damn well knew it. The point was, however, that he could plead ignorance and walk away unscathed.

Of course he wouldn't! A rat and an ingrate Michael might have been for not phoning (and Gerry really didn't mean it!), but he wasn't a swine. They were in this together, all the way.

She couldn't stop worrying. Her nerves were shot. She felt guilty, insecure. Spending time with anyone other than Michael only added to her irritability. Gerry was developing a penchant for scenes. As she had begun dodging old friends, so they had begun dodging her. She was no fun to be with any more.

Only a week before she'd had a blow-up with her housekeeper, of all people. Over nothing. Trivia! Yet she'd acted like a lunatic.

"You've been in my box!" Gerry screamed.

"What box?" The usually doughty Ida looked befuddled.

"The big one in the dressing room. With all my papers. Don't deny it. I have a sixth sense about such things. It's not enough" – Gerry started weeping – "that I give you

445

my clothes, my best perfumes. And God knows what kind of kickbacks you get from the caterers . . ."

That was enough for Ida. Never before had she been accused of any impropriety. Her reply was to quit on the spot.

Gerry regretted it instantly, but she was damned if she would put up with that kind of crap from a cleaning woman. She valued her privacy too much.

And in an odd way, she preferred having Ida out of the house. Life was easier. With Ida around, Gerry had had to put up a front, play the businesswoman. No more! It never occurred to her that, subconsciously, Gerry had engineered the split.

Now, however, she could stay home and mope and worry and grieve and wait for Michael's calls without feeling embarrassed. She was entitled to some relaxation. Some time for herself.

She no longer drank, not even the odd Campari. Liquor made you fat fat fat. It also made you cry. Instead she consumed gallons of black coffee and watched "the soaps" every day. Gerry had never seen daytime television before, life having always been too full. But with Michael away, she could stretch out on the sofa in the den and let the serials roll over her in a warm narcotic ooze composed of love and hate and drugs and incest and accidents and adulteries and abortions. She didn't like or dislike the pro- grammes. They took less effort than reading and managed to kill the time till Michael called.

When he was out of town she didn't bother to dress. She would pull on an old robe, something warm and comfortable, and sip coffee and chew her nails and sip coffee and face the day's major decisions (*As the World Turns* or *One Life to Live*? *Santa Barbara* or *Guiding Light*?) without having to explain anything to anyone.

Except herself.

She was wretchedly unhappy, attributing her misery to Michael's neglect. If only he would be loving again, she'd be the same old Gerry, gay and carefree. But in the back of her mind, various troubles roiled and festered. She kept waiting for the other shoe to drop.

446

When Gerry learned that Lee was planning a story about her, she had a moment of total panic.

"Why should she do such a thing without telling me?" she demanded of Nancy, who replied that the piece was bound to be favourable. Gerry was not assuaged. No reputable journalist would do a story on a friend without at the least admitting it was in the works.

She tried to quizz Lee directly only to find that her protegée wasn't returning her calls. Incredible! Who the hell was Lee to snub Gerry O'Neal? There were moments when, between Lee and Michael, Gerry felt herself becoming a non-person. A nagging voice on the wrong end of a phone. A nobody.

"I smell mischief," she confided to Michael on one of their rare dinners together.

Michael scoffed. "Come on, Ger. You've been written up a million times before. You love it."

"Not by anyone who knows me so well. She has stories going back to when I was in college. And now she doesn't even answer my calls! What else can it be but a a hatchet job?"

"You're a big girl, Gerry." Michael patted her hand. "It's a mistake to over-react."

Michael certainly wasn't intimidated by the prospect, but then – it wasn't his past that was going to be dragged through the mud.

Indeed, nothing could shake his confidence these days. He was coming and going all over the world, the master of a hundred-ring circus.

As Lee had called him in the pages of *Trend*: "The Man with the Golden Touch".

The turning point had been his meeting in Downing Street the month before. Michael couldn't stop boasting about how well the interview had gone. He and the Prime Minister had achieved instant rapport. "She's one smart cookie," Michael said.

Irrationally, Gerry was jealous.

"What did you do to win her approval, Michael? Flirt a bit? Did you allow her to straighten your tie?"

"For Chrissakes, Gerry! The woman's in her sixties! It was strictly business."

Unwittingly, his reference to age set off a riot of emotions. Gerry wasn't all that far from the sixty mark herself. However, knowing Michael's aversion to scenes, she let the slight pass without comment. She merely added it to her stockpile of suffering.

Periodically, Gerry would fantasize scenarios in which *she* dumped *Michael* in some manner that would salvage her pride. No defence like an offence in affairs of the heart.

("I'm sorry, darling." She could picture herself, elegant, Tallulah-ish in a stylized drawing room comedy. "You see, I've found someone new." She would smile a brave smile. He would blink back a tear and kiss her hand.)

But there was no one new. Nor even a likelihood of such. Besides, what man could possibly compete with Michael?

When the opportunity arose for her to make her farewells, when Michael was actually present in the flesh, the scenario melted away. In real life, her efforts were focused not on letting go, but on hanging in there. For as long as humanly possible, if not longer.

Not that Gerry had ever truly believed the two of them were destined to ride off into a perpetual sunset while the orchestra played "Love in Bloom". Even the soaps spared you that kind of fatuity.

But she had aspired to – if not another year (too much to ask for in a wicked world) – then certainly some months yet before their love ran its course. September. If, by hook crook or miracle, she managed to hold on to him through next September, they might celebrate a first anniversary.

The signs were not good.

She had looked at her horoscope in the *Daily News* that very morning, something she never did, on principle. Horoscopes were for mystics, mental defectives and silly young girls with acne. She devoured every word.

The *News* astrologist warned of "long-term far-reaching changes" which Gerry might safely assume to be for the worse.

Did that mean Michael wouldn't call today? She tried to

laugh the message off. Served her right for reading such rubbish.

But would he call? It had been over forty-eight hours since he left for Milan to hustle some maker of fancy Italian footwear.

"Of course I'll try to call," he'd said, "but remember the time difference. I might not be able to catch you."

He'd catch her. Where else would she be but home, aching and vulnerable and waiting? As she was now. It was two o'clock in New York (*Guiding Light* or *Santa Barbara*? *Guiding Light*.) which meant 8 p.m. in Milan. Time for Michael to be freshening up before dinner, time for him to place that call.

Gerry poured herself another cup of coffee and turned on the box.

Wow! Big trouble ahead. Phillip has just told Alex that he's in love with her. Poor ditz! Doesn't she know that good ole Phil is the father of Meredith's baby? A total scumbag! Well, can you beat that! "Adam" – the guy with those awful facial scars, remember? – actually turns out to be Roger Thorpe! Talk about surprises!

The phone rang. She zapped the TV.

"Michael!" she cried. "About time!"

But it wasn't Michael at all. It was Lee Whitfield.

"I've got the whole story," she was saying in a cold distant voice. "All the details. I've checked it out with Eli Austrian. You may wish to make some statement before I break into print."

They made an appointment. Noon the following day.

eleven

For the hundredth time, doubtless the final time, Lee stepped across the threshold into Gerry's study.

Though it was daytime, the blinds were drawn, the television droning. Gerry turned off the set, then switched on an overhead light. The two women sat down facing each other.

Lee stifled a gasp. Extraordinary how much Gerry had deteriorated in past month. And no sign of Michael anywhere. That explained much, of course. Gerry bore the look of an abandoned woman.

Without make-up, the face was a death mask, the skin a cadaverous white. Someone had botched her hair in a godawful dye job and the grey roots were beginning to show. In thirty days Geraldine O'Neal seemed to have aged thirty years. But that was what happened when one ventured beyond the borders of Shangri-la. She looked like a fugitive, Lee thought, a refugee from a fool's paradise.

Only the eyes, deep and haunting, stirred a memory of the beauty that had been.

Lee suppressed a twinge of pity as unprofessional. Detachment was everything. She only wished that she had brought a photographer along. What a picture Gerry made sitting there!

The important thing was not to view Geraldine O'Neal as either a friend or fallen idol, but as the biggest break of her career. Nothing less. Nothing more. Nothing personal.

With that in mind, Lee opened her attaché case, withdrew two sets of typescripts and handed one to Gerry.

"Everything that's written here can be verified," she said.

Gerry took the sheaf and put it in her lap without even a cursory glance. Was it macho? Lee wondered, or had Gerry forgot to put her contact lenses in? The latter, she suspected.

"In the interest of saving time," Lee said, "I'll run

through the highlights, beginning with the Goldman Fellowship fraud . . ."

Succinctly, Lee touched upon key items: Gerry's stint at the Follies, the Suzie Slade imposture, the affairs with eminent men . . .

As she ran down the list of former bed-mates (and many of the names were dynamite), a peculiar expression flitted across Gerry's gaze. Lee proceeded, naming names right up to and including Michael and the resulting ". . . telephone harassment of Alexandra Avesian, which could be a criminal matter. Which brings us to date and a far more serious instance of criminal activity. Specifically, your forgery of the Austrian contract. Don't bother to deny it. I have ample proof. Copies of your practice sheets. Samples of his signatures on letters to you. One can see where they've been traced. May I remind you, these were obtained legally. You authorized me to borrow anything in the house.

"In addition I've spoken to Mr Austrian who assures me he did not – I repeat *not*! sign the contract for Hailsham. Also I spoke to the bank officer who assures me he has. It may interest you to know that I have kept my own counsel thus far. Neither Mr Austrian nor Miss Benson have any idea that a fraud has been perpetrated. They can read about it – along with the rest of the world – in a future issue of *Trend*. So . . ."

"So . . . !" Gerry wet her lips. "You've done your homework. Why bother to come here?"

"To see if you have any corrections or statements for the record. I want to report both sides of the story."

"And that's what I am to you? A story?"

Lee ignored the question. She wasn't the one being interviewed.

"Or any crucial omissions? Anything you care to add?"

That peculiar expression of Gerry's noted earlier now returned. More a grimace than a smile.

"You left Bobby Obermayer's name out of my lovers' list."

Lee shrugged. What kind of asshole did Gerry think she

was, to compromise her publisher? A goof that size could cost Lee her job.

"No other comment?" Lee asked.

Suddenly, the green eyes filled with panic.

"Why do you want to ruin me?" Gerry cried out. Her composure, so tenuous until now, was slipping away. "What have I done that you should destroy my life like this? Have you no pity? No humanity?"

Lee looked at her with contempt.

"We will now hear from the gypsy violins," she said.

Gerry was shaking her head, as though this were all a bad dream.

"It's revenge you're after. That's it, isn't it. Revenge because Michael fell in love with me, not you."

"Don't be stupid, Gerry, I'm just a reporter doing a job."

"This isn't journalism, Lee. It's assassination. We were friends. Does that mean nothing? Why should you attack me like this?"

She was shaking like a leaf. It took all Lee's self-discipline to squelch a triumphant smirk. At last . . . at last she had the great woman on the run!

"Don't flatter yourself, Gerry," she replied. "I assure you, it's nothing personal. You . . . Michael . . . You don't matter one whit to me. Maybe once, but not now. I'm savvy, a pro. And this interview is strictly business." She permitted herself a smile. "I'm not with the *East Jeezus Gazette* any more."

Gerry staggered to her feet. The papers scattered to the floor. Then she dashed out of the room.

Lee deliberated briefly, then decided to wait. She still craved that one devastating quote.

Right now, Gerry was probably finding consolation in a brandy bottle. Or crying her eyes out in the john. Or maybe doing coke. Briefly, it occurred to Lee that O'Neal might have gone for a gun. To shoot whom, though – Lee? or herself?

But Gerry loathed guns. Wouldn't have one in the house. And if it came to a knockdown drag-out fight, Lee had the edge. She worked out with weights every morning.

Ten minutes passed, the silence broken only by the tick

of the wall clock. Waiting made Lee nervous. She popped
a downer. Her stomach was in knots. She ought to have
had lunch before she came.

At last Gerry returned carrying a cup of coffee.

Lee steeled herself in expectation of an onslaught: tears,
pleas, anger, hysteria, the cup of coffee flung in her face.

It never materialized. Instead, Gerry walked briskly
across the room, trampling on the typescript as she went.
Then she sat down in her favourite wing chair, took a deep
swig of coffee and looked into Lee's eyes.

To Lee's astonishment, Gerry had put on lipstick.

Lipstick! Incredible. At the edge of total annihilation, a
jail term staring her in the face, and O'Neal puts on lipstick!
Was there no end to the woman's vanity?

But something else had happened in the interval. Something Lee couldn't put her finger on so easily.

Gerry's aura had changed. The play of life had returned
to her eyes. She seemed suddenly taller. More formidable.

She still looked like something the cat wouldn't want to
drag in – no doubt about that! – but she had pulled herself
together and come up with a recognizable whole. Not the
old perky Gerry, to be sure. Nonetheless a Geraldine
O'Neal in full control. It was as though her old nemesis
had reached deep down within herself, into some part of
her that Lee had never known, like a general in a last-ditch
battle sending for the reserves; reached down and come
up with hidden source of power. She had recharged.

Instinctively, Lee shivered.

Gerry finished her coffee, and began talking in a conversational tone. If she was frightened, her voice didn't betray
it.

"You can send me to jail, Lee, if it will give you any
pleasure. But I doubt it will. I think you are incapable of
pleasure. Or joy or misery or passion or love. You don't
feel anything. You're numb. Dead. Even now, you lack the
flush of victory. I pity you, Lee. Not too much. Just a bit.
I pity you for the narrowness of your life, the poverty of
your emotions. You have no politics, no ideals, no beliefs,
no passions, no loyalties. For all your fancy newsgathering,
you dwell within a gamut than ranges from A to B without

a clue as to what lies beyond. You're an observer of life, rather than a participant."

"I don't need you to lecture me!" Lee broke in, despite her resolve to stay cool. Gerry's needling had hit a raw nerve. "After the kind of mess you've made of your life, you're in no position to rule on any one else. You had it all and you blew it. For what? For a guy. So save me your superior pretensions. I know better than to throw myself away!"

"Yes, you're an emotional miser!" Gerry retorted. "And I'm a spendthrift. Maybe that's the difference between your generation and mine. Your mother and I – for all our differences, all our contrasting styles of life – are really very much alike. We belong to a generation that isn't afraid to believe in romantic love, in great causes, grand passions. In the possibility of self-sublimation. Of personal sacrifice. A generation that not only dreamed of a perfect world, but thought it achievable. A dinosaur generation, I have no doubt, and soon to become extinct. But with all its faults, I prefer mine to yours, if you're any example."

"You're a fool, Gerry."

"And you're not? You can't even claim to be a realist, Lee. Because a realist understands the need for love. For occasional folly. But you . . . oh no! You're too cautious to succumb to your feelings. Too busy looking out for Number One. And oh, how scared you are! Terrified that passion, real passion, will prove to be a messy disruptive business. Which it is and should be. You remind me of a wind-up toy, a mechanical mouse. You turn the key and it starts running furiously but without direction. Seeing neither left nor right. Going nowhere. Zig-zag, zig-zag. Jangled. Purposeless. Till it finally runs smack into a brick wall. And who gives a damn when it smashes up? It was only a mechanical device, after all. It never ran blood . . . never felt life.

"I have no regrets, Lee, for what I've done. Least of all for loving Michael. At the best it was paradise. And at the worst . . . At the worst, I knew I was alive in every atom of my being. That I'm not a mechanical creature, a mere automaton. No, my friend, I wouldn't surrender a single moment of what I've felt these past few months – love, misery, ecstasy, pain, high, low and all the points in between. The gamut from A to Z. Well, I may be a romantic old fool, Lee, but you're the truly ancient one. Immune to passion. Emotionally dead. Life has passed you by and you don't even know it. You're a loser. That's the real difference between you and me. You're a loser. And you always will be."

Lee was speechless. As for Gerry, she picked up the remote control on the television set and began switching channels.

"You want a quote before you leave?" She didn't bother to look up. "I'll give you one from the Duke of Wellington. As the Great Duke said when being shaken down by a whore of his acquaintance, 'Publish and be damned!' "

Then she settled down to watch *One Life to Live*.

twelve

"Don't do that!" he said.

"Don't do what?" She had opened his fly, worked her way down his shorts and was now caressing his penis with the side of her thumb in a slow rhythmic movement. He hardened instantly and wished he hadn't.

"At least don't do it while I'm driving."

"Boo hoo!" she teased. "I thought you liked to live close to the edge. Come on, pet. Don't deny me a few simple pleasures. Yourself either. Wasn't the idea that we should get away from it all? A vacation from real life, you said."

She closed her hand about his cock.

"You're driving me nuts," he said.

"That's the idea, darling. Now you just keep your eye on the road and let me know when we get to Avignon."

With that, she unbuckled her seat belt and moistened her lips.

Jesus God – Michael quivered with delight – she was going down on him! In the middle of a motor route yet. In a car clocking 140 kilometers per hour. Which he made out to be about 85 m.p.h. American. No mealy-mouthed speed limits here. No speed limit on her either. Her tongue was as fast as a hummingbird's.

It felt scary but good. Maybe good because it was so scary. Recklessness was that woman's middle name.

On his left, a red Porsche passed in a roar of motor. Cruising at Indy speed.

Way to go! Then the driver honked twice. He must have had a glimpse of the action. Michael honked back.

She was the one who had suggested the Peugeot. A French car for the French countryside, she'd insisted. She'd even drawn up the itinerary. Provence. The chateaux country. A pilgrimage to Chartres. The most wonderful sights. She knew them all. He didn't. Live and learn.

For a long trip, he preferred a Mercedes. He liked the

456

way the Merc hugged the road. Though this trip wasn't going to be all that long. Another four, five days at most.

Anyhow, the Peugeot was proving to be a good little car – fast, responsive. He could have done with a bit more interior room, though. Especially in the present circumstances.

He tried not to glance down. Even pretended she wasn't there. Which was hard. She was sucking him like a kid with a giant lollipop. Every now and then she'd pause and lick her lips. She seemed to be in full control. Well, so was he. This was not exactly the time and place for a great big orgasm. A few simple pleasures, she had said.

Now and then, her head brushed up against the steering wheel. Her hair tickled his hands.

"Hey," he said. "Slow down. You're going to get us both killed."

Instead, she speeded up. So did he.

He was doing close to 160 when he saw the Avignon turn off.

"Shit!" Michael spun the wheel, hit on the brakes.

The thud of her head was the last thing he remembered. That and a vague recollection of bursting through a barrier, rolling over and over and over . . .

"I ought to break your other leg, Michael Avesian."

Gerry was sitting by his bed, grim and jet-lagged. It was a small provincial hospital in some town he'd never heard of and couldn't begin to pronounce. The care had been excellent and, as the American consul had said, he was lucky to be alive.

He didn't feel lucky. He felt wretched. The whole experience had been a nightmare, compounded by happening in a language he couldn't comprehend.

At least Gerry spoke French.

"Would you ask 'em how soon I can get out of here?"

"I already have. The surgeon says you'll be ambulatory in four or five days, although you'll be on crutches for a while. It was a clean fracture. I see you broke your nose too," she remarked.

"Again." He touched the bandages gingerly. His face

was a mass of bruises. "Maybe this time, they'll straighten it out."

Gerry fought back the tears. She hated hospitals. Hated their smells, their silences, the sudden bursts of noise. At this moment, she hated Michael too.

"How could you, Michael? With your banker, of all people. This was a trip you and I were going to make together!"

He couldn't meet her eyes. "You should thank God it wasn't you in the car!" he said. "But I wish it hadn't been Annie either. She was a decent sort."

Gerry blew her nose. There was no point in being angry at this Benson person. Poor thing! She had paid for loving Michael with her life. Anyhow, she hadn't been the one behind the wheel. *Oh Michael, you rat bastard!* Why was it always the men who walked away unscathed? Hadn't he broken enough hearts already?

"What happened, Michael?"

He cracked his knuckles and sighed. "I had my seat belt on, she didn't. She went into the wheel shaft. Crushed her skull."

But Gerry was puzzled.

"How did she hit the wheel shaft if you were driving? Surely she was in the passenger seat . . ."

"For God's sake, Gerry! Give me a break. I don't want to talk about it. It was horrible! Just the wildest fluke that *both* of us weren't killed. The car was travelling at speed. I guess I'm lucky. I should be grateful. At least that's what they say."

She studied him for a long cool moment.

"Maybe not so lucky after all," she said. "I have bad news for you, my friend."

The moment Lee had left her house that dreadful day, Gerry had collapsed. All her energy had gone into playing a rôle, and now she was drained. For while it was one thing to put on a great front, a bold flourish, it was quite another to contemplate the reality.

She prowled through the house alternately cursing and weeping.

What to do? That crazy vengeful girl would destroy both her and Michael, unless a way could be found to stop her. But short of murder, Gerry hadn't a clue.

Prison! She couldn't picture that, either. The mere idea threw her into a panic. But then, until a few months ago, she couldn't have imagined herself committing a major crime.

She ought to have called Jake, taken legal advice well before now. Except the thought of losing his respect was intolerable. Jake had always thought her a highly moral person.

And what defence could she offer? What could she say in mitigation? *Not guilty, judge, by reason of insanity. I was crazy in love.*

True. That's what this romance had been from the start: total insanity. All for Love, or The World Well Lost, as Dryden put it. Except it hadn't worked out that way. She had managed to jeopardize the world without hanging on to the lover. Where was the quid pro quo?

By mid-afternoon she had pulled herself together sufficiently to try raising Michael. She rang up every big hotel in Milan, in Nice, in Paris. He had disappeared. Not even his office knew where he was.

"A matter of life and death," she told his secretary, who had undergone Gerry's cries of wolf many times before. "Believe me, Sally, this once, I'm not being melodramatic."

Sally apparently took her at her word, for she rang up two days later to say the American Consul in Nîmes had been in touch. Michael was in a hospital near Fontaine-de-Vaucluse. The woman travelling with him was dead.

"That was yesterday. I took the first plane out. I didn't even bother to pack. You know what I thought, Michael, what crazy idea went through my mind? That the dead woman was Sandy. And . . . well, awful as it was, maybe it might turn out for the best. That somehow, we'd be together again. Instead of which . . ."

Instead of which, he'd cosied up to his lending officer.

She dabbed her cheek on a corner of the bed sheet.

459

The linen scratched her skin. She'd forgotten what French starch was like.

"What was it, Michael? A form of debt repayment? Or was it that you just couldn't resist a pretty body?"

But Michael couldn't be goaded. He had more serious things on his mind. "For God's sake, Gerry," he said. "This is no time for recriminations. The poor girl's dead, whereas you and I are alive and in ten kinds of shit. Is Lee really going to publish that fucking article? I can hardly believe it. She had such a schoolgirl crush on you. On me too," he said as an afterthought.

"Oh, she'll do it all right," Gerry said bitterly. "She's blinkered. Driven. Nothing I say can pierce that hide. Besides, it's the biggest break of her career!"

Michael pursed his lips. He was thinking hard.

"Then get Obermayer to squelch it," he said.

"Bobby isn't speaking to me any more. And even if he killed the story, it would make no difference. Lee'd peddle it somewhere else. She's got the goods. Michael. On both of us."

Michael groaned.

"What's the word for 'nightmare'?" he asked.

"*Cauchemar.*"

"*Cauchemar,*" he echoed. "*Quel* fucking *cauchemar.*"

He shut his eyes. She thought he had fallen asleep. After a minute or two, he blinked awake and began speaking in a quick staccato.

"I know this sounds shitty of me, Gerry, and I hope you don't take it amiss, but I sought legal advice on this matter a month ago. I discussed the outline with a criminal lawyer. He gave me to understand that, technically speaking I might avoid prosecution as 'an unindicted co-conspirator'. Like Richard Nixon in Watergate. What did I know and when did I know it? Actually, I knew zilch about details. I never asked, you never told. If I had to – and I pray to God it won't come to that – I could swear in court that I didn't know until today that forgery was involved. And I certainly never authorized it."

She couldn't believe her ears. "You'd weasel out? After all that I've done for you?"

"I'm being practical. And it's high time you were too. If I could lessen your burden, Gerry, I would. You know that. But let's face it, my going to jail won't do you a damn bit of good. It makes no sense for either of us. Why ruin two lives? For what?"

Gerry was too stunned to reply. All she could think was that Michael had been to see a lawyer. Without consulting her. Without confiding. From the very moment she handed him the contract, he had begun seeking ways to cover his ass.

Realistically, what had she expected? He was right: what purpose was served by both of them going to prison? None whatsoever. She'd be the first to concede the point.

And yet, unreasonably, she had expected more. A show of loyalty. Of martyrdom, if need be. A willingness to go down the line.

Instead of which he had already planned that she alone would pay the penalty while he took care of Number One.

She stared at him speechless. He was lying back, brow furrowed, darkly handsome against the pillows. She saw that he was calculating. The mind working at full professional tilt.

And in that instant, as suddenly as she had fallen in love with him one crisp September day, her passion died.

She folded her arms and watched him with an abstract curiosity.

"You know, Gerry," he said after a couple of minutes' thought, "I may have a solution for you. Get your own lawyer on the horn and see if what you've done is extraditable. I don't know what the legal arrangement is between France and the States, but it certainly warrants looking into. How much time, do you think, before the article hits the streets?"

"I have no idea."

"OK! Say you saw her Tuesday, this is Friday. She would have missed this week's issue. Maybe next week's, too. Remember, Trend is first going to have to clear all this stuff with their lawyers. They don't want to be on the wrong side of a libel suit. My bet is you've got between ten days' and two weeks' lead time. So! You might want to consider

461

making a quick quiet trip to New York. Close your bank accounts. Liquidate your ready assets. Grab your valuables. Then head someplace where they can't bring you back. A little island in the sun, maybe. Some tropical paradise. With flexible currency laws. Costa Rica is good. Pretty country. Robert Vesco holed up there for years and he was charged with every crime in the book. Or Brazil. The Brazilians almost never extradite. You might ask your Señor Oliveira what it's like. Or is he Bolivian? I forget. Granted, earning money might be a problem, but you're a smart lady. You'll manage. Maybe you should consider writing your memoirs. They could be a source of extra income."

"Who the hell do you think I am?" Gerry broke in. "The Mayflower Madam? Telling all for a buck?"

"I think you're a clever adaptable woman who knows how to survive. Jesus, Gerry, my own situation aside, I don't want to see you go to jail. Goddam, but I don't! I'm giving you sound advice. Probably better than you'll get from a lawyer, some of whom may be burdened by fine ethical considerations, which – as you know – I'm not. If I were you, darling, I'd get a move on right away." He checked his watch. "Now! With luck, you still have time to catch the afternoon flight from Nice."

"Are you trying to get rid of me, Michael?"

"Be sensible, Gerry. You can't stay here. Think how it looks – the two of us being closeted together. Too dangerous. A prosecutor might conclude that we're advancing the conspiracy. Right now, the safest thing would be for us to avoid all communication. No phone calls . . . no direct contact . . ."

"You *are* trying to get rid of me!"

"I'm trying to save you from yourself," he said after a painful pause. "I can't bear to watch you go down the tubes. Oh Gerry sweetheart! Be sensible for once."

She nodded mutely. Then she put her hand on his cheek. He had a three-day growth of beard.

"Don't they shave you in this joint?" she asked. "Shall I speak to the nurse?"

She leaned over and kissed him. Then put on her coat.

462

"I'll go Michael, although I don't see me fleeing the country to swat flies in Brazil. I'm too old for that kind of change."

"Oh Gerry!" He scraped together a smile. "You old? Never!"

The two women brushed past each other at the hospital door, one going out, one entering, smartly clad.

"*Pardon!*" said the older one, routinely.

The one going in said nothing. She couldn't speak French.

Geraldine O'Neal and Alexandra Avesian.

Gerry took a train to Paris and checked into a small hotel in the Rue des Sts Pères, in the heart of the student quarter. It was a far cry from the considerable splendour of the Plaza Athenée, her usual haunt, but it was clean and comfortable. And cheap.

Arielle Colton, she wrote in the register as an *hommage* to the afternoon soaps, of *East Podunk, USA*. The clerk never blinked. Gerry did. Anonymity made for a change of pace.

In the old days, she recalled, you couldn't pull a gag like that. The desk clerk would have made you surrender your passport and fill out an official government form – in duplicate on flimsy paper, *s'il vous plâit* – before allowing you to spend a night on the premises. The documents were then forwarded to the local police where your passport was checked to be returned the next morning. The rest of the paperwork was filed away for eternity. Gerry could never figure it out. Were the French trying to keep tabs on drug-runners, revolutionaries, illicit lovers? Or simply providing employment for bureacrats?

At the time, she had groused about the procedure, but in retrospect, it struck her as amusing. Romantic in a way. A scene out of an old black-and-white movie, full of foreign intrigue. Bogart playing the lead. Claude Rains as the bad guy. To this day she had no idea of what became of those ancient flimsies, especially the ones bearing her name. Were they still gathering dust in forgotten vaults in some public building or other, she wondered? How well had they withstood the years? Better than she, most likely.

"Your key, Madame Colton."

Gerry grinned and went up to her room.

She spent the next few days exploring the quarter on foot, clocking up the changes. The weather was fine. She wore comfortable shoes. She could almost pretend she was twenty again.

Although she had visited Paris often in the intervening years, her sojourns were inevitably brief and frantic. Business trips, consisting of one appointment after another, with a quick dash through the couture houses if she could squeeze it in. Who had time for nostalgic pilgrimages? Not the celebrated Geraldine O'Neal. In fact, she hadn't strolled through the Latin Quarter in years.

Much had changed. Her old hotel, the former brothel, had been converted into modern apartments with a fast-food Croissanterie on the ground floor. The little bar where she and Jean-Claude used to rendezvous each evening, hot for sex, had become a Benetton store, of all things! She went in and bought a sweater as a souvenir.

On the whole, the district struck her as cleaner, the shops more expensive. Yet the basics remained intact.

The crowded book stores, the grand cafés, the sharp dank smell of greenery around the church of St Germain des Prés, the sailboats in the Luxembourg gardens. The life of the streets.

That had changed least of all.

She spent an entire afternoon sipping Pernod at a café on Boul' Mich, people-watching. It was an excellent vantage point. The boulevard bubbled with the chatter of students, foreigners, artists of both the genuine and hot-air variety, flâneurs, vendors. It was an unending flow. She filled her lungs with the pungent aroma of Gitanes.

At the next table, a group of young people were arguing volubly about the merits of the new Pei Pyramid at the Louvre. It ought to be blown to smithereens, one young man insisted, thumping the table with his fist for emphasis, while across from him, a pretty girl, dark and slender, took violent issue.

464

"Tu es troglodyte!" she said.

Gerry smiled. Herself when young. Always championing the new.

Only now, she was the troglodyte. The anomaly.

A well-dressed American tourist in late middle age. Exactly the type she had mocked when young.

She paid the bill and left. Time to go home. She'd been away a whole week.

The next morning, she went to the American Express office to arrange a flight. The ticket agent recognized her.

"I can get you on the Concorde, Miss O'Neal," he said.

Who did he think she was, a bloody millionaire?

"A regular flight will be fine."

He booked her on Air France. "First Class of course!"

Inwardly, she groaned. She had hoped to go Tourist and save.

"Of course!"

Her last evening in Paris was spent in an unpretentious little restaurant near the hotel. The street was familiar. The restaurant wasn't, but it appeared to be just her kind of place. Lace curtains. Paper tablecloths. Wooden chairs scraping against uncarpeted tile. A hand-written menu in purple ink. The man next to her was eating *tête de veau*, picking around the eye cavities for choice bits of meat. Disgusting, but earthy. Authentic.

Gerry ordered a simple meal plus a half bottle of the house red, then gave herself over to a contemplation of her straits. The outlook was grim. And one fact was abundantly clear: she wouldn't have Michael by her side when the crunch came.

Look out for Number One, he'd advised. Well, *he* certainly had! The news that he'd taken legal advice had been an unpleasant surprise. As was the discovery that she wasn't in love any more.

Extraordinary!

The magic, the smoke-and-mirrors, that indefinable "something" had vanished almost as abruptly as it had begun. Michael Avesian – wunderkind, demon-lover, lord of the dance – had, in the harsh light of morning, turned into the most mortal of men.

She felt like a high roller on the day of a stock-market crash. How could she ever have been so imprudent?

There was no denying Michael's good qualities. He was a genuinely charming fellow and she was fond of him still! But charm was an insufficient explanation. She tried to analyse what it was that had driven her to such excess. It had to be something more than the man himself.

Essentially he had tickled her vanity. Made her feel young. And while he was a consummately attractive person, almost any handsome young man might have filled the bill. For she had fallen in love with something even more dazzling, more intoxicating than Michael Avesian.

She had fallen in love with love.

Again.

As she'd been doing all her life, from Jean-Claude on.

Love was her hashish.

Here lies a hopeless addict, they would incise on her tombstone, *in love with the idea of love.*

All her life, it had been her escape. Her delusion. The greatest possible high. To fall in love, Gerry realized, was to thumb your nose at reality. To feel, however briefly, immortal.

But sooner or later, reality thumbed its nose back.

Pay day, as Michael had said.

As for the question, was it worth it? Who could say!

She ordered a *café filtre* and a brandy. Then she cadged a Gauloise from the diner with the *tête de veau.*

She inhaled gracefully. Maybe she would take up smoking again. At her age, there were so few pleasures left.

It was fitting that the end should come here, in the same country that had launched her romantic career. Here where Jean-Claude had abandoned her so many years ago. Robbed her. Left her pregnant and alone to find her way home.

Suddenly – perhaps it was the Gauloise that had brought on this rush of memory – she knew why this street was familiar.

She had had an abortion in one of these grey five-storey houses. The one opposite, perhaps. Yes! Right above the boutique. Only it wasn't a boutique in those days. There had been, she recalled, a *chevaucherie* on the ground floor. Horsemeat. With a wooden horse's head swinging over the entrance to help the unlettered.

A butcher shop, in short.

And, not to put too fine a point on it, a different kind of butcher shop upstairs.

The memory made her wince. No doctor. No anaesthetic. It had taken both women to hold her down. She had been heartsick. And terribly scared.

Count backwards from one thousand, the older woman had said. It would help. It was better than screaming.

And Gerry had cried out, *"Je n'peux pas compter en fran- çais!"*

I cannot count in French.

But of course she could. And did.

It was the worst hour of her life, that visit to the rue de Buci. And bloody expensive. Practically every franc she'd managed to save at the Folies Bergère.

Yet somehow or other, when the operation was over, Gerry had dragged herself back to her own hotel, up the five flights, drunk some brandy, pulled the typewriter on to the bed and written that funny piece for the *Trib*, recounting her "glamorous" adventures as a show girl. What the hell, she'd needed the money desperately. That piece had paid for her passage home.

Now, it was time to go home again. Home to face the music. Alone.

Alone still. After all these years.

Funny – except not really. But it did seem that was how women always wound up in this world. All by themselves on their lonesomes. Herself for one. Nancy. There must be plenty of others in that boat.

She tried to think of examples among her close friends. But she had no truly close friends who were women.

One thing she'd do when she got back to New York, Gerry vowed. Cultivate some female acquaintances. She knew plenty of smart women. Amusing ones. It was time she got to know them better, strengthen bonds. A regular Girl Scout, that's what she'd be, complete with merit badges. Sorority Sister Gerry O'Neal.

Tough to envision. She'd lived all her life in a man's world.

Still, let's face it, women were a kind of insurance against the day she turned ninety. Who else would be around when she came out of jail? There sure as hell would be no Mr Wonderful in the wings.

Ouch! She grimaced at the prospect of what was in store back in New York. And even if she stayed out of prison through smart lawyering, there was no dodging the scandal. The disgrace.

As Michael said, *quel* fucking *cauchemar*!

She waved for the bill. It was higher than she had anticipated. A fortune, in fact. This new authenticity cost a bundle.

"*C'est correct?*" she asked. "*Je n'peux pas compter en français.*" The waiter totted it up again. Added another three francs.

Wearily, she pulled out a credit card.

God knew what her American Express invoice would come to this month. Astronomic! Looked like she'd have to sell Michael's bracelet after all.

thirteen

"I cannot believe – " Harry McKay had been outraged " – that my daughter is actually considering going back to that . . . that . . ."

". . . low-life?"

"Thank you, Hilda. That low-life husband of yours. When I think of the misery he's caused my little girl . . ."

"Come on, pop. Poor man is lying in some hospital a million miles away with all kinds of broken bones. Of course I'm going to him."

"Broken bones," her father had muttered darkly. "I'll give him broken bones!"

But the worldly new Alexandra refused to be ruffled.

"You've never liked Mikey. Why? What has he ever done to you?"

"Me myself and I?" said the pharmacist. "Not a thing. It's the way he treats my baby girl. It gets my goat, the way he's always bossing you around. Do this. Do that. Move here. Move there. As if you have no mind of your own. What's the matter – Baltimore isn't good enough for the great Mr Avesian? And my daughter should follow him like a lowly slave? The man's a tyrant, I tell you. A low-life tyrant. Am I right, Hilda?"

"Listen to your father," Hilda said.

"You hear that? Your mother's talking sense. Listen to dear old dad. I forbid you to go chasing off to France. And that's an order!"

Alexandra greeted the "order" with a smile. Thirteen years of son-in-law sniping had suddenly fallen into context. Her father couldn't endure the idea of another man bossing her around. He had hoped to preserve that privilege for himself.

"I'll drop you a postcard from the Riviera," she said.

"So here I am, Mikey. I brought you some corn bread from

469

Solly's Bakery. I figure by now you must have had it with French food."

"Thanks, Sandy. That was sweet."

"I'd rather you didn't call me Sandy any more. I prefer to be known as Alexandra."

Michael broke off a piece of corn bread and chewed it thoughtfully, savouring its distinctive taste along with the change in his wife's appearance. She looked terrific. All grown up. Confident.

"Alexandra. I quite like that. And you can call me Michael. Tell me, how are the kids?"

They spent an hour or so catching up on the domestic scene, and Michael finally broke the ice.

"I don't know how you feel about taking me back, after all this. I've behaved miserably, I admit, but it's all over between Gerry and me." He sighed. "It was a kind of craziness, I guess. A need to bust loose. One thing, though. Don't ever bad-mouth her or expect me to do the same. She's a remarkable person. But if you can find it in your heart to forgive me . . ."

"Oh Michael!" Alexandra's eyes grew moist. "You're not the only one who slipped from grace. There was this kid at the country club . . ."

Michael raised his hand in protest.

"Please. I don't want to hear it. What's past is past. Let's turn the page."

She took his hand and they sat for a while in perfect silence.

"What are you trying to do, honey?" she said at last. "Grow a beard? Or don't the nuns know how to shave a man?"

"The skin's very tender from the accident," he said. "It's only three days' growth."

"Uh huh," she said. "Well it feels like Brillo. Remember when we were first married and I used to shave you when you came home from the office, so we could make love without my getting a beard burn?"

Michael laughed. "I remember."

She got up without a word and returned a few minutes later with a straight razor and a bowl of hot water.

470

For a woman who didn't speak a word of French, it struck Michael, his wife was managing remarkably well. He looked at her with a new respect.

Alexandra lathered him up, then held the razor poised.

"I really ought to cut your throat," she said mildly.

"Second best offer I've had today."

As she began shaving him with scrupulous care and deft fingers, he talked about his business troubles.

"I could be in deep shit," he said, "or I could make a fortune. Depends. What's our financial situation like? Can you give me some idea?"

"Well," Alexandra said, "remember those bearer bonds you had in the safe deposit box? They were doing zilch, so I switched them to a little start-up electronics stock that looks promising. The P/E ratio was eighteen to one, not so hot, but the growth capability is tremendous. And for a hedge I bought a hundred thou in CD's. This bank in North Dakota is paying 10.35% . . ."

He listened in disbelief as Alexandra tallied up their holdings, shaving him in smooth even strokes as she talked. When she was done, she patted his face dry with a slick cotton towel.

"Christ! They starch everything in this hospital. Not very comfortable. I think it's time you came home. I'm going to get us on a plane tomorrow." Suddenly she giggled. "Why Michael! Your mouth is hanging open."

"I'm impressed," he said. "Let me amend that. I'm overwhelmed."

She wiped the blade dry, then sat down on the bed beside him.

"Yes, well I've been studying, boning up and you know something? This business stuff is fun. Mr Mintz, my divorce lawyer – or maybe I should make that my ex-divorce lawyer – tells me I've got the stuff that top financial managers are made of. He's talked me into taking some business courses at Johns Hopkins next fall. How 'bout that!" She was proud beyond words. "You always thought I was stupid, didn't you, Michael?"

Michael considered this for a very long time.

"How could you be stupid?" he finally said. "After all, you married me."

She laughed. They kissed.

"Partners?"

"Partners."

When the orderly came with the dinner tray, he found them both cuddled up in bed, fast asleep.

fourteen

His name was Dudley and he was a goddam nuisance.

He grieved. Even when she took him into bed with her, he continued to grieve. A solid block of misery, that's what he was. The Original Heartbreak Kid. Nothing consoled him, not massage. Not petting. Not even having his belly rubbed.

Loneliness. That was Dudley's problem. The little bugger missed Bill.

"I give him into your care," Bill had said the day before leaving for Rome. "One second-hand, gently used cat, pre-owned, as they say in the car ads. No more than three thousand miles on him, and that mostly shuffling between the bowl and the litterbox. He'll be no trouble at all, I promise. He's been neutered."

Lee had tried to fob Dudley off on her mother, but Nancy claimed that her lease precluded pets. "Anyhow," she added, "I'm not sure how much longer I'll stay in New York. My life here has no direction, no focus, you see."

"Dudley could be a focus," Lee suggested. "He's a sweet animal. A Himalayan. You've never had a Himalayan. The most beautiful blue eyes . . ."

"My dear girl! In the course of raising four children, I have been forced to cohabit with two dogs, various cats of mixed parentage, hamsters – or were they gerbils? – Easter bunnies, tropical fish, a pair of love birds and one painted souvenir turtle from Las Vegas. I have paid my dues to the animal kingdom, thank you very much, and look forward to spending my remaining years unencumbered."

"Gee, Mom. All you had to say was No."

So Dudley moved in with Lee, an unhappy and unwelcomed house guest. The first three days he refused to come out from under the bed. He didn't eat. Didn't make a sound. The only evidence of his tenancy were two gleaming blue circles dimly discerned in the corner furthest from her reach.

She tried moving the bed, to force him into the open, but Dudley scuttled from one dark haven to the next with the speed of a wild forest creature pursued by hunters. This was supposed to be a house pet?

She sought advice from her colleagues.

"I'm worried about Dudley. He refuses to eat. I've tempted him with everything, from catnip mice to pâté to something called Tabby Ticklers which are supposedly the feline equivalent of Godiva chocolates. But nothing, nada. I'm afraid he's going to grieve to death. How will I explain that to Bill if he should call?"

"Cats don't grieve," Teddy Goodman said with authority. "Dogs grieve. Cats don't give a flying fuck. He'll come out when he's hungry."

And sure enough, when she returned home that night, Dudley had actually put a dent in the Friskies. He behaved as though caught in the commission of a felony, and beat a swift retreat to his usual hiding place. But the ice was broken. Dudley was eating. Drinking. Crapping. She almost wept with relief.

Dudley would survive. He would not starve himself into an early grave out of heartbreak. But Teddy was wrong about one thing. Dudley did indeed grieve.

Every night when she came home, he would be waiting behind the door, hot with anticipation for his lord and master. Then, seeing that it was only Lee, Dudley would turn tail and skulk away, disappointment visible in every hair in his body.

"Well, fuck you, Dudley!" Lee was wounded. Who needed to be cold-shouldered by a cat? Nonetheless, she found herself growing attached. Poor thing! He missed Bill. What the hell. So did she!

She began coming home earlier in the evening, so Dudley wouldn't feel too neglected. Or bored. Imagine sitting all alone in an apartment from morning till night. You had to feel sorry.

Dudley was a pest. A nuisance. He didn't love her. Worse, he shed those fine silky hairs onto every conceivable surface including the butter dish. She couldn't wear black jerseys any more. Nonetheless, there was something to be said in favour of being greeted, albeit diffidently, by a live sentient creature at the end of the day. "Hey honey, I'm home!" she would call out half-facetiously. Sometimes, big deal, he'd brush up against her leg. Even a second-hand cat was better than an echo.

She bought a laptop computer and took to finishing her assignments on the coffee table while Dudley snoozed or watched television with the sound turned down. He liked television. Maybe he was looking for Bill to put in an appearance on the Morton Downey Jr. show.

Sometimes as she worked, Lee would talk to Dudley, try out phrases. Ideas.

"Let me run this past you, Dud. Which is better? 'A face only a mugger could love', or 'The Poor Man's Pee Wee Herman'? What d'you think, Doodles? Remember, we're talking about a US Senator."

Dudley would yawn. Roll over.

"Yeah . . . I think so too, Duddy." She would slap the copy in and press the save key.

Tonight, however, the words weren't coming. She had the story complete, almost all of it down on floppy disk, but what it needed was that crunchy opening paragraph. Dudley was being no help at all. Looked like they both had writer's block.

Begin with a bombshell. Rule One in exposés.

Fire-brand. Feminist. Fabulous fake. Forger.

Christ no! Even the cat looked ready to vomit.

Behind the glitter that is Geraldine O'Neal is a story that . . .

Hollywood hash! Gimme a break!

Once upon a time – in a Yorkville tenement . . .

Now there was a thought! A literary allusion would give the opener some class, satiric thrust. Cast the story in a wider frame of reference. She began summoning up famous first lines. As always she had excellent recall.

It was the best of times. Now it's the worst of times. Geraldine O'Neal woke one day to find herself turned into a giant cockroach.

Whether she will turn out to be the heroine of her own life . . .
Call me Geraldine!

Call this garbage! Nothing was working tonight. And Dudley had gone into hiding again. After a few more false starts, Lee switched off the computer. She had a raging headache. Why should one lousy para be so hard to write? She felt depressed. She had been depressed all day. All week, for that matter.

She'd run. Run the blues right out of her system. Once, twice around the reservoir.

She changed into T-shirt and sweat pants, then groped under the bed for her running shoes. Suddenly, Dudley pounced out of his hiding place. Scared the hell out of her, he did. Peculiar animal, lurking there quiet and sly, only to spring at her like a beast in the jungle.

Now there was a literary association that almost rang a bell. The beast in the jungle.

She went down the stairs and began running, slowly at first, rhythmically. By the time she reached Central Park she was warmed up.

No beasts in the jungle, she hoped.

She picked up speed, hit her stride. But for some reason, she couldn't lose herself tonight in the act of running. Her thoughts were all over the place.

Gerry. Dudley. The beast in the jungle. The Beast in the Jungle.

Suddenly she remembered. It was a Henry James tale that she had read in freshman English. It had made a profound impression at the time. Even now, after the passage of years, she could recall the story in almost word for word detail.

John Marcher had been the hero's name. Marcher. A wintry name! A wintry soul. And yet he believed himself destined for a remarkable fate, something that would set him aside from the rest of humanity. One day his fate would reveal itself. It would spring upon him like a beast in the jungle.

Until then he must wait and watch and keep himself in readiness. So he did. And while he waited, life passed him by. Life. Love. Tears. Gaiety. The sweetness of the seasons. The quotidian cares. All held in abeyance while he kept his vigil.

Until one day at the graveside of the woman who had once shared his vision, he was startled by the sight of a mourner a few graves away. The man was ravaged by grief. But such grief, such searing devastation as Marcher could scarcely conceive. He had never known such feelings himself.

And in that unguarded moment, the beast in the jungle sprang.

No passion had ever touched him (James wrote), for this was what passion meant; he had survived and maundered and pined, but where was his deep ravage . . . He had seen the outside of life, not learned it within.

The wait was over. John Marcher had discovered his destiny.

The fate he had been marked for, he had met with a vengeance – he had been *the* man to whom nothing on earth was to have happened.

Nothing. Nothing on earth!

It was a story about utter emptiness. About death in life.

A horror story of sorts. The ultimate horror story.

Lee didn't wipe away the tears that coursed down her cheeks.

Was it possible? Was it conceivable that she was a latter-day John Marcher? Of course not. His life was a failure, hers a success. Moreover Marcher was a pitiable figure. Numb. Empty. Untouched. Untouching. "He had seen the outside of life . . ."

Yet Gerry's words kept winging back to her.

You are an observer of life, she had told Lee, not a participant. You dwell within a gamut from A to B.

At the time Lee had dismissed such talk as a lie and slander, a face-saving speech from a woman under assault.

And yet . . . and yet.

And yet in those few minutes, Gerry had struck an open nerve, articulating Lee's deepest fears.

Sometimes, in the dead of night, she had the terrifying notion that life was sweeping by her, slipping beyond her grasp. Rushing away at an inhuman speed, unfelt, unexperienced. Unreal.

Now and then she suspected some essential part of her was missing. She lacked the capacity to feel. To love.

Was it a basic shortcoming, a physiological quirk, like being born tone deaf or colour blind? Or had Lee chosen her path, in the manner of John Marcher, mortgaging the present for some distant expectation, husbanding her feelings against some promise of greatness to come. In her mind, real life was always just around the corner waiting to spring. Like the beast in the jungle. What if she waited in vain?

Use it or lose it. People were always saying that about sex. But it might be equally true of that other organ, the heart. Whatever that meant.

Was it conceivable that Gerry, that wily old fool, had been right after all? That something dynamic, vital, had been lost between her parents' generation and her own? The "dinosaur generation" Gerry had called it. Yet at twenty-five, Lee was already living better than her mother ever had, ever would. With a still brighter future before her. What, then, was the loss? Love? Passion? Gallantry? A quixotic dedication to impossible ideals? What jazz musicians called "soul"?

Antique concepts, the lot of them. Anathema to any fast-tracker worthy of the name. Except the fast track had become the narrow track. The gamut from A to B.

Lee had never thought of herself as a curiosity. *Trend Magazine* teemed with people like her. As did Wall Street and broadcasting and publishing and real estate and every other hot profession, from fashion design to drug dealing. People working harder. Working smarter. Getting theirs while supplies last.

Driven? Yes. But surely better to be driven than be a dinosaur.

Lee had always taken pride in belonging to a generation that was gutsier, savvier, better educated, more ambitious and (especially for women) quicker to move up through the ranks.

Those were the gains. The same gains Gerry O'Neal had struggled so hard to achieve. Lee wouldn't surrender a one.

But maybe there were losses, too. Passion among them. It struck her that Gerry, and her own mother too, experienced life at a richer, more rewarding level. They had better reserves. Where did they find the strength?

Lee ouldn't squash the image of Gerry in that final interview. She had left the room a broken woman and come back a few minutes later replenished, as though she had made a large withdrawal from a bank. Or drunk from a magic reservoir.

Lee had been confounded. She had gone to the house secure in the knowledge that she was stronger than Gerry, that she had the upper hand. And while Lee had anticipated any number of reactions – tears, hysteria, rage, guilt, despair – she had not foreseen such resilience.

Lee didn't understand.

But then, there were a number of things she didn't understand any more. She didn't understand the simplest declarative sentence.

John loves Mary.

A very simple sentence. But what did it mean? She hadn't a clue.

Every week Lee wrote about passion, lust, violence, folly. But always from the outside. Never from direct experience. Never putting herself in someone else's skin. Seeing all. Understanding nothing.

Would she ever know what it was like to be swept away – by a man, an idea? Would she ever be caught up in something larger than herself? Or would all her life be lived outside the grand arena, in the narrow grey catwalk that Gerry had called "the gamut between A and B"?

She recalled her unpublished piece on the homeless denizens of the Port Authority. It was the biggest story she had ever tackled and she had botched it. Something was missing, Fletch had said. He hadn't specified what. Lee had been furious. How hard she had worked on that article, getting every detail right: the smells, the sores, the tough luck yarns, the taste of cheap wine. She had laid her subjects out bare as a surgeon. The only thing she failed to see was the heart.

She knew now what was missing. Passion. Life.

Lee had observed that scene as though it were a spectator sport, maintaining an antiseptic distance throughout. Never once in the course of those two weeks had she permitted herself to imagine the heartbreak of those lives. Of what it must feel to be lost and lonely and unloved.

She hadn't dared, too threatened by the fear of her own vulnerability. Fear of losing control.

She had lacked the courage to think of them as human beings. Tried instead to reduce them to anecdotes. Vignettes. Rungs of the ladder to be climbed. She had hoped to exploit them, and they had spited her. They had refused to come alive in her prose.

"No wings," Fletch had said.

No emotion. No passion. No wonder. Lee Whitfield had done such a great job of damming those feelings up inside her, perhaps they had dried up and disappeared.

As she rounded the Central Park reservoir, she imagined herself back once again in the bowels of the Port Authority. Not simply to recall those hellish days, but to live them as she had not done before. Little by little she forced her feelings out. They came slowly at first – in droplets, in chary trickles, underground streams seeking the sea until at last her imagination flowed free and unchannelled. Only then did she dare to ask herself what it was like, what it was really like to be lost. And alone. And unloved.

To her astonishment, Lee discovered she already knew.

She knew why she was running. And what she was running from.

Well, John Marcher wasn't the only one entitled to an epiphany. She headed for home. Dudley was waiting behind the door. Still hoping, after all this time.

She showered, made coffee, took three aspirins, then switched on the computer.

She felt physically drained, yet oddly powerful. Creative.

If Bill Frazier were around, she might discuss this with

him – the relation between feeling and writing. Between life and art. But Bill was in Rome. At the moment, her only confidants were the cat and the computer.

And while these reflections were no doubt of interest to Dudley, they'd have to wait. Lee still had a living to fetch.

"OK Dud," she said. "Back to work."

Lee sat down and began to write.

fifteen

Gerry stepped out of the terminal and headed for the taxi ranks.

It was 90° in the shade. The pavement sank beneath her heels. The air smelled like a Turkish wrestler's jock strap with a soupçon of gasworks thrown in. At the kerb, twelve gypsy cabs were having a Who-can-honk-the-loudest competition while a Carey coach belched carbon monoxide straight into her lungs.

Gerry drew a deep breath. It was good to be home.

More or less.

She managed to out-elbow the crowds for the first available cab, and once safely inside, tore into the new copy of *Trend*.

The cover story was entitled 'Death of the Hamptons', with a picture of a million-dollar dune house.

Important news from the front! *Trend Magazine* had officially declared South Hampton extinct as a watering hole and designated Block Island as the place to be.

She felt both relieved and insulted. For this, Geraldine O'Neal had been bumped off the cover? Relegated to the back of the book?

Swiftly, she thumbed through the pages. An exposé of price-fixing in the auction houses. '*How to Hire a Nanny.*' '*Mafia Chic*', a fashion spread featuring John Gotti. '*Shopaholics! the Tragedy of New York's Super-rich.*' Movie reviews. Book reviews. Wine reviews. Who's who on Broadway. What's what in the galleries. Wall Street gossip. Fifth Avenue glitz. A write-up of a restaurant that featured Alaskan cuisine, whatever that was, by someone other than that nice Bill Frazier.

Apart from the change in restaurant critics, the only item of interest was the absence of any reference to Geraldine O'Neal.

She heaved a hugh sigh. Another week of grace. She'd

go home, get a good night's sleep, then call Jake first thing in the morning.

First thing in the morning, a messenger arrived at her door with a manila envelope. Gerry opened it. A swirl of confetti tumbled out.

Except it wasn't confetti at all, but strips of duplicating paper that had been put through a shredder, and in among the scraps, a hand-written note. Gerry read the note once, twice, three times. Read it again more closely. Let out a yell.

She spent the next quarter-hour on the phone. Then she dressed in an immaculate white Chanel suit, topping it off with Michael's diamond bracelet. She looked great. Her last call was to Big Apple Limousine.

"I want your Rolls Royce Silver Cloud," she said. "Stock the bar with Dom Perignon. And I have to be where I'm going by lunch-time."

Nice days such as this, like many another working woman, Nancy would buy something to eat from a street vendor, then sit down in front of the ornamental fountains and watch the world go by.

Through Gerry's good offices, she had obtained a job editing copy for a children's book publisher. Although low-paid, the work was proving pleasant enough.

Despite the ferocious warning on the wall (IF YOU HAVE TO ASK WHAT IS THE PROBLEM, YOU ARE THE PROBLEM), the atmosphere at Pippin Press was benign and unhurried.

She worked seven hours a day in a long narrow room crammed with standard reference books and the full line of Pippin's publications. When things were slow, she would skim through the titles (*The NASA Story*, *The Best of Mayan Myths*) and marvel. Amazing what kids were into these days. Smart didn't begin to describe.

Her job was to ensure that the manuscripts were couched in clear and proper English prior to typesetting, and see that the contents "tracked". Her current assignment, *The Great Big Book of Birds*, was a case in point. You couldn't have a reference to the Baltimore Oriole on one page and the Baltimore oriole on another. Emerson may have japed that consistency was the hobgoblin of little minds but here at Pippin, it reigned supreme. Which led to the other notice posted on the walls. WHEN IN DOUBT, CHECK IT OUT. She checked it out. Cap "O" was correct when referring to the baseball team, lower case "o" when it came to the bird.

The oriole problem resolved, Nancy had moved on to penguins this morning. There were different varieties of penguins, she learned, some of which paired for life. Now wasn't that sweet! On the other hand . . .

If you thought all penguins look alike, the author had written, *you could be right. Consider the Chinstrap Penguin . . .*

"Imagine that," Nancy had remarked to Christabel who sat across the table from her. "There's a breed of penguins that look so much the same that the males and females can't tell each other apart."

"How do they mate?" Christabel asked.

"Trial and error, apparently. If everything fits, they know they've got the penguin of the opposite sex."

Christabel had giggled. "Sounds like a description of life in the East Village."

Well, that was true, Nancy thought as she sat in the noonday sunshine, munching falafel. There were parts of Manhattan, not only the Village, where you hadn't a clue as to a passerby's gender. As David used to say, *"If I don't know what sex it is, I don't want to know."*

Although in Cedar City, the question rarely arose.

One thing for sure, New York was no place like home. In fact, though she was loath to admit it, urban life was proving a bit of a disappointment. The theatre, the lectures, the concerts, all the things she had dreamed of in Cedar City, were here all right. More events than there were hours in the day. But what wasn't out of reach financially was often impossible logistically. It was a city for the young and/or the rich. The folkways puzzled her. You had to plan everything so far in advance. Where else, she wondered, would people stand in line for hours just to see a movie? Or pay to be insulted by a headwaiter?

And even if you did get in to the entertainment of your choice, try getting a cab to take you home to Queens!

However – as Lee, as everyone, cautioned her – you never never take the subway at night.

The injunction was part of a growing list. The Nevers, as Nancy had come to think of them.

Never open your door to strangers.

Never walk through Central Park after sunset.

Never assume the cab driver knows where he's going.

Never eat mussels from Jamaica Bay.

Never put your handbag down for a second.

Never buy anything electronic from a 'Lost our lease/going out of business' frontage, even if it is on Fifth Avenue.

Never make eye contact when riding public transportation.

Never enter an elevator without checking the mirror.

Funny, Nancy thought. She had come to New York in search of personal freedom and found constrictions on every side.

She finished her falafel and wiped her fingers on a paper napkin. A few feet away, two chauffeurs were exchanging obscenities concerning the rights to an illegal parking space. Across the street, construction workers were operating pneumatic drills. Briefly, Nancy shut her eyes and listened to the music of New York. The shrill of sirens, the blare of ghetto blasters, the honking of horns at the stoplight. It was a deafening montage.

She got up, packed the remains of her lunch into an empty paper cup and went to the corner litter bin. A CLEANER NEW YORK IS UP TO YOU. As she reached the kerb, a Sixth Avenue bus screeched to a halt in a hot filthy blast.

VVOOOOM! then VVOOOOM VVOOOM VVOOM for good measure.

Nancy wiped the grime from her face with a tissue, adding a new never-never to the list.

Never never wear a white skirt.

Some forty floors above the ornamental fountains, two

485

young women were sitting down to a window table in one of the city's most elegant restaurants.

"So, Miss Fairchild!"

"So, Miss Ballantine!"

"We meet again."

They exchanged complicitous smiles. Then the one with the white blonde hair slipped an envelope across the table. It was stuffed with cash. "A bonus. Don't spend it all in one place."

Miss Ballantine thumbed through the contents with fast capable fingers.

"Very considerate. Technically, he didn't have to. The agency's already paid my fee."

"No, he didn't have to. But you may as well share the wealth."

"I'm glad he's satisfied," Miss Ballantine said. "I like to give value for money."

"To use an old Icelandic expression, my man's as happy as a hog in shit." She clapped for the waiter. "This calls for champagne."

Across town, Lee Whitfield ate lunch at her desk (tuna on rye and diet Coke) while she put the finishing touches on her story.

As the limo service had promised, Gerry arrived before one. She wouldn't have recognized the spot except for the sign:

FUTURE SITE OF HAILSHAM USA.

The New Jersey meadow had been transformed since the day when she had first met Michael. Gone were the grassy swards, the rural quiet, the picnic table so artfully set. The bucolic acres had been bulldozed to smithereens. That was progress, she supposed.

Just inside the gate, a fleet of heavy duty trucks were ready to roll, their sides emblazoned with AVESIAN ENTERPRISES in red white and blue. Dust everywhere. Dust and cranes and masonry and the kind of purposeful human frenzy that gave the place the appearance of a

486

battlefield. And loud! Good God, noisier than Broadway and 42nd!

She leaned out the limo window and hollered: "Where's the man?"

"Upstairs!" The foreman pointed skyward.

And sure enough, there was Michael, seated in the cab of a forty foot high cherry-picker, arms waving, barking orders into a walkie-talkie, reminding her of nothing so much as a Hollywood director in charge of a very major motion picture.

He waved, and had the crane operator winch him down to ground level. She brushed the dust off her white suit.

"My secretary told me you were coming," he shouted above the din. He was wearing a work-shirt and chinos. His leg was still in a cast. A tape covered the bridge of his nose. There was a layer of dust in his hair. Gerry felt wildly overdressed. The foreman was insisting she put on a hard hat.

"I should have worn jeans," she said to Michael.

He grinned. "You look marvellous. A touch of class. Forgive me if I don't rise to greet you, but it's a bitch getting in and out. Ever been up in one of these things? More fun than a helicopter."

Gerry shook her head. Then climbed in beside him carrying the wicker basket. It was a tight squeeze.

"I brought lunch,' she said. "Champagne, pâté. It's about time we had another picnic."

All the way down to Jersey in the limo, she'd rehearsed the agenda. First the good news. Well, of course, he'd be delirious. Drinks. Congratulations all around.

Then the bad news. "It's over, my dear," she would tell him. As if he didn't know. But she felt a crying need to make it official. On her terms. At the time and place of her choosing. Her ego demanded nothing less. Men didn't leave Geraldine O'Neal in the lurch. Never never never! It was vital that she perpetuate the myth.

Her game plan, however, hadn't encompassed an audience of construction workers with bulldozers for background music. In her mind, the site had stayed as idyllic as on that summer day when they'd first met.

Michael might have sensed her quandary, for he cupped his hands around his mouth. "I'm going to have the operator crane us up again. If I'm correct, you're due for another guided tour. Anyhow, it's quieter in the balcony. We can talk."

They rose above the dust line and from her vantage point, Gerry tried to grasp the scope of works in progress. Astonishing what had been achieved in such short time! Already the faint outlines of the castle were taking shape. Briefly, she shut her eyes and envisioned the whole.

"The topiary garden is going there," Michael said, pointing to a levelled patch on the horizon. "Importing the trees turned out to be impractical, so I did the next best thing. I imported a team of Kentish gardeners."

Gerry gaped. She had forgotten how vast the project was, and how complex. There was a long way to go, a very long way. But still . . .

"My God!" Gerry blurted out. "It's actually happening."

"Oh ye of little faith!" He laughed and popped the champagne. She poured it into paper cups. Michael seemed happier than she had seen him in months. More content in himself.

"So how's the nose, the leg?"

She didn't ask him, how's the wife? though she had a gut level hunch that they had reconciled.

"Leg's fine. I asked 'em not to reset the nose. I want to see a familiar face in the mirror."

The two small-talked gracefully for a few minutes more. Then Michael put on his go-to-meeting face. "Sally says you have something vital to show me."

"Fabulous news." She handed him Lee's note.

" 'It never happened,' " he read. " 'It never will happen. I never saw these. There are no other copies. Please forgive.' " Michael chewed on his lip. "Is this for real?"

Gerry nodded. "Definitely. All the documents were enclosed, shredded. It's for real, Michael, but don't ask me what came over Lee. I haven't a clue. Maybe something I said. Maybe conscience. I don't know. I don't care." Suddenly, the joy broke through her voice. "Jesus God! but I'm relieved. Like getting a million-pound monkey off my back. It's over. The whole fucking *cauchemar*, as you say. It's over and we're free!"

She poured more champagne and moved on to her second topic.

"And I'm free, too, Michael. This is very hard for me to say, my darling, and I don't want to cause you unnecessary pain. But it's been coming for quite a while, my love, and I can't put it off any longer. You know me. I have such a short attention span when it comes to men. What I'm saying is, it's over between us as well." Her eyes glistened with tears. As she spoke, she knew that almost every other word was true. "I've loved you so much, Michael. As much as I've ever loved any one. I doubt that I'll ever care that way again. You were like a fever in my blood, a kind of divine craziness. It was superb while it lasted. You made me happier than I deserve. But now the spark, the drunkenness – whatever you call it – is gone forever, I'm afraid. It's not the sort of thing one can muster at will. If I could stay in love, I would, believe me. I'm sorry, Michael!" She put out her hand. "We ran the line out as long as we could. It's time to say goodbye."

He sat there for a while, his face a compendium of feelings: regret, relief, and a half-dozen stages in between.

Then he took her hand.

"Gerry," he began, "there is no way I can ever repay you for . . ."

"Forget that wretched forgery!" she broke in. "I never want to think about it again."

"I wasn't even thinking of that, Gerry. I'm grateful for much much more. You were my window onto a larger world . . ."

"Please," she stopped him with an embarrassed shrug. "I detest sentimental scenes, especially when conducted by anyone other than myself. Besides, I have to be getting back to the city. Dear God!" she groaned. "You'd never think I have a business to run. I've been so damn negligent these last few months."

He continued to hold her hand, smiling faintly. His finger toyed with the clasp of the diamond bracelet.

"You'll keep the bracelet, won't you, as a memento of

what we've meant to each other? At least be that sentimental."

Gerry's eyes welled with tears. "My darling, nothing
would induce me to part with it. And I promise to think
of you whenever I wear it which will be often. Now, please,
I'd like to go before I dissolve into a total marshmallow."

Michael called out instructions for the crane operator.
They descended in silence, hand in hand, till they reached
ground level.

Gerry turned for one last look, as though to fix him in
her memory forever.

"Here we are, Michael," she said softly. "Down to earth
at last."

He held her hand a moment longer, than raised it to his
lips like a Continental gentleman saluting royalty.

"Goodbye, Madame Ambassador."

She wept most of the way home. It was cathartic. Then
she dried her eyes and fell to planning the new life that
lay ahead.

"Here you go." Lee handed the manuscript to Fletch. "One
genuine cover article. You'll love it. It has wings. It flies."

He looked down and scowled. "What the hell is this,
Whitfield? I was expecting the O'Neal piece this week."

Lee widened those artless eyes of hers and sighed. She
appeared to be thoroughly disappointed.

"I tried, Fletch. I busted my ass but there was no story
there. Nothing you couldn't find in a press release. As you
said yourself, O'Neal is ancient history. Whereas this . . . !
I know you turned down the first piece I wrote on the Port
Authority. But believe me, this version is nothing like. It's
real. Vital. It should be. I put my heart's blood into it. Just
read it, is all I ask."

"Interesting title," Fletch said. " 'Begging for My Life.' "

Gerry returned home close to five o'clock, tired but with a
sense of renewal. Tomorrow, it would be back to work at
full tilt.

She kicked off her heels and threw down her jacket. Her

490

suit was streaked with red dust, mortally wounded for all she knew.

What kind of idiot wears a white Chanel suit to a construction site? she asked herself. Idiots in love with grand gestures. She decided to shower and change, then find someone to take her to dinner. But first, a Campari-and-soda on the rocks.

Gerry was getting the ice out when she heard a commotion in the street. Then the doorbell rang. She answered it in stockinged feet.

On the steps were two uniformed cops, one a woman, both looking terribly serious. And a wiry young man in a brown polyester suit.

"Yes, officer?" she addressed the policewoman with a smile.

Behind them a sound truck had pulled up and was jockeying for space in front of her "hydrant".

"Geraldine O'Neal?" Mr Shiny Suit asked. He flashed an ID. "I have a warrant here for your arrest."

Gerry stared from the ID (he was a Stephen Waitkus from the District Attorney's office) to the warrant to the man, dumbstruck. There was some mistake here. Some cosmic mistake.

Could Lee have betrayed her in spite of everything? Had she sent Gerry the note this very morning only to lull her into a false sense of security? It was too monstrous to conceive of! Too implausible. Easier to believe she was going crazy.

That was it, Gerry decided. She was going crazy. In which case, everything made sense.

"You are Gerry O'Neal, aren't you?" the young man was saying, then taking her silence for confirmation, brushed past her into the hall. Gerry followed in a daze, with the police bringing up the rear.

"I don't believe this . . . !" she gasped.

"You have the right to remain silent . . ." Waitkus intoned.

She stood mesmerized, her worst dream come true, while he reeled off Miranda in a nasal voice. He was gloating.

Quel cauchemar! Quel fucking *cauchemar!*

". . . may be used against you . . ."

No! It couldn't have been Lee. That was unthinkable. They were nailing her for some minor offence. Speeding, maybe. Or taxes. That was it. Jake had warned her a million times that she was heading for trouble.

But that didn't give this snotty young kid the right to treat her like Public Enemy Number One.

"What is going on here?" she burst out. "Will someone tell me?"

Waitkus mumbled a paragraph of legalese, then suddenly snorted. Arresting a celebrity clearly gave him a charge. He'd be dining out on it for weeks.

"Come off it, Gerry. Don't play the innocent. We've already picked up Yoshimura . . ."

"Oh my God!"

Her heart sank into her toes. I am going crazy, she thought.

". . . and Commissioner McFeeley. The District Attorney is only sorry he couldn't be here himself."

That said, he clapped a proprietary hand on her arm. "Now be a good girl, Gerry. Put on your shoes and let's go."

Gerry shot an alarmed glance on to the street. A camera crew was assembled on her doorstep. Sweet Jeezus. She was going to be on *Live at Five*! And there was CBS turning the corner. With PIX right behind. Microphones were popping up left and right as though World War Three had broken out. Gerry drew back in horror.

The sight of the minicams jolted her like a whiff of ozone.

This was television. She, Geraldine O'Neal, was going out live. Into millions of homes. And there would be replays on the national news. At seven. Then again at eleven.

No way! Not looking like this! Grimy. Bedraggled. She didn't even have lipstick on!

The District Attorney, never a man to miss a headline, must have set it up, tipping off the media in advance. He was playing to the stands as always. But she was a performer too.

"Wait! A! Minute!" Gerry swung around and plucked Waitkus's hand off her sleeve as if it were lint. "If you think I'm going out there, in front of the press, looking like something the cat dragged in, you are sorely mistaken. First, I'm going to call my lawyer. Then I'm going upstairs to change into clean clothes. The woman officer can accompany me . . ."

"Just hold it right there, pal!" Waitkus said. "You're not calling the shots any more."

"Oh no?" Gerry's voice went dark with menace. "Now you listen to me, sonny, and listen hard. I am going to do exactly as I said – wash, dress and put on make up. Otherwise, you're going to have to drag me across the threshold. And you betcha that I'll be screaming 'Police brutality' every step of the way. Now let me tell you something else, Stevie baby. The people in this city know me and love me. I'm a revered figure, almost an icon. I am also, may I remind you, a woman. Why do you think the DA didn't come himself? Because he wanted someone else to be the patsy. Ask yourself, do you want to be remembered as Stephen Waitkus, the guy who used strong-arm tactics on poor defenceless Geraldine O'Neal? Why, the woman was old enough to be his mother! For shame, Stephen! that's what people will say. For shame!"

Waitkus rolled his eyes. Gerry flounced upstairs without waiting for a reply and changed into a crisp linen suit and high heels.

He was standing at the foot of the staircase when she came down, foot tapping, fingers drumming edgily on the table top. The five minutes must have seemed an eternity.

"OK, Gerry," he said. "Let's cut the crap and get a move on."

She drew herself up, a peacock in full preen, then glared at him.

"Madame Ambassador to you, sonny boy."

sixteen

"There's been a ghastly mistake. I am the victim of the DA's imagination."

Thus Gerry to the army of reporters, who duly noted that the former ambassador appeared smiling and confident.

But now, sitting in Jake Matthews' office, she was besieged by doubt. If Jake's face was any barometer, the prospects were stormy.

"One gets the impression," he was saying, "that you transcended the barrier that separates the Public Relations consultant from the professional fixer. Not much doubt about what took place."

He skimmed through his notes.

"On November 23rd you and your client, Mr Taki Yoshimura drove to the Cross County Shopping Center in Yonkers in a rented car. You were behind the wheel. At 11:15, you parked in front of a store called Dizzy Donnie's Discounts. Shortly after, a meeting took place in the back seat of your car between Mr Yoshimura and Commissioner McFeeley, who had arrived separately. During that meeting, money changed hands between the two men. A substantial amount. Correct so far?"

Gerry cast down her eyes. Jake continued.

"And the very next week, by an astounding coincidence, the good commissioner announces a plan to install new turnstiles in the city subways. What can any one deduce other than the bribery of a public official?" He put down the report with a baffled expression. " 'Say it ain't so, Joe,' " he pleaded.

"I wish I could, Jake. For what it's worth, I swear I had no idea there was going to be a pay-off that day. I was flabbergasted."

"What did you think, Gerry? That they were schlepping out to Yonkers to buy ties?"

"I didn't think, regrettably. I suppose I didn't want to. And once it happened, I could hardly blow the whistle. I offer no defence, Jake, except galloping stupidity and the assurance that I'd never done such a thing before in my life." She hated the wounded expression on Jake's face. It made her feel like a worm.

"I was crazy, Jake. In over my head. You see, Michael and I were leaving for London in a few days. So there I was, desperate for money, and Taki was turning up the pressure. I couldn't afford to lose him as a client. Anyhow he offered me a bonus if I could set up a meeting with the commissioner. Just a discreet little meeting, he said. At the conscious level, I pretended it was normal business procedure. But subconsciously? Oh, Christ! Part of me figured, what the hell – these guys are all thieves anyhow and it was going to happen with or without me. And, to be frank, the cloak-and-dagger aspects appealed to my sense of adventure. Yonkers struck me as so utterly outrageous, the last place on earth where anyone who was anyone would know me. It never dawned on me I was under surveillance! I still can't fathom how District Attorney Mariano found out. Granted, he never liked me. We had a little contretemps in the theatre one night. But to have me staked out? That's carrying a grudge too far."

"It wasn't Mariano. You were being watched by a private investigator from Securi-Guard Corp. They put a plant in your office last summer."

Gerry's was incredulous. "A traitor on my payroll?"

"Exactly. When you rented the car that morning, their insider sounded the alert. Securi-Guard operatives followed you to Yonkers and recorded the entire transaction on film. Then they turned the evidence over to Mariano's office. Quite properly, I may add."

"It must have given the DA great joy, having me handed to him on a platter like that."

"Apparently so. When I called him to discuss a possible dismissal of charges, he came out with the most extraordinary remark. He said, 'Never miss a chance to fuck a fucker.' He claims it's a direct quote from Geraldine O'Neal. The mole in your office, incidentally, was a woman named Leslie Ballantine. Ring a bell?"

Gerry shook her head vigorously, then it struck her.

"I had a trainee named Leslie Balsam. Balsam . . . Ballantine. Close enough. She quit without notice last December.
Jesus!" Gerry punched her palm in frustration. "I should
have figured there was something phoney about her. She
was willing to work for beans, which was pretty rare in this
money-grubbing age. She said something about wanting to
sit at the feet of the master. That it would be a 'learning
experience' as the jargon goes. I was enormously flattered." Gerry groaned. "Well, fuck all! Undone by ego yet
again!"

"Looks like it was a learning experience for both of you."

"But who would put her up to such a thing? Who hates
me that much? We're talking huge buck expenditure on
the off chance that I'd do something illegal."

"We're talking Lawrence Winterbourne," Jake replied,
"who has a vested interest in declaring you an unfit trustee."

"I see." Gerry leaned back to absorb this latest blow.
"Well, I wouldn't have thought him capable of such ingen-
uity. Can we fight this, Jake?. Can I hang in there as
trustee?"

"I wouldn't, Gerry. One thing you don't need at this
point is to have your name dragged further in the mire.
Winterbourne's attorney has already been to see me. He's
Harlow Farnsworth of Slater-Blaney, a reputable man from
a reputable firm. We had a detailed discussion, the gist of
which is, Winterbourne will decline to sue if you make
over the trusteeship to the two people of his choice . . ."

"Who are?"

"Farnsworth and a young woman named Risha Lindstrom."

"That figures!" Gerry said sourly. "I've been the victim
of a conspiracy. You know what that screwball is going to
do, once he gets his mitts on the money? And we're talking
multiple millions! He'll piss it away trying to prove that
Columbus didn't discover America or some such crap. The
man's looney toons."

Jake shrugged.

"As you yourself said in this very office not so long ago,
everyone is entitled to one great folly in life."

496

"Do me a favour," Gerry grumbled. "Don't ever quote me to myself. OK, I surrender. What choice do I have? Tell Winterbourne's lawyer to draw up the papers. I'll miss the income, though, especially now. It wasn't a fortune, but I could live on it if I had to. What's my next move, Jake? Do I get myself a job in a hamburger joint?"

"Nope. You get yourself a top criminal lawyer." Jake scribbled a name and pushed it across the desk to her. "When it comes to white-collar crime, this one's the best. He's already been apprised of the situation and will be happy to represent you."

Gerry deciphered Jake's scrawl and rolled her eyes. "Bernard Popkin. Isn't he the guy who got the Wizard of Wall Street off the hook? My dear, there's no way I can afford that kind of talent."

"Don't worry about it, Gerry. Bernie will adjust this fee."

"To what?" Gerry asked. "To all the money west of the Mississippi? Get real, Jake. We're talking million-dollar law."

"I repeat, don't worry about it. It will all be taken care of. Bernie's joining my firm as special counsel."

"In other words, my defence is on the house?"

Jake gave an almost imperceptible nod.

Gerry sat very still for a minute, twisting her garnet ring. Then she leaned across the desk and kissed him.

"You're the best of the good guys, Jake. Just like your father. And he was the best that ever was. And now, my pet," she averted her eyes, "I must dash. Off to the hairdressers. Can't have those grey roots showing on TV. I'm appearing on Ted Koppel's show tonight, did I mention? Or is it Letterman? I'll have my secretary let you know."

First the bad news, Gerry had thought sitting in the precinct house on the night of her arrest. She could conceivably wind up doing hard time. Now the good news. She was back in the limelight once more.

Her arrest had been a media event.

GERRY JAILED! screamed the *Post*, not on page six either, but in a 72-point headline. Not strictly accurate. She was out on bail within hours. Most coverage was cautious however, with Gerry's long career being given its respectful due. *The Times's* heading, "Ex-Ambassador Named in Corruption Inquiry", at least offered the presumption of innocence. And the *Daily News's* "The Great Lady Stumbles" could be read as a compliment of sorts.

One thing was certain: the name O'Neal was now on everyone's lips. Granted, this wasn't the means by which she had hoped to reassert herself in the public consciousness. But fame of any kind, be it acclaim or notoriety, was a thousand per cent better than oblivion.

From the moment she'd marched into the fusillade of upthrust microphones and minicams (looking marvellous, by all accounts), her life had been transformed.

The first concrete benefit was reaped the morning after her arrest when Gerry was awakened by the aroma of fresh coffee. She went downstairs to find her housekeeper had returned.

"Ida!" Gerry exclaimed. "Does this mean. . . . I mean, will you . . . would you..?" She was ready to go down on her knees.

But Ida wasted no time on generalities. She was too busy peering into the refrigerator, running her fingers over the counter, examining the contents of the garbage pail.

"Disgusting!" Ida pronounced. "Dust and grease an inch thick! You just can't get decent help these days. Now will you please get out of my kitchen, Miss O'Neal, and let me get on with my work?"

By nine that morning, the phone was ringing off the hook.

Did Gerry have any statements for Public Radio? Would she appear on 20/20? Could *Vanity Fair* send a photographer around? Was she free for a phone-in show? For a slot on "Good Morning America"? For dinner "any time you can possibly make it"?

Out of the woodwork they came: reporters, journalists, publishers with proposals, old lovers, recent acquaintances, people she hadn't seen in twenty years, people she didn't want to see for another twenty. Total strangers stopped her in the street to scavenge autographs or unburden themselves of their opinions. "I loved you when you were on 'What's My Line'," one old-timer said. Go tell her she had the wrong celebrity.

Close friends and colleagues displayed fierce loyalty, proclaiming her innocence to all who would listen. Old favours came home to roost. "I'd take a bullet for you," one woman wrote her from Kansas, "for any one of a hundred reasons."

In a way, it was like the old days, a heady mix of controversy and adulation, the sense of being on the front lines.

But if those who believed her innocent were quick to rally round, those convinced of her guilt were even more fervid in their pursuit. People loved to run with the devil.

"You must come on Saturday," one eager hostess gushed, "Claus von Bulow will be there and it would be super to seat the two of you together! You have so much in common."

Gerry declined, preferring to escort a group of ghetto kids to a night game at Yankee Stadium. It was a shameless piece of public relations, especially when she posed for photographers in a baseball cap. But what the hell, Gerry reasoned, why not do for herself what others paid her to do for them!

"To be frank," she told a Newsday reporter with a gallant smile, her arm about one of her teenage charges, "my own problems pale by comparison with what boys like Scott here face every day of their young lives. Drugs. Discrimination. Broken homes. Rotten housing. I try to help a little."

"This lady's some dude!" Scott volunteered, a comment which duly appeared in the story, leaving the reader to wonder if the majesty of law had nothing better to do with its resources than persecute poor Gerry O'Neal.

And still the calls came.

"Why Bobby Obermayer, you old reprobate! I thought we weren't on speaking terms."

"Don't be an asshole, Gerry. Why do you think I posted your bail, if not out of friendship?"

"Because you want something."

"Well, that too . . ." Bobby admitted. "I was thinking of

maybe your memoirs exclusive for my magazine group. Our readers would love to know your side of the story."

"The unexpurgated version?" Gerry squelched a smile. Little did he know that one of his lowly employees had already ploughed the ground most thoroughly. She told him she'd consider his proposition.

Lee Whitfield phoned in due course. They had a stilted conversation.

"I feel awful about what happened," Lee said.

"Me too. Looks like you made the supreme sacrifice for nothing. Thanks anyhow. And just when I thought it was safe to go back in the water," she mocked. "If I didn't know better, I'd say it was kismet."

"I'm truly sorry," Lee said. "You and Michael have split up, I gather."

"You can still see the skid marks," Gerry said.

"I'm sorry about that too. If there's any way I help . . ."

Gerry was quiet for so long, Lee thought she might have left her dangling. Then she said something that surprised.

"The oddest thought just struck me. You've committed the most appalling breach of professional ethics."

Lee was piqued. She had phoned in good faith.

"I didn't steal anything, Gerry. OK, I abused your trust in going through your box and I was less than forthright the past few months. But I did enter your house legitimately. The rest of the story, the nuts-and-bolts part, was honest legwork."

"I'm not questioning how you got the story," Gerry said with a mordant laugh, "but how you suppressed it. Your duty as a journalist was to publish the truth, instead of which you've aided and abetted a felon. For which I'm eternally grateful, believe me. I trust it hasn't damaged your career."

It had and it hadn't.

Fletch had been incredulous.

"Two days after you swear there's no story in O'Neal, all hell breaks loose. Hottest item since the Bess Mess and it was right under your nose. You goofed, Whitfield. You missed the big one."

"I'm a reporter," she shot back, "not a detective agency. Or a fortune teller either. Who could have foreseen a development like that? I refuse to discuss it further. Meanwhile, what's happening with my piece on the homeless?"

Fletch chewed on a corner of his horn rims. "My wife . . ." he began and Lee's spirits sank. To such an arbiter of taste as the immaculate Mrs. B., it must have been an ugly reminder of the other New York.

"My wife wept," Fletch concluded.

Lee exhaled, limp with relief. Had Fletch been moved too? she wondered. Or was he making a calculated decision?

"Top management's been after me," he added in an uncharacteristic burst of confidence. "They say the magazine should be seen to uphold what's called 'values'. Values, schmalues . . . as long as we sell copies is my feeling. But I think they have a point. Kinder, gentler society and all that crap, a return to commitment. It's in keeping with the current psyche. Even 'The Incredible Hulk' is being toned down, I hear."

"A kinder gentler Hulk?"

"You got it. Compassion is in. That's what my wife liked about your piece. Well written, intensely felt, plus you give the impression you really care. Great timing, kid. You sure know how to tap a trend. It'll be the cover for the Independence Day issue. Everyone's out in the Hamptons that weekend, sunning, sailing, eating lobsters from Dean and Deluca. Make the bastards feel grateful for what they have and at the same time truly superior. Keep up the good work!"

Lee felt a combination of flattered and miffed.

"I didn't write that story to tap a trend, Fletch. I wrote it from the heart."

He glared at her as though she'd said a dirty word.

Some time after, Lee had dinner with Jake.

"What will become of Gerry?" she asked. "I'm reluctant to discuss it with her directly, it's such a scary subject."

Jake looked uneasy. "Is this for publication?"

Lee shook her head. "Strictly off the cuff, Scout's

honour. I'm inquiring as a friend, Jake. Of both yours and of hers. You were the first people to be nice to me in this town."

"Well, there's no secret about it. Gerry is being tried separately from Yoshimura and the Commissioner at her lawyer's insistence. Three alternatives. She could be acquitted. She could plea bargain on a lesser charge, though that's unlikely since the District Attorney is after her scalp. Anyhow, she insists she wasn't at fault. Or – she could be found guilty as charged."

"And if convicted?"

"With luck, a light sentence or even probation since it's a first offence. It depends. She might hit a sympathetic judge."

"But she could go to prison?"

Jake looked ineffably sad. "I'm afraid so, Lee. As I say, that would depend on the judge."

Lee shut her eyes, trying to picture Gerry behind bars. The eagle caged, so to speak. Her mind boggled. This was a woman accustomed to luxury and beauty and freedom.

"But that's so unfair," she cried. "All kinds of muggers and murderers walk the streets, whereas Gerry is such a non-violent person. She won't survive in jail, I don't think."

"Oh she'll survive," Jake said confidently. "Adversity brings out the best in her. Always has. This is a woman of great courage."

Lee was stunned by the assurance with which he spoke. He sounded proprietary, as if he understood Gerry better than anyone. Almost as though she belonged to him.

But then, Jake had always been something of an enigma. Apart from the obvious, that he was one of the few black lawyers to have scaled the heights on Wall Street, Lee knew nothing of his background. Nothing – except for some kind of intimate connection with Geraldine O'Neal. Wild ideas began forming.

"You've known her a long time, haven't you, Jake?"

"As long as I can remember," he replied in a low husky voice. "You see, my father was Lionel Matthews."

The name was not familiar, although Lee had a sense

502

that she should have recognized it at once, that Jake was conveying a message of supreme importance.

"That should mean something," she said, "and it doesn't. Please tell me, Jake. What is Gerry to you? I'm asking as a friend."

Jake hesitated, but the urge to unburden himself won out.

"What I tell you is to go no farther than across the width of this table," Jake warned. "Swear it."

Lee thought of the story she had voluntarily destroyed and nodded slowly. With conviction.

"I swear. Believe me, Jake. I can be silent as a tomb when I want to. You can't imagine the things I know and never told."

Jake shut his eyes for a moment, then crossed an invisible threshold.

Lionel Matthews was one of the most dynamic figures of the civil rights movement in the early sixties, he told Lee. An intimate of Martin Luther King's. A charter member of CORE. A man of fierce energy and passionate commitment.

He was also the great love of Gerry's life.

Lee listened, incredulous. Had she dug so deeply into Gerry's past to miss the most significant story of all? There had been no hint of him in the contents of the cardboard box, no letters or notes. Not even a snapshot. Whatever had happened between Geraldine O'Neal and Lionel Matthews, considerable effort had been expended to keep the memory suppressed.

Suddenly, Lee shivered. That day in the dressing room, she had been aware of a hiatus, a time when Gerry seemingly vanished from the face of the earth. A nervous breakdown, Lee had speculated. A love affair gone awry. But now her mind flooded with other possibilities.

Was it conceivable? There was Gerry's secrecy to be accounted for. Jake's age. The closeness of their relationship. The gaping hole in the O'Neal chronology. The supposition was too crazy for words!

"She's not . . . ?" Lee gasped. "She couldn't be . . . !"

"My mother?" Jake finished the sentence. "No. My real

503

mother died when I was born. Yet in many other ways, yes. You could say she brought me up. I was little more than a toddler when I first saw her. I remember her visiting our house, smelling of some wonderful perfume, wearing a pretty yellow dress. She was like a figure out of a movie or a story book. In those days, you know, white women didn't visit black men's homes, least of all in small-town Mississippi. In those days, segregation was king."

Following the fiasco at the *New York Globe*, Gerry was a columnist without a column. No newspaper would touch her. Her stand on abortion had made her too controversial a figure for the syndicated papers. Her response was to seek out an issue even more emotive.

A few weeks earlier, the Russians had crossed the ultimate frontier to launch the first man into space. Yet here in her own country, there were millions of people for whom even a Woolworth lunch counter was out of bounds. The irony was bitter.

As Lee herself was to do many years later in the Port Authority, Gerry chose not merely to observe the story from the outside, but actually to live the life. It could only be done from the vantage point of total anonymity. Gerry dyed her hair a mousey brown, got some fake ID and, confiding her plans to no one, went to Washington and joined the Freedom Riders.

What would now be a routine journey was, in that turbulent era, a dangerous passage. A gamble with death. The Freedom Riders were pioneers, the first of the interracial groups to venture south in the 1960s. Setting out from the capitol, they crisscrossed the heartland of Dixie by bus, defying Jim Crow laws every step of the way. Lunch counters, waiting rooms, barber shops, drinking fountains, movie houses, toilets: wherever they went suddenly became the front line of the civil rights battle. They refused to take No for an answer.

The response was one of unabated fury. And not just from Southern diehards. Official Washington didn't want to know. "Looking for trouble," was the broad consensus as the Establishment washed its hands of the affair. It was early days in the Civil Rights movement. The Freedom Riders were on their own.

By local standards, *they* were the law-breakers, these men and women of the buses. Scum of the earth to be greeted at best by jeering crowds and pelted garbage and obscenities. At worst by sheriffs with dogs and cattle prods. By angry rabble with shotguns and rope.

From the very first day, Gerry breached the line that separates the disinterested journalist from passionate participant. This was more than a story. It was the closest she came to a holy cause. And if any doubt lingered of the depths of her commitment, it vanished when she met Lionel Matthews. The effect was instant, galvanizing. Mutual. A flash of lightning on a hot summer night.

"They dared much together," was how one veteran of the struggle recalled it.

Ultimately, they dared too much.

When the Freedom Ride was completed, Gerry stayed on. To her lover alone, she confessed her identity. She rented a house in the town where he lived, wanting only to be near him. With him. To share his life and dreams. But where Lionel Matthews was cautious, she was not.

"What is it," she said, "for us to walk down the street hand in hand, like any two people in love?"

"What is it? It's suicide, my darling. You're a New Yorker. You don't understand how things stand here."

"I understand that if we sit back and play their game, abide by their conventions, then we let them win, Lionel."

She wanted to marry, then move away. Live abroad, if necessary. But Jake's father felt his destiny was here in the South. In a state where miscegenation was a crime. It sufficed, he argued, that they were bound together in each other's eyes. Marriage was but another convention. In their situation, a luxury.

Gerry remained adamant. She wanted nothing less than a public expression of their bond. Some gesture of defiance. At heart, Jake's father must have yearned for it too.

"A ring," she said. "You must buy me a ring."

What better symbol of the permanence of love than an unbroken circle around her finger?

Her notion was simple. They would stroll down Main Street one fine Monday afternoon and go to the jewellery store in the Courthouse Square. "Then you will buy me a ring and place it on my finger. Now where is the crime in that!"

The day came. They walked across the square hand in hand, pretending to be oblivious of the hostile eyes, the angry voices shouting obscenities and threats. Their steps never faltered.

Inside the shop, Gerry chose a tiny garnet in a antique gold setting. The stone was the colour of blood. It was the colour of Lionel's blood when he died in her arms moments later.

And even as she knelt on the pavement, his brains splattered on her dress, someone in the crowd yelled, "OK nigger-lover! Now it's your turn."

"According to the police report," Jake said, "my father was shot down while resisting 'arrest'. The charge, by the way, was robbing a jewellery store."

As for Gerry, she was trussed up by a gang of rednecks, thrown into the back of a pick-up truck, beaten and dumped on US Route 78, the same road she had ridden proudly but a few months earlier.

"Whatever else happened to her on that ride, I don't know," Jake concluded. "And I don't want to know. I don't even want to imagine."

Lee felt physically ill. But she had to ask.

"She never said anything, never wrote a word about her experiences. How extraordinary! She's such a public person on the whole. Too painful, of course. Too guilt-making. Tell me, Jake, do you blame her for your father's death?"

He shook his head and it was a while before he found his voice.

"No. Maybe because I was almost too young to remember. And his death turned out to be a turning point. It galvanized public opinion, not only in Washington but around the world. No, I can't blame Gerry for something she did out of love. But the point is, Gerry blames herself. She feels her recklessness condemned him to death. But

506

that's wrong. Gerry didn't murder my father. They did. The racists. The bigots. Not Gerry. That's the important thing. And he didn't die in vain."

"Oh God! What a traumatic experience!"

"Clearly. For she never spoke of it to anyone. Once the nightmare was over, she returned to New York. Ostensibly her life went on as usual. Except for me."

Gerry had taken over financial responsibility for Lionel's family. Supported his aging parents in their last years. Sent Jake first to prep school, then college, ultimately to Harvard Law.

"She felt she owed you," Lee said.

"And I owe her. You could say, we both owe each other," Jake concluded. "More than either of us can ever pay. And now that you know our secret, I beg you to forget it. I couldn't bear to have her hurt again."

Lee wiped her streaming eyes.

Forget it? In her heart she never would.

"For the record, I already have."

She walked home that evening. Not jogged, but walked. Slowly and thoughtfully, sorting things out.

What an extraordinary woman Gerry had turned out to be after all. A combination of sleaze and nobility. Of foolishness and strength. Of vanity and idealism.

And what a life! The gamut – from A to Z.

seventeen

"Herman Herman Herman!" she yelled down the hall. "Round up the usual suspects. It's party time."

Her assistant trotted in.

"The complete 'A'-list?" he asked.

"Absolutely, with certain exceptions. Michael Avesian. Lawrence Winterbourne. Include them out. And I want everyone in the office to attend. Plus use your judgement on the 'B'-list, the 'C'-list. Clients, associates, the works! Though God knows who will actually show up. Probably be like Gatsby's funeral, God forbid. But at least I'll know who my friends are."

"Food and drink?"

"Have Sherry-Lehmann do the booze and tell them to lay on plenty of champagne. A buffet, I think. Call Petrossian's for caviare. Let's have Memphis do the catering, William Greenburg handle desserts. Now – you taking this all down? – I want a string quartet to play while we're dining. Mozart would be nice. You might phone up Juilliard and ask for gifted students. Let the kids earn a few bucks. Then book a jazz group starting around midnight. Now flowers . . . Call Costos, but tell him nothing funereal, mind you. This is not a wake. I want everything to look gay, very gay. All other details you can work out with Ida. OK Herman, get cracking."

"Two small questions, Gerry: where and when? It's sometimes useful to have it on the invitations."

"Where? My home. As for when? The night before the trial begins. It'll be a kind of send-off. And across the top of the invitation, I want them to print the following." She gave a wicked laugh. " 'Not with a whimper but with a bang!' "

It would be false to say she wasn't scared as the trial date neared. She was. Only a fool could be complacent.

When she was younger, she occasionally pictured herself

being martyred for a grand cause. Geraldine O'Neal – feminist, fire-brand, civil-rights warrior – breaking unjust laws, then making eloquent speeches in the dock. That at least would have had a claim to nobility. Even the Austrian forgery could be defended, if not excused, as the folly of a woman in love.

Now, however, she stood an excellent chance of being convicted for what she herself regarded as one of the sleaziest crimes in the book. One in which she had never meant to take part.

The irony was, that nobody much cared whether she was culpable or not. Society had grown surprisingly non-judgemental, it struck her, with sympathy generally being voiced in terms of "just your luck to get caught".

Her major error, it would appear, was that she hadn't even turned a decent profit. As a white-collar criminal, she was a washout. Crime not only paid, she was reminded on every hand. It normally paid a helluva lot more than she had received.

Look at insider traders, people pointed out. The junk-bond tsars. They'd racked up billions, money to boggle the mind. Look at the defence contractors with their 1000% markups, the borough presidents now languishing in jail, the White House familiars cashing in on their connections. As a Hollywood mogul once put it, "You take a million here, a million there and sooner or later it all adds up." Look at the union leaders with their sweetheart contracts, the heads of School Boards on the take, developers blowing up buildings in the dead of night. Rich rich rich. And Gerry was broke.

"Look at Oliver North," the head of a lecture bureau enthused on the phone. "He gets twenty-five thousand a pop. For what? reading a prepared speech and pumping a few hands. Time to cash in on your celebrity, Miss O'Neal. Sign with us and I can guarantee you fifteen thou per appearance. I'm speaking before commission, of course."

"Of course," Gerry mouthed and told him she'd think it over.

The wages of sin it appeared, was steady employment on the rubber-chicken circuit. At the moment she was contemplating a host of book proposals (she said she'd think them over, too) and ABC was talking Movie of the Week.

"Who do you like for the part?" the TV packager asked her. "Stephanie Powers or Lee Remick? Jane Seymour may be a bit too young."

"What would they call this epic?" Gerry wanted to know.

"Working title's 'Beauty and the Bribe', but that's not final, though the promo people want it to have a mellifluous flow."

"Like 'The Mayflower Madam'?"

"Don't knock it, Gerry. Biddle made a fortune on that flick. Even Gary Hart's bimbo did a deal for a hundred thou plus."

"My my," Gerry clucked. "That's quite a payoff for a one-night stand."

"My point exactly. So imagine what a woman of your stature could fetch. At least as good, is my bet. Plus the possibility of overseas sales. Think about it."

She promised to do so and added that proposition to the growing pile of Undecideds.

Doubtless, she would write something. Do something. Autobiography seemed the most likely prospect. If she were acquitted, it would be a ringing vindication of her life. An affirmation of her youthful ideals.

And if convicted?

One thing for certain, she wouldn't whine and pule and play the victim. She despised mawkish behaviour. No! Geraldine O'Neal would take her punishment "like a man". Which was how, in many ways, she had always lived.

The more she thought of it, the more the possibility intrigued. Going to jail, after all, was one of the few experiences she had yet to embrace. Looked upon in a certain light, one might almost call it the consummate experience. Cellini. Dostoevsky. Gandhi. Even John Dean! Viewed from that angle, you might say everyone who was anyone had been to jail for one reason or other. And as those examples proved beyond dispute, a brief stretch in prison could be salubrious. Not by any means life's sad grey denouement, but a turning point that led to exciting new

510

directions. She would emerge a better, more vibrant woman. With a dynamite book tucked under her belt.

My Life by Geraldine O'Neal. Or better yet: *My Life So Far*. Because there would be more of life yet to come.

With a cover photo by Scavullo.

Already she could picture the popular response, the critical acclaim. Powerful! Gripping! Shooting up to Number Two on *The New York Times* Best Seller list.

Why be modest? Number One.

Feeling positively braced by the prospect of the next twist in her career, Gerry prepared for her farewell party.

A few days earlier, she had gone to a small discreet office in the Pan Am building. "Pawn shop" would be too crass a term for these muted surroundings. The proprietor, an elderly Viennese, preferred to think of himself as more of a "helpmeet" for ladies in distress.

"I'd like to sell this diamond bracelet," she said.

The jeweller studied it. "A handsome piece," he said.

"Given me by a handsome man."

"I'm sure it must cause you pain to part with it."

Gerry smiled sweetly. "Not if the money is right."

After much haggling, they agreed on a price.

"That's a pretty little garnet ring you have, Miss O'Neal. One doesn't see those Victorian settings so much any more. I can make you an offer."

"You don't have enough money," she said as she got up. "Now, Mr Weigl, if you'll be so good as to give me the proceeds for the diamond bracelet in cash. . . . ?"

eighteen

She didn't know why she had bothered to engage a string quartet. They could hardly be heard above the din.

"Dear God!" Gerry poked her nose into the kitchen where Ida was handling logistics. "When I said 'order enough food for an army', I had no idea that two armies would show up. I don't think the chow will hold out. Phone Petrossian's, quick, for more caviare. And order some deli from the Stage. A couple of hundred pastramis on rye, just in case."

She had counted on a quarter, conceivably half the invitees actually making the scene. But everyone? The complete Rolodex, from Brooke Astor to the Zambian Ambassador?

They had come out of friendship. For curiosity's sake. Because they felt the end of an era was at hand. Because New Yorkers were party animals at heart.

Whatever the motives, and Gerry couldn't care less, they were arriving in unprecedented numbers, pouring into the house, flowing through the rooms, spilling out into the garden. Everything was turning out marvellously, including the weather. Gerry belted down a glass of champagne and sallied forth.

"Gerry, my pet. You look sumptuous. Is that from our salon?"

"You know I wouldn't shop anywhere else."

"I want to talk to you." Eli Austrian led her to a stone bench in the garden. Gerry plucked a flower, sniffed it then tucked it into Eli's lapel.

"The last rose of summer," she said. "Mustn't let it go to waste."

Eli looked troubled.

"Your Michael Avesian has been a very naughty boy," he said.

"My Michael Avesian? Not mine any more. Why? Is

512

this something to do with Hailsham? Did the deal fall through?"

"Michael refused to sign the contract," Eli said. "At the very last minute, he backed out. Totally kaput. There's not going to be a Hailsham USA after all. No glittering shops in the wilds of New Jersey. No hands linked across the Atlantic in friendship. It seems the return wasn't fast enough for our ambitious young friend."

"But that's impossible, Eli. Every penny he had was tied up in that project."

"Believe me, there was less of Michael's capital involved than you may think. He was playing mostly with other people's money. Banks, backers. The man was leveraged up to the hilt. And now he's waltzed off with at least a ten million dollar net profit and left us all in the lurch. I feel like the farmer's daughter in those old jokes. Seduced and abandoned."

"But . . . but . . . For God's sakes, Eli. I'm utterly mystified. What is going on down at Hailsham? Last I saw, it was full speed ahead."

"Michael sold it to Lawrence Winterbourne for over twenty million bucks. In cash, believe it or not! Hailsham Castle is about to become – if I have this correct – the Leif Ericson International Institute of Nordic Studies."

"I'll be damned!" Gerry thumped her palm against her forehead. "I will be goddamned."

"Undoubtedly," Eli said.

She burst out laughing.

"I'm a widow too," said the woman with the silver hair and matching dinner suit. "My Ben died last year. Heart. A dear person, a wonderful sportsman. Gerry sent the most extravagant wreath."

"You and Gerry are old friends, I gather."

"To tell you the truth," said the former Suzie Slade, "I hardly know her. And if you can keep a secret, I'll let you in on something else. If not for me, Geraldine O'Neal would have never had a career."

"You don't say!"

"I do say. Gerry stole my column at the *Globe*. And the

513

Globe is what launched her reputation. If not for that break, our mutual friend would be sweating out a civil-service pension."

"Really!" Nancy Schroeder Whitfield's eyebrows shot up.

"Really! Though I don't begrudge her her success. She's a decent sort behind all that swagger. And thoughtful. Every year on our anniversary she'd remember us with flowers."

"Birds," Nancy mumbled. "With me it was birds."

But Suzie Slade Klugman's attention was elsewhere. She was waving furiously across the room. "Ah! My old publisher, Bobby Obermayer. I haven't seen him since the day I was married. If you'll excuse me . . ."

Nancy helped herself to a generous spoonful of caviare. May as well get it in now, while supplies last. Then she beckoned to the waiter for champagne.

"Farnsworth, isn't it? Harlow Farnsworth? I didn't expect to see you here. I'm Bernie Popkin. We met at the ABA convention last year."

"Pleasure to see you again." The old gentleman pumped the younger man's hand. "I understand that you're representing our hostess in this unfortunate case."

"So I am. But aren't you Lawrence Winterbourne's lawyer?" Popkin asked. "Frankly, I'm astonished to find you here. I should think the Winterbourne name is anathema in this house."

"I'm present in my eligible bachelor role," Farnsworth said. "Miss O'Neal asked me to escort a friend of hers, a lovely woman who recently lost her husband. That's her over there – " he cast an imaginary fishing rod in the direction of the woman in the silver dinner suit "– the one chatting with Obermayer. Apparently Geraldine thought Suzie and I would hit off. I'm a recent widower myself."

"I see," Bernard Popkin said. "What times we live in, eh?"

Harlow Farnsworth laughed. "Once a fixer, always a fixer."

"What have we here?" Jake Matthews came over and

clapped an arm about each man. "Lawyers talking shop? This is a party, gentlemen, a social occasion. Harlow, the Cardinal read your piece on fly-making in last month's *Field and Stream* and he's itching to meet you."

"Always eager to meet a fellow fly-caster, especially when he's a Prince of the Church."

"*Camellos?*"

Lee had been trying out her Spanish on Señor Oliveira. She was wondering if she might have misunderstood. "*Camellos?*" she repeated.

"*Si si,*" the little Bolivian struggled to make his point. "*Los camellos . . . dromedarios . . .*"

"*Camellos!*" Lee nodded. Well, if that didn't beat all. She could hardly wait to tell Gerry.

"A privilege to meet you, Your Eminence. I'm told you enjoy fly-casting.."

"Avidly!" Cardinal Novak replied. "With the panting enthusiasm of the city born. I grew up not ten blocks from here, Mr Farnsworth, so, except for pulling tyres out of the East River, fishing is an acquired taste. But it has soul. I leave the golf course to presidents and CEO's. Whenever I can spare the time, I head for the nearest good trout stream."

"An apt pastime for a man of the cloth. After all, you are a fisher of men . . ."

The Cardinal beamed. "And of women too, with due respect to our hostess, who happens to be one of my parishioners. But never happier than when fishing for trout. Jake here tells me you have a remarkable collection of nineteenth century flies . . ."

The two gentlemen swapped fishing stories on an ascending scale. Then Farnsworth grinned. "You must come down to the Institute, Your Eminence, and try your luck there."

"The Institute?"

"The Leif Ericson Institute, of which I'm a director. We have acquired a vast site in New Jersey and by the greatest good luck, there's an excellent trout stream on the grounds."

"Gerry!"
"Nancy!"
"I must talk to you before I leave."
"It's not even midnight."
"I'm taking a plane out in the morning."
"There's a room I use for storage at the top of the house. Meet you there in ten minutes."

"Hi!" The scrumptious red-head repairing her lipstick looked at the gorgeous blonde who was tending a broken nail. "Don't we know each other from somewhere?"
"You look familiar," the blonde said. "Who you here with?"
"The fat guy, Eli Austrian."
"I used to date Eli myself. But now I'm with Bobby Obermayer."
"Oh yeah? How is he?"
"Compared to what?"
"Compared to Austrian."
The blonde made a face. "Schmuckos, the lot of them. Overgrown children. I get more action playing Nintendo."
"Yeah . . . but rich schmuckos." The red-head stood up and rested her hand on the other woman's bare shoulder. "And at least Eli gives stock market tips. My name's Bambi, by the way."
"I'm Yvonne. Maybe we could do lunch tomorrow."
Bambi smiled. Nibbled her lips. "And afterwards a matineé?"

"We met at another of Gerry's parties a while back," said the young man with the red suspenders. "Remember?"
"I do indeed, Steve. We talked book concepts, as I recall."
"Let's talk again, Lee. That piece of yours on life in the Port Authority was a stunner. My rumour mill tells me that it will be short-listed for a Pulitzer Prize. Maybe we

516

could put a book together in time for the Spring List. What do you think?"

Lee smiled. "I'll have my agent call you in the morning."

"So!" Gerry unfolded a spindly bridge chair in the attic and motioned Nancy to do the same. At this remove, the party babble was reduced to a low-level hum. Only the music managed to make itself known. The soft insistent rhythms of jazz.

"I'm sorry we didn't see more of each other, Nancy. You arrived at an awkward time of my life. And then we had that awful scene. You were so bitter that afternoon, if 'bitter' isn't too harsh a word."

"Don't forget 'angry' and 'jealous'," Nancy appended.

"What I want to know is, are you still?"

Nancy cocked an ear to the fragments of music trickling in from the hall.

"That sounds like Quincy Jones playing piano."

"It is," Gerry said. "Quincy and I are old friends."

Nancy listened for a while. "David would have enjoyed being here." Then she folded her hands.

"I've thought about that afternoon a great deal, Gerry. About the two of us, and how at one point our lives seemed interchangeable. The road not taken. I think it's Robert Frost's most powerful image, one that haunted me for years. I always believed that, given the Goldman fellow-ship, I would have had the brilliant career . . ."

"And I . . ?"

Nancy laughed, a brisk sensible laugh. "And you would have been – oh, I don't know. An anonymous housewife. A civil servant. Except it wouldn't have worked out that way. The truth is, we both of us did exactly as we pleased. I wanted to marry David. If I hadn't married David, I would doubtless have married someone else. That was what I wanted. Whereas you . . . if you hadn't launched your career with the fellowship, you would have done it some other way. Because that was what you wanted. We chose our own paths, Gerry and it's stupid to second guess. Conceivably, you might have opted for a less turbulent life and I might have gone for the gold. I doubt it. But even if

517

we'd swapped places and dreams and ambitions, would either of us have been happier? I doubt that too. No, I'm not bitter any more."

Gerry's eyes welled, spilled over. Nancy had the decency to look away.

"Oh Christ," Gerry sniffled. "I'm wrecking my mascara. You don't happen to have a hanky, do you?"

Nancy fished in her bag and produced a towelette.

"Good old Nan. Always prepared."

"That's what comes of raising four children."

Gerry blotted her face dry and mustered a smile.

"So here we are at another fork in the road, although this one's rosier for you than for me. You're free, Nan. You can do whatever you choose, go wherever you like. Carve out a whole new life."

"Hardly," came the reply. "I'm limited by financial realities."

Gerry pulled her ear thoughtfully.

"Remember about twenty years ago I sent you an Audubon print for Christmas? I don't know if you realize it, but that was a hand-coloured aquatint from the 1827 edition. Only three hundred copies in existence. They've appreciated wildly. Sell it. It'll bring a small fortune. Then go ahead and indulge in whatever your pet fantasy happens to be. Start law school. Take a trip around the world. Move to London. Dig for artifacts in Mexico. Or blow it all on a Russian sable coat, if that's your pleasure. Whatever thrills."

"I wouldn't dream of selling the Audubon," Nancy said. "It was a gift. It has sentimental value."

"Bah humbug!" Gerry said. "The whole point of goodies is that they can be exchanged for something better. Do it. I assure you, my feelings won't be hurt."

Nancy grinned. "Anyhow, I'm really not interested in sables. I know exactly what I want to do. Tomorrow morning I will take a plane home . . ."

"And when you get there?"

"I'm going to run for Mayor of Cedar City!"

"You're serious!"

"You betcha!" Nancy's voice brimmed with youthful

enthusiasm. She was bursting with plans. The current mayor was a thief. The snow removal a disgrace. The social services required total overhaul. If anyone could change the face of Cedar City, she was that person.

"I'm a somebody there. Admired. Respected. I've got over thirty years of networking behind me. Of friends. Fans. Partisans. Buddies. People who owe me favours from back when . . ."

She flung open the door to the hall. The babble of voices swelled from downstairs, eddied and swirled.

"Same as you." Nancy smiled. "You'd better get back. Your network is waiting."

The two women embraced, then descended the steps hand in hand.

"Be sure to take some pastrami sandwiches before you go," were Gerry's last words. "Nobody can eat that airline swill."

"Where have you been hiding?" Bernie Popkin asked. "I was beginning to wonder if you'd jumped bail."

"And miss tomorrow's show?" Gerry asked. A tipsy young man giggled, then thrust a glass of champagne into her hand. "A wonderful party," he was saying. "So extravagant. Tell me, Ms O'Neal, will this go down as a deductible expense?"

Gerry stared at him. "I know you from some place . . ."

"Karl Wummer of the IRS. I audited your books last Christmas."

"Terrific! Enjoy yourself."

She moved on.

"Jesus," she complained to Herman Herman Herman. "When I said invite everybody, you didn't have to be so literal."

Jake came over.

"I've been talking to Cardinal Novak and he gave me the impression that you're back in the arms of the church."

Gerry giggled. "Would you believe I've actually been to confession? So I have, darling. My first sacrament in over forty years. But if you really must know, I didn't do it for the sake of my soul. I did it for Andy. He's been after me for ages, so what's the harm? It gave him such pleasure, poor lamb."

Bobby Obermayer overheard the exchange. "Still, religion's not a bad idea at our age, Gerry. It doesn't hurt to hedge your bets."

Gerry laughed. "Why Bobby! You know me better than that. I've never hedged a bet in my life."

At one o'clock, Ida sent out for a hundred more pastramis. By two, the ranks of the guests were thinning out. When the party had dwindled down to old and intimate friends, the Cardinal went over to the band and requested *Woodchoppers' Ball*.

"Do you still remember how to jitterbug, Geraldine?"

She kicked off her shoes. "I certainly do."

The music flowed, warm and bright as old brandy. They cut a modest rug. Not with the same unbridled zest as when they were teenagers. Who had those bones any more? those supple muscles? But not all that bad either, considering.

Then it was three o'clock and even the hardiest guests were departing. Tomorrow was a normal working day.

"Not you!" Gerry caught Lee by the wrist. Lee had a sense of *déjà vu*. "Wait for me in my study upstairs."

"You are about to enjoy a spectacle very few people have ever been privy to," Gerry said, as she settled down in the sofa, feet tucked under her. "You are about to witness Geraldine O'Neal making a formal apology. I've treated you very badly, Lee. I'm sorry."

Lee fidgeted, uncomfortable at the prospect of a Gerry in sackcloth and ashes.

"What's past is past," she said. "We've both treated each other badly, one might say."

"Ah, but I began it," Gerry insisted. "Going after Michael the way I did, especially when I knew how enamoured you were. I don't know what possessed me. Of course he was enormously attractive, but I think part of the challenge lay in proving to myself that I could beat out someone half my age. Yes, vanity mostly. That old competitive urge. When you've spent all your life in the jungle, you sometimes forget how to retract your claws."

Lee winced. "All I had was a schoolgirl crush. I was never really in love. In retrospect you did me a favour. Michael is . . . well, not quite good enough for either of us, I like to think. You've heard what he's been up to?"

"You mean, his selling out to Winterbourne? Disgraceful. The Leif Ericson Institute indeed!"

"Oh that!" Lee said. "That's yesterday's news. I mean the stuff with the camels."

"Camels?" Gerry blinked in incomprehension.

"Yes, camels . . . dromedaries . . . ships of the desert." Lee grinned. It gave her pleasure to have scooped Gerry on something so delicious. Gerry who was always one up. "It seems Michael read in the paper a few weeks ago that the Arabs have more camels than they know what to do with. Apparently, they're all so busy riding around in Mercedes these days, that camels are a drag on the market. Anyhow, Michael's in Saudi right now, buying up the lot at knockdown prices. Plus saddles. Plus hiring riders and handlers."

"Whatever on earth for?"

"He plans to introduce camel-racing into the United States. Never been done before. He sees it as a switch from thoroughbreds, the sport of the future. At least that's the handle according to What's-his-name? You know . . . the little Bolivian with the big moustache?"

"My downstairs neighbour, Señor Oliveira?"

"The same. Apparently this camel thing is going to be a huge enterprise. Bigger than Hailsham. Oliveira tells me that Michael's already leased three hundred prime acres near Las Vegas."

"With his own money?" Gerry asked smartly.

"I suspect Señor Oliveira has also been privileged to invest."

"By providing the bulk of the capital! Fantastic! Well, that's another one Michael owes me. The two of 'em met at one of my parties last year. Same way Michael met Larry Winterbourne. Talk about exploiting connections! I suppose I should be offended but still . . . what a gorgeous con!"

Gerry burst out laughing. The image of Michael haggling with a Arab camel trader was irresistible. They'd both be in paradise.

"One Great American camel scam coming up! I love it. Can you think of anything more outrageous? With Michael making fulsome speeches to prospective investors about the link between our two great cultures. Although I don't know why I should be surprised. It's quite in character. I knew he was a hustler the moment I met him."

"In which case, how could you fall in love with him?"

"Because the chemistry was there. The magic. Across a crowded room, so to speak."

Lee shrugged. "I'll never understand you, Gerry. You knew what he was and yet you chose to deceive yourself."

Gerry looked surprised. "Why, of course, Lee. And Michael did the same, I daresay. My dear, if we didn't deceive ourselves constantly about the objects of our infatuation, no one would ever have a love affair. Which to my mind is the most exciting thing in life."

"In other words, there comes a time when you make a rational decision to behave irrationally."

"Exactly," Gerry said. "You will the craziness to happen, the whole intoxicating scene. Otherwise you might never know."

Lee grew reflective.

"I'm on the brink of a major decision in my own life, and I often wonder. Tell me, Gerry, after all you've been through with Michael, the anguish, the misery – was it worth it?"

Gerry sighed. "Yes . . . no . . . I don't know. I wish I had an easy answer. Would I do it again, that particular form of idiocy? I'm not sure. Presumably, I'm too old for that sort of nonsense. But on the other hand, I wouldn't forfeit a single moment of what we had. After all, what's life without risk, without passion? Without romance?" She paused. "Without men! My God, Lee! Suppose they send me to a women's prison? Well, of course they will, won't they? That is, assuming the worst. Can you picture me in those circumstances? Without a man in sight? *Quel* fucking *cauchemar!* Maybe I'll throw myself on the mercy of the court and the judge will send me to Sing Sing instead. At least the male/female ratio is good."

Lee smothered a laugh. "Bernie Popkin tells me that they've had to import an out-of-town judge, because you were palsy with the entire city judiciary."

Gerry preened. "In some cases, more than just palsy. However, on that topic my lips are sealed. Who knows what I'll get tomorrow. With my luck, Hanging Judge Jeffreys. Cross your fingers for me, Lee. Now enough of this boring, depressing shit. So! Tell me what is this big decision of yours all about?"

She was going to Rome, Lee said, to be with Bill Frazier. After much cogitation, she had taken a leave of absence from *Trend*. Fletch was furious, but there you were, she explained. One had to explore the alternatives. Life was too short. And since you couldn't stretch the length of it, at least you could try and stretch the width. The gamut from A to Z.

"Are you in love with Bill?" Gerry asked.

"I don't know. But there's only one way to find out. You could say I've made a rational decision to behave irrationally. And on that note, Gerry, I must go. Look at the time! You have to be in court in a few hours."

"No no . . ." Gerry stretched out her hand. "Stay and talk. The night's still young. We could go down to the kitchen and have someone fix us a bite."

Lee stood up slowly. "Get some rest, Gerry. The help's gone home. It's four in the morning. The party's over."

"No." Gerry shook her head, a trace of a smile about her lips. "The party is never over."

"All rise," the bailiff called out in stentorian tones.

Gerry fluffed up her hair.

"Do I look OK?" she asked her lawyer.

"Sensational," came the reply.

Which was more or less what the gal from CBS News had said a few minutes earlier, broadcasting from the steps of the courthouse.

"Gerry O'Neal has just arrived here at 100 Center Street, looking every inch the Queen of New York. For her first day in court, she's wearing a brilliant red Chanel suit, long diamond ear-rings and a confident smile . . ."

The diamonds were fake, if the reporter really wanted to know but the smile – oh! the smile was rapidly turning genuine.

For entering the courtroom on the bailiff's cue, looking dashing in flowing black robes, was the man (and it was a man, thank God!) who held her fate in his hands.

Gerry sucked in her breath. What a marvellous face, craggy but with laugh lines around his mouth. And that wonderful thatch of grey hair. Tall. Dignified. Yet kind of sexy, in a way. And Irish, too! Gerry could hardly believe her luck. Well, sure an' begorra she was Oirish herself.

More or less . . .

Oh yes, there was a decided affinity here. She could feel the vibes.

"All rise," Bernie Popkin nudged her with his elbow. "That means you too, Gerry. Face the bench."

Geraldine O'Neal got to her feet. Bestowed a radiant smile upon the judge. Her heart skipped.

Eyes met. Locked. Across a crowded courtroom, so to speak.

Then Judge Daniel X. McCafferty smiled back.